HERMAN MELVILLE was born in New York in 1819. The bankruptcy and death of his merchant father in 1832 deprived him of a routine career and alienated him forever from a conventional optimistic view of life. He taught school, sailed to Liverpool before the mast, then shipped on a Pacific whaling voyage. He deserted at the Marquesas Islands, living for a month among the cannibal Typee natives (July, 1842). An Australian whaleship took him to Tahiti, where he was jailed with the rest of the crew for mutiny, but he escaped and spent some months as a beachcomber. A third whaleship took him on to Hawaii, where he lived for some months before he sailed home in the crew of the frigate *United States*. From these adventures came his popular but increasingly imaginative travel romances: *Typee* (1846), *Omoo* (1847), the allegorical *Mardi* (1849), *Redburn* (1849), *White-Jacket* (1850), and his masterpiece, *Moby-Dick* (1851). Melville married in 1847 and lived in Pittsfield, Massachusetts. His later works of fiction were not sea romances and sold poorly. He gave up professional writing and for twenty years served as a customs inspector in New York. The author died in 1891. *Billy Budd, Sailor,* a short novel written in Melville's last years, was published for the first time in 1924, on the crest of a Melville revival that began about 1920 and continues to the present day—a revival that has established him among the greatest American writers.

BILLY BUDD

and
Other Tales

❈ by ❈

HERMAN MELVILLE

❈

With an Afterword
by WILLARD THORP

Revised and Updated Bibliography

A SIGNET CLASSIC

SIGNET CLASSIC
Published by the Penguin Group
Penguin Books USA Inc., 375 Hudson Street,
New York, New York 10014, U.S.A.
Penguin Books Ltd, 27 Wrights Lane,
London W8 5TZ, England
Penguin Books Australia Ltd, Ringwood,
Victoria, Australia
Penguin Books Canada Ltd, 10 Alcorn Ave., Suite 300,
Toronto, Canada M4V 3B2
Penguin Books (N.Z.) Ltd, 182–190 Wairau Road,
Auckland 10, New Zealand

Penguin Books Ltd, Registered Offices:
Harmondsworth, Middlesex, England

Published by Signet Classic, an imprint of New American Library,
a division of Penguin Books USA Inc.

35   34   33   32   31   30   29   28   27

Cover painting, "The Fort and Ten Pound Island, Goucester, Mass.," by Fitz Hugh Lave.
Courtesy of Kennedy Galleries, New York.

REGISTERED TRADEMARK—MARCA REGISTRADA

Printed in the United States of America

CONTENTS

Billy Budd

(An inside narrative)

DEDICATED TO

JACK CHASE

ENGLISHMAN

Wherever that great heart may now be
Here on Earth or harbored in Paradise
Captain of the maintop in the year 1843
in the U.S. Frigate *United States*

PREFACE

THE year 1797, the year of this narrative, belongs to a period which, as every thinker now feels, involved a crisis for Christendom not exceeded in its undetermined momentousness at the time by any other era whereof there is record. The opening proposition made by the Spirit of that Age involved rectification of the Old World's hereditary wrongs. In France, to some extent, this was bloodily effected. But what then? Straightway the Revolution itself became a wrongdoer, one more oppressive than the kings. Under Napoleon it enthroned upstart kings, and initiated that prolonged agony of continual war whose final throe was Waterloo. During those years not the wisest could have foreseen that the outcome of all would be what to some thinkers apparently it has since turned out to be—a political advance along nearly the whole line for Europeans.

Now, as elsewhere hinted, it was something caught from the Revolutionary Spirit that at Spithead emboldened the man-of-war's men to rise against real abuses, long-standing ones, and afterwards at the Nore to make inordinate and aggressive demands—successful resistance to which was confirmed only when the ringleaders were hung for an admonitory spectacle to the anchored fleet. Yet, in a way analogous to the operation of the Revolution at large, the Great Mutiny, though by Englishmen naturally deemed monstrous at the time, doubtless gave the first latent prompting to most important reforms in the British navy.

1

In the time before steamships, or then more frequently than now, a stroller along the docks of any considerable seaport would occasionally have his attention arrested by a group of bronzed mariners, man-of-war's men or merchant-sailors in holiday attire ashore on liberty. In certain instances they would flank, or, like a bodyguard, quite surround, some superior figure of their own class, moving along with them like Aldebaran among the lesser lights of his constellation. That signal object was the "Handsome Sailor" of the less prosaic time alike of the military and merchant navies. With no perceptible trace of the vainglorious about him, rather with the offhand unaffectedness of natural regality, he seemed to accept the spontaneous homage of his shipmates. A somewhat remarkable instance recurs to me. In Liverpool, now half a century ago, I saw under the shadow of the great dingy street-wall of Prince's Dock (an obstruction long since removed) a common sailor, so intensely black that he must needs have been a native African of the unadulterate blood of Ham. A symmetric figure much above the average height. The two ends of a gay silk handkerchief thrown loose about the neck danced upon the displayed ebony of his chest; in his ears were big hoops of gold, and a Scotch Highland bonnet with a tartan band set off his shapely head.

It was a hot noon in July, and his face, lustrous with perspiration, beamed with barbaric good humor. In jovial sallies right and left, his white teeth flashing into view, he rollicked along, the center of a company of his shipmates. These were made up of such an assortment of tribes and complexions as would have well fitted them to be marched up by Anacharsis Cloots before the bar of the first French

Assembly as Representatives of the Human Race. At each spontaneous tribute rendered by the wayfarers to this black pagoda of a fellow—the tribute of a pause and stare, and less frequent an exclamation—the motley retinue showed that they took that sort of pride in the evoker of it which the Assyrian priests doubtless showed for their grand sculptured Bull when the faithful prostrated themselves.

To return.

If in some cases a bit of a nautical Murat in setting forth his person ashore, the handsome sailor of the period in question evinced nothing of the dandified Billy-be-Damn, an amusing character all but extinct now, but occasionally to be encountered, and in a form yet more amusing than the original, at the tiller of the boats on the tempestuous Erie Canal, or, more likely, vaporing in the groggeries along the towpath. Invariably a proficient in his perilous calling, he was also more or less of a mighty boxer or wrestler. It was strength and beauty. Tales of his prowess were recited. Ashore he was the champion, afloat the spokesman; on every suitable occasion always foremost. Close-reefing topsails in a gale, there he was, astride the weather yard-arm-end, foot in the Flemish horse as "stirrup," both hands tugging at the "earing" as at a bridle, in very much the attitude of young Alexander curbing the fiery Bucephalus. A superb figure, tossed up as by the horns of Taurus against the thunderous sky, cheerily hallooing to the strenuous file along the spar.

The moral nature was seldom out of keeping with the physical make. Indeed, except as toned by the former, the comeliness and power, always attractive in masculine conjunction, hardly could have drawn the sort of honest homage the Handsome Sailor in some examples received from his less gifted associates.

Such a cynosure, at least in aspect, and something such too in nature, though with important variations made apparent as the story proceeds, was welkin-eyed Billy Budd, or Baby Budd as more familiarly under circumstances hereafter to be given he at last came to be called, aged twenty-one, a foretopman of the British fleet toward the close of the last decade of the eighteenth century. It was not very long prior to the time of the narration that follows that he had entered the King's Service, having been impressed on the Narrow Seas from a homeward-bound English merchantman into a seventy-four outward-bound, H.M.S. *Indomitable;* which ship, as was not unusual in those hurried days having been obliged to put to sea short of her proper complement of men. Plump upon Billy at first sight in the gangway the boarding officer Lieutenant Ratcliffe pounced, even before the merchantman's crew was formally mustered on the quarter-deck for his deliberate inspection. And him only he elected. For whether it was because the other men when ranged before him showed to ill advantage after Billy, or whether he had some scruples in view of the merchantman being rather short-handed, however it might be, the officer contented himself with his first spontaneous choice. To the surprise of the ship's company, though much to the lieutenant's satisfaction, Billy made no demur. But, indeed, any demur would have been as idle as the protest of a goldfinch popped into a cage.

Noting this uncomplaining acquiescence, all but cheerful one might say, the shipmates turned a surprise glance of silent reproach at the sailor. The shipmaster was one of those worthy mortals found in every vocation, even the humbler ones—the sort of person whom everybody agrees in calling "a respectable man." And—nor so strange to report as it may appear to be—though a plowman of the troubled waters, lifelong contending with the intractable elements, there was nothing this honest soul at heart loved better than simple peace and quiet. For the rest, he was fifty or thereabouts, a little inclined to corpulence, a prepossessing face, unwhiskered, and of an agreeable color— a rather full face, humanely intelligent in expression. On a fair day with a fair wind and all going well, a certain musical chime in his voice seemed to be the veritable unobstructed outcome of the innermost man. He had much prudence, much conscientiousness, and there were occasions when these virtues were the cause of overmuch disquietude in him. On a passage, so long as his craft was in any proximity to land, no sleep for Captain Graveling. He took to heart those serious responsibilities not so heavily borne by some shipmasters.

Now while Billy Budd was down in the forecastle getting his kit together, the *Indomitable*'s lieutenant, burly and bluff, nowise disconcerted by Captain Graveling's omitting

to proffer the customary hospitalities on an occasion so
unwelcome to him, an omission simply caused by preoccu-
pation of thought, unceremoniously invited himself into the
cabin, and also to a flask from the spirit-locker, a receptacle
which his experienced eye instantly discovered. In fact he
was one of those sea dogs in whom all the hardship and
peril of naval life in the great prolonged wars of his time
never impaired the natural instinct for sensuous enjoyment.
His duty he always faithfully did; but duty is sometimes a
dry obligation, and he was for irrigating its aridity, whenso-
ever possible, with a fertilizing decoction of strong waters.
For the cabin's proprietor there was nothing left but to
play the part of the enforced host with whatever grace and
alacrity were practicable. As necessary adjuncts to the flask,
he silently placed tumbler and water-jug before the irrepres-
sible guest. But excusing himself from partaking just then,
he dismally watched the unembarrassed officer deliberately
diluting his grog a little, then tossing it off in three swallows,
pushing the empty tumbler away, yet not so far as to be
beyond easy reach, at the same time settling himself in his
seat and smacking his lips with high satisfaction, looking
straight at the host.

These proceedings over, the master broke the silence,
and there lurked a rueful reproach in the tone of his voice:
"Lieutenant, you are going to take my best man from me,
the jewel of 'em."

"Yes, I know," rejoined the other, immediately drawing
back the tumbler preliminary to a replenishing. "Yes, I
know. Sorry."

"Beg pardon, but you don't understand, Lieutenant. See
here now. Before I shipped that young fellow, my forecastle
was a rat-pit of quarrels. It was black times, I tell you
aboard the *Rights* here. I was worried to that degree my
pipe had no comfort for me. But Billy came, and it was
like a Catholic priest striking peace in an Irish shindy. Not
that he preached to them or said or did anything in particular, but a virtue went out of him, sugaring the sour ones.
They took to him like hornets to treacle; all but the buffer
of the gang, the big shaggy chap with the fire-red whiskers.
He indeed, out of envy, perhaps, of the newcomer, and
thinking such a 'sweet and pleasant fellow,' as he mockingly
designated him to the others, could hardly have the spirit

of a gamecock, must needs bestir himself in trying to get up
an ugly row with him. Billy forebore with him and reasoned
with him in a pleasant way—he is something like myself,
Lieutenant, to whom aught like a quarrel is hateful—but
nothing served. So, in the second dog watch one day the
Red Whiskers, in presence of the others, under pretense of
showing Billy just whence a sirloin steak was cut—for the
fellow had once been a butcher—insultingly gave him a dig
under the ribs. Quick as lightning Billy let fly his arm.
I dare say he never meant to do quite as much as he did,
but anyhow he gave the burly fool a terrible drubbing. It
took about half a minute, I should think. And, Lord bless
you, the lubber was astonished at the celerity. And will you
believe it, Lieutenant, the Red Whiskers now really loves
Billy—loves him, or is the biggest hypocrite that ever I
heard of. But they all love him. Some of 'em do his washing, darn his old trousers for him; the carpenter is at odd
times making a pretty little chest of drawers for him. Anybody will do anything for Billy Budd; and it's the happy
family here. But now, Lieutenant, if that young fellow goes
—I know how it will be aboard the *Rights*. Not again very
soon shall I, coming up from dinner, lean over the capstan
smoking a quiet pipe—no, not very soon again, I think.
Aye, Lieutenant, you are going to take away the jewel of
'em; you are going to take away my peacemaker!" And
with that the good soul had really some ado in checking a
rising sob.

"Well," said the officer, who had listened with amused
interest to all this, and now waxing merry with his tipple,
"well, blessed are the peacemakers, especially the fighting
peacemakers! And such are the seventy-four beauties some
of which you see poking their noses out of the portholes of
yonder warship lying to for me," pointing through the cabin
window at the *Indomitable*. "But courage! don't you look
so downhearted, man. Why, I pledge you in advance the
royal approbation. Rest assured that His Majesty will be
delighted to know that in a time when his hardtack is not
sought for by sailors with such avidity as should be, a time
also when some shipmasters privily resent the borrowing
from them a tar or two for the services, His Majesty, I say,
will be delighted to learn that *one* shipmaster at least cheerfully surrenders to the King the flower of his flock, a sailor

who with equal loyalty makes no dissent.—But where's my
beauty? Ah," looking through the cabin's open door, "here
he comes; and, by Jove—lugging along his chest—Apollo
with his portmanteau!—My man," stepping out to him,
"you can't take that big box aboard a warship. The boxes
there are mostly shot-boxes. Put your duds in a bag, lad.
Boot and saddle for the cavalrymen, bag and hammock for
the man-of-war's man."

The transfer from chest to bag was made. And, after
seeing his man into the cutter and then following him down,
the lieutenant pushed off from the *Rights-of-Man*. That
was the merchant ship's name, though by her master and
crew abbreviated in sailor fashion into *The Rights*. The
hard-headed Dundee owner was a staunch admirer of
Thomas Paine, whose book in rejoinder to Burke's arraign-
ment of the French Revolution had then been published for
some time and had gone everywhere. In christening his
vessel after the title of Paine's volume the man of Dundee
was something like his contemporary shipowner, Stephen
Girard of Philadelphia, whose sympathies, alike with his
native land and its liberal philosophers, he evinced by
naming his ships after Voltaire, Diderot, and so forth.

But now, when the boat swept under the merchantman's
stern, and officer and oarsmen were noting—some bitterly
and others with a grin—the name emblazoned there, just
then it was that the new recruit jumped up from the bow
where the coxswain had directed him to sit, and waving his
hat to his silent shipmates sorrowfully looking over at him
from the taffrail, bade the lads a genial good-bye. Then,
making a salutation as to the ship herself, "And good-bye
to you too, old *Rights of Man*."

"Down, sir!" roared the lieutenant, instantly assuming all
the rigor of his rank, though with difficulty repressing a
smile.

To be sure, Billy's action was a terrible breach of naval
decorum. But in that decorum he had never been instructed, in consideration of which the lieutenant would
hardly have been so energetic in reproof but for the
concluding farewell to the ship. This he rather took as
meant to convey a covert sally on the new recruit's part,
a sly slur at impressment in general, and that of himself
in especial. And yet, more likely, if satire it was in effect,

it was hardly so by intention, for Billy, though happily
endowed with the gaiety of high health, youth, and a free
heart, was yet by no means of a satirical turn. The will
to it and the sinister dexterity were alike wanting. To deal
in double meanings and insinuations of any sort was quite
foreign to his nature.

As to his enforced enlistment, that he seemed to take
pretty much as he was wont to take any vicissitude of
weather. Like the animals, though no philosopher, he was,
without knowing it, practically a fatalist. And it may be
that he rather liked this adventurous turn in his affairs,
which promised an opening into novel scenes and martial
excitements.

Aboard the *Indomitable* our merchant-sailor was forthwith rated as an able seaman and assigned to the starboard watch of the foretop. He was soon at home in the
service, not at all disliked for his unpretentious good looks
and a sort of genial happy-go-lucky air. No merrier man
in his mess, in marked contrast to certain other individuals
included like himself among the impressed portion of the
ship's company; for these when not actively employed
were sometimes, and more particularly in the last dog
watch when the drawing near of twilight induced reverie,
apt to fall into a saddish mood which in some partook
of sullenness. But they were not so young as our foretopman, and no few of them must have known a hearth of
some sort; others may have had wives and children left,
too probably, in uncertain circumstances, and hardly any
but must have had acknowledged kith and kin, while for
Billy, as will shortly be seen, his entire family was practically invested in himself.

2

Though our new-made foretopman was well received
in the top and on the gun decks, hardly here was he that
cynosure he had previously been among those minor
ship's companies of the merchant marine, with which companies only had he hitherto consorted.

He was young, and, despite his all but fully developed
frame, in aspect looked even younger than he really was,
owing to a lingering adolescent expression in the as yet
smooth face all but feminine in purity of natural com-

plexion but where, thanks to his seagoing, the lily was
quite suppressed and the rose had some ado visibly to flush
through the tan.

To one essentially such a novice in the complexities of
factitious life, the abrupt transition from his former and
simpler sphere to the ampler and more knowing world of
a great warship—this might well have abashed him had
there been any conceit or vanity in his composition. Among
her miscellaneous multitude, the *Indomitable* mustered
several individuals who, however inferior in grade, were
of no common natural stamp, sailors more signally sus-
ceptive of that air which continuous martial discipline and
repeated presence in battle can in some degree impart even
to the average man. As the *handsome sailor* Billy Budd's
position aboard the seventy-four was something analogous
to that of a rustic beauty transplanted from the provinces
and brought into competition with the highborn dames of
the court. But this change of circumstances he scarce
noted. As little did he observe that something about him
provoked an ambiguous smile in one or two harder faces
among the bluejackets. Nor less unaware was he of the
peculiar favorable effect his person and demeanor had
upon the more intelligent gentlemen of the quarter-deck.
Nor could this well have been otherwise. Cast in a mould
peculiar to the finest physical examples of those Englishmen in whom the Saxon strain would seem not at all to
partake of any Norman or other admixture, he showed in
face that humane look of reposeful good nature which the
Greek sculptor in some instances gave to his heroic strong
man, Hercules. But this again was subtly modified by
another and pervasive quality. The ear, small and shapely,
the arch of the foot, the curve in mouth and nostril, even
the indurated hand dyed to the orange-tawny of the
toucan's bill, a hand telling alike of the halyards and
tar bucket; but, above all, something in the mobile expression, and every chance attitude and movement, something suggestive of a mother eminently favored by Love
and the Graces; all this strangely indicated a lineage in
direct contradiction to his lot. The mysteriousness here
became less mysterious through a matter of fact elicited
when Billy at the capstan was being formally mustered
into the service. Asked by the officer, a small brisk little

gentleman, as it chanced among other questions, his place of birth, he replied, "Please, sir, I don't know."

"Don't know where you were born?—Who was your father?"

"God knows, sir."

Struck by the straightforward simplicity of these replies, the officer next asked, "Do you know anything about your beginning?"

"No, sir. But I have heard that I was found in a pretty silk-lined basket hanging one morning from the knocker of a good man's door in Bristol."

"Found say you? Well," throwing back his head and looking up and down the new recruit; "well, it turns out to have been a pretty good find. Hope they'll find some more like you, my man; the fleet sadly needs them."

Yes, Billy Budd was a foundling, a presumable by-blow, and, evidently, no ignoble one. Noble descent was as evident in him as in a blood horse.

For the rest, with little or no sharpness of faculty or any trace of the wisdom of the serpent, nor yet quite a dove, he possessed that kind and degree of intelligence going along with the unconventional rectitude of a sound human creature, one to whom not yet has been proffered the questionable apple of knowledge. He was illiterate; he could not read, but he could sing, and like the illiterate nightingale was sometimes the composer of his own song.

Of self-consciousness he seemed to have little or none, or about as much as we may reasonably impute to a dog of Saint Bernard's breed.

Habitually living with the elements and knowing little more of the land than as a beach, or, rather, that portion of the terraqueous globe providentially set apart for dance-houses, doxies, and tapsters, in short what sailors call a "fiddlers' green," his simple nature remained unsophisticated by those moral obliquities which are not in every case incompatible with that manufacturable thing known as respectability. But are sailors, frequenters of fiddlers' greens, without vices? No; but less often than with landsmen do their vices, so called, partake of crookedness of heart, seeming less to proceed from viciousness than exuberance of vitality after long constraint; frank manifestations in accordance with natural law. By his original constitution aided by the cooperating influences of his lot, Billy in many respects was little more than a sort of upright barbarian, much such perhaps as Adam presumably might have been ere the urbane Serpent wriggled himself into his company.

And here be it submitted that, apparently going to corroborate the doctrine of man's fall, a doctrine now popularly ignored, it is observable that where certain virtues pristine and unadulterate peculiarly characterize anybody in the external uniform of civilization, they will upon scrutiny seem not to be derived from custom or convention, but rather to be out of keeping with these, as if indeed exceptionally transmitted from a period prior to Cain's city and citified man. The character marked by such qualities has to an unvitiated taste an untampered-with flavor like that of berries, while the man thoroughly civilized even in a fair specimen of the breed has to the same moral palate a questionable smack as of a compounded wine. To any stray inheritor of these primitive qualities found, like Kaspar Hauser, wandering dazed in any Christian capital of our time, the good-natured poet's famous invocation, near two thousand years ago, of the good rustic out of his latitude in the Rome of the Caesars, still appropriately holds:

> Honest and poor, faithful in word and thought,
> What has thee, Fabian, to the city brought.

Though our Handsome Sailor had as much of masculine beauty as one can expect anywhere to see, nevertheless, like the beautiful woman in one of Hawthorne's minor tales, there was just one thing amiss in him. No visible blemish indeed, as with the lady; no, but an occasional liability to a vocal defect. Though in the hour of elemental uproar or peril he was everything that a sailor should be, yet under sudden provocation of strong heart-feeling his voice, otherwise singularly musical, as if expressive of the harmony within, was apt to develop an organic hesitancy, in fact more or less of a stutter or even worse. In this particular Billy was a striking instance that the arch interferer, the envious marplot of Eden, still has more or less to do with every human consignment to this planet of earth. In every case, one way or another he is sure to slip in his little card, as much as to remind us—I too have a hand here.

The avowal of such an imperfection in the Handsome Sailor should be evidence not alone that he is not presented as a conventional hero, but also that the story in which he is the main figure is no romance.

3

At the time of Billy Budd's arbitrary enlistment into the *Indomitable* that ship was on her way to join the Mediterranean fleet. No long time elapsed before the junction was effected. As one of that fleet the seventy-four participated in its movements, though at times, on account of her superior sailing qualities, in the absence of frigates, despatched on separate duty as a scout and at times on less temporary service. But with all this the story has little concernment, restricted as it is to the inner life of one particular ship and the career of an individual sailor.

It was the summer of 1797. In the April of that year had occurred the commotion at Spithead, followed in May by a second and yet more serious outbreak in the fleet at the Nore. The latter is known, and without exaggeration in the epithet, as the Great Mutiny. It was indeed a demonstration more menacing to England than the contemporary manifestoes and conquering and proselyting armies of the French Directory.

To the British Empire the Nore mutiny was what a strike in the fire brigade would be to London threatened by general arson. In a crisis when the kingdom might well have anticipated the famous signal that some years later published along the naval line of battle what it was that upon occasion England expected of Englishmen, *that* was the time when at the mastheads of the three-deckers and seventy-fours moored in her own roadstead—a fleet, the right arm of a Power then all but the sole free conservative one of the Old World—the bluejackets, to be numbered by thousands, ran up with huzzahs the British colors with the union and cross wiped out; by that cancellation transmuting the flag of founded law and freedom defined into the enemy's red meteor of unbridled and unbounded revolt. Reasonable discontent growing out of practical grievances in the fleet had been ignited into irrational combustion as by live cinders blown across the Channel from France in flames.

The event converted into irony for a time those spirited strains of Dibdin—as a song-writer no mean auxiliary to the English Government at the European conjuncture —strains celebrating, among other things, the patriotic devotion of the British tar:

And as for my life, 'tis the King's!

Such an episode in the Island's grand naval story her naval historians naturally abridge, one of them (G. P. R. James) candidly acknowledging that fain would he pass it over did not "impartiality forbid fastidiousness." And yet his mention is less a narration than a reference, having to do hardly at all with details. Nor are these readily to be found in the libraries. Like some other events in every age befalling states everywhere including America, the Great Mutiny was of such character that national pride along with views of policy would fain shade it off into the historical background. Such events cannot be ignored, but there is a considerate way of historically treating them. If a well-constituted individual refrains from blazoning aught amiss or calamitous in his family, a nation in the like circumstance may without reproach be equally discreet.

Though after parleyings between Government and the ringleaders, and concessions by the former as to some glaring abuses, the first uprising—that at Spithead—with difficulty was put down, or matters for the time pacified; yet at the Nore the unforeseen renewal of insurrection on a yet larger scale, and emphasized in the conferences that ensued by demands deemed by the authorities not only inadmissible but aggressively insolent, indicated—if the Red Flag did not sufficiently do so—what was the spirit animating the men. Final suppression, however, there was, but only made possible perhaps by the unswerving loyalty of the marine corps and voluntary resumption of loyalty among influential sections of the crews.

To some extent the Nore Mutiny may be regarded as analogous to the distempering irruption of contagious fever in a frame constitutionally sound, and which anon throws it off.

At all events, of these thousands of mutineers were

some of the tars who not so very long afterwards—whether
wholly prompted thereto by patriotism, or pugnacious
instinct, or by both—helped to win a coronet for Nelson
at the Nile, and the naval crown of crowns for him at
Trafalgar. To the mutineers those battles and especially
Trafalgar were a plenary absolution and a grand one:
For all that goes to make up scenic naval display, heroic
magnificence in arms, those battles, especially Trafalgar,
stand unmatched in human annals.

4

*Concerning "The greatest sailor since our
world began."*—TENNYSON

In this matter of writing, resolve as one may to keep
to the main road, some bypaths have an enticement not
readily to be withstood. I am going to err into such a
bypath. If the reader will keep me company I shall be
glad. At the least we can promise ourselves that pleasure
which is wickedly said to be in sinning, for a literary sin
the divergence will be.

Very likely it is no new remark that the inventions of
our time have at last brought about a change in sea
warfare in degree corresponding to the revolution in all
warfare effected by the original introduction from China
into Europe of gunpowder. The first European firearm, a
clumsy contrivance, was, as is well known, scouted by
no few of the knights as a base implement, good enough
peradventure for weavers too craven to stand up crossing
steel with steel in frank fight. But as ashore knightly valor,
though shorn of its blazonry, did not cease with the knights,
neither on the seas, though nowadays in encounters there
a certain kind of displayed gallantry be fallen out of date
as hardly applicable under changed circumstances, did
the nobler qualities of such naval magnates as Don John
of Austria, Doria, Van Tromp, Jean Bart, the long line
of British Admirals and the American Decaturs of 1812,
become obsolete with their wooden walls.

Nevertheless, to anybody who can hold the Present at
its worth without being inappreciative of the Past, it may
be forgiven, if to such an one the solitary old hulk at
Portsmouth, Nelson's *Victory,* seems to float there, not
alone as the decaying monument of a fame incorruptible,

but also as a poetic reproach, softened by its picturesque-
ness, to the *Monitors* and yet mightier hulls of the European ironclads. And this not altogether because such craft
are unsightly, unavoidably lacking the symmetry and
grand lines of the old battleships, but equally for other
reasons.

There are some, perhaps, who, while not altogether
inaccessible to that poetic reproach just alluded to, may
yet on behalf of the new order be disposed to parry it; and
this to the extent of iconoclasm, if need be. For example,
prompted by the sight of the star inserted in the *Victory*'s
quarter-deck designating the spot where the Great Sailor
fell, these martial utilitarians may suggest considerations
implying that Nelson's ornate publication of his person
in battle was not only unnecessary, but not military, nay,
savored of foolhardiness and vanity. They may add, too,
that at Trafalgar it was in effect nothing less than a challenge to death, and death came; and that but for his
bravado the victorious admiral might possibly have survived the battle, and so, instead of having his sagacious
dying injunctions overruled by his immediate successor
in command, he himself when the contest was decided
might have brought his shattered fleet to anchor, a proceeding which might have averted the deplorable loss of
life by shipwreck in the elemental tempest that followed
the martial one.

Well, should we set aside the more disputable point
whether for various reasons it was possible to anchor the
fleet, then plausibly enough the Benthamites of war may
urge the above.

But the *might-have-been* is but boggy ground to build
on. And, certainly, in foresight as to the larger issue of an
encounter, and anxious preparations for it—buoying the
deadly way and mapping it out, as at Copenhagen—few
commanders have been so painstakingly circumspect as
this same reckless declarer of his person in fight.

Personal prudence, even when dictated by quite other
than selfish considerations, surely is no special virtue in a
military man; while an excessive love of glory, impassion-
ing a less burning impulse, the honest sense of duty, is
the first. If the name *Wellington* is not so much of a
trumpet to the blood as the simpler name *Nelson,* the

reason for this may perhaps be inferred from the above. Alfred in his funeral ode on the victor of Waterloo ventures not to call him the greatest soldier of all time, though in the same ode he invokes Nelson as "the greatest sailor since our world began."

At Trafalgar Nelson on the brink of opening the fight sat down and wrote his last brief will and testament. If under the presentiment of the most magnificent of all victories to be crowned by his own glorious death, a sort of priestly motive led him to dress his person in the jeweled vouchers of his own shining deeds; if thus to have adorned himself for the altar and the sacrifice were indeed vainglory, then affectation and fustian is each more heroic line in the great epics and dramas, since in such lines the poet but embodies in verse those exaltations of sentiment that a nature like Nelson, the opportunity being given, vitalizes into acts.

5

Yes, the outbreak at the Nore was put down. But not every grievance was redressed. If the contractors, for example, were no longer permitted to ply some practices peculiar to their tribe everywhere, such as providing shoddy cloth, rations not sound or false in the measure, not the less impressment, for one thing, went on. By custom sanctioned for centuries, and judicially maintained by a Lord Chancellor as late as Mansfield, that mode of manning the fleet, a mode now fallen into a sort of abeyance but never formally renounced, it was not practicable to give up in those years. Its abrogation would have crippled the indispensable fleet, one wholly under canvas, no steam power, its innumerable sails and thousands of cannon, everything in short, worked by muscle alone; a fleet the more insatiate in demand for men, because then multiplying its ships of all grades against contingencies present and to come of the convulsed Continent.

Discontent foreran the two mutinies, and more or less it lurkingly survived them. Hence it was not unreasonable to apprehend some return of trouble sporadic or general. One instance of such apprehensions: In the same year with this story, Nelson, then Vice Admiral Sir Horatio, being with the fleet off the Spanish coast, was directed by the

admiral in command to shift his pennant from the *Captain*
to the *Theseus,* and for this reason: that the latter ship,
having newly arrived on the station from home, where
it had taken part in the Great Mutiny, danger was apprehended from the temper of the men, and it was thought
that an officer like Nelson was the one, not indeed to
terrorize the crew into base subjection, but to win them,
by force of his mere presence, back to an allegiance, if
not as enthusiastic as his own, yet as true. So it was that
for a time on more than one quarter-deck anxiety did exist.
At sea, precautionary vigilance was strained against relapse.
At short notice an engagement might come on. When it did,
the lieutenants assigned to batteries felt it incumbent on
them, in some instances, to stand with drawn swords
behind the men working the guns.

6

But on board the seventy-four in which Billy now swung
his hammock, very little in the manner of the men and
nothing obvious in the demeanor of the officers would have
suggested to an ordinary observer that the Great Mutiny
was a recent event. In their general bearing and conduct
the commissioned officers of a warship naturally take their
tone from the commander, that is if he have that ascendancy of character that ought to be his.

Captain the Honorable Edward Fairfax Vere, to give his
full title, was a bachelor of forty or thereabouts, a sailor
of distinction even in a time prolific of renowned seamen.
Though allied to the higher nobility his advancement had
not been altogether owing to influences connected with
that circumstance. He had seen much service, been in
various engagements, always acquitting himself as an
officer mindful of the welfare of his men, but never tolerat-
ing an infraction of discipline; thoroughly versed in the
science of his profession, and intrepid to the verge of
temerity, though never injudiciously so. For his gallantry
in the West Indian waters as flag-lieutenant under Rodney
in that admiral's crowning victory over De Grasse, he was
made a post-captain.

Ashore in the garb of a civilian scarce anyone would
have taken him for a sailor, more especially that he never
garnished unprofessional talk with nautical terms, and,

grave in his bearing, evinced little appreciation of mere
humor. It was not out of keeping with these traits that
on a passage when nothing demanded his paramount
action, he was the most undemonstrative of men. Any
landsman observing this gentleman not conspicuous by
his stature and wearing no pronounced insignia, emerging
from his cabin to the open deck, and noting the silent
deference of the officers retiring to leeward, might have
taken him for the King's guest, a civilian aboard the King's
ship, some highly honorable discreet envoy on his way to
an important post. But in fact this unobtrusiveness of
demeanor may have proceeded from a certain unaffected
modesty of manhood sometimes accompanying a resolute
nature, a modesty evinced at all times not calling for
pronounced action, and which, shown in any rank of life,
suggests a virtue aristocratic in kind.

As with some other engaged in various departments of
the world's more heroic activities, Captain Vere, though
practical enough upon occasion, would at times betray a
certain dreaminess of mood. Standing alone on the weather
side of the quarter-deck, one hand holding by the rigging,
he would absently gaze off at the blank sea. At the presen-
tation to him then of some minor matter interrupting the
current of his thoughts he would show more or less irasci-
bility, but instantly he would control it.

In the navy he was popularly known by the appellation
"Starry Vere." How such a designation happened to fall
upon one who, whatever his sterling qualities, was without
any brilliant ones, was in this wise: A favorite kinsman,
Lord Denton, a free-hearted fellow, had been the first
to meet and congratulate him upon his return to England
from his West Indian cruise; and but the day previous
turning over a copy of Andrew Marvell's poems had
lighted, not for the first time however, upon the lines en-
titled "Appleton House," the name of one of the seats
of their common ancestor, a hero in the German wars of
the seventeenth century, in which poem occur the lines,

> This 'tis to have been from the first
> In a domestic heaven nursed,
> Under the discipline severe
> Of Fairfax and the starry Vere.

And so, upon embracing his cousin fresh from Rodney's

great victory wherein he had played so gallant a part,
brimming over with just family pride in the sailor of their
house, he exuberantly exclaimed, "Give ye joy, Ed; give
ye joy, my starry Vere!" This got currency, and the novel
prefix serving in familiar parlance readily to distinguish
the *Indomitable*'s captain from another Vere his senior,
a distant relative an officer of like rank in the navy, it
remained permanently attached to the surname.

7

In view of the part that the commander of the *Indomitable* plays in scenes shortly to follow, it may be well to
fill out that sketch of him outlined in the previous chapter.

Aside from his qualities as a sea officer Captain Vere
was an exceptional character. Unlike no few of England's
renowned sailors, long and arduous service, with signal
devotion to it, had not resulted in absorbing and *salting*
the entire man. He had a marked leaning toward everything intellectual. He loved books, never going to sea
without a newly replenished library, compact but of the
best. The isolated leisure, in some cases so wearisome,
falling at intervals to commanders even during a war cruise,
never was tedious to Captain Vere. With nothing of that
literary taste which less heeds the thing conveyed than the
vehicle, his bias was toward those books to which every
serious mind of superior order occupying any active post
of authority in the world naturally inclines: books treating
of actual men and events no matter of what era—history,
biography, and unconventional writers, who, free from
cant and convention, like Montaigne, honestly and in the
spirit of common sense philosophize upon realities.

In this love of reading he found confirmation of his own
more reasoned thoughts—confirmation which he had vainly
sought in social converse—so that, as touching most
fundamental topics, there had got to be established in him
some positive convictions, which he forefelt would abide
in him essentially unmodified so long as his intelligent part
remained unimpaired. In view of the troubled period in
which his lot was cast this was well for him. His settled
convictions were as a dike against those invading waters
of novel opinion, social, political, and otherwise, which
carried away as in a torrent no few minds in those days,

minds by nature not inferior to his own. While other
members of that aristocracy to which by birth he belonged
were incensed at the innovators mainly because their
theories were inimical to the privileged classes, not alone
Captain Vere disinterestedly opposed them because they
seemed to him incapable of embodiment in lasting institutions, but at war with the peace of the world and the true
welfare of mankind.

With minds less stored than his and less earnest, some
officers of his rank, with whom at times he would necessarily consort, found him lacking in the companionable
quality, a dry and bookish gentleman as they deemed.
Upon any chance withdrawal from their company one
would be apt to say to another, something like this: "Vere
is a noble fellow, Starry Vere. Spite the gazettes, Sir
Horatio" meaning him with the Lord title "is at bottom
scarce a better seaman or fighter. But between you and me
now don't you think there is a queer streak of the pedantic
running through him? Yes, like the King's yarn in a coil
of navy-rope?"

Some apparent ground there was for this sort of
confidential criticism, since not only did the captain's discourse never fall into the jocosely familiar, but in illustrat-
ing of any point touching the stirring personages and
events of the time he would be as apt to cite some historic
character or incident of antiquity as that he would cite
from the moderns. He seemed unmindful of the circumstance that to his bluff company such remote allusions,
however pertinent they might really be, were altogether
alien to men whose reading was mainly confined to the
journals. But considerateness in such matters is not easy
to natures constituted like Captain Vere's. Their honesty
prescribes to them directness, sometimes far-reaching like
that of a migratory fowl that in its flight never heeds when
it crosses a frontier.

8

The lieutenants and other commissioned gentlemen
forming Captain Vere's staff it is not necessary here to
particularize, nor needs it to make any mention of any
of the warrant officers. But among the petty officers was
one who, having much to do with the story, may as well

be forthwith introduced. His portrait I essay, but shall never hit it. This was John Claggart, the master-at-arms. But that sea title may to landsmen seem somewhat equivocal. Originally, doubtless, that petty officer's function was the instruction of the men in the use of arms, sword or cutlass. But very long ago, owing to the advance in gunnery making hand-to-hand encounters less frequent and giving to niter and sulphur the preeminence over steel, that function ceased; the master-at-arms of a great warship becoming a sort of chief of police charged among other matters with the duty of preserving order on the populous lower gun decks.

Claggart was a man about five-and-thirty, somewhat spare and tall, yet of no ill figure upon the whole. His hand was too small and shapely to have been accustomed to hard toil. The face was a notable one, the features all except the chin cleanly cut as those on a Greek medallion; yet the chin, beardless as Tecumseh's, had something of strange protuberant heaviness in its make that recalled the prints of the Rev. Dr. Titus Oates, the historic deponent with the clerical drawl in the time of Charles II and the fraud of the alleged Popish Plot. It served Claggart in his office that his eye could cast a tutoring glance. His brow was of the sort phrenologically associated with more than average intellect; silken jet curls partly clustering over it, making a foil to the pallor below, a pallor tinged with a faint shade of amber akin to the hue of time-tinted marbles of old. This complexion, singularly contrasting with the red or deeply bronzed visages of the sailors, and in part the result of his official seclusion from the sunlight, though it was not exactly displeasing, nevertheless seemed to hint of something defective or abnormal in the constitution and blood. But his general aspect and manner were so suggestive of an education and career incongruous with his naval function that when not actively engaged in it he looked like a man of high quality, social and moral, who for reasons of his own was keeping incog. Nothing was known of his former life. It might be that he was an Englishman, and yet there lurked a bit of accent in his speech suggesting that possibly he was not such by birth, but through naturalization in early childhood. Among certain grizzled sea gossips of the gun decks and forecastle

went a rumor perdue that the master-at-arms was a
chevalier who had volunteered into the king's navy by way
of compounding for some mysterious swindle whereof he
had been arraigned at the King's Bench. The fact that
nobody could substantiate this report was, of course,
nothing against its secret currency. Such a rumor once
started on the gun decks in reference to almost anyone
below the rank of a commissioned officer would, during
the period assigned to this narrative, have seemed not
altogether wanting in credibility to the tarry old wiseacres
of a man-of-war crew. And indeed a man of Claggart's
accomplishments, without prior nautical experience entering the navy at mature life, as he did, and necessarily
allotted at the start to the lowest grade in it; a man too
who never made allusion to his previous life ashore, these
were circumstances which in the dearth of exact knowledge
as to his true antecedents opened to the invidious a vague
field for unfavorable surmise.

But the sailors' dog-watch gossip concerning him derived
a vague plausibility from the fact that now for some period
the British navy could so little afford to be squeamish in
the matter of keeping up the muster rolls, that not only
were press gangs notoriously abroad both afloat and ashore,
but there was little or no secret about another matter,
namely that the London police were at liberty to capture
any questionable fellow at large, and summarily ship him
to the dockyard or fleet. Furthermore, even among voluntary enlistments there were instances where the motive
thereto partook neither of patriotic impulse nor yet of a
random desire to experience a bit of sea life and martial
adventure. Insolvent debtors of minor grade, together
with the promiscuous lame ducks of morality, found in
the navy a convenient and secure refuge. Secure, because
once enlisted aboard a King's ship, they were as much in
sanctuary as the transgressor of the Middle Ages harboring himself under the shadow of the altar. Such sanctioned
irregularities, which for obvious reasons the government
would hardly think to parade at the time and which consequently, and as affecting the least influential class of
mankind, have all but dropped into oblivion, lend color
to something for the truth whereof I do not vouch, and
hence have some scruple in stating; something I remember

having seen in print, though the book I cannot recall; but the same thing was personally communicated to me now more than forty years ago by an old pensioner in a cocked hat with whom I had a most interesting talk on the terrace at Greenwich, a Baltimore Negro, a Trafalgar man. It was to this effect: In the case of a warship short of hands whose speedy sailing was imperative, the deficient quota, in lack of any other way of making it good, would be eked out by drafts culled direct from the jails. For reasons previously suggested it would not perhaps be easy at the present day directly to prove or disprove the allegation. But allowed as a verity, how significant would it be of England's straits at the time, confronted by those wars which like a flight of harpies rose shrieking from the din and dust of the fallen Bastille. That era appears measurably clear to us who look back at it, and but read of it. But to the grandfathers of us graybeards, the more thoughtful of them, the genius of it presented an aspect like that of Camöen's Spirit of the Cape, an eclipsing menace mysterious and prodigious. Not America was exempt from apprehension. At the height of Napoleon's unexampled conquests, there were Americans who had fought at Bunker Hill who looked forward to the possibility that the Atlantic might prove no barrier against the ultimate schemes of this French upstart from the revolutionary chaos who seemed in act of fulfilling judgment prefigured in the Apocalypse.

But the less credence was to be given to the gun-deck talk touching Claggart, seeing that no man holding his office in a man-of-war can ever hope to be popular with the crew. Besides, in derogatory comments upon anyone against whom they have a grudge, or for any reason or no reason mislike, sailors are much like landsmen—they are apt to exaggerate or romance it.

About as much was really known to the *Indomitable*'s tars of the master-at-arms' career before entering the service as an astronomer knows about a comet's travels prior to its first observable appearance in the sky. The verdict of the sea quidnuncs has been cited only by way of showing what sort of moral impression the man made upon rude uncultivated natures whose conceptions of human wickedness were necessarily of the narrowest, limited to

ideas of vulgar rascality—a thief among the swinging hammocks during a night watch, or the man-brokers and land-
sharks of the sea ports.

It was no gossip, however, but fact, that though, as
before hinted, Claggart upon his entrance into the navy
was, as a novice, assigned to the least honorable section
of a man-of-war's crew, embracing the drudgery, he did
not long remain there.

The superior capacity he immediately evinced, his constitutional sobriety, ingratiating deference to superiors,
together with a peculiar ferreting genius manifested on a
singular occasion, all this capped by a certain austere
patriotism abruptly advanced him to the position of master-
at-arms.

Of this maritime chief of police the ship's corporals,
so called, were the immediate subordinates, and compliant
ones, and this, as is to be noted in some business departments ashore, almost to a degree inconsistent with entire
moral volition. His place put various converging wires of
underground influence under the chief's control, capable
when astutely worked through his understrappers of operating to the mysterious discomfort, if nothing worse, of any
of the sea commonalty.

9

Life in the foretop well agreed with Billy Budd. There,
when not actually engaged on the yards yet higher aloft,
the topmen, who as such had been picked out for youth
and activity, constituted an aerial club lounging at ease
against the smaller stunsails rolled up into cushions,
spinning yarns like the lazy gods, and frequently amused
with what was going on in the busy world of the decks
below. No wonder then that a young fellow of Billy's disposition was well content in such society. Giving no cause
of offense to anybody, he was always alert at a call. So in
the merchant service it had been with him. But now such
a punctiliousness in duty was shown that his topmates
would sometimes good-naturedly laugh at him for it. This
heightened alacrity had its cause, namely, the impression
made upon him by the first formal gangway punishment
he had ever witnessed, which befell the day following his
impressment. It had been incurred by a little fellow, young,

a novice, an after-guardsman absent from his assigned
post when the ship was being put about—a dereliction
resulting in a rather serious hitch to that maneuver, one
demanding instantaneous promptitude in letting go and
making fast. When Billy saw the culprit's naked back
under the scourge gridironed with red welts, and worse;
when he marked the dire expression on the liberated man's
face as with his woolen shirt flung over him by the execu-
tioner he rushed forward from the spot to bury himself
in the crowd, Billy was horrified. He resolved that never
through remissness would he make himself liable to such
a visitation or do or omit aught that might merit even
verbal reproof. What then was his surprise and concern
when ultimately he found himself getting into petty trouble
occasionally about such matters as the stowage of his bag
or something amiss in his hammock, matters under the
police oversight of the ship's corporals of the lower decks,
and which brought down on him a vague threat from one
of them.

So heedful in all things as he was, how could this be?
He could not understand it, and it more than vexed him.
When he spoke to his young topmates about it they were
either lightly incredulous or found something comical in
his unconcealed anxiety. "Is it your bag, Billy?" said one;
"well, sew yourself up in it, bully boy, and then you'll be
sure to know if anybody meddles with it."

Now there was a veteran aboard who because his years
began to disqualify him for more active work had been
recently assigned duty as mainmastman in his watch, looking to the gear belayed at the rail roundabout that great
spar near the deck. At off times the foretopman had picked
up some acquaintance with him, and now in his trouble
it occurred to him that he might be the sort of person to
go to for wise counsel. He was an old Dansker long
anglicized in the service, of few words, many wrinkles, and
some honorable scars. His wizened face, time-tinted and
weather-stained to the complexion of an antique parch-
ment, was here and there peppered blue by the chance
explosion of a gun cartridge in action. He was an *Agamemnon* man; some two years prior to the time of this story
having served under Nelson when but Sir Horatio in that
ship immortal in naval memory, and which, dismantled

and in part broken up to her bare ribs, is seen a grand
skeleton in Haydon's etching. As one of a boarding party
from the *Agamemnon* he had received a cut slantwise
along one temple and cheek, leaving a long pale scar like
a streak of dawn's light falling athwart the dark visage.
It was on account of that scar and the affair in which it
was known that he had received it, as well as from his
blue-peppered complexion, that the Dansker went among
the *Indomitable*'s crew by the name of "Board-her-in-the-
smoke."

Now the first time that his small weazel eyes happened
to light on Billy Budd, a certain grim internal merriment
set all his ancient wrinkles into antic play. Was it that his
eccentric unsentimental old sapience, primitive in its kind,
saw or thought it saw something which in contrast with the
warship's environment looked oddly incongruous in the
Handsome Sailor? But after slyly studying him at intervals,
the old Merlin's equivocal merriment was modified; for
now when the twain would meet it would start in his face
a quizzing sort of look, but it would be but momentary
and sometimes replaced by an expression of speculative
query as to what might eventually befall a nature like that,
dropped into a world not without some man traps and
against whose subtleties simple courage lacking experience
and address and without any touch of defensive ugliness
is of little avail; and where such innocence as man is
capable of does yet in a moral emergency not always
sharpen the faculties or enlighten the will.

However it was, the Dansker in his ascetic way rather
took to Billy. Nor was this only because of a certain philosophic interest in such a character. There was another
cause. While the old man's eccentricities, sometimes bordering on the ursine, repelled the juniors, Billy, undeterred
thereby, revering him as a salt hero would make advances,
never passing the old *Agamemnon*-man without a salutation marked by that respect which is seldom lost on the
aged, however crabbed at times or whatever their station
in life.

There was a vein of dry humor, or what not, in the mast-
man; and, whether in freak of patriarchal irony touching
Billy's youth and athletic frame or for some other and
more recondite reason, from the first in addressing him he

always substituted "Baby" for "Billy," the Dansker in fact being the originator of the name by which the foretopman eventually became known aboard ship.

Well then, in his mysterious little difficulty going in quest of the wrinkled one, Billy found him off duty in a dog watch ruminating by himself seated on a shot-box of the upper gun deck now and then surveying with a somewhat cynical regard certain of the more swaggering promenaders there. Billy recounted his trouble, again wondering how it all happened. The salt seer attentively listened, accompanying the foretopman's recital with queer twitchings of his wrinkles and problematical little sparkles of his small ferret eyes. Making an end of his story, the foretopman asked, "And now, Dansker, do tell me what you think of it."

The old man, shoving up the front of his tarpaulin and deliberately rubbing the long slant scar at the point where it entered the thin hair, laconically said, "Baby Budd, *Jimmy Legs*" (meaning the master-at-arms) "is down on you."

"Jimmy Legs!" ejaculated Billy, his welkin eyes expanding; "what for? Why he calls me *the sweet and pleasant young fellow,* they tell me."

"Does he so?" grinned the grizzled one; then said "Ay, Baby Lad, a sweet voice has *Jimmy Legs.*"

"No, not always. But to me he has. I seldom pass him but there comes a pleasant word."

"And that's because he's down upon you, Baby Budd."

Such reiteration along with the manner of it, incomprehensible to a novice, disturbed Billy almost as much as the mystery for which he had sought explanation. Something less unpleasingly oracular he tried to extract; but the old sea-Chiron, thinking perhaps that for the nonce he had sufficiently instructed his young Achilles, pursed his lips, gathered all his wrinkles together, and would commit himself to nothing further.

Years, and those experiences which befell certain shrewder men subordinated lifelong to the will of superiors, all this had developed in the Dansker the pithy guarded cynicism that was his leading characteristic.

10

The next day an incident served to confirm Billy Budd in his incredulity as to the Dansker's strange summing up of the case submitted. The ship at noon going large before the wind was rolling on her course, and he below at dinner and engaged in some sportful talk with the members of his mess chanced in a sudden lurch to spill the entire contents of his soup pan upon the new scrubbed deck. Claggart, the master-at-arms, official rattan in hand, happened to be passing along the battery in a bay of which the mess was lodged, and the greasy liquid streamed just across his path. Stepping over it, he was proceeding on his way without comment, since the matter was nothing to take notice of under the circumstances, when he happened to observe who it was that had done the spilling. His countenance changed. Pausing, he was about to ejaculate something hasty at the sailor, but checked himself, and, pointing down to the streaming soup, playfully tapped him from behind with his rattan, saying in a low musical voice peculiar to him at times: "Handsomely done, my lad! And handsome is as handsome did it too!" And with that passed on. Not noted by Billy, as not coming within his view, was the involuntary smile, or rather grimace, that accompanied Claggart's equivocal words. Aridly it drew down the thin corners of his shapely mouth. But everybody taking his remark as meant for humorous, and at which therefore as coming from a superior they were bound to laugh, "with counterfeited glee" acted accordingly; and Billy, tickled, it may be, by the allusion to his being the Handsome Sailor, merrily joined in; then addressing his messmates exclaimed: "There now, who says that Jimmy Legs is down on me!" "And who said he was, Beauty?" demanded one Donald with some surprise. Whereat the foretopman looked a little foolish recalling that it was only one person, Board-her-in-the-smoke, who had suggested what to him was the smoky idea that this master-at-arms was in any peculiar way hostile to him. Meantime that functionary, resuming his path, must have momentarily worn some expression less guarded than that of the bitter smile, and usurping the face from the heart, some distorting expression perhaps, for a drummer-boy, heedlessly frolicking along from the opposite direction and chancing to come into light collision with his person, was strangely disconcerted by his aspect. Nor was the impression lessened when the official, impulsively giving him a sharp cut with the rattan, vehemently exclaimed: "Look where you go!"

11

What was the matter with the master-at-arms? And, be the matter what it might, how could it have direct relation to Billy Budd, with whom, prior to the affair of the spilled soup, he had never come into any special contact official or otherwise? What indeed could the trouble have to do with one so little inclined to give offense as the merchant ship's *peacemaker,* even him who in Claggart's own phrase was "the sweet and pleasant young fellow"? Yes, why should *Jimmy Legs,* to borrow the Dansker's expression, be *down* on the Handsome Sailor? But, at heart and not for nothing, as the late chance encounter may indicate to the discerning, down on him, secretly down on him, he assuredly was.

Now to invent something touching the more private career of Claggart, something involving Billy Budd, of which something the latter should be wholly ignorant, some romantic incident implying that Claggart's knowledge of the young bluejacket began at some period anterior to catching sight of him on board the seventy-four—all this, not so difficult to do, might avail in a way more or less interesting to account for whatever of enigma may appear to lurk in the case. But in fact there was nothing of the sort. And yet the cause, necessarily to be assumed as the sole one assignable, is in its very realism as much charged with that prime element of Radcliffian romance, *the mysterious,* as any that the ingenuity of the author of the *Mysteries of Udolpho* could devise. For what can more partake of the mysterious than an antipathy spontaneous and profound, such as is evoked in certain exceptional mortals by the mere aspect of some other mortal however harmless he may be, if not called forth by this very harmlessness itself?

Now there can exist no irritating juxtaposition of dissimilar personalities comparable to that which is possible aboard a great warship fully manned and at sea. There,

every day among all ranks, almost every man comes into
more or less of contact with almost every other man.
Wholly there to avoid even the sight of an aggravating
object one must needs give it Jonah's toss or jump overboard himself. Imagine how all this might eventually
operate on some peculiar human creature the direct re-
verse of a saint.

But for the adequate comprehending of Claggart by
a normal nature these hints are insufficient. To pass from
a normal nature to him one must cross "the deadly space
between." And this is best done by indirection.

Long ago an honest scholar my senior said to me in
reference to one who like himself is now no more, a
man so unimpeachably respectable that against him
nothing was ever openly said though among the few
something was whispered, "Yes, X—— is a nut not to be
cracked by the tap of a lady's fan. You are aware that I
am the adherent of no organized religion, much less of
any philosophy built into a system. Well, for all that, I
think that to try and get into X——, enter his labyrinth
and get out again, without a clue derived from some source
other than what is known as *knowledge of the world*—
that were hardly possible, at least for me."

"Why," said I, "X——, however singular a study to
some, is yet human, and knowledge of the world assuredly
implies the knowledge of human nature, and in most of
its varieties."

"Yes, but a superficial knowledge of it, serving ordinary
purposes. But for anything deeper, I am not certain
whether to know the world and to know human nature
be not two distinct branches of knowledge, which, while
they may coexist in the same heart, yet either may exist
with little or nothing of the other. Nay, in an average man
of the world, his constant rubbing with it blunts that fine
spiritual insight indispensable to the understanding of the
essential in certain exceptional characters, whether evil
ones or good. In a matter of some importance I have seen
a girl wind an old lawyer about her little finger. Nor was
it the dotage of senile love. Nothing of the sort. But he
knew law better than he knew the girl's heart. Coke and
Blackstone hardly shed so much light into obscure spiritual

places as the Hebrew prophets. And who were they? Mostly recluses."

At the time my inexperience was such that I did not quite see the drift of all this. It may be that I see it now. And, indeed, if that lexicon which is based on Holy Writ were any longer popular, one might with less difficulty define and denominate certain phenomenal men. As it is, one must turn to some authority not liable to the charge of being tinctured with the Biblical element.

In a list of definitions included in the authentic translation of Plato, a list attributed to him, occurs this: "Natural Depravity: a depravity according to nature." A definition which, though savoring of Calvinism, by no means involves Calvin's dogmas as to total mankind. Evidently its intent makes it applicable but to individuals. Not many are the examples of this depravity, which the gallows and jail supply. At any rate, for notable instances, since these have no vulgar alloy of the brute in them but invariably are dominated by intellectuality, one must go elsewhere. Civilization, especially if of the austerer sort, is auspicious to it. It folds itself in the mantle of respectability. It has its certain negative virtues serving as silent auxiliaries. It never allows wine to get within its guard. It is not going too far to say that it is without vices or small sins. There is a phenomenal pride in it that excludes them from anything mercenary or avaricious. In short the depravity here meant partakes nothing of the sordid or sensual. It is serious, but free from acerbity. Though no flatterer of mankind it never speaks ill of it.

But the thing which in eminent instances signalizes so exceptional a nature is this: though the man's even temper and discreet bearing would seem to intimate a mind peculiarly subject to the law of reason, not the less in his heart he would seem to riot in complete exemption from that law, having apparently little to do with reason further than to employ it as an ambidexter implement for effecting the irrational. That is to say: Toward the accomplishment of an aim which in wantonness of malignity would seem to partake of the insane, he will direct a cool judgment sagacious and sound.

These men are true madmen, and of the most dangerous sort, for their lunacy is not continuous but occasional, evoked by some special object; it is probably secretive, which is as much to say it is self-contained, so that when, moreover, most active, it is to the average mind not distinguishable from sanity, and for the reason above suggested, that, whatever its aims may be—and the aim is never declared—the method and the outward proceeding are always perfectly rational.

Now something such an one was Claggart, in whom was the mania of an evil nature, not engendered by vicious training or corrupting books or licentious living but born with him and innate, in short "a depravity according to nature."

12

Lawyers, Experts, Clergy
An Episode

By the way, can it be the phenomenon, disowned or at least concealed, that in some criminal cases puzzles the courts? For this cause have our juries at times not only to endure the prolonged contentions of lawyers with their fees, but also the yet more perplexing strife of the medical experts with theirs?—But why leave it to them? Why not subpoena as well the clerical proficients? their vocation bringing them into peculiar contact with so many human beings, and sometimes in their least guarded hour, in interviews very much more confidential than those of physician and patient; this would seem to qualify them to know something about those intricacies involved in the question of moral responsibility; whether in a given case, say, the crime proceeded from mania in the brain or rabies of the heart. As to any differences among themselves these clerical proficients might develop on the stand, these could hardly be greater than the direct contradictions exchanged between the remunerated medical experts.

Dark sayings are these, some will say. But why? Is it because they somewhat savor of Holy Writ in its phrase "mysteries of iniquity"? If they do, such savor was far from being intended, for little will it commend these pages to many a reader of today.

The point of the present story turning on the hidden nature of the master-at-arms has necessitated this chapter.

With an added hint or two in connection with the incident
at the mess, the resumed narrative must be left to vindicate,
as it may, its own credibility.

13

Pale ire, envy and despair

That Claggart's figure was not amiss, and his face, save
the chin, well molded, has already been said. Of these
favorable points he seemed not insensible, for he was not
only neat but careful in his dress. But the form of Billy
Budd was heroic; and if his face was without the intellectual look of the pallid Claggart's, not the less was it lit,
like his, from within, though from a different source. The
bonfire in his heart made luminous the rose-tan in his
cheek.

In view of the marked contrast between the persons of
the twain, it is more than probable that when the master-
at-arms in the scene last given applied to the sailor the
proverb *Handsome is as handsome does* he there let escape
an ironic inkling, not caught by the young sailors who
heard it, as to what it was that had first moved him against
Billy, namely, his significant personal beauty.

Now envy and antipathy, passions irreconcilable in
reason, nevertheless in fact may spring conjoined like
Chang and Eng in one birth. Is Envy then such a monster?
Well, though many an arraigned mortal has in hopes of
mitigated penalty pleaded guilty to horrible actions, did
ever anybody seriously confess to envy? Something there
is in it universally felt to be more shameful than even
felonious crime. And not only does everybody disown it
but the better sort are inclined to incredulity when it is in
earnest imputed to an intelligent man. But since its lodgment is in the heart, not the brain, no degree of intellect
supplies a guarantee against it. But Claggart's was no
vulgar form of the passion. Nor, as directed toward Billy
Budd, did it partake of that streak of apprehensive jealousy
that marred Saul's visage perturbedly brooding on the
comely young David. Claggart's envy struck deeper. If
askance he eyed the good looks, cheery health, and frank
enjoyment of young life in Billy Budd, it was because these
went along with a nature that, as Claggart magnetically

felt, had in its simplicity never willed malice or experienced
the reactionary bite of that serpent. To him, the spirit
lodged within Billy and looking out from his welkin eyes
as from windows, that ineffability it was which made the
dimple in his dyed cheek, suppled his joints, and, dancing
in his yellow curls, made him preeminently the Handsome
Sailor. One person excepted, the master-at-arms was perhaps the only man in the ship intellectually capable of
adequately appreciating the moral phenomenon presented
in Billy Budd. And the insight but intensified his passion,
which, assuming various secret forms within him, at times
assumed that of cynic disdain—disdain of innocence——
To be nothing more than innocent! Yet in an esthetic way
he saw the charm of it, the courageous free-and-easy
temper of it, and fain would have shared it, but he de-
spaired of it.

With no power to annul the elemental evil in him,
though readily enough he could hide it; apprehending the
good, but powerless to be it; a nature like Claggart's sur-
charged with energy as such natures almost invariably are,
what recourse is left to it but to recoil upon itself, and,
like the scorpion for which the Creator alone is responsible, act out to the end the part allotted it.

14

Passion, and passion in its profoundest, is not a thing
demanding a palatial stage whereon to play its part. Down
among the groundlings, among the beggars and rakers of
the garbage, profound passion is enacted. And the circumstances that provoke it, however trivial or mean, are
no measure of its power. In the present instance the stage
is a scrubbed gun deck, and one of the external provoca-
tions a man-of-war's-man's spilled soup.

Now when the master-at-arms noticed whence came that
greasy fluid streaming before his feet, he must have taken
it—to some extent willfully, perhaps—not for the mere
accident it assuredly was, but for the sly escape of a
spontaneous feeling on Billy's part more or less answering
to the antipathy on his own. In effect a foolish demonstration he must have thought, and very harmless, like the
futile kick of a heifer, which yet, were the heifer a shod
stallion, would not be so harmless. Even so was it that

into the gall of Claggart's envy he infused the vitriol of
his contempt. But the incident confirmed to him certain
telltale reports purveyed to his ear by "Squeak," one of his
more cunning corporals, a grizzled little man, so nick-
named by the sailors on account of his squeaky voice and
sharp visage ferreting about the dark corners of the lower
decks after interlopers, satirically suggesting to them the
idea of a rat in a cellar.

From his Chief's employing him as an implicit tool in
laying little traps for the worriment of the foretopman—
for it was from the master-at-arms that the petty persecu-
tions heretofore adverted to had proceeded—the corporal,
having naturally enough concluded that his master could
have no love for the sailor, made it his business, faithful
understrapper that he was, to foment the ill blood by
perverting to his chief certain innocent frolics of the good-
natured foretopman, besides inventing for his mouth sundry contumelious epithets he claimed to have overheard
him let fall. The master-at-arms never suspected the
veracity of these reports, more especially as to the epithets,
for he well knew how secretly unpopular may become a
master-at-arms, at least a master-at-arms of those days
zealous in his function, and how the bluejackets shoot at
him in private their raillery and wit; the nickname by
which he goes among them (*Jimmy Legs*) implying under
the form of merriment their cherished disrespect and dislike.

But in view of the greediness of hate for patrolmen, it
hardly needed a purveyor to feed Claggart's passion. An
uncommon prudence is habitual with the subtler depravity, for it has everything to hide. And in case of an injury
but suspected, its secretiveness voluntarily cuts it off from
enlightenment or disillusion; and, not unreluctantly, action
is taken upon surmise as upon certainty. And the retalia-
tion is apt to be in monstrous disproportion to the supposed offense; for when in anybody was revenge in its
exactions aught else but an inordinate usurer? But how
with Claggart's conscience? For though consciences are
unlike as foreheads, every intelligence, not excluding the
Scriptural devils who "believe and tremble," has one. But
Claggart's conscience, being but the lawyer to his will,
made ogres of trifles, probably arguing that the motive im-

puted to Billy in spilling the soup just when he did,
together with the epithets alleged, these, if nothing more,
made a strong case against him; nay, justified animosity
into a sort of retributive righteousness. The Pharisee is the
Guy Fawkes prowling in the hid chambers underlying the
Claggarts. And they can really form no conception of an
unreciprocated malice. Probably, the master-at-arms' clandestine persecution of Billy was started to try the temper
of the man; but it had not developed any quality in him
that enmity could make official use of or even pervert into
plausible self-justification; so that the occurrence at the
mess, petty if it were, was a welcome one to that peculiar
conscience assigned to be the private mentor of Claggart.
And, for the rest, not improbably it put him upon new
experiments.

15

Not many days after the last incident narrated something befell Billy Budd that more graveled him than aught
that had previously occurred.

It was a warm night for the latitude, and the foretopman,
whose watch at the time was properly below, was dozing
on the uppermost deck, whither he had ascended from
his hot hammock, one of hundreds suspended so closely
wedged together over a lower gun deck that there was
little or no swing to them. He lay as in the shadow of a
hillside, stretched under the lee of the booms, a piled ridge
of spare spars amidships between foremast and mainmast
and among which the ship's largest boat, the launch, was
stowed. Alongside of three other slumberers from below,
he lay near that end of the booms which approaches the
foremast, his station aloft on duty as a foretopman being
just over the deck station of the forecastlemen, entitling
him according to usage to make himself more or less at
home in that neighborhood.

Presently he was stirred into semiconsciousness by
somebody, who must have previously sounded the sleep
of the others, touching his shoulder, and then, as the
foretopman raised his head, breathing into his ear in a
quick whisper, "Slip into the lee forechains, Billy; there
is something in the wind. Don't speak. Quick, I will meet
you there," and disappeared.

Now Billy, like sundry other essentially good-natured ones, had some of the weaknesses inseparable from essential good nature, and among these was a reluctance, almost an incapacity, of plumply saying *no* to an abrupt proposition not obviously absurd on the face of it, nor obviously unfriendly, nor iniquitous. And being of warm blood he had not the phlegm tacitly to negative any proposition by unresponsive inaction. Like his sense of fear, his apprehension as to aught outside of the honest and natural was seldom very quick. Besides, upon the present occasion, the drowse from his sleep still hung upon him.

However it was, he mechanically rose, and, sleepily wondering what could be in the wind, betook himself to the designated place, a narrow platform, one of six, outside of the high bulwarks and screened by the great deadeyes and multiple columned lanyards of the shrouds and backstays, and, in a great warship of that time, of dimensions commensurate to the hull's magnitude, a tarry balcony in short overhanging the sea, and so secluded that one mariner of the *Indomitable,* a nonconformist old tar of a serious turn, made it even in daytime his private oratory.

In this retired nook the stranger soon joined Billy Budd. There was no moon as yet; a haze obscured the starlight. He could not distinctly see the stranger's face. Yet from something in the outline and carriage, Billy took him to be, and correctly, one of the after-guard.

"Hist! Billy," said the man in the same quick cautionary whisper as before; "you were impressed, weren't you? Well, so was I," and he paused, as to mark the effect. But Billy, not knowing exactly what to make of this, said nothing. Then the other: "We are not the only impressed ones, Billy. There's a gang of us.—Couldn't you—help—at a pinch?"

"What do you mean?" demanded Billy, here thoroughly shaking off his drowse.

"Hist, hist!" the hurried whisper now growing husky, "see here"—and the man held up two small objects faintly twinkling in the nightlight—"see, they are yours, Billy, if you'll only——"

But Billy broke in, and in his resentful eagerness to deliver himself his vocal infirmity somewhat intruded: "D-D-Damme, I don't know what you are d-driving at, or what

you mean, but you had better g-g-go where you belong!"
For the moment the fellow, as confounded, did not stir;
and Billy, springing to his feet, said, "If you d-don't start
I'll t-t-toss you back over the r-rail!" There was no mis-
taking this, and the mysterious emissary decamped, disappearing in the direction of the mainmast in the shadow
of the booms.

"Hallo, what's the matter?" here came growling from
a forecastleman awakened from his deck doze by Billy's
raised voice. And as the foretopman reappeared and was
recognized by him: "Ah, Beauty, is it you? Well, something must have been the matter for you st-st-stuttered."

"Oh," rejoined Billy, now mastering the impediment,
"I found an after-guardsman in our part of the ship here
and I bid him be off where he belongs."

"And is that all you did about it, foretopman?" gruffly
demanded another, an irascible old fellow of brick-colored
visage and hair, and who was known to his associate forecastlemen as "Red Pepper." "Such sneaks I should like
to marry to the gunner's daughter!" by that expression
meaning that he would like to subject them to disciplinary
castigation over a gun.

However, Billy's rendering of the matter satisfactorily
accounted to these inquirers for the brief commotion,
since of all the sections of a ship's company the forecastlemen, veterans for the most part and bigoted in their
sea prejudices, are the most jealous in resenting territorial
encroachments, especially on the part of any of the after-
guard, of whom they have but a sorry opinion, chiefly
landsmen, never going aloft except to reef or furl the
mainsail, and in no wise competent to handle a marlinspike
or turn in a deadeye, say.

16

This incident sorely puzzled Billy Budd. It was an entirely new experience, the first time in his life that he had
ever been personally approached in underhand intriguing
fashion. Prior to this encounter he had known nothing
of the after-guardsman, the two men being stationed wide
apart, one forward and aloft during his watch, the other
on deck and aft.

What could it mean? And could they really be guineas,

those two glittering objects the interloper had held up to
his eyes? Where could the fellow get guineas? Why even
spare buttons are not so plentiful at sea. The more he
turned the matter over, the more he was nonplused, and
made uneasy and discomfited. In his disgustful recoil from
an overture which though he but ill comprehended he instinctively knew must involve evil of some sort, Billy Budd
was like a young horse fresh from the pasture suddenly
inhaling a vile whiff from some chemical factory and by
repeated snortings tries to get it out of his nostrils and
lungs. This frame of mind barred all desire of holding
further parley with the fellow, even were it but for the
purpose of gaining some enlightenment as to his design
in approaching him. And yet he was not without natural
curiosity to see how such a visitor in the dark would look
in broad day.

He espied him the following afternoon in his first dog
watch below, one of the smokers on that forward part of
the upper gun deck allotted to the pipe. He recognized him
by his general cut and build, more than by his round
freckled face and glassy eyes of pale blue, veiled with
lashes all but white. And yet Billy was a bit uncertain
whether indeed it were he—yonder chap about his own
age chatting and laughing in free-hearted way, leaning
against a gun, a genial young fellow enough to look at,
and something of a rattlebrain, to all appearance. Rather
chubby too for a sailor, even an after-guardsman. In short
the last man in the world, one would think, to be over-
burthened with thoughts, especially those perilous thoughts
that must needs belong to a conspirator in any serious
project, or even to the underling of such a conspirator.

Although Billy was not aware of it, the fellow, with a
sidelong watchful glance, had perceived Billy first, and
then noting that Billy was looking at him thereupon nodded
a familiar sort of friendly recognition as to an old acquaintance, without interrupting the talk he was engaged
in with the group of smokers. A day or two afterwards,
chancing in the evening promenade on a gun deck to pass
Billy, he offered a flying word of good fellowship, as it
were, which, by its unexpectedness and equivocalness
under the circumstances, so embarrassed Billy that he
knew not how to respond to it, and let it go unnoticed.

Billy was now left more at a loss than before. The ineffectual speculations into which he was led were so disturbingly alien to him that he did his best to smother them. It never entered his mind that here was a matter which, from its extreme questionableness, it was his duty as a loyal bluejacket to report in the proper quarter. And, probably, had such a step been suggested to him, he would have been deterred from taking it by the thought, one of novice magnanimity, that it would savor overmuch of the dirty work of a telltale. He kept the thing to himself. Yet upon one occasion he could not forbear a little disburthening himself to the old Dansker, tempted thereto perhaps by the influence of a balmy night when the ship lay becalmed; the twain, silent for the most part, sitting together on deck, their heads propped against the bulwarks. But it was only a partial and anonymous account that Billy gave, the unfounded scruples above referred to preventing full disclosure to anybody. Upon hearing Billy's version, the sage Dansker seemed to divine more than he was told, and, after a little meditation during which his wrinkles were pursed as into a point, quite effacing for the time that quizzing expression his face sometimes wore—"Didn't I say so, Baby Budd?"

"Say what?" demanded Billy.

"Why, *Jimmy Legs* is *down* on you."

"And what," rejoined Billy in amazement, "has *Jimmy Legs* to do with that cracked after-guardsman?"

"Ho, it was an after-guardsman then. A cat's-paw, a cat's-paw!" And with that exclamation, which, whether it had reference to a light puff of air just then coming over the calm sea, or subtler relation to the after-guardsman, there is no telling, the old Merlin gave a twisting wrench with his black teeth at his plug of tobacco, vouchsafing no reply to Billy's impetuous question, though now repeated, for it was his wont to relapse into grim silence when interrogated in skeptical sort as to any of his sententious oracles, not always very clear ones, rather partaking of that obscurity which invests most Delphic deliverances from any quarter.

Long experience had very likely brought this old man to that bitter prudence which never interferes in aught and never gives advice.

17

Yes, despite the Dansker's pithy insistence as to the
master-at-arms being at the bottom of these strange experiences of Billy on board the *Indomitable,* the young
sailor was ready to ascribe them to almost anybody but
the man who, to use Billy's own expression, "always had
a pleasant word for him." This is to be wondered at. Yet
not so much to be wondered at. In certain matters, some
sailors even in mature life remain unsophisticated enough.
But a young seafarer of the disposition of our athletic
foretopman is much of a child-man. And yet a child's utter
innocence is but its blank ignorance, and the innocence
more or less wanes as intelligence waxes. But in Billy Budd
intelligence, such as it was, had advanced, while yet his
simple-mindedness remained for the most part unaffected.
Experience is a teacher indeed, yet did Billy's years make
his experience small. Besides, he had none of that intuitive
knowledge of the bad which in natures not good or in-
completely so foreruns experience, and therefore may pertain, as in some instances it too clearly does pertain, even
to youth.

And what could Billy know of man except of man as a
mere sailor? And the old-fashioned sailor, the veritable
man-before-the-mast, the sailor from boyhood up, he,
though indeed of the same species as a landsman, is in
some respects singularly distinct from him. The sailor is
frankness, the landsman is finesse. Life is not a game with
the sailor, demanding the long head; no intricate game of
chess where few moves are made in straightforwardness,
and ends are attained by indirection; an oblique, tedious,
barren game hardly worth that poor candle burnt out in
playing it.

Yes, as a class, sailors are in character a juvenile race.
Even their deviations are marked by juvenility. And this
more especially holding true with the sailors of Billy's time.
Then, too, certain things which apply to all sailors do more
pointedly operate here and there upon the junior one.
Every sailor, too, is accustomed to obey orders without
debating them; his life afloat is externally ruled for him; he
is not brought into that promiscuous commerce with mankind where unobstructed free agency on equal terms—

equal superficially, at least—soon teaches one that unless
upon occasion he exercise a distrust keen in proportion
to the fairness of the appearance, some foul turn may
be served him. A ruled undemonstrative distrustfulness is
so habitual, not with businessmen so much, as with men
who know their kind in less shallow relations than business,
namely, certain men-of-the-world, that they come at last
to employ it all but unconsciously, and some of them
would very likely feel real surprise at being charged with
it as one of their general characteristics.

18

But after the little matter at the mess Billy Budd no
more found himself in strange trouble at times about his
hammock or his clothes bag or what not. While, as to
that smile that occasionally sunned him, and the pleasant
passing word, these were, if not more frequent, yet if
anything more pronounced than before.

But, for all that, there were certain other demonstrations
now. When Claggart's unobserved glance happened to
light on belted Billy rolling along the upper gun deck in the
leisure of the second dog watch, exchanging passing broad-
sides of fun with other young promenaders in the crowd,
that glance would follow the cheerful sea-Hyperion with
a settled meditative and melancholy expression, his eyes
strangely suffused with incipient feverish tears. Then would
Claggart look like the man of sorrows. Yes, and sometimes the melancholy expression would have in it a touch
of soft yearning, as if Claggart could even have loved
Billy but for fate and ban. But this was an evanescence,
and quickly repented of, as it were, by an immitigable
look, pinching and shriveling the visage into the momentary semblance of a wrinkled walnut. But sometimes catching sight in advance of the foretopman coming in his
direction, he would, upon their nearing, step aside a little
to let him pass, dwelling upon Billy for the moment with
the glittering dental satire of a Guise. But upon any
abrupt unforeseen encounter a red light would [flash]
forth from his eye like a spark from an anvil in a dusk
smithy. That quick fierce light was a strange one, darted
from orbs which in repose were of a color nearest approaching a deeper violet, the softest of shades.

Though some of these caprices of the pit could not but be observed by their object, yet were they beyond the construing of such a nature. And the thews of Billy were hardly compatible with that sort of sensitive spiritual organization which in some cases instinctively conveys to ignorant innocence an admonition of the proximity of the malign. He thought the master-at-arms acted in a manner rather queer at times. That was all. But the occasional frank air and pleasant word went for what they purported to be, the young sailor never having heard as yet of the "too fair-spoken man."

Had the foretopman been conscious of having done or said anything to provoke the ill will of the official, it would have been different with him, and his sight might have been purged if not sharpened. As it was, innocence was his blinder.

So was it with him in yet another matter. Two minor officers—the armorer and captain of the hold, with whom he had never exchanged a word, his position in the ship not bringing him into contact with them—these men now for the first began to cast upon Billy when they chanced to encounter him that peculiar glance which evidences that the man from whom it comes has been some way tampered with and to the prejudice of him upon whom the glance lights. Never did it occur to Billy as a thing to be noted or a thing suspicious, though he well knew the fact, that the armorer and captain of the hold, with the ship's yeoman, apothecary, and others of that grade, were, by naval usage, messmates of the master-at-arms, men with ears convenient to his confidential tongue.

But the general popularity that our Handsome Sailor's manly forwardness upon occasion, and his irresistible good nature, indicating no mental superiority tending to excite an invidious feeling—this good will on the part of most of his shipmates made him the less to concern himself about such mute aspects toward him as those whereto allusion has just been made.

As to the after-guardsman, though Billy for reasons already given necessarily saw little of him, yet when the two did happen to meet, invariably came the fellow's off-hand cheerful recognition, sometimes accompanied by a passing pleasant word or two. Whatever that equivocal

young person's original design may really have been, or
the design of which he might have been the deputy, certain it was from his manner upon these occasions that he
had wholly dropped it.

It was as if his precocity of crookedness (and every
vulgar villain is precocious) had for once deceived him,
and the man he had sought to entrap as a simpleton had,
through his very simplicity, ignominiously baffled him.

But shrewd ones may opine that it was hardly possible
for Billy to refrain from going up to the after-guardsman
and bluntly demanding to know his purpose in the initial
interview, so abruptly closed in the forechains. Shrewd
ones may also think it but natural in Billy to set about
sounding some of the other impressed men of the ship in
order to discover what basis, if any, there was for the
emissary's obscure suggestions as to plotting disaffection
aboard. Yes, the shrewd may so think. But something
more, or, rather, something else, than mere shrewdness
is perhaps needful for the due understanding of such a
character as Billy Budd's.

As to Claggart, the monomania in the man—if that indeed it were, as involuntarily disclosed by starts in the
manifestations detailed, yet in general covered over by his
self-contained and rational demeanor—this, like a subterranean fire was eating its way deeper and deeper in him.
Something decisive must come of it.

19

After the mysterious interview in the forechains, the
one so abruptly ended there by Billy, nothing especially
germane to the story occurred until the events now about
to be narrated.

Elsewhere it has been said that in the lack of frigates
(of course better sailers than line-of-battle ships) in the
English squadron up the Straits at the period, the *Indomitable* was occasionally employed not only as an available
substitute for a scout, but at times on detached service
of more important kind. This was not alone because of
her sailing qualities, not common in a ship of her rate,
but quite as much, probably, that the character of her
commander, it was thought, specially adapted him for any
duty where under unforeseen difficulties a prompt initiative

might have to be taken in some matter demanding knowledge and ability in addition to those qualities implied in good seamanship. It was on an expedition of the latter sort, a somewhat distant one, and when the *Indomitable* was almost at her furthest remove from the fleet, that in the latter part of an afternoon watch she unexpectedly came in sight of a ship of the enemy. It proved to be a frigate. The latter perceiving through the glass that the weight of men and metal would be heavily against her, invoking her light heels crowded sail to get away. After a chase urged almost against hope and lasting until about the middle of the first dog watch, she signally succeeded in effecting her escape.

Not long after the pursuit had been given up, and ere the excitement incident thereto had altogether waned away, the master-at-arms ascending from his cavernous sphere made his appearance cap in hand by the mainmast respectfully waiting the notice of Captain Vere, then solitary walking the weather side of the quarter-deck, doubtless somewhat chafed at the failure of the pursuit. The spot where Claggart stood was the place allotted to men of lesser grades seeking some more particular interview either with the officer of the deck or the captain himself. But from the latter it was not often that a sailor or petty officer of those days would seek a hearing; only some exceptional cause would, according to established custom, have warranted that.

Presently, just as the commander absorbed in his reflections was on the point of turning aft in his promenade, he became sensible of Claggart's presence, and saw the doffed cap held in deferential expectancy. Here be it said that Captain Vere's personal knowledge of this petty officer had only begun at the time of the ship's last sailing from home, Claggart then for the first, in transfer from a ship detained for repairs, supplying on board the *Indomitable* the place of a previous master-at-arms disabled and ashore.

No sooner did the commander observe who it was that now deferentially stood awaiting his notice, than a peculiar expression came over him. It was not unlike that which uncontrollably will flit across the countenance of one at unawares encountering a person who though known to him indeed has hardly been long enough known for thorough knowledge, but something in whose aspect nevertheless now for the first provokes a vaguely repellent distaste. But coming to a stand, and resuming much of his wonted official manner, save that a sort of impatience lurked in the intonation of the opening word, he said: "Well? what is it, Master-at-Arms?"

With the air of a subordinate grieved at the necessity of being a messenger of ill tidings, and while conscientiously determined to be frank, yet equally resolved upon shunning overstatement, Claggart, at this invitation or rather summons to disburthen, spoke up. What he said, conveyed in the language of no uneducated man, was to the effect following if not altogether in these words, namely, that during the chase and preparations for the possible encounter he had seen enough to convince him that at least one sailor aboard was a dangerous character in a ship mustering some who not only had taken a guilty part in the late serious troubles, but others also who, like the man in question, had entered His Majesty's service under another form than enlistment.

At this point Captain Vere with some impatience interrupted him: "Be direct, man; say impressed men."

Claggart made a gesture of subservience and proceeded.

Quite lately he (Claggart) had begun to suspect that on the gun decks some sort of movement prompted by the sailor in question was covertly going on, but he had not thought himself warranted in reporting the suspicion so long as it remained indistinct. But, from what he had that afternoon observed in the man referred to, the suspicion of something clandestine going on had advanced to a point less removed from certainty. He deeply felt, he added, the serious responsibility assumed in making a report involving such possible consequences to the individual mainly concerned, besides tending to augment those natural anxieties which every naval commander must feel in view of extraordinary outbreaks so recent as those which, he sorrowfully said it, it needed not to name.

Now at the first broaching of the matter Captain Vere, taken by surprise, could not wholly dissemble his disquietude. But as Claggart went on, the former's aspect changed into restiveness under something in the witness's manner in giving his testimony. However, he refrained from interrupting him. And Claggart, continuing, concluded with this:

"God forbid, your honor, that the *Indomitable*'s should be the experience of the——"

"Never mind that!" here peremptorily broke in the superior, his face altering with anger, instinctively divining the ship that the other was about to name, one in which the Nore Mutiny had assumed a singularly tragical character that for a time jeopardized the life of its commander. Under the circumstances he was indignant at the purposed allusion. When the commissioned officers themselves were on all occasions very heedful how they referred to the recent events, for a petty officer unnecessarily to allude to them in the presence of his captain, this struck him as a most immodest presumption. Besides, to his quick sense of self-respect, it even looked under the circumstances something like an attempt to alarm him. Nor at first was he without some surprise that one who so far as he had hitherto come under his notice had shown considerable tact in his function should in this particular evince such lack of it.

But these thoughts and kindred dubious ones flitting across his mind were suddenly replaced by an intuitional surmise which though as yet obscure in form served practically to affect his reception of the ill tidings. Certain it is that, long versed in everything pertaining to the complicated gun-deck life, which like every other form of life has its secret mines and dubious side, the side popularly disclaimed, Captain Vere did not permit himself to be unduly disturbed by the general tenor of his subordinate's report. Furthermore, if in view of recent events prompt action should be taken at the first palpable sign of recurring insubordination, for all that, not judicious would it be, he thought, to keep the idea of lingering disaffection alive by undue forwardness in crediting an informer even if his own subordinate and charged among other things with police surveillance of the crew. This feeling would not perhaps have so prevailed with him were it not that upon a prior occasion the patriotic zeal officially evinced by Claggart had somewhat irritated him as appearing rather supersensible and strained. Furthermore, something even

in the official's self-possessed and somewhat ostentatious
manner in making his specifications strangely reminded
him of a bandsman, a perjurious witness in a capital case
before a court-martial ashore of which when a lieutenant
he, Captain Vere, had been a member.

Now the peremptory check given to Claggart in the
matter of the arrested allusion was quickly followed up by
this: "You say that there is at least one dangerous man
aboard. Name him."

"William Budd. A foretopman, your honor———"

"William Budd," repeated Captain Vere with unfeigned
astonishment; "and mean you the man that Lieutenant
Ratcliffe took from the merchantman not very long ago—
the young fellow who seems to be so popular with the
men—Billy, the Handsome Sailor, as they call him?"

"The same, your honor; but, for all his youth and good
looks, a deep one. Not for nothing does he insinuate himself into the good will of his shipmates, since at the least
all hands will at a pinch say a good word for him at all
hazards. Did Lieutenant Ratcliffe happen to tell your
honor of that adroit fling of Budd's, jumping up in the
cutter's bow under the merchantman's stern when he was
being taken off? It is even masked by that sort of good-
humored air that at heart he resents his impressment. You
have but noted his fair cheek. A man trap may be under
his ruddy-tipped daisies."

Now the Handsome Sailor, as a signal figure among the
crew, had naturally enough attracted the captain's attention from the first. Though in general not very demons-
trative to his officers, he had congratulated Lieutenant
Ratcliffe upon his good fortune in lighting on such a fine
specimen of the *genus homo,* who in the nude might have
posed for a statue of young Adam before the Fall. As to
Billy's adieu to the ship *Rights-of-Man,* which the boarding
lieutenant had indeed reported to him but in a deferential
way more as a good story than aught else, Captain Vere,
though mistakenly understanding it as a satiric sally, had
but thought so much the better of the impressed man for
it, as a military sailor, admiring the spirit that could take
an arbitrary enlistment so merrily and sensibly. The foretopman's conduct, too, so far as it had fallen under the
captain's notice, had confirmed the first happy augury,

while the new recruit's qualities as a *sailorman* seemed to
be such that he had thought of recommending him to the
executive officer for promotion to a place that would more
frequently bring him under his own observation, namely,
the captaincy of the mizzentop, replacing there in the starboard watch a man not so young whom partly for that
reason he deemed less fitted for the post. Be it parenthe-
sized here that since the mizzentopmen, having not to
handle such breadths of heavy canvas as the lower sails
on the mainmast and foremast, a young man if of the
right stuff not only seems best adapted to duty there,
but in fact is generally selected for the captaincy of that
top, and the company under him are light hands and often
but striplings. In sum, Captain Vere had from the beginning deemed Billy Budd to be what in the naval parlance
of the time was called a *"King's bargain,"* that is to say,
for His Britannic Majesty's navy a capital investment at
small outlay or none at all.

After a brief pause during which the reminiscences
above mentioned passed vividly through his mind and he
weighed the import of Claggart's last suggestion conveyed
in the phrase "pitfall under the daisies," and the more he
weighed it the less reliance he felt in the informer's good
faith, suddenly he turned upon him and in a low voice:
"Do you come to me, Master-at-Arms, with so foggy a
tale? As to Budd, cite me an act or spoken word of his
confirmatory of what you in general charge against him.
Stay," drawing nearer to him, "heed what you speak. Just
now, and in a case like this, there is a yardarm-end for the
false witness."

"Ah, your honor!" sighed Claggart, mildly shaking his
shapely head as in sad deprecation of such unmerited se-
verity of tone. Then, bridling—erecting himself as in
virtuous self-assertion, he circumstantially alleged certain
words and acts, which collectively, if credited, led to pre-
sumptions mortally inculpating Budd. And for some of
these averments, he added, substantiating proof was not
far.

With gray eyes impatient and distrustful essaying to
fathom to the bottom Claggart's calm violet ones, Captain
Vere again heard him out, then for the moment stood
ruminating. The mood he evinced, Claggart, himself for

the time liberated from the other's scrutiny, steadily regarded with a look difficult to render—a look curious of
the operation of his tactics, a look such as might have
been that of the spokesman of the envious children of
Jacob deceptively imposing upon the troubled patriarch
the blood-dyed coat of young Joseph.

Though something exceptional in the moral quality of
Captain Vere made him, in earnest encounter with a
fellow man, a veritable touchstone of that man's essential
nature, yet now as to Claggart and what was really going
on in him his feeling partook less of intuitional conviction
than of strong suspicion clogged by strange dubieties. The
perplexity he evinced proceeded less from aught touching
the man informed against—as Claggart doubtless opined—
than from considerations how best to act in regard to the
informer. At first indeed he was naturally for summoning
that substantiation of his allegations which Claggart said
was at hand. But such a proceeding would result in the
matter at once getting abroad, which in the present stage
of it, he thought, might undesirably affect the ship's company. If Claggart was a false witness—that closed the
affair. And therefore before trying the accusation he would
first practically test the accuser, and he thought this could
be done in a quiet undemonstrative way.

The measure he determined upon involved a shifting
of the scene, a transfer to a place less exposed to observation than the broad quarter-deck. For although the few
gun-room officers there at the time had, in due observance
of naval etiquette, withdrawn to leeward the moment
Captain Vere had begun his promenade on the deck's
weather side; and though during the colloquy with Claggart they of course ventured not to diminish the distance,
and though throughout the interview Captain Vere's voice
was far from high and Claggart's silvery and low, and
the wind in the cordage and the wash of the sea helped
the more to put them beyond earshot; nevertheless, the
interview's continuance already had attracted observation
from some topmen aloft and other sailors in the waist or
further forward.

Having determined upon his measures, Captain Vere
forthwith took action. Abruptly turning to Claggart he
asked, "Master-at-Arms, is it now Budd's watch aloft?"

"No, your honor." Whereupon, "Mr. Wilkes!" summoning the nearest midshipman, "tell Albert to come to me." Albert was the captain's hammock-boy, a sort of sea-valet in whose discretion and fidelity his master had much confidence. The lad appeared. "You know Budd the foretopman?"

"I do, sir."

"Go find him. It is his watch off. Manage to tell him out of earshot that he is wanted aft. Contrive it that he speaks to nobody. Keep him in talk yourself. And not till you get well aft here, not till then let him know that the place where he is wanted is my cabin. You understand. Go.—Master-at-Arms, show yourself on the decks below, and when you think it time for Albert to be coming with his man, stand by quietly to follow the sailor in."

20

Now when the foretopman found himself closeted there, as it were, in the cabin with the captain and Claggart, he was surprised enough. But it was a surprise unaccompanied by apprehension or distrust. To an immature nature essentially honest and humane, forewarning intimations of subtler danger from one's kind come tardily if at all. The only thing that took shape in the young sailor's mind was this: Yes, the captain, I have always thought, looks kindly upon me. Wonder if he's going to make me his coxswain. I should like that. And maybe now he is going to ask the master-at-arms about me.

"Shut the door there, sentry," said the commander; "stand without, and let nobody come in.—Now, Master-at-Arms, tell this man to his face what you told of him to me," and stood prepared to scrutinize the mutually confronting visages.

With the measured step and calm collected air of an asylum physician approaching in the public hall some patient beginning to show indications of a coming paroxysm, Claggart deliberately advanced within short range of Billy, and, mesmerically looking him in the eye, briefly recapitulated the accusation.

Not at first did Billy take it in. When he did, the rose-tan of his cheek looked struck as by white leprosy. He stood like one impaled and gagged. Meanwhile the ac-

cuser's eyes removing not as yet from the blue dilated
ones, underwent a phenomenal change, their wonted rich
violet color blurring into a muddy purple, those lights
of human intelligence losing human expression, gelidly
protruding like the alien eyes of certain uncatalogued
creatures of the deep. The first mesmeric glance was one
of serpent fascination; the last was as the hungry lurch of
the torpedo-fish.

"Speak, man!" said Captain Vere to the transfixed one,
struck by his aspect even more than by Claggart's. "Speak!
defend yourself." Which appeal caused but a strange dumb
gesturing and gurgling in Billy, amazement at such an accusation so suddenly sprung on inexperienced nonage; this,
and, it may be, horror of the accuser, serving to bring
out his lurking defect and in this instance for the time
intensifying it into a convulsed tongue-tie; while the intent
head and entire form straining forward in an agony of
ineffectual eagerness to obey the injunction to speak and
defend himself, gave an expression to the face like that of
a condemned Vestal priestess in the moment of being
buried alive, and in the first struggle against suffocation.

Though at the time Captain Vere was quite ignorant of
Billy's liability to vocal impediment, he now immediately
divined it, since vividly Billy's aspect recalled to him that
of a bright young schoolmate of his whom he had once
seen struck by much the same startling impotence in the
act of eagerly rising in the class to be foremost in response
to a testing question put to it by the master. Going close
up to the young sailor, and laying a soothing hand on his
shoulder, he said: "There is no hurry, my boy. Take your
time, take your time." Contrary to the effect intended, these
words so fatherly in tone doubtless touching Billy's heart
to the quick, prompted yet more violent efforts at utterance
—efforts soon ending for the time in confirming the
paralysis, and bringing to his face an expression which was
as a crucifixion to behold. The next instant, quick as the
flame from a discharged cannon at night, his right arm
shot out, and Claggart dropped to the deck. Whether in-
tentionally or but owing to the young athlete's superior
height, the blow had taken effect full upon the forehead,
so shapely and intellectual-looking a feature in the master-
at-arms, so that the body fell over lengthwise, like a heavy

plank tilted from erectness. A gasp or two, and he lay
motionless.

"Fated boy," breathed Captain Vere in tone so low as
to be almost a whisper, "what have you done! But here,
help me."

The twain raised the felled one from the loins up into
a sitting position. The spare form flexibly acquiesced, but
inertly. It was like handling a dead snake. They lowered it
back. Regaining erectness Captain Vere with one hand
covering his face stood to all appearance as impassive as
the object at his feet. Was he absorbed in taking in all the
bearings of the event and what was best, not only now at
once to be done, but also in the sequel? Slowly he uncovered his face, and the effect was as if the moon emerging from eclipse should reappear with quite another
aspect than that which had gone into hiding. The father
in him, manifested toward Billy thus far in the scene, was
replaced by the military disciplinarian. In his official tone
he bade the foretopman retire to a stateroom aft (pointing
it out) and there remain till thence summoned. This order
Billy in silence mechanically obeyed. Then, going to the
cabin door where it opened on the quarter-deck, Captain
Vere said to the sentry without, "Tell somebody to send
Albert here." When the lad appeared his master so con-
trived it that he should not catch sight of the prone one.
"Albert," he said to him, "tell the surgeon I wish to see
him. You need not come back till called." When the surgeon entered—a self-poised character of that grave sense
and experience that hardly anything could take him aback
—Captain Vere advanced to meet him, thus unconsciously
intercepting his view of Claggart, and, interrupting the
other's wonted ceremonious salutation, said, "Nay, tell
me how it is with yonder man," directing his attention to
the prostrate one.

The surgeon looked, and for all his self-command, somewhat started at the abrupt revelation. On Claggart's always
pallid complexion, thick black blood was now oozing
from nostril and ear. To the gazer's professional eye it
was unmistakably no living man that he saw.

"Is it so then?" said Captain Vere, intently watching
him. "I thought it. But verify it." Whereupon the customary
tests confirmed the surgeon's first glance, who now, looking

up in unfeigned concern, cast a look of intense inquisitive-
ness upon his superior. But Captain Vere, with one hand
to his brow, was standing motionless. Suddenly, catching
the surgeon's arm convulsively, he exclaimed, pointing
down to the body—"It is the divine judgment on Ananias!
Look!"

Disturbed by the excited manner he had never before
observed in the *Indomitable*'s captain, and as yet wholly
ignorant of the affair, the prudent surgeon nevertheless
held his peace, only again looking an earnest interrogation
as to what it was that had resulted in such a tragedy.

But Captain Vere was now again motionless, standing
absorbed in thought. But again starting, he vehemently exclaimed—"Struck dead by an angel of God! Yet the angel
must hang!"

At these passionate interjections, mere incoherences to
the listener as yet unapprised of the antecedents, the surgeon was profoundly discomposed. But now, as recollecting
himself, Captain Vere in less passionate tone briefly related the circumstances leading up to the event.

"But come, we must despatch," he added. "Help me
to remove him (meaning the body) to yonder compartment," designating one opposite that where the foretopman
remained immured. Anew disturbed by a request that,
as implying a desire for secrecy, seemed unaccountably
strange to him, there was nothing for the subordinate
to do but comply.

"Go now," said Captain Vere with something of his
wonted manner—"go now. I shall presently call a drumhead court. Tell the lieutenants what happened, and tell
Mr. Mordant," meaning the captain of marines, "and
charge them to keep the matter to themselves."

21

Full of disquietude and misgiving, the surgeon left
the cabin. Was Captain Vere suddenly affected in his
mind, or was it but a transient excitement, brought about
by so strange and extraordinary a happening? As to the
drumhead court, it struck the surgeon as impolitic, if nothing more. The thing to do, he thought, was to place Billy
Budd in confinement and in a way dictated by usage, and
postpone further action in so extraordinary a case to such

time as they should rejoin the squadron, and then refer it to the admiral. He recalled the unwonted agitation of Captain Vere and his excited exclamations so at variance with his normal manner. Was he unhinged? But assuming that he is, it is not so susceptible of proof. What then can he do? No more trying situation is conceivable than that of an officer subordinate under a captain whom he suspects to be, not mad indeed, but yet not quite unaffected in his intellect. To argue his order to him would be insolence. To resist him would be mutiny.

In obedience to Captain Vere he communicated what had happened to the lieutenants and captain of marines, saying nothing as to the captain's state. They fully shared his own surprise and concern. Like him too they seemed to think that such a matter should be referred to the admiral.

22

Who in the rainbow can show the line where the violet tint ends and the orange tint begins? Distinctly we see the difference of the colors, but when exactly does the one first blendingly enter into the other? So with sanity and insanity. In pronounced cases, there is no question about them. But in some supposed cases, in various degrees supposedly less pronounced, to draw the exact line of demarcation few will undertake—though for a fee some professional experts will. There is nothing namable but that some men will undertake to do it for pay.

Whether Captain Vere, as the surgeon professionally and privately surmised, was really the sudden victim of any degree of aberration, one must determine for himself by such light as this narrative may afford.

That the unhappy event which has been narrated could not have happened at a worse juncture was but too true. For it was close on the heel of the suppressed insurrections, an aftertime very critical to naval authority, demanding from every English sea commander two qualities not readily interfusible—prudence and rigor. Moreover, there was something crucial in the case.

In the jugglery of circumstances preceding and attending the event on board the *Indomitable*, and in the light of that martial code whereby it was formally to be judged, innocence and guilt personified in Claggart and Budd in effect changed places. In a legal view the apparent victim of the tragedy was he who had sought to victimize a man blameless; and the indisputable deed of the latter, navally regarded, constituted the most heinous of military crimes. Yet more. The essential right and wrong involved in the matter, the clearer that might be, so much the worse for the responsibility of a loyal sea commander inasmuch as he was not authorized to determine the matter on that primitive basis.

Small wonder then that the *Indomitable*'s captain, though in general a man of rapid decision, felt that circumspectness not less than promptitude was necessary. Until he could decide upon his course, and in each detail, and not only so, but until the concluding measure was upon the point of being enacted, he deemed it advisable, in view of all the circumstances, to guard as much as possible against publicity. Here he may or may not have erred. Certain it is, however, that subsequently in the confidential talk of more than one or two gun rooms and cabins he was not a little criticized by some officers, a fact imputed by his friends and vehemently by his cousin Jack Denton to professional jealousy of "Starry Vere." Some imaginative ground for invidious comment there was. The maintenance of secrecy in the matter, the confining all knowledge of it for a time to the place where the homicide occurred, the quarter-deck cabin—in these particulars lurked some resemblance to the policy adopted in those tragedies of the palace which have occurred more than once in the capital founded by Peter the Barbarian.

The case indeed was such that fain would the *Indomitable*'s captain have deferred taking any action whatever respecting it further than to keep the foretopman a close prisoner till the ship rejoined the squadron and then submitting the matter to the judgment of his admiral.

But a true military officer is in one particular like a true monk. Not with more of self-abnegation will the latter keep his vows of monastic obedience than the former his vows of allegiance to martial duty.

Feeling that unless quick action was taken on it, the deed of the foretopman, so soon as it should be known on the gun decks, would tend to awaken any slumbering embers of the Nore among the crew, a sense of the urgency of the case overruled in Captain Vere every other consideration. But though a conscientious disciplinarian he was no lover of authority for mere authority's sake. Very far was he from embracing opportunities for monopolizing to himself the perils of moral responsibility, none at least that could properly be referred to an official superior or shared with him by his official equals or even subordinates. So thinking, he was glad it would not be at variance with usage to turn the matter over to a summary court of his own officers, reserving to himself as the one on whom the ultimate accountability would rest, the right of maintaining a supervision of it, or formally or informally interposing at need. Accordingly a drumhead court was summarily convened, he electing the individuals composing it, the first lieutenant, the captain of marines, and the sailing master.

In associating an officer of marines with the sea lieutenants in a case having to do with a sailor, the commander perhaps deviated from general custom. He was prompted thereto by the circumstance that he took that soldier to be a judicious person, thoughtful, and not altogether incapable of grappling with a difficult case unprecedented in his prior experience. Yet even as to him he was not without some latent misgiving, for withal he was an extremely good-natured man, an enjoyer of his dinner, a sound sleeper, and inclined to obesity. A man who though he would always maintain his manhood in battle might not prove altogether reliable in a moral dilemma involving aught of the tragic. As to the first lieutenant and the sailing master, Captain Vere could not but be aware that, though honest natures, of approved gallantry upon occasion, their intelligence was mostly confined to the matter of active seamanship and the fighting demands of their profession. The court was held in the same cabin where the unfortunate affair had taken place. This cabin, the commander's, embraced the entire area under the poop deck. Aft, and on either side, was a small stateroom, the one room temporarily a jail and the other a dead-house, and a yet smaller compartment leaving a space between, expanding forward into a goodly oblong of length coinciding with the ship's beam. A skylight of moderate dimension was overhead, and at each end of the oblong space were two sashed porthole windows easily convertible back into embrasures for short carronades.

All being quickly in readiness, Billy Budd was arraigned, Captain Vere necessarily appearing as the sole witness in the case, and as such temporarily sinking his rank, though singularly maintaining it in a matter apparently trivial, namely, that he testified from the ship's weather side, with that object having caused the court to sit on the lee side. Concisely he narrated all that had led up to the catastrophe, omitting nothing in Claggart's accusation and deposing as to the manner in which the prisoner had received it. At this testimony the three officers glanced with no little surprise at Billy Budd, the last man they would have suspected either of the mutinous design alleged by Claggart or the undeniable deed he himself had done.

The first lieutenant, taking judicial primacy and turning toward the prisoner, said, "Captain Vere has spoken. Is it or is it not as Captain Vere says?" In response came syllables not so much impeded in the utterance as might have been anticipated. They were these: "Captain Vere tells the truth. It is just as Captain Vere says, but it is not as the master-at-arms said. I have eaten the King's bread and I am true to the King."

"I believe you, my man," said the witness, his voice indicating a suppressed emotion not otherwise betrayed.

"God will bless you for that, your honor!" not without stammering said Billy, and all but broke down. But immediately was recalled to self-control by another question, to which with the same emotional difficulty of utterance he said, "No, there was no malice between us. I never bore malice against the master-at-arms. I am sorry that he is dead. I did not mean to kill him. Could I have used my tongue I would not have struck him. But he foully lied to my face and in presence of my captain, and I had to say something, and I could only say it with a blow, God help me!"

In the impulsive aboveboard manner of the frank one the court saw confirmed all that was implied in words that just previously had perplexed them, coming as they did from the testifier to the tragedy and promptly following

Billy's impassioned disclaimer of mutinous intent—Captain Vere's words, "I believe you, my man."

Next it was asked of him whether he knew of or suspected aught savoring of incipient trouble (meaning mutiny, though the explicit term was avoided) going on in any section of the ship's company.

The reply lingered. This was naturally imputed by the court to the same vocal embarrassment which had retarded or obstructed previous answers. But in main it was otherwise here, the question immediately recalling to Billy's mind the interview with the after-guardsman in the forechains. But an innate repugnance to playing a part at all approaching that of an informer against one's own shipmates—the same erring sense of uninstructed honor which had stood in the way of his reporting the matter at the time though as a loyal man-of-war-man it was incumbent on him, and failure so to do if charged against him and proven, would have subjected him to the heaviest of penalties—this, with the blind feeling now his, that nothing really was being hatched, prevailed with him. When the answer came it was a negative.

"One question more," said the officer of marines, now first speaking and with a troubled earnestness. "You tell us that what the master-at-arms said against you was a lie. Now why should he have so lied, so maliciously lied, since you declare there was no malice between you?"

At that question unintentionally touching on a spiritual sphere wholly obscure to Billy's thoughts, he was nonplused, evincing a confusion indeed that some observers, such as can readily be imagined, would have construed into involuntary evidence of hidden guilt. Nevertheless he strove some way to answer, but all at once relinquished the vain endeavor, at the same time turning an appealing glance toward Captain Vere, as deeming him his best helper and friend. Captain Vere, who had been seated for a time, rose to his feet, addressing the interrogator. "The question you put to him comes naturally enough. But how can he rightly answer it? or anybody else? unless indeed it be he who lies within there," designating the compartment where lay the corpse. "But the prone one there will not rise to our summons. In effect, though, as it seems to me, the point you make is hardly material. Quite aside from any con-

ceivable motive actuating the master-at-arms, and irre-
spective of the provocation to the blow, a martial court
must needs in the present case confine its attention to the
blow's consequence, which consequence justly is to be
deemed not otherwise than as the striker's deed."

This utterance, the full significance of which it was not
at all likely that Billy took in, nevertheless caused him to
turn a wistful interrogative look toward the speaker, a
look in its dumb expressiveness not unlike that which a
dog of generous breed might turn upon his master, seeking
in his face some elucidation of a previous gesture ambiguous to the canine intelligence. Nor was the same
utterance without marked effect upon the three officers,
more especially the soldier. Couched in it seemed to them
a meaning unanticipated, involving a prejudgment on
the speaker's part. It served to augment a mental dis-
turbance previously evident enough.

The soldier once more spoke, in a tone of suggestive
dubiety addressing at once his associates and Captain
Vere: "Nobody is present—none of the ship's company, I
mean—who might shed lateral light, if any is to be had,
upon what remains mysterious in this matter."

"That is thoughtfully put," said Captain Vere; "I see
your drift. Aye, there is a mystery; but, to use a Scriptural
phrase, it is 'a mystery of iniquity,' a matter for psy-
chologic theologians to discuss. But what has a military
court to do with it? Not to add that for us any possible
investigation of it is cut off by the lasting tongue-tie of—
him—in yonder," again designating the mortuary stateroom. "The prisoner's deed—with that alone we have
to do."

To this, and particularly the closing reiteration, the
marine soldier, knowing not how aptly to reply, sadly
abstained from saying aught. The first lieutenant, who at
the outset had not unnaturally assumed primacy in the
court, now overrulingly instructed by a glance from Captain Vere, a glance more effective than words, resumed
that primacy. Turning to the prisoner, "Budd," he said,
and scarce in equable tones, "Budd, if you have aught
further to say for yourself, say it now."

Upon this the young sailor turned another quick glance
toward Captain Vere; then, as taking a hint from that

aspect, a hint confirming his own instinct that silence was now best, replied to the lieutenant "I have said all, sir."

The marine—the same who had been the sentinel without the cabin door at the time that the foretopman, followed by the master-at-arms, entered it—he, standing by the sailor throughout these judicial proceedings, was now directed to take him back to the after compartment originally assigned to the prisoner and his custodian. As the twain disappeared from view, the three officers, as partially liberated from some inward constraint associated with Billy's mere presence, simultaneously stirred in their seats. They exchanged looks of troubled indecision, yet feeling that decide they must and without long delay. As for Captain Vere, he for the time stood unconsciously with his back toward them, apparently in one of his absent fits, gazing out from a sashed porthole to windward upon the monotonous blank of the twilight sea. But the court's silence continuing, broken only at moments by brief consultations in low earnest tones, this seemed to arm him and energize him. Turning, he to-and-fro paced the cabin athwart, in the returning ascent to windward climbing the slant deck in the ship's lee roll, without knowing it symbolizing thus in his action a mind resolute to surmount difficulties even if against primitive instincts strong as the wind and the sea. Presently he came to a stand before the three. After scanning their faces he stood less as mustering his thoughts for expression than as one only deliberating how best to put them to well-meaning men not intellectually mature, men with whom it was necessary to demonstrate certain principles that were axioms to himself. Similar impatience as to talking is perhaps one reason that deters some minds from addressing any popular assemblies.

When speak he did, something both in the substance of what he said and his manner of saying it, showed the influence of unshared studies modifying and tempering the practical training of an active career. This, along with his phraseology now and then, was suggestive of the grounds whereon rested that imputation of a certain pedantry socially alleged against him by certain naval men of wholly practical cast, captains who nevertheless would frankly concede that His Majesty's navy mustered no more efficient officer of their grade than "Starry Vere."

What he said was to this effect: "Hitherto I have been but the witness, little more; and I should hardly think now to take another tone, that of your coadjutor, for the time, did I not perceive in you—at the crisis too—a troubled hesitancy, proceeding, I doubt not, from the clash of military duty with moral scruple—scruple vitalized by compassion. For the compassion, how can I otherwise than share it? But, mindful of paramount obligations, I strive against scruples that may tend to enervate decision. Not, gentlemen, that I hide from myself that the case is an exceptional one. Speculatively regarded, it well might be referred to a jury of casuists. But for us here acting not as casuists or moralists, it is a case practical, and under martial law practically to be dealt with.

"But your scruples: do they move as in a dusk? Challenge them. Make them advance and declare themselves. Come now: do they import something like this: If, mindless of palliating circumstances, we are bound to regard the death of the master-at-arms as the prisoner's deed, then does that deed constitute a capital crime whereof the penalty is a mortal one? But in natural justice is nothing but the prisoner's overt act to be considered? How can we adjudge to summary and shameful death a fellow creature innocent before God, and whom we feel to be so?—Does that state it aright? You sign sad assent. Well, I too feel that, the full force of that. It is Nature. But do these buttons that we wear attest that our allegiance is to Nature? No, to the King. Though the ocean, which is inviolate Nature primeval, though this be the element where we move and have our being as sailors, yet as the King's officers lies our duty in a sphere correspondingly natural? So little is that true that, in receiving our commissions, we in the most important regards ceased to be natural free agents. When war is declared are we, the commissioned fighters, previously consulted? We fight at command. If our judgments approve the war, that is but coincidence. So in other particulars. So now. For suppose condemnation to follow these present proceedings. Would it be so much we ourselves that would condemn as it would be martial law operating through us? For that law and the rigor of it, we are not responsible. Our vowed responsibility is in this:

That however pitilessly that law may operate, we nevertheless adhere to it and administer it.

"But the exceptional in the matter moves the hearts within you. Even so too is mine moved. But let not warm hearts betray heads that should be cool. Ashore in a criminal case will an upright judge allow himself off the bench to be waylaid by some tender kinswoman of the accused seeking to touch him with her tearful plea? Well the heart here denotes the feminine in man, is as that piteous woman and, hard though it be, she must here be ruled out."

He paused, earnestly studying them for a moment, then resumed.

"But something in your aspect seems to urge that it is not solely the heart that moves in you, but also the conscience, the private conscience. But tell me whether or not, occupying the position we do, private conscience should not yield to that imperial one formulated in the code under which alone we officially proceed?"

Here the three men moved in their seats, less convinced than agitated by the course of an argument troubling but the more the spontaneous conflict within.

Perceiving which, the speaker paused for a moment, then, abruptly changing his tone, went on.

"To steady us a bit, let us recur to the facts.—In wartime at sea a man-of-war's-man strikes his superior in grade, and the blow kills. Apart from its effect, the blow itself is, according to the Articles of War, a capital crime. Furthermore——"

"Aye, sir," emotionally broke in the officer of marines, "in one sense it was. But surely Budd purposed neither mutiny nor homicide."

"Surely not, my good man. And before a court less arbitrary and more merciful than a martial one that plea would largely extenuate. At the Last Assizes it shall acquit. But how here? We proceed under the law of the Mutiny Act. In feature no child can resemble his father more than that Act resembles in spirit the thing from which it derives —War. In His Majesty's service—in this ship indeed— there are Englishmen forced to fight for the King against their will. Against their conscience, for aught we know. Though as their fellow creatures some of us may appreciate

their position, yet as navy officers, what reck we of it? Still
less recks the enemy. Our impressed men he would fain
cut down in the same swath with our volunteers. As
regards the enemy's naval conscripts, some of whom may
even share our own abhorrence of the regicidal French
Directory, it is the same on our side. War looks but to the
frontage, the appearance. And the Mutiny Act, War's
child, takes after the father. Budd's intent or nonintent is
nothing to the purpose.

"But while, put to it by those anxieties in you which I
cannot but respect, I only repeat myself—while thus
strangely we prolong proceedings that should be summary
—the enemy may be sighted and an engagement result.
We must do; and one of two things must we do—condemn
or let go."

"Can we not convict and yet mitigate the penalty?"
asked the junior lieutenant here speaking, and falteringly,
for the first.

"Lieutenant, were that clearly lawful for us under the
circumstances, consider the consequences of such clem-
ency. The people" (meaning the ship's company) "have
native sense; most of them are familiar with our naval
usage and tradition, and how would they take it? Even
could you explain to them—which our official position
forbids—they, long molded by arbitrary discipline, have
not that kind of intelligent responsiveness that might
qualify them to comprehend and discriminate. No, to the
people the foretopman's deed, however it be worded in
the announcement, will be plain homicide committed in
a flagrant act of mutiny. What penalty for that should
follow, they know. But it does not follow. *Why?* they will
ruminate. You know what sailors are. Will they not revert
to the recent outbreak at the Nore? Aye. They know the
well-founded alarm—the panic it struck throughout England. Your clement sentence they would account pusillani-
mous. They would think that we flinch, that we are afraid
of them—afraid of practicing a lawful rigor singularly
demanded at this juncture lest it should provoke new
troubles. What shame to us such a conjecture on their
part, and how deadly to discipline. You see then, whither,
prompted by duty and the law, I steadfastly drive. But I
beseech you, my friends, do not take me amiss. I feel as

you do for this unfortunate boy. But did he know our hearts, I take him to be of that generous nature that he would feel even for us on whom in this military necessity so heavy a compulsion is laid."

With that, crossing the deck he resumed his place by the sashed porthole, tacitly leaving the three to come to a decision. On the cabin's opposite side the troubled court sat silent. Loyal lieges, plain and practical, though at bottom they dissented from some points Captain Vere had put to them, they were without the faculty, hardly had the inclination, to gainsay one whom they felt to be an earnest man, one, too, not less their superior in mind than in naval rank. But it is not improbable that even such of his words as were not without influence over them, less came home to them than his closing appeal to their instinct as sea officers in the forethought he threw out as to the practical consequences to discipline, considering the unconfirmed tone of the fleet at the time, should a man-of-war's-man's violent killing at sea of a superior in grade be allowed to pass for aught else than a capital crime demanding prompt infliction of the penalty.

Not unlikely they were brought to something more or less akin to that harassed frame of mind which in the year 1842 actuated the commander of the U.S. brig-of-war *Somers* to resolve, under the so-called Articles of War, Articles modeled upon the English Mutiny Act, to resolve upon the execution at sea of a midshipman and two petty officers as mutineers designing the seizure of the brig. Which resolution was carried out though in a time of peace and within not many days sail of home—an act vindicated by a naval court of inquiry subsequently convened ashore. History, and here cited without comment. True, the circumstances on board the *Somers* were different from those on board the *Indomitable*. But the urgency felt, well-warranted or otherwise, was much the same.

Says a writer whom few know, "Forty years after a battle it is easy for a noncombatant to reason about how it ought to have been fought. It is another thing personally and under fire to direct the fighting while involved in the obscuring smoke of it. Much so with respect to other emergencies involving considerations both practical and moral, and when it is imperative promptly to act. The greater the

fog the more it imperils the steamer, and speed is put on
though at the hazard of running somebody down. Little
ween the snug card-players in the cabin of the responsibilities of the sleepless man on the bridge."

In brief, Billy Budd was formally convicted and sen-
tenced to be hung at the yardarm in the early morning
watch, it being now night. Otherwise, as is customary in
such cases, the sentence would forthwith have been carried
out. In wartime, on the field or in the fleet, a mortal punishment decreed by a drumhead court—on the field sometimes decreed by but a nod from the general—follows
without delay on the heel of conviction, without appeal.

23

It was Captain Vere himself who of his own motion
communicated the finding of the court to the prisoner, for
that purpose going to the compartment where he was in
custody and bidding the marine there to withdraw for the
time.

Beyond the communication of the sentence, what took
place at this interview was never known. But in view of
the character of the twain briefly closeted in that stateroom, each radically sharing in the rarer qualities of our
nature—so rare indeed as to be all but incredible to
average minds however much cultivated—some conjectures may be ventured.

It would have been in consonance with the spirit of
Captain Vere should he on this occasion have concealed
nothing from the condemned one—should he indeed have
frankly disclosed to him the part he himself had played
in bringing about the decision, at the same time revealing
his actuating motives. On Billy's side it is not improbable
that such a confession would have been received in much
the same spirit that prompted it. Not without a sort of
joy indeed he might have appreciated the brave opinion
of him implied in his captain making such a confidant of
him. Nor as to the sentence itself could he have been
insensible that it was imparted to him as to one not afraid
to die. Even more may have been. Captain Vere in the
end may have developed the passion sometimes latent
under an exterior stoical or indifferent. He was old enough
to have been Billy's father. The austere devotee of military

duty letting himself melt back into what remains primeval in our formalized humanity may in the end have caught Billy to his heart even as Abraham may have caught young Isaac on the brink of resolutely offering him up in obedience to the exacting behest. But there is no telling the sacrament, seldom if in any case revealed to the gadding world, wherever under circumstances at all akin to those here attempted to be set forth two of great Nature's nobler order embrace. There is privacy at the time, inviolable to the survivor, and holy oblivion, the sequel to each diviner magnanimity, providentially covers all at last.

The first to encounter Captain Vere in act of leaving the compartment was the senior lieutenant. The face he beheld, for the moment one expressive of the agony of the strong, was to that officer, though a man of fifty, a startling revelation. That the condemned one suffered less than he who mainly had effected the condemnation was apparently indicated by the former's exclamation in the scene soon perforce to be touched upon.

24

Of a series of incidents within a brief term rapidly following each other, the adequate narration may take up a term less brief, especially if explanation or comment here and there seem requisite to the better understanding of such incidents. Between the entrance into the cabin of him who never left it alive, and him who when he did leave it left it as one condemned to die, between this and the closeted interview just given, less than an hour and a half had elapsed. It was an interval long enough, however, to awaken speculations among no few of the ship's company as to what it was that could be detaining in the cabin the master-at-arms and the sailor; for a rumor that both of them had been seen to enter it and neither of them had been seen to emerge, this rumor had got abroad upon the gun decks and in the tops; the people of a great warship being in one respect like villagers taking microscopic note of every outward movement or nonmovement going on. When, therefore, in weather not at all tempestuous all hands were called in the second dog watch, a summons under such circumstances not usual in those hours, the crew were not wholly unprepared for some announcement extraordinary, one having connection too with the continued absence of the two men from their wonted haunts.

There was a moderate sea at the time, and the moon, newly risen and near to being at its full, silvered the white spar-deck wherever not blotted by the clear-cut shadows horizontally thrown of fixtures and moving men. On either side the quarter-deck the marine guard under arms was drawn up; and Captain Vere, standing in his place surrounded by all the wardroom officers, addressed his men. In so doing his manner showed neither more nor less than that property pertaining to his supreme position aboard his own ship. In clear terms and concise he told them what had taken place in the cabin: that the master-at-arms was dead; that he who had killed him had been already tried by a summary court and condemned to death; and that the execution would take place in the early morning watch. The word *mutiny* was not named in what he said. He refrained too from making the occasion an opportunity for any preachment as to the maintenance of discipline, thinking perhaps that under existing circumstances in the navy the consequence of violating discipline should be made to speak for itself.

Their captain's announcement was listened to by the throng of standing sailors in a dumbness like that of a seated congregation of believers in hell listening to the clergyman's announcement of his Calvinistic text.

At the close, however, a confused murmur went up. It began to wax. All but instantly, then, at a sign, it was pierced and suppressed by shrill whistles of the boatswain and his mates piping down one watch.

To be prepared for burial Claggart's body was delivered to certain petty officers of his mess. And here, not to clog the sequel with lateral matters, it may be added that, at a suitable hour, the master-at-arms was committed to the sea with every funeral honor properly belonging to his naval grade.

In this proceeding, as in every public one growing out of the tragedy, strict adherence to usage was observed. Nor in any point could it have been at all deviated from, either with respect to Claggart or Billy Budd, without begetting undesirable speculations in the ship's company, sailors,

and more particularly men-of-war's men, being of all men
the greatest sticklers for usage.

For similar cause, all communication between Captain
Vere and the condemned one ended with the closeted interview already given, the latter being now surrendered
to the ordinary routine preliminary to the end. This transfer
under guard from the captain's quarters was effected without unusual precautions—at least no visible ones.

If possible not to let the men so much as surmise that
their officers anticipate aught amiss from them is the tacit
rule in a military ship. And the more that some sort of
trouble should really be apprehended, the more do the
officers keep that apprehension to themselves, though
not the less unostentatious vigilance may be augmented.

In the present instance the sentry placed over the
prisoner had strict orders to let no one have communication with him but the chaplain. And certain unobtrusive
measures were taken absolutely to insure this point.

25

In a seventy-four of the old order the deck known as the
upper gun deck was the one covered over by the spar-deck,
which last, though not without its armament, was for the
most part exposed to the weather. In general it was at all
hours free from hammocks; those of the crew swinging
on the lower gun deck and berth deck, the latter being
not only a dormitory but also the place for the stowing
of the sailors' bags, and on both sides lined with the large
chests or movable pantries of the many messes of the men.

On the starboard side of the *Indomitable*'s upper gun
deck, behold Billy Budd under sentry lying prone in irons
in one of the bays formed by the regular spacing of the
guns comprising the batteries on either side. All these
pieces were of the heavier caliber of that period. Mounted
on lumbering wooden carriages, they were hampered with
cumbersome harness of breeching and strong side tackles
for running them out. Guns and carriages, together with the
long rammers and shorter lintstocks lodged in loops overhead—all these, as customary, were painted black; and the
heavy hempen breechings, tarred to the same tint, wore
the like livery of the undertakers. In contrast with the
funereal hue of these surroundings the prone sailor's ex-

terior apparel, white jumper and white duck trousers, each
more or less soiled, dimly glimmered in the obscure light
of the bay like a patch of discolored snow in early April
lingering at some upland cave's black mouth. In effect
he is already in his shroud or the garments that shall serve
him in lieu of one. Over him but scarce illuminating him,
two battle lanterns swing from two massive beams of the
deck above. Fed with the oil supplied by the war contractors (whose gains, honest or otherwise, are in every land
an anticipated portion of the harvest of death) with
flickering splashes of dirty yellow light, they pollute
the pale moonshine, all but ineffectually struggling in
obstructed flecks through the open ports from which the
tompioned cannon protrude. Other lanterns at intervals
serve but to bring out somewhat the obscurer bays, which,
like small confessionals or side-chapels in a cathedral,
branch from the long dim-vistaed broad aisle between the
two batteries of that covered tier.

Such was the deck where now lay the Handsome Sailor.
Through the rose-tan of his complexion no pallor could
have shown. It would have taken days of sequestration
from the winds and the sun to have brought about the
effacement of that. But the skeleton in the cheekbone at
the point of its angle was just beginning delicately to be
defined under the warm-tinted skin. In fervid hearts self-
contained some brief experiences devour our human tissue
as secret fire in a ship's hold consumes cotton in the bale.

But now lying between the two guns, as nipped in the
vice of fate, Billy's agony, mainly proceeding from a
generous young heart's virgin experience of the diabolical
incarnate and effective in some men—the tension of that
agony was over now. It survived not the something healing
in the closeted interview with Captain Vere. Without
movement, he lay as in a trance. That adolescent expression previously noted as his, taking on something
akin to the look of a slumbering child in the cradle when
the warm hearth-glow of the still chamber at night plays
on the dimples that at whiles mysteriously form in the
cheek, silently coming and going there. For now and then
in the gyved one's trance a serene happy light born of some
wandering reminiscence or dream would diffuse itself over
his face, and then wane away only anew to return.

The Chaplain coming to see him and finding him thus, and perceiving no sign that he was conscious of his presence, attentively regarded him for a space, then, slipping aside, withdrew for the time, peradventure feeling that even he, the minister of Christ, though receiving his stipend from Mars had no consolation to proffer which could result in a peace transcending that which he beheld. But in the small hours he came again. And the prisoner now awake to his surroundings noticed his approach and civilly, all but cheerfully, welcomed him. But it was to little purpose that in the interview following the good man sought to bring Billy Budd to some godly understanding that he must die, and at dawn. True, Billy himself freely referred to his death as a thing close at hand; but it was something in the way that children will refer to death in general, who yet among their other sports will play a funeral with hearse and mourners.

Not that like children Billy was incapable of conceiving what death really is. No; but he was wholly without irrational fear of it, a fear more prevalent in highly civilized communities than those so-called barbarous ones which in all respects stand nearer to unadulterate Nature. And, as elsewhere said, a barbarian Billy radically was; as much so, for all the costume, as his countrymen the British captives, living trophies, made to march in the Roman triumph of Germanicus. Quite as much so as those later barbarians, young men probably, and picked specimens among the earlier British converts to Christianity, at least nominally such and taken to Rome (as today converts from lesser isles of the sea may be taken to London) of whom the pope of that time, admiring the strangeness of their personal beauty so unlike the Italian stamp, their clear ruddy complexion and curled flaxen locks, exclaimed, "Angles" (meaning *English,* the modern derivative) "Angles do you call them? And is it because they look so like angels?" Had it been later in time one would think that the Pope had in mind Fra Angelico's seraphs, some of whom, plucking apples in gardens of the Hesperides, have the faint rose-bud complexion of the more beautiful English girls.

If in vain the good chaplain sought to impress the young barbarian with ideas of death akin to those conveyed in

the skull, dial, and crossbones on old tombstones, equally
futile to all appearance were his efforts to bring home to
him the thought of salvation and a Saviour. Billy listened,
but less out of awe or reverence perhaps than from a
certain natural politeness, doubtless at bottom regarding
all that in much the same way that most mariners of his
class take any discourse abstract or out of the common
tone of the workaday world. And this sailor-way of taking
clerical discourse is not wholly unlike the way in which
the pioneer of Christianity, full of transcendent miracles,
was received long ago on tropic isles by any superior
savage so called—a Tahitian, say, of Captain Cook's time
or shortly after that time. Out of natural courtesy he received, but did not appropriate. It was like a gift placed
in the palm of an outreached hand upon which the fingers
do not close.

But the *Indomitable*'s chaplain was a discreet man,
possessing the good sense of a good heart. So he insisted
not in his vocation here. At the instance of Captain Vere,
a lieutenant had apprised him of pretty much everything
as to Billy; and since he felt that innocence was even a
better thing than religion wherewith to go to Judgment,
he reluctantly withdrew, but in his emotion not without
first performing an act strange enough in an Englishman,
and under the circumstances yet more so in any regular
priest. Stooping over, he kissed on the fair cheek his fellow
man, a felon in martial law, one who, though on the
confines of death, he felt he could never convert to a
dogma; nor for all that did he fear for his future.

Marvel not that having been made acquainted with the
young sailor's essential innocence (an irruption of heretic
thought hard to suppress) the worthy man lifted not a
finger to avert the doom of such a martyr to martial discipline. So to do would not only have been as idle as invoking the desert, but would also have been an audacious
transgression of the bounds of his function, one as exactly
prescribed to him by military law as that of the boatswain
or any other naval officer. Bluntly put, a chaplain is the
minister of the Prince of Peace serving in the host of the
God of War—Mars. As such, he is as incongruous as that
musket of Blücher, etc., at Christmas. Why then is he
there? Because he indirectly subserves the purpose attested

by the cannon; because too he lends the sanction of the religion of the meek to that which practically is the abrogation of everything but brute Force.

26

The night so luminous on the spar-deck but otherwise on the cavernous ones below, levels so like the tiered galleries in a coal mine—the luminous night passed away. But, like the prophet in the chariot disappearing in heaven and dropping his mantle to Elisha, the withdrawing night transferred its pale robe to the breaking day. A meek shy light appeared in the East, where stretched a diaphanous fleece of white furrowed vapor. That light slowly waxed. Suddenly *eight bells* was struck aft, responded to by one louder metallic stroke from forward. It was four o'clock in the morning. Instantly the silver whistles were heard summoning all hands to witness punishment. Up through the great hatchways rimmed with racks of heavy shot, the watch below came pouring, overspreading with the watch already on deck the space between the mainmast and foremast, including that occupied by the capacious launch and the black booms tiered on either side of it, boat and booms making a summit of observation for the powder-boys and younger tars. A different group comprising one watch of topmen leaned over the rail of that sea-balcony, no small one in a seventy-four, looking down on the crowd below. Man or boy none spake but in whisper, and few spake at all. Captain Vere—as before, the central figure among the assembled commissioned officers—stood nigh the break of the poop deck facing forward. Just below him on the quarter-deck the marines in full equipment were drawn up much as at the scene of the promulgated sentence.

At sea in the old time, the execution by halter of a military sailor was generally from the foreyard. In the present instance, for special reasons the mainyard was assigned. Under an arm of that lee yard the prisoner was presently brought up, the chaplain attending him. It was noted at the time, and remarked upon afterwards, that in this final scene the good man evinced little or nothing of the perfunctory. Brief speech indeed he had with the condemned one, but the genuine Gospel was less on his tongue than in his aspect and manner toward him. The final

preparations personal to the latter being speedily brought to
an end by two boatswain's mates, the consummation impended. Billy stood facing aft. At the penultimate moment,
his words, his only ones, words wholly unobstructed in
the utterance, were these—"God bless Captain Vere!"
Syllables so unanticipated coming from one with the
ignominious hemp about his neck—a conventional felon's
benediction directed aft toward the quarters of honor;
syllables, too, delivered in the clear melody of a singing
bird on the point of launching from the twig, had a
phenomenal effect, not unenhanced by the rare personal
beauty of the young sailor spiritualized now through late
experiences so poignantly profound.

Without volition as it were, as if indeed the ship's populace were but the vehicles of some vocal current electric,
with one voice from alow and aloft came a resonant sympathetic echo—"God bless Captain Vere!" And yet at
that instant Billy alone must have been in their hearts,
even as he was in their eyes.

At the pronounced words and the spontaneous echo
that voluminously rebounded them, Captain Vere, either
through stoic self-control or a sort of momentary paralysis
induced by emotional shock, stood erectly rigid as a
musket in the ship-armorer's rack.

The hull deliberately recovering from the periodic roll
to leeward was just regaining an even keel, when the last
signal, a preconcerted dumb one, was given. At the same
moment it chanced that the vapory fleece hanging low in the
East was shot through with a soft glory as of the fleece of
the Lamb of God seen in mystical vision, and simultaneously therewith, watched by the wedged mass of upturned
faces, Billy ascended, and, ascending, took the full rose of
the dawn.

In the pinioned figure arrived at the yard-end, to the
wonder of all no motion was apparent, none save that
created by the ship's motion, in moderate weather so
majestic in a great ship ponderously cannoned.

27

A digression

When, some days afterward, in reference to the singularity just mentioned, the purser, a rather ruddy rotund

person more accurate as an accountant than profound as a philosopher, said at mess to the surgeon, "What testimony to the force lodged in will power," the latter—saturnine, spare and tall, one in whom a discreet causticity went along with a manner less genial than polite, replied, "Your pardon, Mr. Purser. In a hanging scientifically conducted—and under special orders I myself directed how Budd's was to be effected—any movement following the completed suspension and originating in the body suspended, such movement indicates mechanical spasm in the muscular system. Hence the absence of that is no more attributable to will power as you call it than to horsepower —begging your pardon."

"But this muscular spasm you speak of, is not that in a degree more or less invariable in these cases?"

"Assuredly so, Mr. Purser."

"How then, my good sir, do you account for its absence in this instance?"

"Mr. Purser, it is clear that your sense of the singularity in this matter equals not mine. You account for it by what you call will power, a term not yet included in the lexicon of science. For me, I do not, with my present knowledge, pretend to account for it at all. Even should we assume the hypothesis that at the first touch of the halyards the action of Budd's heart, intensified by extraordinary emotion at its climax, abruptly stopped—much like a watch when in carelessly winding it up you strain at the finish, thus snapping the chain—even under that hypothesis how account for the phenomenon that followed?"

"You admit, then, that the absence of spasmodic movement was phenomenal."

"It was phenomenal, Mr. Purser, in the sense that it was an appearance the cause of which is not immediately to be assigned."

"But tell me, my dear sir," pertinaciously continued the other, "was the man's death effected by the halter, or was it a species of euthanasia?"

" 'Euthanasia,' Mr. Purser, is something like your 'will power': I doubt its authenticity as a scientific term— begging your pardon again. It is at once imaginative and metaphysical,—in short, Greek. But," abruptly changing

his tone, "there is a case in the sick bay that I do not care
to leave to my assistants. Beg your pardon, but excuse
me." And rising from the mess he formally withdrew.

28

The silence at the moment of execution and for a
moment or two continuing thereafter, a silence but emphasized by the regular wash of the sea against the hull or
the flutter of a sail caused by the helmsman's eyes being
tempted astray, this emphasized silence was gradually
disturbed by a sound not easily to be verbally rendered.
Whoever has heard the freshet-wave of a torrent suddenly swelled by pouring showers in tropical mountains,
showers not shared by the plain; whoever has heard the
first muffled murmur of its sloping advance through pre-
cipitous woods, may form some conception of the sound
now heard. The seeming remoteness of its source was
because of its murmurous indistinctness since it came
from close by, even from the men massed on the ship's
open deck. Being inarticulate, it was dubious in significance further than it seemed to indicate some capricious
revulsion of thought or feeling such as mobs ashore are
liable to, in the present instance possibly implying a sullen
revocation on the men's part of their involuntary echoing
of Billy's benediction. But ere the murmur had time to wax
into clamor it was met by a strategic command, the more
telling that it came with abrupt unexpectedness.

"Pipe down the starboard watch, Boatswain, and see
that they go."

Shrill as the shriek of the sea hawk the whistles of the
boatswain and his mates pierced that ominous low sound,
dissipating it; and yielding to the mechanism of discipline
the throng was thinned by one half. For the remainder,
most of them were set to temporary employments connected with trimming the yards and so forth, business
readily to be got up to serve occasion by any officer-of-the-
deck.

Now each proceeding that follows a mortal sentence
pronounced at sea by a drumhead court is characterized
by promptitude not perceptibly merging into hurry, though
bordering that. The hammock, the one which had been
Billy's bed when alive, having already been ballasted with

shot and otherwise prepared to serve for his canvas coffin, the last offices of the sea-undertakers, the sailmaker's mates, were now speedily completed. When everything was in readiness a second call for all hands, made necessary by the strategic movement before mentioned, was sounded, and now to witness burial.

The details of this closing formality it needs not to give. But when the tilted plank let slide its freight into the sea, a second strange human murmur was heard, blended now with another inarticulate sound proceeding from certain larger seafowl, whose attention having been attracted by the peculiar commotion in the water resulting from the heavy sloped dive of the shotted hammock into the sea, flew screaming to the spot. So near the hull did they come that the stridor or bony creak of their gaunt double-jointed pinions was audible. As the ship under light airs passed on, leaving the burial spot astern, they still kept circling it low down with the moving shadow of their outstretched wings and the croaked requiem of their cries.

Upon sailors as superstitious as those of the age preceding ours, men-of-war's men, too, who had just beheld the prodigy of repose in the form suspended in air and now foundering in the deeps; to such mariners the action of the seafowl, though dictated by mere animal greed for prey, was big with no prosaic significance. An uncertain movement began among them, in which some encroachment was made. It was tolerated but for a moment. For suddenly the drum beat to quarters, which familiar sound, happening at least twice every day, had upon the present occasion a signal peremptoriness in it. True martial discipline long continued superinduces in average man a sort of impulse of docility whose operation at the official sound of command much resembles in its promptitude the effect of an instinct.

The drumbeat dissolved the multitude, distributing most of them along the batteries of the two covered gun decks. There, as wont, the guns' crews stood by their respective cannon erect and silent. In due course the first officer, sword under arm and standing in his place on the quarter-deck, formally received the successive reports of the sworded lieutenants commanding the sections of bat-teries below, the last of which reports being made, the

summed report he delivered with the customary salute to
the commander. All this occupied time, which in the
present case was the object of beating to quarters at an
hour prior to the customary one. That such variance from
usage was authorized by an officer like Captain Vere, a
martinet as some deemed him, was evidence of the necessity for unusual action implied in what he deemed to be
temporarily the mood of his men. "With mankind," he
would say, "forms, measured forms, are everything; and
that is the import couched in the story of Orpheus with
his lyre spellbinding the wild denizens of the wood." And
this he once applied to the disruption of forms going on
across the Channel and the consequences thereof.

At this unwonted muster at quarters, all proceeded as at
the regular hour. The band on the quarter-deck played a
sacred air, after which the chaplain went through the customary morning service. That done, the drum beat the
retreat, and, toned by music and religious rites subserving
the discipline and purpose of war, the men in their wonted
orderly manner dispersed to the places allotted them when
not at the guns.

And now it was full day. The fleece of low-hanging
vapor had vanished, licked up by the sun that late had so
glorified it. And the circumambient air in the clearness of
its serenity was like smooth white marble in the polished
block not yet removed from the marble dealer's yard.

29

The symmetry of form attainable in pure fiction cannot
so readily be achieved in a narration essentially having
less to do with fable than with fact. Truth uncompromis-
ingly told will always have its ragged edges; hence the
conclusion of such a narration is apt to be less finished
than an achitectural finial.

How it fared with the Handsome Sailor during the year
of the Great Mutiny has been faithfully given. But though
properly the story ends with his life, something in way of
sequel will not be amiss. Three brief chapters will suffice.

In the general rechristening under the Directory of the
craft originally forming the navy of the French monarchy,
the *St. Louis* line-of-battle ship was named the *Athéiste*.
Such a name, like some other substituted ones in the

Revolutionary fleet, while proclaiming the infidel audacity of the ruling power was yet, though not so intended to be, the aptest name, if one consider it, ever given to a warship, far more so indeed than the *Devastation*, the *Erebus* (the *Hell*) and similar names bestowed upon fighting ships.

On the return passage to the English fleet from the detached cruise during which occurred the events already recorded, the *Indomitable* fell in with the *Athéiste*. An engagement ensued, during which Captain Vere, in the act of putting his ship alongside the enemy with a view of throwing his boarders across her bulwarks, was hit by a musket ball from a porthole of the enemy's main cabin. More than disabled he dropped to the deck and was carried below to the same cockpit where some of his men already lay. The senior lieutenant took command. Under him the enemy was finally captured and though much crippled was by rare good fortune successfully taken into Gibraltar, an English port not very distant from the scene of the fight. There Captain Vere with the rest of the wounded was put ashore. He lingered for some days, but the end came. Unhappily he was cut off too early for the Nile and Trafalgar. The spirit that spite its philosophic austerity may yet have indulged in the most secret of all passions, ambition, never attained to the fullness of fame.

Not long before death, while lying under the influence of that magical drug which, soothing the physical frame, mysteriously operates on the subtler element in man, he was heard to murmur words inexplicable to his attendant —"Billy Budd, Billy Budd." That these were not the accents of remorse would seem clear from what the attendant said to the *Indomitable*'s senior officer of marines, who, as the most reluctant to condemn of the members of the drumhead court, too well knew, though here he kept the knowledge to himself, who Billy Budd was.

30

Some few weeks after the execution, among other matters under the head of *News from the Mediterranean*, there appeared in a naval chronicle of the time, an authorized weekly publication, an account of the affair. It was doubtless for the most part written in good faith, though the medium, partly rumor, through which the facts must have reached the writer, served to deflect and in part falsify them. The account was as follows:

"On the tenth of the last month a deplorable occurrence took place on board H.M.S. *Indomitable*. John Claggart, the ship's master-at-arms, discovering that some sort of plot was incipient among an inferior section of the ship's company, and that the ringleader was one William Budd, he, Claggart, in the act of arraigning the man before the captain was vindictively stabbed to the heart by the suddenly drawn sheath knife of Budd.

"The deed and the implement employed sufficiently suggest that, though mustered into the service under an English name, the assassin was no Englishman, but one of those aliens adopting English cognomens whom the present extraordinary necessities of the service have caused to be admitted into it in considerable numbers.

"The enormity of the crime and the extreme depravity of the criminal appear the greater in view of the character of the victim, a middle-aged man respectable and discreet, belonging to that minor official grade, the petty officers, upon whom, as none know better than the commissioned gentlemen, the efficiency of His Majesty's navy so largely depends. His function was a responsible one, at once onerous and thankless, and his fidelity in it the greater because of his strong patriotic impulse. In this instance, as in so many other instances in these days, the character of this unfortunate man signally refutes, if refutation were needed, that peevish saying attributed to the late Dr. Johnson, that patriotism is the last refuge of a scoundrel.

"The criminal paid the penalty of his crime. The promptitude of the punishment has proved salutary. Nothing amiss is now apprehended aboard H.M.S. *Indomitable*."

The above, appearing in a publication now long ago superannuated and forgotten, is all that hitherto has stood in human record to attest what manner of men respectively were John Claggart and Billy Budd.

31

Everything is for a term remarkable in navies. Any tangible object associated with some striking incident of the service is converted into a monument. The spar from which the foretopman was suspended was for some few years kept trace of by the bluejackets. Their knowledge followed it from ship to dockyard and again from dockyard to ship, still pursuing it even when at last reduced to a mere dockyard boom. To them a chip of it was as a piece of the Cross. Ignorant though they were of the secret facts of the tragedy, and not thinking but that the penalty was somehow unavoidably inflicted from the naval point of view, for all that they instinctively felt that Billy was a sort of man as incapable of mutiny as of willful murder. They recalled the fresh young image of the Handsome Sailor, that face never deformed by a sneer or subtler vile freak of the heart within. Their impression of him was doubtless deepened by the fact that he was gone, and in a measure mysteriously gone. At the time on the gun decks of the *Indomitable* the general estimate of his nature and its unconscious simplicity eventually found rude utterance from another foretopman, one of his own watch, gifted, as some sailors are, with an artless poetic temperament; the tarry hands made some lines which, after circulating among the shipboard crew for a while, finally got rudely printed at Portsmouth as a ballad. The title given to it was the sailor's.

Billy in the Darbies

Good of the Chaplain to enter Lone Bay
And down on his marrow-bones here and pray
For the likes just o' me, Billy Budd.—But look:
Through the port comes the moonshine astray!
It tips the guard's cutlass and silvers this nook;
But 'twill die in the dawning of Billy's last day.
A jewel-block they'll make of me tomorrow,
Pendant pearl from the yardarm-end
Like the eardrop I gave to Bristol Molly—
Oh, 'tis me, not the sentence they'll suspend.
Aye, Aye, all is up; and I must up too
Early in the morning, aloft from alow.
On an empty stomach, now, never it would do.
They'll give me a nibble—bit o' biscuit ere I go.
Sure, a messmate will reach me the last parting cup;
But, turning heads away from the hoist and the belay,
Heaven knows who will have the running of me up!
No pipe to those halyards.—But aren't it all sham?

A blur's in my eyes; it is dreaming that I am.
A hatchet to my hawser? all adrift to go?
The drum roll to grog, and Billy never know?
But Donald he has promised to stand by the plank;
So I'll shake a friendly hand ere I sink.
But—no! It is dead then I'll be, come to think.—
I remember Taff the Welshman when he sank.
And his cheek it was like the budding pink
But me they'll lash me in hammock, drop me deep.
Fathoms down, fathoms down, how I'll dream fast asleep.
I feel it stealing now. Sentry, are you there?
Just ease this darbies at the wrist, and roll me over fair,
I am sleepy, and the oozy weeds about me twist.

END OF BOOK

April 19th, 1891

The Piazza Tales

THE PIAZZA

"With fairest flowers,
Whilst summer lasts, and I live here, Fidele—"

WHEN I removed into the country, it was to occupy an old-fashioned farmhouse, which had no piazza—a deficiency the more regretted because not only did I like piazzas, as somehow combining the coziness of indoors with the freedom of outdoors, and it is so pleasant to inspect your thermometer there, but the country round about was such a picture that in berry time no boy climbs hill or crosses vale without coming upon easels planted in every nook, and sunburnt painters painting there. A very paradise of painters. The circle of the stars cut by the circle of the mountains. At least, so looks it from the house; though, once upon the mountains, no circle of them can you see. Had the site been chosen five rods off, this charmed ring would not have been.

The house is old. Seventy years since, from the heart of the Hearth Stone Hills, they quarried the Kaaba, or Holy Stone, to which, each Thanksgiving, the social pilgrims used to come. So long ago that, in digging for the foundation, the workmen used both spade and ax, fighting the troglodytes of those subterranean parts—sturdy roots of a sturdy wood, encamped upon what is now a long landslide of sleeping meadow, sloping away off from my poppybed. Of that knit wood but one survivor stands—an elm, lonely through steadfastness.

Whoever built the house, he builded better than he knew, or else Orion in the zenith flashed down his

89

Damocles' sword to him some starry night and said,
"Build there." For how, otherwise, could it have entered
the builder's mind, that, upon the clearing being made,
such a purple prospect would be his?—nothing less than
Greylock, with all his hills about him, like Charlemagne
among his peers.

Now, for a house, so situated in such a country, to have
no piazza for the convenience of those who might desire
to feast upon the view, and take their time and ease about
it, seemed as much of an omission as if a picture gallery
should have no bench; for what but picture galleries are
the marble halls of these same limestone hills?—galleries
hung, month after month anew, with pictures ever fading
into pictures ever fresh. And beauty is like piety—you
cannot run and read it; tranquillity and constancy, with,
nowadays, an easy chair, are needed. For though, of old,
when reverence was in vogue and indolence was not, the
devotees of Nature doubtless used to stand and adore—
just as, in the cathedrals of those ages, the worshipers of
a higher Power did—yet, in these times of failing faith
and feeble knees, we have the piazza and the pew.

During the first year of my residence, the more leisurely
to witness the coronation of Charlemagne (weather permitting, they crown him every sunrise and sunset), I
chose me, on the hillside bank near by, a royal lounge
of turf—a green velvet lounge, with long, moss-padded
back; while at the head, strangely enough, there grew
(but, I suppose, for heraldry) three tufts of blue violets in
a field argent of wild strawberries; and a trellis, with honey-
suckle, I set for canopy. Very majestical lounge, indeed. So
much so that here, as with the reclining majesty of Den-
mark in his orchard, a sly earache invaded me. But, if
damps abound at times in Westminster Abbey because it
is so old, why not within this monastery of mountains,
which is older?

A piazza must be had.

The house was wide, my fortune narrow, so that, to
build a panoramic piazza, one round and round, it could
not be—although, indeed, considering the matter by rule
and square, the carpenters, in the kindest way, were anxious
to gratify my furthest wishes, at I've forgotten how much
a foot.

Upon but one of the four sides would prudence grant me what I wanted. Now, which side?

To the east, that long camp of the Hearth Stone Hills, fading far away towards Quito, and every fall, a small white flake of something peering suddenly, of a coolish morning, from the topmost cliff—the season's new-dropped lamb, its earliest fleece; and then the Christmas dawn, draping those dun highlands with red-barred plaids and tartans—goodly sight from your piazza, that. Goodly sight; but, to the north is Charlemagne—can't have the Hearth Stone Hills with Charlemagne.

Well, the south side. Apple trees are there. Pleasant, of a balmy morning in the month of May, to sit and see that orchard, white-budded, as for a bridal; and, in October, one green arsenal yard, such piles of ruddy shot. Very fine, I grant; but, to the north is Charlemagne.

The west side, look. An upland pasture, alleying away into a maple wood at top. Sweet, in opening spring, to trace upon the hillside, otherwise gray and bare—to trace, I say, the oldest paths by their streaks of earliest green. Sweet, indeed, I can't deny; but, to the north is Charlemagne.

So Charlemagne, he carried it. It was not long after 1848, and, somehow, about that time, all round the world these kings, they had the casting vote, and voted for themselves.

No sooner was ground broken than all the neighborhood, neighbor Dives, in particular, broke, too—into a laugh. Piazza to the north! Winter piazza! Wants, of winter midnights, to watch the Aurora Borealis, I suppose; hope he's laid in good store of polar muffs and mittens.

That was in the lion month of March. Not forgotten are the blue noses of the carpenters, and how they scouted at the greenness of the cit, who would build his sole piazza to the north. But March don't last forever; patience, and August comes. And then, in the cool elysium of my northern bower, I, Lazarus in Abraham's bosom, cast down the hill a pitying glance on poor old Dives, tormented in the purgatory of his piazza to the south.

But, even in December, this northern piazza does not repel—nipping cold and gusty though it be, and the north wind, like any miller, bolting by the snow in finest flour—

for then, once more, with frosted beard, I pace the sleety deck, weathering Cape Horn.

In summer, too, Canute-like, sitting here, one is often reminded of the sea. For not only do long ground swells roll the slanting grain, and little wavelets of the grass ripple over upon the low piazza, as their beach, and the blown down of dandelions is wafted like the spray, and the purple of the mountains is just the purple of the billows, and a still August noon broods upon the deep meadows as a calm upon the Line, but the vastness and the lonesomeness are so oceanic, and the silence and the sameness, too, that the first peep of a strange house, rising beyond the trees, is for all the world like spying, on the Barbary coast, an unknown sail.

And this recalls my inland voyage to fairyland. A true voyage, but, take it all in all, interesting as if invented.

From the piazza, some uncertain object I had caught, mysteriously snugged away, to all appearance, in a sort of purpled breast pocket, high up in a hopperlike hollow or sunken angle among the northwestern mountains—yet, whether, really, it was on a mountainside or a mountaintop could not be determined; because, though, viewed from favorable points, a blue summit, peering up away behind the rest, will, as it were, talk to you over their heads, and plainly tell you that, though he (the blue summit) seems among them, he is not of them (God forbid!), and, indeed, would have you know that he considers himself—as, to say truth, he has good right—by several cubits their superior, nevertheless, certain ranges, here and there double-filed, as in platoons, so shoulder and follow up upon one another, with their irregular shapes and heights, that, from the piazza, a nigher and lower mountain will, in most states of the atmosphere, effacingly shade itself away into a higher and further one; that an object, bleak on the former's crest, will, for all that, appear nested in the latter's flank. These mountains, somehow, they play at hide-and-seek, and all before one's eyes.

But, be that as it may, the spot in question was, at all events, so situated as to be only visible, and then but vaguely, under certain witching conditions of light and shadow.

Indeed, for a year or more, I knew not there was such

a spot, and might, perhaps, have never known, had it not
been for a wizard afternoon in autumn—late in autumn
—a mad poet's afternoon, when the turned maple woods
in the broad basin below me, having lost their first ver-
milion tint, dully smoked, like smoldering towns, when
flames expire upon their prey; and rumor had it that this
smokiness in the general air was not all Indian summer
—which was not used to be so sick a thing, however mild
—but, in great part, was blown from far-off forests, for
weeks on fire, in Vermont; so that no wonder the sky was
ominous as Hecate's caldron—and two sportsmen, crossing a red stubble buckwheat field, seemed guilty Macbeth
and foreboding Banquo; and the hermit sun, hutted in an
Adullum cave, well towards the south, according to his
season, did little else but, by indirect reflection of narrow
rays shot down a Simplon Pass among the clouds, just
steadily paint one small, round strawberry mole upon the
wan cheek of northwestern hills. Signal as a candle. One
spot of radiance, where all else was shade.

Fairies there, thought I; some haunted ring where fairies
dance.

Time passed, and the following May, after a gentle
shower upon the mountains—a little shower islanded in
misty seas of sunshine; such a distant shower—and sometimes two, and three, and four of them, all visible together
in different parts—as I love to watch from the piazza,
instead of thunderstorms as I used to, which wrap old
Greylock like a Sinai, till one thinks swart Moses must be
climbing among scathed hemlocks there; after, I say, that
gentle shower, I saw a rainbow, resting its further end just
where, in autumn, I had marked the mole. Fairies there,
thought I; remembering that rainbows bring out the
blooms, and that, if one can but get to the rainbow's end,
his fortune is made in a bag of gold. Yon rainbow's end,
would I were there, thought I. And none the less I wished
it, for now first noticing what seemed some sort of glen,
or grotto, in the mountainside; at least, whatever it was,
viewed through the rainbow's medium it glowed like the
Potosi mine. But a workaday neighbor said no doubt it
was but some old barn—an abandoned one, its broadside
beaten in, the acclivity its background. But I, though I
had never been there, I knew better.

A few days after, a cheery sunrise kindled a golden sparkle in the same spot as before. The sparkle was of that vividness it seemed as if it could only come from glass. The building, then—if building, after all, it was—could, at least, not be a barn, much less an abandoned one, stale hay ten years musting in it. No; if aught built by mortal, it must be a cottage; perhaps long vacant and dismantled, but this very spring magically fitted up and glazed.

Again, one noon, in the same direction, I marked, over dimmed tops of terraced foliage, a broader gleam, as of a silver buckler held sunwards over some croucher's head; which gleam, experience in like cases taught, must come from a roof newly shingled. This, to me, made pretty sure the recent occupancy of that far cot in fairyland.

Day after day, now, full of interest in my discovery, what time I could spare from reading the *Midsummer Night's Dream*, and all about Titania, wishfully I gazed off towards the hills; but in vain. Either troops of shadows, and imperial guard, with slow pace and solemn, defiled along the steeps, or, routed by pursuing light, fled broadcast from east to west—old wars of Lucifer and Michael; or the mountains, though unvexed by these mirrored sham fights in the sky, had an atmosphere otherwise unfavorable for fairy views. I was sorry, the more so because I had to keep my chamber for some time after—which chamber did not face those hills.

At length, when pretty well again, and sitting out in the September morning upon the piazza and thinking to myself, when, just after a little flock of sheep, the farmer's banded children passed, a-nutting, and said, "How sweet a day"—it was, after all, but what their fathers call a weather-breeder—and, indeed, was become so sensitive through my illness as that I could not bear to look upon a Chinese creeper of my adoption, and which, to my delight, climbing a post of the piazza, had burst out in starry bloom, but now, if you removed the leaves a little, showed millions of strange, cankerous worms, which, feeding upon those blossoms, so shared their blessed hue as to make it unblessed evermore—worms whose germs had doubtless lurked in the very bulb which, so hopefully, I had planted: in this ingrate peevishness of my weary convalescence was

I sitting there, when, suddenly looking off, I saw the golden mountain window, dazzling like a deep-sea dolphin. Fairies there, thought I, once more, the queen of fairies at her fairy-window, at any rate, some glad mountain girl; it will do me good, it will cure this weariness, to look on her. No more; I'll launch my yawl—ho, cheerly, heart!— and push away for fairyland, for rainbow's end, in fairy-land.

How to get to fairyland, by what road, I did not know, nor could any one inform me, not even one Edmund Spenser, who had been there—so he wrote me— further than that to reach fairyland it must be voyaged to, and with faith. I took the fairy-mountain's bearings, and the first fine day, when strength permitted, got into my yawl—high-pommeled, leather one—cast off the fast, and away I sailed, free voyager as an autumn leaf. Early dawn, and, sallying westward, I sowed the morning before me.

Some miles brought me nigh the hills, but out of present sight of them. I was not lost, for roadside goldenrods, as guideposts, pointed, I doubted not, the way to the golden window. Following them, I came to a lone and languid region, where the grass-grown ways were traveled but by drowsy cattle, that, less waked than stirred by day, seemed to walk in sleep. Browse they did not—the enchanted never eat. At least, so says Don Quixote, that sagest sage that ever lived.

On I went, and gained at last the fairy-mountain's base, but saw yet no fairy ring. A pasture rose before me. Letting down five moldering bars—so moistly green they seemed fished up from some sunken wreck—a wigged old Aries, long-visaged and with crumpled horn, came snuffing up, and then, retreating, decorously led on along a milky-way of whiteweed, past dim-clustering Pleiades and Hyades, of small forget-me-nots, and would have led me further still his astral path but for golden flights of yellow-birds—pilots, surely, to the golden window, to one side flying before me, from bush to bush, toward deep woods —which woods themselves were luring—and, somehow, lured, too, by their fence, banning a dark road, which, however dark, led up. I pushed through, when Aries, renouncing me now for some lost soul, wheeled, and went his wiser way. Forbidding and forbidden ground—to him.

A winter wood road, matted all along with wintergreen. By the side of pebbly waters—waters the cheerier for their solitude; beneath swaying fir boughs, petted by no season but still green in all, on I journeyed—my horse and I; on, by an old sawmill bound down and hushed with vines that his grating voice no more was heard; on, by a deep flume clove through snowy marble, vernal-tinted, where freshet eddies had, on each side, spun out empty chapels in the living rock; on, where Jacks-in-the-pulpit, like their Baptist namesake, preached but to the wilderness; on, where a huge, criss-grain block, fern-bedded, showed where, in forgotten times, man after man had tried to split it, but lost his wedges for his pains—which wedges yet rusted in their holes; on, where, ages past, in steplike ledges of a cascade, skull-hollow pots had been churned out by ceaseless whirling of a flintstone—ever wearing, but itself unworn; on, by wild rapids pouring into a secret pool, but, soothed by circling there awhile, issued forth serenely; on, to less broken ground and by a little ring, where, truly, fairies must have danced, or else some wheel-tire been heated—for all was bare; still on, and up, and out into a hanging orchard, where maidenly looked down upon me a crescent moon, from morning.

My horse hitched low his head. Red apples rolled before him—Eve's apples, seek-no-furthers. He tasted one, I another; it tasted of the ground. Fairyland not yet, thought I, flinging my bridle to a humped old tree, that crooked out an arm to catch it. For the way now lay where path was none, and none might go but by himself, and only go by daring. Through blackberry brakes that tried to pluck me back, though I but strained toward fruitless growths of mountain laurel, up slippery steeps to barren heights, where stood none to welcome. Fairyland not yet, thought I, though the morning is here before me.

Footsore enough and weary, I gained not then my journey's end, but came erelong to a craggy pass, dipping towards growing regions still beyond. A zigzag road, half overgrown with blueberry bushes, here turned among the cliffs. A rent was in their ragged sides; through it a little track branched off, which, upwards threading that short defile, came breezily out above, to where the mountain-

top, part sheltered northward by a taller brother, sloped
gently off a space ere darkly plunging; and here, among
fantastic rocks, reposing in a herd, the foot track wound,
half beaten, up to a little, low-storied, grayish cottage,
capped, nunlike, with a peaked roof.

On one slope the roof was deeply weather-stained, and,
nigh the turfy eaves-trough, all velvet-napped; no doubt
the snail-monks founded mossy priories there. The other
slope was newly shingled. On the north side, doorless and
windowless, the clapboards, innocent of paint, were yet
green as the north side of lichened pines, or copperless
hulls of Japanese junks becalmed. The whole base, like
those of the neighboring rocks, was rimmed about with
shaded streaks of richest sod; for, with hearthstones in
fairyland, the natural rock, though housed, preserves to
the last, just as in open fields, its fertilizing charm; only, by
necessity, working now at a remove, to the sward without. So, at least, says Oberon, grave authority in fairy
lore. Though, setting Oberon aside, certain it is that, even
in the common world, the soil close up to farmhouses, as
close up to pasture rocks, is, even though untended, ever
richer than it is a few rods off—such gentle, nurturing heat
is radiated there.

But with this cottage the shaded streaks were richest in
its front and about its entrance, where the groundsill, and
especially the doorsill, had, through long eld, quietly
settled down.

No fence was seen, no inclosure. Near by—ferns, ferns,
ferns; further—woods, woods, woods; beyond—mountains,
mountains, mountains; then—sky, sky, sky. Turned out
in aerial commons, pasture for the mountain moon. Nature,
and but nature, house and all; even a low cross-pile of
silver birch, piled openly, to season; up among whose
silvery sticks, as through the fencing of some sequestered
grave, sprang vagrant raspberry bushes—willful assertors
of their right of way.

The foot track, so dainty narrow, just like a sheep track,
led through long ferns that lodged. Fairyland at last,
thought I; Una and her lamb dwell here. Truly, a small
abode—mere palanquin, set down on the summit, in a
pass between two worlds, participant of neither.

A sultry hour, and I wore a light hat, of yellow sinnet,

with white duck trousers—both relics of my tropic seagoing. Clogged in the muffling ferns, I softly stumbled, staining the knees a sea green.

Pausing at the threshold, or rather where threshold once
had been, I saw, through the open doorway, a lonely girl,
sewing at a lonely window. A pale-cheeked girl and fly-
specked window, with wasps about the mended upper
panes. I spoke. She shyly started, like some Tahiti girl,
secreted for a sacrifice, first catching sight, through palms,
of Captain Cook. Recovering, she bade me enter; with her
apron brushed off a stool; then silently resumed her own.
With thanks I took the stool; but now, for a space, I, too,
was mute. This, then, is the fairy-mountain house, and
here the fairy queen sitting at her fairy-window.

I went up to it. Downwards, directed by the tunneled
pass, as through a leveled telescope, I caught sight of a
far-off, soft, azure world. I hardly knew it, though I came
from it.

"You must find this view very pleasant," said I, at last.

"Oh, sir," tears starting in her eyes, "the first time I
looked out of this window, I said 'never, never shall I
weary of this.'"

"And what wearies you of it now?"

"I don't know," while a tear fell; "but it is not the view,
it is Marianna."

Some months back, her brother, only seventeen, had
come hither, a long way from the other side, to cut wood
and burn coal, and she, elder sister, had accompanied
him. Long had they been orphans, and now sole inhabitants
of the sole house upon the mountain. No guest came, no
traveler passed. The zigzag, perilous road was only used
at seasons by the coal wagons. The brother was absent
the entire day, sometimes the entire night. When, at evening, fagged out, he did come home, he soon left his
bench, poor fellow, for his bed, just as one, at last, wearily
quits that, too, for still deeper rest. The bench, the bed,
the grave.

Silent I stood by the fairy-window, while these things
were being told.

"Do you know," said she at last, as stealing from her
story, "do you know who lives yonder?—I have never
been down into that country—away off there, I mean; that

house, that marble one," pointing far across the lower
landscape; "have you not caught it? there, on the long
hillside: the field before, the woods behind; the white
shines out against their blue; don't you mark it? the only
house in sight."

I looked, and, after a time, to my surprise, recognized,
more by its position than its aspect or Marianna's description, my own abode, glimmering much like this mountain
one from the piazza. The mirage haze made it appear less
a farmhouse than King Charming's palace.

"I have often wondered who lives there; but it must
be some happy one; again this morning was I thinking
so."

"Some happy one," returned I, starting; "and why do
you think that? You judge some rich one lives there?"

"Rich or not, I never thought, but it looks so happy, I
can't tell how, and it is so far away. Sometimes I think I
do but dream it is there. You should see it in a sunset."

"No doubt the sunset gilds it finely, but not more than
the sunrise does this house, perhaps."

"This house? The sun is a good sun, but it never gilds
this house. Why should it? This old house is rotting. That
makes it so mossy. In the morning, the sun comes in at
this old window, to be sure—boarded up, when first we
came; a window I can't keep clean, do what I may—and
half burns, and nearly blinds me at my sewing, besides
setting the flies and wasps astir—such flies and wasps as
only lone mountain houses know. See, here is the curtain
—this apron—I try to shut it out with then. It fades it, you
see. Sun gild this house? not that ever Marianna saw."

"Because when this roof is gilded most, then you stay
here within."

"The hottest, weariest hour of day, you mean? Sir, the
sun gilds not this roof. It leaked so, brother newly shingled
all one side. Did you not see it? The north side, where the
sun strikes most on what the rain has wetted. The sun is
a good sun, but this roof, it first scorches, and then rots.
An old house. They went West, and are long dead, they
say, who built it. A mountain house. In winter no fox
could den in it. That chimney-place has been blocked up
with snow, just like a hollow stump."

"Yours are strange fancies, Marianna."

"They but reflect the things."

"Then I should have said, 'These are strange things,' rather than, 'Yours are strange fancies.' "

"As you will," and took up her sewing.

Something in those quiet words, or in that quiet act, it made me mute again; while, noting through the fairy-window a broad shadow stealing on, as cast by some gigantic condor floating at brooding poise on outstretched wings, I marked how, by its deeper and inclusive dusk, it wiped away into itself all lesser shades of rock or fern.

"You watch the cloud," said Marianna.

"No, a shadow; a cloud's, no doubt—though that I cannot see. How did you know it? Your eyes are on your work."

"It dusked my work. There, now the cloud is gone, Tray comes back."

"How?"

"The dog, the shaggy dog. At noon, he steals off, of himself, to change his shape— returns, and lies down awhile, nigh the door. Don't you see him? His head is turned round at you, though when you came he looked before him."

"Your eyes rest but on your work; what do you speak of?"

"By the window, crossing."

"You mean this shaggy shadow—the nigh one? And, yes, now that I mark it, it is not unlike a large, black Newfoundland dog. The invading shadow gone, the invaded one returns. But I do not see what casts it."

"For that, you must go without."

"One of those grassy rocks, no doubt."

"You see his head, his face?"

"The shadow's? You speak as if *you* saw it, and all the time your eyes are on your work."

"Tray looks at you," still without glancing up; "this is his hour; I see him."

"Have you, then, so long sat at this mountain window, where but clouds and vapors pass, that to you shadows are as things, though you speak of them as of phantoms; that, by familiar knowledge working like a second sight, you can, without looking for them, tell just where they are, though, as having micelike feet, they creep about, and come and go; that to you these lifeless shadows are as living friends, who, though out of sight, are not out of mind, even in their faces—is it so?"

"That way I never thought of it. But the friendliest one, that used to soothe my weariness so much, coolly quivering on the ferns, it was taken from me, never to return, as Tray did just now. The shadow of a birch. The tree was struck by lightning, and brother cut it up. You saw the cross-pile outdoors—the buried root lies under it, but not the shadow. That is flown, and never will come back, nor ever anywhere stir again."

Another cloud here stole along, once more blotting out the dog, and blackening all the mountain; while the stillness was so still deafness might have forgot itself, or else believed that noiseless shadow spoke.

"Birds, Marianna, singing birds, I hear none; I hear nothing. Boys and bobolinks, do they never come a-berrying up here?"

"Birds I seldom hear; boys, never. The berries mostly ripe and fall—few but me the wiser."

"But yellowbirds showed me the way—part way, at least."

"And then flew back. I guess they play about the mountainside but don't make the top their home. And no doubt you think that, living so lonesome here, knowing nothing, hearing nothing—little, at least, but sound of thunder and the fall of trees—never reading, seldom speaking, yet ever wakeful, this is what gives me my strange thoughts—for so you call them—this weariness and wakefulness together. Brother, who stands and works in open air, would I could rest like him; but mine is mostly but dull woman's work—sitting, sitting, restless sitting."

"But do you not go walk at times? These woods are wide."

"And lonesome; lonesome, because so wide. Sometimes, 'tis true, of afternoons, I go a little way, but soon come back again. Better feel lone by hearth than rock. The shadows hereabouts I know—those in the woods are strangers."

"But the night?"

"Just like the day. Thinking, thinking—a wheel I cannot stop; pure want of sleep it is that turns it."

"I have heard that, for this wakeful weariness, to say one's prayers, and then lay one's head upon a fresh hop pillow——"

"Look!"

Through the fairy-window, she pointed down the steep to a small garden patch near by—mere pot of rifled loam, half rounded in by sheltering rocks—where, side by side, some feet apart, nipped and puny, two hopvines climbed two poles, and, gaining their tip ends, would have then joined over in an upward clasp, but the baffled shoots, groping awhile in empty air, trailed back whence they sprung.

"You have tried the pillow, then?"

"Yes."

"And prayer?"

"Prayer and pillow."

"Is there no other cure, or charm?"

"Oh, if I could but once get to yonder house, and but look upon whoever the happy being is that lives there! A foolish thought: why do I think it? Is it that I live so lonesome, and know nothing?"

"I, too, know nothing, and therefore cannot answer; but for your sake, Marianna, well could wish that I were that happy one of the happy house you dream you see; for then you would behold him now, and, as you say, this weariness might leave you."

—Enough. Launching my yawl no more for fairyland, I stick to the piazza. It is my box-royal, and this amphi-theater, my theater of San Carlo. Yes, the scenery is magi-cal—the illusion so complete. And Madam Meadow Lark, my prima donna, plays her grand engagement here; and, drinking in her sunrise note, which, Memnon-like, seems struck from the golden window, how far from me the weary face behind it.

But every night when the curtain falls, truth comes in with darkness. No light shows from the mountain. To and fro I walk the piazza deck, haunted by Marianna's face, and many as real a story.

BARTLEBY

I AM a rather elderly man. The nature of my avocations for the last thirty years has brought me into more than ordinary contact with what would seem an interesting and somewhat singular set of men, of whom, as yet, nothing that I know of has ever been written—I mean the law-copyists, or scriveners. I have known very many of them, professionally and privately, and, if I pleased, could relate divers histories at which good-natured gentlemen might smile and sentimental souls might weep. But I waive the biographies of all other scriveners for a few passages in the life of Bartleby, who was a scrivener, the strangest I ever saw or heard of. While of other law-copyists I might write the complete life, of Bartleby nothing of that sort can be done. I believe that no materials exist for a full and satisfactory biography of this man. It is an irreparable loss to literature. Bartleby was one of those beings of whom nothing is ascertainable except from the original sources, and, in his case, those are very small. What my own astonished eyes saw of Bartleby, *that* is all I know of him, except, indeed, one vague report, which will appear in the sequel.

Ere introducing the scrivener as he first appeared to me, it is fit I make some mention of myself, my employees, my business, my chambers and general surroundings, because some such description is indispensable to an adequate understanding of the chief character about to be presented. *Imprimis:* I am a man who, from his youth upwards, has been filled with a profound conviction that the easiest way of life is the best. Hence, though I belong to a profession proverbially energetic and nervous even to turbulence at times, yet nothing of that sort have I ever suffered to invade my peace. I am one of those unambitious lawyers who never addresses a jury or in any way draws down public applause, but, in the cool tranquillity of a snug retreat, do a snug business among rich men's bonds, and mortgages, and title deeds. All who know me consider me an eminently *safe* man. The late John Jacob Astor, a personage little given to poetic enthusiasm, had no hesitation in pronouncing my first grand point to be prudence, my next, method. I do not speak it in vanity, but simply record the fact that I was not unemployed in my profession by the late John Jacob Astor, a name which, I admit, I love to repeat, for it hath a rounded and orbicular sound to it, and rings like unto bullion. I will freely add that I was not insensible to the late John Jacob Astor's good opinion.

Some time prior to the period at which this little history begins my avocations had been largely increased. The good old office, now extinct in the State of New York, of a Master in Chancery, had been conferred upon me. It was not a very arduous office, but very pleasantly remunerative. I seldom lose my temper, much more seldom indulge in dangerous indignation at wrongs and outrages, but I must be permitted to be rash here and declare that I consider the sudden and violent abrogation of the office of Master in Chancery, by the new Constitution, as a —— premature act, inasmuch as I had counted upon a life lease of the profits, whereas I only received those of a few short years. But this is by the way.

My chambers were upstairs at No. —— Wall Street. At

one end they looked upon the white wall of the interior
of a spacious skylight shaft, penetrating the building from
top to bottom.

This view might have been considered rather tame than
otherwise, deficient in what landscape painters call "life."
But, if so, the view from the other end of my chambers
offered at least a contrast, if nothing more. In that direction, my windows commanded an unobstructed view of a
lofty brick wall, black by age and everlasting shade, which
wall required no spyglass to bring out its lurking beauties,
but, for the benefit of all nearsighted spectators, was pushed
up to within ten feet of my windowpanes. Owing to the
great height of the surrounding buildings, and my chambers' being on the second floor, the interval between this
wall and mine not a little resembled a huge square cistern.

At the period just preceding the advent of Bartleby, I
had two persons as copyists in my employment, and a
promising lad as an office boy. First, Turkey; second,
Nippers; third, Ginger Nut. These may seem names the
like of which are not usually found in the Directory. In
truth, they were nicknames, mutually conferred upon each
other by my three clerks, and were deemed expressive
of their respective persons or characters. Turkey was a
short, pursy Englishman, of about my own age—that is,
somewhere not far from sixty. In the morning, one might
say, his face was of a fine florid hue, but after twelve
o'clock, meridian—his dinner hour—it blazed like a grate
full of Christmas coals; and continued blazing—but, as it
were, with a gradual wane—till six o'clock, P.M., or thereabouts; after which I saw no more of the proprietor of
the face, which, gaining its meridian with the sun, seemed
to set with it, to rise, culminate, and decline the following
day, with the like regularity and undiminished glory. There
are many singular coincidences I have known in the course
of my life, not the least among which was the fact, that,
exactly when Turkey displayed his fullest beams from his
red and radiant countenance, just then, too, at that critical
moment, began the daily period when I considered his
business capacities as seriously disturbed for the remainder
of the twenty-four hours. Not that he was absolutely idle
or averse to business then; far from it. The difficulty was,
he was apt to be altogether too energetic. There was a

strange, inflamed, flurried, flighty recklessness of activity
about him. He would be incautious in dipping his pen
into his inkstand. All his blots upon my documents were
dropped there after twelve o'clock, meridian. Indeed, not
only would he be reckless and sadly given to making blots
in the afternoon, but some days he went further and was
rather noisy. At such times, too, his face flamed with
augmented blazonry, as if cannel coal had been heaped
on anthracite. He made an unpleasant racket with his
chair; spilled his sandbox; in mending his pens, impatiently
split them all to pieces and threw them on the floor in a
sudden passion; stood up and leaned over his table, boxing
his papers about in a most indecorous manner, very sad
to behold in an elderly man like him. Nevertheless, as he
was in many ways a most valuable person to me, and all the
time before twelve o'clock, meridian, was the quickest,
steadiest creature, too, accomplishing a great deal of work
in a style not easily to be matched—for these reasons I
was willing to overlook his eccentricities, though indeed,
occasionally, I remonstrated with him. I did this very
gently, however, because, though the civilest, nay, the
blandest and most reverential of men in the morning, yet,
in the afternoon he was disposed, upon provocation, to be
slightly rash with his tongue—in fact, insolent. Now,
valuing his morning services as I did, and resolved not to
lose them—yet, at the same time, made uncomfortable by
his inflamed ways after twelve o'clock—and being a man
of peace, unwilling by my admonitions to call forth un-
seemly retorts from him, I took upon me one Saturday
noon (he was always worse on Saturdays) to hint to him,
very kindly, that perhaps, now that he was growing old,
it might be well to abridge his labors; in short, he need not
come to my chambers after twelve o'clock, but, dinner
over, had best go home to his lodgings and rest himself
till teatime. But no; he insisted upon his afternoon devo-
tions. His countenance became intolerably fervid, as he
oratorically assured me—gesticulating with a long ruler
at the other end of the room—that if his services in the
morning were useful, how indispensable, then, in the afternoon?

"With submission, sir," said Turkey, on this occasion,
"I consider myself your right-hand man. In the morning

I but marshal and deploy my columns, but in the afternoon
I put myself at their head, and gallantly charge the foe,
thus"—and he made a violent thrust with the ruler.

"But the blots, Turkey," intimated I.

"True; but, with submission, sir, behold these hairs!
I am getting old. Surely, sir, a blot or two of a warm
afternoon is not to be severely urged against gray hairs.
Old age—even if it blot the page—is honorable. With
submission, sir, we *both* are getting old."

This appeal to my fellow feeling was hardly to be resisted. At all events, I saw that go he would not. So I made
up my mind to let him stay, resolving, nevertheless, to see
to it that, during the afternoon, he had to do with my less
important papers.

Nippers, the second on my list, was a whiskered, sallow,
and upon the whole rather piratical-looking young man of
about five and twenty. I always deemed him the victim of
two evil powers—ambition and indigestion. The ambition
was evinced by a certain impatience of the duties of a mere
copyist, an unwarrantable usurpation of strictly professional affairs, such as the original drawing up of legal
documents. The indigestion seemed betokened in an occasional nervous testiness and grinning irritability, causing
the teeth to audibly grind together over mistakes committed in copying; unnecessary maledictions, hissed rather
than spoken, in the heat of business; and especially by a
continual discontent with the height of the table where he
worked. Though of a very ingenious mechanical turn,
Nippers could never get this table to suit him. He put
chips under it, blocks of various sorts, bits of pasteboard,
and at last went so far as to attempt an exquisite adjust-
ment by final pieces of folded blotting paper. But no invention would answer. If, for the sake of easing his back,
he brought the table lid at a sharp angle well up towards
his chin, and wrote there like a man using the steep roof
of a Dutch house for his desk, then he declared that it
stopped the circulation in his arms. If now he lowered
the table to his waistbands and stooped over it in writing,
then there was a sore aching in his back. In short, the
truth of the matter was Nippers knew not what he wanted.
Or, if he wanted anything, it was to be rid of a scrivener's
table altogether. Among the manifestations of his diseased

ambition was a fondness he had for receiving visits from certain ambiguous-looking fellows in seedy coats, whom he called his clients. Indeed, I was aware that not only was he, at times, considerable of a ward politician, but he occasionally did a little business at the Justices' courts, and was not unknown on the steps of the Tombs. I have good reason to believe, however, that one individual who called upon him at my chambers, and who, with a grand air, he insisted was his client, was no other than a dun, and the alleged title deed, a bill. But, with all his failings, and the annoyances he caused me, Nippers, like his compatriot Turkey, was a very useful man to me; wrote a neat, swift hand; and, when he chose, was not deficient in a gentlemanly sort of deportment. Added to this, he always dressed in a gentlemanly sort of way, and so, incidentally, reflected credit upon my chambers. Whereas, with respect to Turkey, I had much ado to keep him from being a reproach to me. His clothes were apt to look oily, and smell of eating houses. He wore his pantaloons very loose and baggy in summer. His coats were execrable, his hat not to be handled. But while the hat was a thing of indifference to me, inasmuch as his natural civility and deference, as a dependent Englishman, always led him to doff it the moment he entered the room, yet his coat was another matter. Concerning his coats, I reasoned with him, but with no effect. The truth was, I suppose, that a man with so small an income could not afford to sport such a lustrous face and a lustrous coat at one and the same time. As Nippers once observed, Turkey's money went chiefly for red ink. One winter day, I presented Turkey with a highly respectable-looking coat of my own—a padded gray coat of a most comfortable warmth, and which buttoned straight up from the knee to the neck. I thought Turkey would appreciate the favor and abate his rashness and obstreperousness of afternoons. But no; I verily believe that buttoning himself up in so downy and blanket-like a coat had a pernicious effect upon him—upon the same principle that too much oats are bad for horses. In fact, precisely as a rash, restive horse is said to feel his oats, so Turkey felt his coat. It made him insolent. He was a man whom prosperity harmed.

Though, concerning the self-indulgent habits of Turkey,

I had my own private surmises, yet, touching Nippers, I
was well persuaded that, whatever might be his faults in
other respects, he was, at least, a temperate young man.
But indeed, nature herself seemed to have been his vintner,
and, at his birth, charged him so thoroughly with an irritable, brandylike disposition that all subsequent potations
were needless. When I consider how, amid the stillness of
my chambers, Nippers would sometimes impatiently rise
from his seat, and, stooping over his table, spread his arms
wide apart, seize the whole desk, and move it, and jerk it,
with a grim, grinding motion on the floor, as if the table
were a perverse voluntary agent, intent on thwarting and
vexing him, I plainly perceive that, for Nippers, brandy-
and-water were altogether superfluous.

It was fortunate for me that, owing to its peculiar cause
—indigestion—the irritability and consequent nervousness
of Nippers were mainly observable in the morning, while
in the afternoon he was comparatively mild. So that,
Turkey's paroxysms only coming on about twelve o'clock,
I never had to do with their eccentricities at one time. Their
fits relieved each other, like guards. When Nippers's was
on, Turkey's was off; and vice versa. This was a good
natural arrangement, under the circumstances.

Ginger Nut, the third on my list, was a lad some twelve
years old. His father was a carman, ambitious of seeing
his son on the bench instead of a cart before he died.
So he sent him to my office, as student at law, errand boy,
cleaner and sweeper, at the rate of one dollar a week. He
had a little desk to himself, but he did not use it much.
Upon inspection, the drawer exhibited a great array of
the shells of various sorts of nuts. Indeed, to this quick-
witted youth, the whole noble science of the law was contained in a nutshell. Not the least among the employments
of Ginger Nut, as well as one which he discharged with the
most alacrity, was his duty as cake and apple purveyor
for Turkey and Nippers. Copying law papers being proverbially a dry, husky sort of business, my two scriveners were
fain to moisten their mouths very often with Spitzenbergs,
to be had at the numerous stalls nigh the Custom House
and Post Office. Also, they sent Ginger Nut very frequently
for that peculiar cake—small, flat, round, and very spicy—
after which he had been named by them. Of a cold morn-

ing, when business was but dull, Turkey would gobble up
scores of these cakes, as if they were mere wafers—indeed,
they sell them at the rate of six or eight for a penny—the
scrape of his pen blending with the crunching of the crisp
particles in his mouth. Of all the fiery afternoon blunders
and flurried rashnesses of Turkey was his once moistening
a ginger cake between his lips and clapping it on to a
mortgage for a seal. I came within an ace of dismissing him
then. But he mollified me by making an Oriental bow,
and saying:

"With submission, sir, it was generous of me to find you
in stationery on my own account."

Now my original business—that of a conveyancer and
title hunter, and drawer-up of recondite documents of all
sorts—was considerably increased by receiving the Master's office. There was now great work for scriveners. Not
only must I push the clerks already with me, but I must
have additional help.

In answer to my advertisement, a motionless young man
one morning stood upon my office threshold, the door
being open, for it was summer. I can see that figure now—
pallidly neat, pitiably respectable, incurably forlorn! It was
Bartleby.

After a few words touching his qualifications, I engaged
him, glad to have among my corps of copyists a man of so
singularly sedate an aspect, which I thought might operate
beneficially upon the flighty temper of Turkey and the
fiery one of Nippers.

I should have stated before that ground-glass folding
doors divided my premises into two parts, one of which
was occupied by my scriveners, the other by myself. According to my humor, I threw open these doors or closed
them. I resolved to assign Bartleby a corner by the folding
doors, but on my side of them, so as to have this quiet man
within easy call, in case any trifling thing was to be done.
I placed his desk close up to a small side window in that
part of the room, a window which originally had afforded
a lateral view of certain grimy back yards and bricks, but
which, owing to subsequent erections, commanded at
present no view at all, though it gave some light. Within
three feet of the panes was a wall, and the light came
down from far above, between two lofty buildings, as from

a very small opening in a dome. Still further to a satisfactory arrangement, I procured a high green folding
screen, which might entirely isolate Bartleby from my
sight, though not remove him from my voice. And thus,
in a manner, privacy and society were conjoined.

At first, Bartleby did an extraordinary quantity of writing. As if long famishing for something to copy, he seemed
to gorge himself on my documents. There was no pause
for digestion. He ran a day and night line, copying by
sunlight and by candlelight. I should have been quite
delighted with his application, had he been cheerfully industrious. But he wrote on silently, palely, mechanically.

It is, of course, an indispensable part of a scrivener's
business to verify the accuracy of his copy, word by word.
Where there are two or more scriveners in an office, they
assist each other in this examination, one reading from
the copy, the other holding the original. It is a very dull,
wearisome, and lethargic affair. I can readily imagine that,
to some sanguine temperaments, it would be altogether
intolerable. For example, I cannot credit that the mettle-
some poet, Byron, would have contentedly sat down with
Bartleby to examine a law document of, say five hundred
pages, closely written in a crimpy hand.

Now and then, in the haste of business, it had been
my habit to assist in comparing some brief document
myself, calling Turkey or Nippers for this purpose. One
object I had in placing Bartleby so handy to me behind
the screen was to avail myself of his services on such trivial
occasions. It was on the third day, I think, of his being
with me, and before any necessity had arisen for having
his own writing examined, that, being much hurried to
complete a small affair I had in hand, I abruptly called to
Bartleby. In my haste and natural expectancy of instant
compliance, I sat with my head bent over the original
on my desk, and my right hand sideways, and somewhat
nervously extended with the copy, so that, immediately
upon emerging from his retreat, Bartleby might snatch
it and proceed to business without the least delay.

In this very attitude did I sit when I called to him,
rapidly stating what it was I wanted him to do—namely,
to examine a small paper with me. Imagine my surprise,
nay, my consternation, when, without moving from his

privacy, Bartleby, in a singularly mild, firm voice, replied, "I would prefer not to."

I sat awhile in perfect silence, rallying my stunned faculties. Immediately it occurred to me that my ears had deceived me, or Bartleby had entirely misunderstood my meaning. I repeated my request in the clearest tone I could assume; but in quite as clear a one came the previous reply, "I would prefer not to."

"Prefer not to," echoed I, rising in high excitement, and crossing the room with a stride. "What do you mean? Are you moon-struck? I want you to help me compare this sheet here—take it," and I thrust it towards him.

"I would prefer not to," said he.

I looked at him steadfastly. His face was leanly composed; his gray eyes dimly calm. Not a wrinkle of agitation rippled him. Had there been the least uneasiness, anger, impatience or impertinence in his manner; in other words, had there been anything ordinarily human about him, doubtless I should have violently dismissed him from the premises. But as it was I should have as soon thought of turning my pale plaster-of-Paris bust of Cicero out of doors. I stood gazing at him awhile, as he went on with his own writing, and then reseated myself at my desk. This is very strange, thought I. What had one best do? But my business hurried me. I concluded to forget the matter for the present, reserving it for my future leisure. So calling Nippers from the other room, the paper was speedily examined.

A few days after this, Bartleby concluded four lengthy documents, being quadruplicates of a week's testimony taken before me in my High Court of Chancery. It became necessary to examine them. It was an important suit, and great accuracy was imperative. Having all things arranged, I called Turkey, Nippers and Ginger Nut, from the next room, meaning to place the four copies in the hands of my four clerks, while I should read from the original. Accordingly, Turkey, Nippers, and Ginger Nut had taken their seats in a row, each with his document in his hand, when I called to Bartleby to join this interesting group.

"Bartleby! quick, I am waiting."

I heard a slow scrape of his chair legs on the uncarpeted

floor, and soon he appeared standing at the entrance of his hermitage.

"What is wanted?" said he, mildly.

"The copies, the copies," said I, hurriedly. "We are going to examine them. There"—and I held towards him the fourth quadruplicate.

"I would prefer not to," he said, and gently disappeared behind the screen.

For a few moments I was turned into a pillar of salt, standing at the head of my seated column of clerks. Recovering myself, I advanced towards the screen and demanded the reason for such extraordinary conduct.

"*Why* do you refuse?"

"I would prefer not to."

With any other man I should have flown outright into a dreadful passion, scorned all further words, and thrust him ignominiously from my presence. But there was something about Bartleby that not only strangely disarmed me, but, in a wonderful manner, touched and disconcerted me. I began to reason with him.

"These are your own copies we are about to examine. It is labor saving to you, because one examination will answer for your four papers. It is common usage. Every copyist is bound to help examine his copy. Is it not so? Will you not speak? Answer!"

"I prefer not to," he replied in a flutelike tone. It seemed to me that, while I had been addressing him, he carefully revolved every statement that I made; fully comprehended the meaning; could not gainsay the irresistible conclusion; but, at the same time, some paramount consideration prevailed with him to reply as he did.

"You are decided, then, not to comply with my request —a request made according to common usage and common sense?"

He briefly gave me to understand that on that point my judgment was sound. Yes: his decision was irreversible.

It is seldom the case that, when a man is browbeaten in some unprecedented and violently unreasonable way, he begins to stagger in his own plainest faith. He begins, as it were, vaguely to surmise that, wonderful as it may be, all the justice and all the reason is on the other side. Accordingly, if any disinterested persons are present, he

turns to them for some reinforcement for his own faltering
mind.

"Turkey," said I, "what do you think of this? Am I not
right?"

"With submission, sir," said Turkey, in his blandest
tone, "I think that you are."

"Nippers," said I, "what do *you* think of it?"

"I think I should kick him out of the office."

(The reader of nice perceptions, will here perceive that,
it being morning, Turkey's answer is couched in polite
and tranquil terms, but Nippers replies in ill-tempered
ones. Or, to repeat a previous sentence, Nippers's ugly
mood was on duty, and Turkey's off.)

"Ginger Nut," said I, willing to enlist the smallest
suffrage in my behalf, "what do *you* think of it?"

"I think, sir, he's a little *luny*," replied Ginger Nut, with
a grin.

"You hear what they say," said I, turning towards the
screen, "come forth and do your duty."

But he vouchsafed no reply. I pondered a moment in
sore perplexity. But once more business hurried me. I
determined again to postpone the consideration of this
dilemma to my future leisure. With a little trouble we
made out to examine the papers without Bartleby, though
at every page or two Turkey deferentially dropped his
opinion that this proceeding was quite out of the common;
while Nippers, twitching in his chair with a dyspeptic
nervousness, ground out between his set teeth occasional
hissing maledictions against the stubborn oaf behind the
screen. And for his (Nippers's) part, this was the first
and the last time he would do another man's business
without pay.

Meanwhile Bartleby sat in his hermitage, oblivious to
everything but his own peculiar business there.

Some days passed, the scrivener being employed upon
another lengthy work. His late remarkable conduct led
me to regard his ways narrowly. I observed that he never
went to dinner; indeed, that he never went anywhere. As
yet I had never, of my personal knowledge, known him to
be outside of my office. He was a perpetual sentry in the
corner. At about eleven o'clock, though, in the morning,
I noticed that Ginger Nut would advance towards the

opening in Bartleby's screen, as if silently beckoned thither by a gesture invisible to me where I sat. The boy would then leave the office jingling a few pence, and reappear with a handful of gingernuts, which he delivered in the hermitage, receiving two of the cakes for his trouble.

He lives, then, on gingernuts, thought I; never eats a dinner, properly speaking; he must be a vegetarian, then; but no, he never eats even vegetables, he eats nothing but gingernuts. My mind then ran on in reveries concerning the probable effects upon the human constitution of living entirely on gingernuts. Gingernuts are so called because they contain ginger as one of their peculiar constituents, and the final flavoring one. Now, what was ginger? A hot, spicy thing. Was Bartleby hot and spicy? Not at all. Ginger, then, had no effect upon Bartleby. Probably he preferred it should have none.

Nothing so aggravates an earnest person as a passive resistance. If the individual so resisted be of a not inhumane temper, and the resisting one perfectly harmless in his passivity, then, in the better moods of the former, he will endeavor charitably to construe to his imagination what proves impossible to be solved by his judgment. Even so, for the most part, I regarded Bartleby and his ways. Poor fellow! thought I, he means no mischief; it is plain he intends no insolence; his aspect sufficiently evinces that his eccentricities are involuntary. He is useful to me. I can get along with him. If I turn him away, the chances are he will fall in with some less indulgent employer, and then he will be rudely treated, and perhaps driven forth miserably to starve. Yes. Here I can cheaply purchase a delicious self-approval. To befriend Bartleby, to humor him in his strange willfulness, will cost me little or nothing, while I lay up in my soul what will eventually prove a sweet morsel for my conscience. But this mood was not invariable with me. The passiveness of Bartleby sometimes irritated me. I felt strangely goaded on to encounter him in new opposition—to elicit some angry spark from him answerable to my own. But, indeed, I might as well have essayed to strike fire with my knuckles against a bit of Windsor soap. But one afternoon the evil impulse in me mastered me, and the following little scene ensued:

"Bartleby," said I, "when those papers are all copied, I will compare them with you."

"I would prefer not to."

"How? Surely you do not mean to persist in that mulish vagary?"

No answer.

I threw open the folding doors near by, and, turning upon Turkey and Nippers, exclaimed:

"Bartleby a second time says he won't examine his papers. What do you think of it, Turkey?"

It was afternoon, be it remembered. Turkey sat glowing like a brass boiler, his bald head steaming, his hands reeling among his blotted papers.

"Think of it?" roared Turkey. "I think I'll just step behind his screen and black his eyes for him!"

So saying, Turkey rose to his feet and threw his arms into a pugilistic position. He was hurrying away to make good his promise when I detained him, alarmed at the effect of incautiously rousing Turkey's combativeness after dinner.

"Sit down, Turkey," said I, "and hear what Nippers has to say. What do you think of it, Nippers? Would I not be justified in immediately dismissing Bartleby?"

"Excuse me, that is for you to decide, sir. I think his conduct quite unusual, and indeed, unjust, as regards Turkey and myself. But it may only be a passing whim."

"Ah," exclaimed I, "you have strangely changed your mind, then—you speak very gently of him now."

"All beer," cried Turkey; "gentleness is effects of beer —Nippers and I dined together today. You see how gentle *I* am, sir. Shall I go and black his eyes?"

"You refer to Bartleby, I suppose. No, not today, Turkey," I replied; "pray, put up your fists."

I closed the doors and again advanced towards Bartleby. I felt additional incentives tempting me to my fate. I burned to be rebelled against again. I remembered that Bartleby never left the office.

"Bartleby," said I, "Ginger Nut is away; just step around to the Post Office, won't you? (it was but a three minutes' walk), and see if there is anything for me."

"I would prefer not to."

"You *will* not?"

"*I prefer* not."

I staggered to my desk and sat there in a deep study. My blind inveteracy returned. Was there any other thing in which I could procure myself to be ignominiously repulsed by this lean, penniless wight?—my hired clerk? What added thing is there, perfectly reasonable, that he will be sure to refuse to do?

"Bartleby!"

No answer.

"Bartleby," in a louder tone.

No answer.

"Bartleby," I roared.

Like a very ghost, agreeably to the laws of magical invocation, at the third summons he appeared at the entrance of his hermitage.

"Go to the next room, and tell Nippers to come to me."

"I prefer not to," he respectfully and slowly said, and mildly disappeared.

"Very good, Bartleby," said I, in a quiet sort of serenely severe self-possessed tone, intimating the unalterable purpose of some terrible retribution very close at hand. At the moment I half intended something of the kind. But upon the whole, as it was drawing towards my dinner hour, I thought it best to put on my hat and walk home for the day, suffering much from perplexity and distress of mind.

Shall I acknowledge it? The conclusion of this whole business was that it soon became a fixed fact of my chambers, that a pale young scrivener by the name of Bartleby had a desk there; that he copied for me at the usual rate of four cents a folio (one hundred words); but he was permanently exempt from examining the work done by him, that duty being transferred to Turkey and Nippers, out of compliment, doubtless, to their superior acuteness; moreover, said Bartleby was never, on any account, to be dispatched on the most trivial errand of any sort; and that even if entreated to take upon him such a matter, it was generally understood that he would "prefer not to"—in other words, that he would refuse point-blank.

As days passed on, I became considerably reconciled to Bartleby. His steadiness, his freedom from all dissipation, his incessant industry (except when he chose to throw himself into a standing reverie behind his screen), his great

stillness, his unalterableness of demeanor under all circumstances, made him a valuable acquisition. One prime thing
was this—*he was always there*—first in the morning, continually through the day, and the last at night. I had a
singular confidence in his honesty. I felt my most precious
papers perfectly safe in his hands. Sometimes, to be sure,
I could not, for the very soul of me, avoid falling into sudden spasmodic passions with him. For it was exceeding
difficult to bear in mind all the time those strange peculi-
arities, privileges, and unheard-of exemptions, forming the
tacit stipulations on Bartleby's part under which he remained in my office. Now and then, in the eagerness of
dispatching pressing business, I would inadvertently sum-
mon Bartleby, in a short, rapid tone, to put his finger, say,
on the incipient tie of a bit of red tape with which I was
about compressing some papers. Of course, from behind
the screen the usual answer, "I prefer not to," was sure
to come; and then, how could a human creature, with the
common infirmities of our nature, refrain from bitterly
exclaiming upon such perverseness—such unreasonable-
ness. However, every added repulse of this sort which I
received only tended to lessen the probability of my repeating the inadvertence.

Here it must be said that, according to the custom of
most legal gentlemen occupying chambers in densely
populated law buildings, there were several keys to my
door. One was kept by a woman residing in the attic, which
person weekly scrubbed and daily swept and dusted my
apartments. Another was kept by Turkey for convenience'
sake. The third I sometimes carried in my own pocket.
The fourth I knew not who had.

Now, one Sunday morning I happened to go to Trinity
Church, to hear a celebrated preacher, and finding myself
rather early on the ground I thought I would walk round
to my chambers for a while. Luckily I had my key with
me, but upon applying it to the lock, I found it resisted
by something inserted from the inside. Quite surprised, I
called out, when to my consternation a key was turned
from within, and, thrusting his lean visage at me, and holding the door ajar, the apparition of Bartleby appeared,
in his shirt sleeves, and otherwise in a strangely tattered
deshabille, saying quietly that he was sorry, but he was

deeply engaged just then, and—preferred not admitting me at present. In a brief word or two, he moreover added, that perhaps I had better walk around the block two or three times, and by that time he would probably have concluded his affairs.

Now, the utterly unsurmised appearance of Bartleby, tenanting my law chambers of a Sunday morning, with his cadaverously gentlemanly *nonchalance,* yet withal firm and self-possessed, had such a strange effect upon me that incontinently I slunk away from my own door and did as desired. But not without sundry twinges of impotent rebellion against the mild effrontery of this unaccountable scrivener. Indeed, it was his wonderful mildness, chiefly, which not only disarmed me but unmanned me, as it were. For I consider that one, for the time, is sort of unmanned when he tranquilly permits his hired clerk to dictate to him and order him away from his own premises. Furthermore, I was full of uneasiness as to what Bartleby could possibly be doing in my office in his shirt sleeves, and in an otherwise dismantled condition, of a Sunday morning. Was anything amiss going on? Nay, that was out of the question. It was not to be thought of for a moment that Bartleby was an immoral person. But what could he be doing there?— copying? Nay again, whatever might be his eccentricities, Bartleby was an eminently decorous person. He would be the last man to sit down to his desk in any state approaching to nudity. Besides, it was Sunday; and there was something about Bartleby that forbade the supposition that he would by any secular occupation violate the proprieties of the day.

Nevertheless, my mind was not pacified, and, full of a restless curiosity, at last I returned to the door. Without hindrance I inserted my key, opened it, and entered. Bartleby was not to be seen. I looked round anxiously, peeped behind his screen, but it was very plain that he was gone. Upon more closely examining the place, I surmised that for an indefinite period Bartleby must have ate, dressed, and slept in my office, and that, too, without plate, mirror, or bed. The cushioned seat of a rickety old sofa in one corner bore that faint impress of a lean, reclining form. Rolled away under his desk I found a blanket; under the empty grate, a blacking box and brush;

on a chair, a tin basin, with soap and a ragged towel; in a newspaper a few crumbs of gingernuts and a morsel of cheese. Yes, thought I, it is evident enough that Bartleby has been making his home here, keeping bachelor's hall all by himself. Immediately then the thought came sweeping across me, what miserable friendliness and loneliness are here revealed. His poverty is great, but his solitude, how horrible! Think of it. Of a Sunday, Wall Street is deserted as Petra, and every night of every day it is an emptiness. This building, too, which of weekdays hums with industry and life, at nightfall echoes with sheer vacancy, and all through Sunday is forlorn. And here Bartleby makes his home, sole spectator of a solitude which he has seen all populous—a sort of innocent and transformed Marius brooding among the ruins of Carthage!

For the first time in my life a feeling of overpowering stinging melancholy seized me. Before, I had never experienced aught but a not unpleasing sadness. The bond of a common humanity now drew me irresistibly to gloom. A fraternal melancholy! For both I and Bartleby were sons of Adam. I remembered the bright silks and sparkling faces I had seen that day, in gala trim, swanlike sailing down the Mississippi of Broadway; and I contrasted them with the pallid copyist, and thought to myself, Ah, happiness courts the light, so we deem the world is gay, but misery hides aloof, so we deem that misery there is none. These sad fancyings—chimeras, doubtless, of a sick and silly brain—led on to other and more special thoughts, concerning the eccentricities of Bartleby. Presentiments of strange discoveries hovered round me. The scrivener's pale form appeared to me laid out, among uncaring strangers in its shivering winding sheet.

Suddenly I was attracted by Bartleby's closed desk, the key in open sight left in the lock.

I mean no mischief, seek the gratification of no heartless curiosity, thought I; besides, the desk is mine, and its contents, too, so I will make bold to look within. Everything was methodically arranged, the papers smoothly placed. The pigeonholes were deep, and, removing the files of documents, I groped into their recesses. Presently I felt something there, and dragged it out. It was an old

bandanna handkerchief, heavy and knotted. I opened it,
and saw it was a savings bank.

I now recalled all the quiet mysteries which I had noted
in the man. I remembered that he never spoke but to
answer; that, though at intervals he had considerable time
to himself, yet I had never seen him reading—no, not even
a newspaper; that for long periods he would stand looking
out, at his pale window behind the screen, upon the dead
brick wall; I was quite sure he never visited any refectory
or eating house, while his pale face clearly indicated that
he never drank beer like Turkey, or tea and coffee even,
like other men; that he never went anywhere in particular
that I could learn; never went out for a walk, unless, indeed,
that was the case at present; that he had declined telling
who he was, or whence he came, or whether he had any
relatives in the world; that though so thin and pale, he
never complained of ill health. And more than all I remembered a certain unconscious air of pallid—how shall
I call it?—of pallid haughtiness, say, or rather an austere
reserve about him, which had positively awed me into my
tame compliance with his eccentricities, when I had feared
to ask him to do the slightest incidental thing for me, even
though I might know, from his long-continued motion-
lessness, that behind his screen he must be standing in one
of those dead-wall reveries of his.

Revolving all these things, and coupling them with the
recently discovered fact that he made my office his constant
abiding place and home, and not forgetful of his morbid
moodiness—revolving all these things, a prudential feeling
began to steal over me. My first emotions had been those
of pure melancholy and sincerest pity; but just in proportion as the forlornness of Bartleby grew and grew to my
imagination, did that same melancholy merge into fear,
that pity into repulsion. So true it is, and so terrible too,
that up to a certain point the thought or sight of misery
enlists our best affections; but, in certain special cases,
beyond that point it does not. They err who would assert
that invariably this is owing to the inherent selfishness of
the human heart. It rather proceeds from a certain hopelessness of remedying excessive and organic ill. To a
sensitive being, pity is not seldom pain. And when at last it

is perceived that such pity cannot lead to effectual succor, common sense bids the soul be rid of it. What I saw that morning persuaded me that the scrivener was the victim of innate and incurable disorder. I might give alms to his body, but his body did not pain him—it was his soul that suffered, and his soul I could not reach.

I did not accomplish the purpose of going to Trinity Church that morning. Somehow, the things I had seen disqualified me for the time from churchgoing. I walked homeward, thinking what I would do with Bartleby. Finally, I resolved upon this—I would put certain calm questions to him the next morning, touching his history, etc., and if he declined to answer them openly and unreservedly (and I supposed he would prefer not), then to give him a twenty-dollar bill over and above whatever I might owe him, and tell him his services were no longer required; but that if in any other way I could assist him, I would be happy to do so, especially if he desired to return to his native place, wherever that might be, I would willingly help to defray the expenses. Moreover, if, after reaching home, he found himself at any time in want of aid, a letter from him would be sure of a reply.

The next morning came.

"Bartleby," said I, gently calling to him behind his screen.

No reply.

"Bartleby," said I, in a still gentler tone, "come here; I am not going to ask you to do anything you would prefer not to do—I simply wish to speak to you."

Upon this he noiselessly slid into view.

"Will you tell me, Bartleby, where you were born?"

"I would prefer not to."

"Will you tell me *anything* about yourself?"

"I would prefer not to."

"But what reasonable objection can you have to speak to me? I feel friendly towards you."

He did not look at me while I spoke, but kept his glance fixed upon my bust of Cicero, which, as I then sat, was directly behind me, some six inches above my head.

"What is your answer, Bartleby," said I, after waiting a considerable time for a reply, during which his countenance remained immovable, only there was the faintest conceivable tremor of the white attenuated mouth.

"At present I prefer to give no answer," he said, and retired into his hermitage.

It was rather weak in me I confess, but his manner, on this occasion, nettled me. Not only did there seem to lurk in it a certain calm disdain, but his perverseness seemed ungrateful, considering the undeniable good usage and indulgence he had received from me.

Again I sat ruminating what I should do. Mortified as I was at his behavior, and resolved as I had been to dismiss him when I entered my office, nevertheless I strangely felt something superstitious knocking at my heart, and forbidding me to carry out my purpose, and denouncing me for a villain if I dared to breathe one bitter word against this forlornest of mankind. At last, familiarly drawing my chair behind his screen, I sat down and said: "Bartleby, never mind, then, about revealing your history; but let me entreat you, as a friend, to comply as far as may be with the usages of this office. Say now, you will help to examine papers tomorrow or next day: in short, say now, that in a day or two you will begin to be a little reasonable:—say so, Bartleby."

"At present I would prefer not to be a little reasonable," was his mildly cadaverous reply.

Just then the folding doors opened and Nippers approached. He seemed suffering from an unusually bad night's rest, induced by severer indigestion than common. He overheard those final words of Bartleby.

"*Prefer not,* eh?" gritted Nippers—"I'd *prefer* him, if I were you, sir," addressing me—"I'd *prefer* him; I'd give him preferences, the stubborn mule! What is it, sir, pray, that he *prefers* not to do now?"

Bartleby moved not a limb.

"Mr. Nippers," said I, "I'd prefer that you would withdraw for the present."

Somehow, of late, I had got into the way of involuntarily using this word "prefer" upon all sorts of not exactly suitable occasions. And I trembled to think that my contact with the scrivener had already and seriously affected me in a mental way. And what further and deeper aberration might it not yet produce? This apprehension had not been without efficacy in determining me to summary measures.

As Nippers, looking very sour and sulky, was departing, Turkey blandly and deferentially approached.

"With submission, sir," said he, "yesterday I was thinking about Bartleby here, and I think that if he would but prefer to take a quart of good ale every day, it would do much towards mending him, and enabling him to assist in examining his papers."

"So you have got the word, too," said I, slightly excited.

"With submission, and word, sir?" asked Turkey, respectfully crowding himself into the contracted space behind the screen, and by so doing making me jostle the scrivener. "What word, sir?"

"I would prefer to be left alone here," said Bartleby, as if offended at being mobbed in his privacy.

"*That's* the word, Turkey," said I—"*that's* it."

"Oh, *prefer?* oh yes—queer word. I never use it myself. But, sir, as I was saying, if he would but prefer——"

"Turkey," interrupted I, "you will please withdraw."

"Oh certainly, sir, if you prefer that I should."

As he opened the folding door to retire, Nippers at his desk caught a glimpse of me, and asked whether I would prefer to have a certain paper copied on blue paper or white. He did not in the least roguishly accent the word prefer. It was plain that it involuntarily rolled from his tongue. I thought to myself, surely I must get rid of a demented man, who already has in some degree turned the tongues, if not the heads, of myself and clerks. But I thought it prudent not to break the dismission at once.

The next day I noticed that Bartleby did nothing but stand at his window in his dead-wall reverie. Upon asking him why he did not write, he said that he had decided upon doing no more writing.

"Why, how now? what next?" exclaimed I, "do no more writing?"

"No more."

"And what is the reason?"

"Do you not see the reason for yourself?" he indifferently replied.

I looked steadfastly at him, and perceived that his eyes looked dull and glazed. Instantly it occurred to me that his unexampled diligence in copying by his dim window for the first few weeks of his stay with me might have temporarily impaired his vision.

I was touched. I said something in condolence with him. I hinted that of course he did wisely in abstaining from writing for a while; and urged him to embrace that opportunity of taking wholesome exercise in the open air. This, however, he did not do. A few days after this, my other clerks being absent, and being in a great hurry to dispatch certain letters by the mail, I thought that, having nothing else earthly to do, Bartleby would surely be less inflexible than usual, and carry these letters to the Post Office. But he blankly declined. So, much to my inconvenience, I went myself.

Still added days went by. Whether Bartleby's eyes improved or not, I could not say. To all appearance, I thought they did. But when I asked him if they did, he vouchsafed no answer. At all events, he would do no copying. At last, in reply to my urgings, he informed me that he had permanently given up copying.

"What!" exclaimed I; "suppose your eyes should get entirely well—better than ever before—would you not copy then?"

"I have given up copying," he answered, and slid aside.

He remained as ever, a fixture in my chamber. Nay—if that were possible—he became still more of a fixture than before. What was to be done? He would do nothing in the office; why should he stay there? In plain fact, he had now become a millstone to me, not only useless as a necklace, but afflictive to bear. Yet I was sorry for him. I speak less than truth when I say that, on his own account, he occasioned me uneasiness. If he would but have named a single relative or friend, I would instantly have written and urged their taking the poor fellow away to some convenient retreat. But he seemed alone, absolutely alone in the universe. A bit of wreck in the mid-Atlantic. At length, necessities connected with my business tyrannized over all other considerations. Decently as I could, I told Bartleby that in six days' time he must unconditionally leave the office. I warned him to take measures, in the interval, for procuring some other abode. I offered to assist him in this endeavor, if he himself would but take the first step towards a removal. "And when you finally quit me, Bartleby," added I, "I shall see that you go not away entirely unprovided. Six days from this hour, remember."

At the expiration of that period, I peeped behind the screen, and lo! Bartleby was there.

I buttoned up my coat, balanced myself, advanced slowly towards him, touched his shoulder, and said, "The time has come; you must quit this place; I am sorry for you; here is money; but you must go."

"I would prefer not," he replied, with his back still towards me.

"You *must*."

He remained silent.

Now I had an unbounded confidence in this man's common honesty. He had frequently restored to me sixpences and shillings carelessly dropped upon the floor, for I am apt to be very reckless in such shirt-button affairs. The proceeding, then, which followed will not be deemed extraordinary.

"Bartleby," said I, "I owe you twelve dollars on account; here are thirty-two; the odd twenty are yours— Will you take it?" and I handed the bills towards him.

But he made no motion.

"I will leave them here, then," putting them under a weight on the table. Then taking my hat and cane and going to the door, I tranquilly turned and added—"After you have removed your things from these offices, Bartleby, you will of course lock the door—since everyone is now gone for the day but you—and if you please, slip your key underneath the mat, so that I may have it in the morning. I shall not see you again; so good-bye to you. If, hereafter, in your new place of abode, I can be of any service to you, do not fail to advise me by letter. Good-bye, Bartleby, and fare you well."

But he answered not a word; like the last column of some ruined temple, he remained standing mute and solitary in the middle of the otherwise deserted room.

As I walked home in a pensive mood, my vanity got the better of my pity. I could not but highly plume myself on my masterly management in getting rid of Bartleby. Masterly I call it, and such it must appear to any dispassionate thinker. The beauty of my procedure seemed to consist in its perfect quietness. There was no vulgar bullying, no bravado of any sort, no choleric hectoring and striding to and fro across the apartment, jerking out vehement commands for Bartleby to bundle himself off with his beggarly traps. Nothing of the kind. Without loudly bidding Bartleby depart—as an inferior genius might have done—I *assumed* the ground that depart he must, and upon that assumption built all I had to say. The more I thought over my procedure, the more I was charmed with it. Nevertheless, next morning, upon awakening, I had my doubts—I had somehow slept off the fumes of vanity. One of the coolest and wisest hours a man has is just after he awakes in the morning. My procedure seemed as sagacious as ever—but only in theory. How it would prove in practice—there was the rub. It was truly a beautiful thought to have assumed Bartleby's departure; but, after all, that assumption was simply my own, and none of Bartleby's. The great point was, not whether I had assumed that he would quit me, but whether he would prefer so to do. He was more a man of preferences than assumptions.

After breakfast, I walked downtown, arguing the probabilities pro and con. One moment I thought it would prove a miserable failure, and Bartleby would be found all alive at my office as usual; the next moment it seemed certain that I should find his chair empty. And so I kept veering about. At the corner of Broadway and Canal Street, I saw quite an excited group of people standing in earnest conversation.

"I'll take odds he doesn't," said a voice as I passed.

"Doesn't go?—done!" said I, "put up your money."

I was instinctively putting my hand in my pocket to produce my own, when I remembered that this was an election day. The words I had overheard bore no reference to Bartleby but to the success or nonsuccess of some candidate for the mayoralty. In my intent frame of mind, I had, as it were, imagined that all Broadway shared in my excitement, and were debating the same question with me. I passed on, very thankful that the uproar of the street screened my momentary absent-mindedness.

As I had intended, I was earlier than usual at my office door. I stood listening for a moment. All was still. He must be gone. I tried the knob. The door was locked.

Yes, my procedure had worked to a charm; he indeed must be vanished. Yet a certain melancholy mixed with this: I was almost sorry for my brilliant success. I was fumbling under the door mat for the key, which Bartleby was to have left there for me, when accidentally my knee knocked against a panel, producing a summoning sound, and in response a voice came to me from within—"Not yet; I am occupied."

It was Bartleby.

I was thunderstruck. For an instant I stood like the man who, pipe in mouth, was killed one cloudless afternoon long ago in Virginia by summer lightning; at his own warm open window he was killed, and remained leaning out there upon the dreamy afternoon, till someone touched him, when he fell.

"Not gone!" I murmured at last. But again obeying that wondrous ascendancy which the inscrutable scrivener had over me, and from which ascendancy, for all my chafing, I could not completely escape, I slowly went downstairs and out into the street, and while walking round the block considered what I should next do in this unheard-of perplexity. Turn the man out by an actual thrusting I could not; to drive him away by calling him hard names would not do; calling in the police was an unpleasant idea; and yet, permit him to enjoy his cadaverous triumph over me—this, too, I could not think of. What was to be done? or, if nothing could be done, was there anything further that I could *assume* in the matter? Yes, as before I had prospectively assumed that Bartleby would depart, so now I might retrospectively assume that departed he was. In the legitimate carrying out of this assumption I might enter my office in a great hurry, and, pretending not to see Bartleby at all, walk straight against him as if he were air. Such a proceeding would in a singular degree have the appearance of a home thrust. It was hardly possible that Bartleby could withstand such an application of the doctrine of assumptions. But upon second thoughts the success of the plan seemed rather dubious. I resolved to argue the matter over with him again.

"Bartleby," said I, entering the office, with a quietly severe expression, "I am seriously displeased. I am pained, Bartleby. I had thought better of you. I had imagined you of such a gentlemanly organization that in any delicate dilemma a slight hint would suffice—in short, an assumption. But it appears I am deceived. Why," I added, unaffectedly starting, "you have not even touched that money yet," pointing to it, just where I had left it the evening previous.

He answered nothing.

"Will you, or will you not, quit me?" I now demanded in a sudden passion, advancing close to him.

"I would prefer *not* to quit you," he replied, gently emphasizing the *not*.

"What earthly right have you to stay here? Do you pay any rent? Do you pay my taxes? Or is this property yours?"

He answered nothing.

"Are you ready to go on and write now? Are your eyes recovered? Could you copy a small paper for me this morning? or help examine a few lines? or step round to the Post Office? In a word, will you do anything at all to give a coloring to your refusal to depart the premises?"

He silently retired into his hermitage.

I was now in such a state of nervous resentment that I thought it but prudent to check myself at present from further demonstrations. Bartleby and I were alone. I remembered the tragedy of the unfortunate Adams and the still more unfortunate Colt in the solitary office of the latter; and how poor Colt, being dreadfully incensed by Adams, and imprudently permitting himself to get wildly excited, was at unawares hurried into his fatal act —an act which certainly no man could possibly deplore more than the actor himself. Often it had occurred to me in my ponderings upon the subject that had that altercation taken place in the public street, or at a private residence, it would not have terminated as it did. It was the circumstance of being alone in a solitary office, upstairs, of a building entirely unhallowed by humanizing domestic associations—an uncarpeted office, doubtless, of a dusty, haggard sort of appearance—this it must have been which greatly helped to enhance the irritable desperation of the hapless Colt.

But when this old Adam of resentment rose in me and tempted me concerning Bartleby, I grappled him and threw him. How? Why, simply by recalling the divine injunction: "A new commandment give I unto you, that ye love one another." Yes, this it was that saved me. Aside from higher considerations, charity often operates as a vastly wise and prudent principle—a great safeguard to its possessor. Men have committed murder for jealousy's sake, and anger's sake, and hatred's sake, and selfishness' sake, and spiritual pride's sake; but no man that ever I heard of ever committed a diabolical murder for sweet charity's sake. Mere self-interest, then, if no better motive can be enlisted, should, especially with high-tempered men, prompt all beings to charity and philanthropy. At any rate, upon the occasion in question, I strove to drown my exasperated feelings towards the scrivener by benevolently construing his conduct. Poor fellow, poor fellow! thought I, he don't mean anything, and besides, he has seen hard times, and ought to be indulged.

I endeavored, also, immediately to occupy myself, and at the same time to comfort my despondency. I tried to fancy that in the course of the morning, at such time as might prove agreeable to him, Bartleby, of his own free accord, would emerge from his hermitage and take up some decided line of march in the direction of the door. But no. Half-past twelve o'clock came; Turkey began to glow in the face, overturn his inkstand, and become generally obstreperous; Nippers abated down into quietude and courtesy; Ginger Nut munched his noon apple; and Bartleby remained standing at his window in one of his profoundest dead-wall reveries. Will it be credited? Ought I to acknowledge it? That afternoon I left the office without saying one further word to him.

Some days now passed during which, at leisure intervals, I looked a little into "Edwards on the Will," and "Priestley on Necessity." Under the circumstances, those books induced a salutary feeling. Gradually I slid into the persuasion that these troubles of mine touching the scrivener had been all predestinated from eternity, and Bartleby was billeted upon me for some mysterious purpose of an all-wise Providence, which it was not for a mere mortal like me to fathom. Yes, Bartleby, stay there behind your screen, thought I; I shall persecute you no more; you are harmless and noiseless as any of these old chairs; in short, I never feel so private as when I know you are here. At last I see it, I feel it; I penetrate to the predestinated purpose of my life. I am content. Others may have loftier parts to enact, but my mission in this world, Bartleby, is to furnish you with office room for such period as you may see fit to remain.

I believe that this wise and blessed frame of mind would have continued with me had it not been for the unsolicited and uncharitable remarks obtruded upon me by my professional friends who visited the rooms. But thus it often is that the constant friction of illiberal minds wears out at last the best resolves of the more generous. Though, to be sure, when I reflected upon it it was not strange that people entering my office should be struck by the peculiar aspect of the unaccountable Bartleby, and so be tempted to throw out some sinister observations concerning him. Sometimes an attorney having business with me, and calling at my office, and finding no one but the scrivener there, would undertake to obtain some sort of precise information from him touching my whereabouts; but without heeding his idle talk, Bartleby would remain standing immovable in the middle of the room. So, after contemplating him in that position for a time, the attorney would depart no wiser than he came.

Also, when a reference was going on, and the room full of lawyers and witnesses, and business driving fast, some deeply-occupied legal gentleman present, seeing Bartleby wholly unemployed, would request him to run round to his (the legal gentleman's) office and fetch some papers for him. Thereupon Bartleby would tranquilly decline, and yet remain idle as before. Then the lawyer would give a great stare, and turn to me. And what could I say? At last I was made aware that all through the circle of my professional acquaintance a whisper of wonder was running round, having reference to the strange creature I kept at my office. This worried me very much. And as the idea came upon me of his possibly turning out a long-lived man, and keep occupying my chambers, and denying my authority; and perplexing my visitors; and scandalizing my professional reputation; and casting a general gloom over the premises; keeping soul and body together to the last upon his savings (for doubtless he spent but half a dime a day), and in the end perhaps outlive me, and

claim possession of my office by right of his perpetual
occupancy—as all these dark anticipations crowded upon
me more and more, and my friends continually intruded
their relentless remarks upon the apparition in my room,
a great change was wrought in me. I resolved to gather all
my faculties together and forever rid me of this intolerable
incubus.

Ere revolving any complicated project, however, adapted
to this end, I first simply suggested to Bartleby the propriety of his permanent departure. In a calm and serious
tone, I commended the idea to his careful and mature
consideration. But, having taken three days to meditate
upon it, he apprised me that his original determination remained the same; in short, that he still preferred to abide
with me.

What shall I do? I now said to myself, buttoning up my
coat to the last button. What shall I do? what ought I to
do? what does conscience say I *should* do with this man,
or, rather, ghost. Rid myself of him, I must; go, he shall.
But how? You will not thrust him, the poor, pale, passive
mortal—you will not thrust such a helpless creature out
of your door? you will not dishonor yourself by such
cruelty? No, I will not, I cannot do that. Rather would I
let him live and die here, and then mason up his remains
in the wall. What, then, will you do? For all your coaxing,
he will not budge. Bribes he leaves under your own paper-
weight on your table; in short, it is quite plain that he
prefers to cling to you.

Then something severe, something unusual, must be
done. What! surely you will not have him collared by a
constable, and commit his innocent pallor to the common
jail? And upon what ground could you procure such a
thing to be done?—a vagrant, is he? What! he a vagrant, a
wanderer, who refuses to budge? It is because he will *not*
be a vagrant, then, that you seek to count him *as* a vagrant.
That is too absurd. No visible means of support: there I
have him. Wrong again: for indubitably he *does* support
himself, and that is the only unanswerable proof that any
man can show of his possessing the means so to do. No
more, then. Since he will not quit me, I must quit him. I
will change my offices; I will move elsewhere, and give him

fair notice that if I find him on my new premises I will then proceed against him as a common trespasser.

Acting accordingly, next day I thus addressed him: "I find these chambers too far from the City Hall; the air is unwholesome. In a word, I propose to remove my offices next week, and shall no longer require your services. I tell you this now, in order that you may seek another place."

He made no reply, and nothing more was said.

On the appointed day I engaged carts and men, proceeded to my chambers, and, having but little furniture, everything was removed in a few hours. Throughout, the scrivener remained standing behind the screen, which I directed to be removed the last thing. It was withdrawn; and, being folded up like a huge folio, left him the motionless occupant of a naked room. I stood in the entry watching him a moment, while something from within me upbraided me.

I re-entered, with my hand in my pocket—and—and my heart in my mouth.

"Good-bye, Bartleby; I am going—good-bye; and God some way bless you; and take that," slipping something in his hand. But it dropped upon the floor, and then— strange to say—I tore myself from him whom I had so longed to be rid of.

Established in my new quarters, for a day or two I kept the door locked, and started at every footfall in the passages. When I returned to my rooms after any little absence, I would pause at the threshold for an instant and attentively listen ere applying my key. But these fears were needless. Bartleby never came nigh me.

I thought all was going well, when a perturbed-looking stranger visited me, inquiring whether I was the person who had recently occupied rooms at No. — Wall Street.

Full of forebodings, I replied that I was.

"Then, sir," said the stranger, who proved a lawyer, "you are responsible for the man you left there. He refuses to do any copying; he refuses to do anything; he says he prefers not to; and he refuses to quit the premises."

"I am very sorry, sir," said I, with assumed tranquillity, but an inward tremor, "but, really, the man you allude to is nothing to me—he is no relation or apprentice of mine, that you should hold me responsible for him."

"In mercy's name, who is he?"

"I certainly cannot inform you. I know nothing about him. Formerly I employed him as a copyist; but he has done nothing for me now for some time past."

"I shall settle him, then—good morning, sir."

Several days passed, and I heard nothing more; and, though I often felt a charitable prompting to call at the place and see poor Bartleby, yet a certain squeamishness, of I know not what, withheld me.

All is over with him, by this time, thought I at last, when, through another week, no further intelligence reached me. But, coming to my room the day after, I found several persons waiting at my door in a high state of nervous excitement.

"That's the man—here he comes," cried the foremost one, whom I recognized as the lawyer who had previously called upon me alone.

"You must take him away, sir, at once," cried a portly person among them, advancing upon me, and whom I knew to be the landlord of No. — Wall Street. "These gentlemen, my tenants, cannot stand it any longer; Mr. B——," pointing to the lawyer, "has turned him out of his room, and he now persists in haunting the building generally, sitting upon the banisters of the stairs by day, and sleeping in the entry by night. Everybody is concerned; clients are leaving the offices; some fears are entertained of a mob; something you must do, and that without delay."

Aghast at this torrent, I fell back before it, and would fain have locked myself in my new quarters. In vain I persisted that Bartleby was nothing to me—no more than to anyone else. In vain—I was the last person known to have anything to do with him, and they held me to the terrible account. Fearful, then, of being exposed in the papers (as one person present obscurely threatened), I considered the matter, and at length said that if the lawyer would give me a confidential interview with the scrivener, in his (the lawyer's) own room, I would, that afternoon, strive my best to rid them of the nuisance they complained of.

Going upstairs to my old haunt, there was Bartleby silently sitting upon the banister at the landing.

"What are you doing here, Bartleby?" said I.

"Sitting upon the banister," he mildly replied.

I motioned him into the lawyer's room, who then left us.

"Bartleby," said I, "are you aware that you are the cause of great tribulation to me, by persisting in occupying the entry after being dismissed from the office?"

No answer.

"Now one of two things must take place. Either you must do something, or something must be done to you. Now what sort of business would you like to engage in? Would you like to re-engage in copying for someone?"

"No; I would prefer not to make any change."

"Would you like a clerkship in a dry-goods store?"

"There is too much confinement about that. No, I would not like a clerkship; but I am not particular."

"Too much confinement," I cried; "why you keep yourself confined all the time!"

"I would prefer not to take a clerkship," he rejoined, as if to settle that little item at once.

"How would a bartender's business suit you? There is no trying of the eyesight in that."

"I would not like it at all; though, as I said before, I am not particular."

His unwonted wordiness inspirited me. I returned to the charge.

"Well, then, would you like to travel through the country collecting bills for the merchants? That would improve your health."

"No, I would prefer to be doing something else."

"How, then, would going as a companion to Europe, to entertain some young gentleman with your conversation—how would that suit you?"

"Not at all. It does not strike me that there is anything definite about that. I like to be stationary. But I am not particular."

"Stationary you shall be, then," I cried, now losing all patience, and, for the first time in all my exasperating connection with him, fairly flying into a passion. "If you do not go away from these premises before night, I shall feel bound—indeed, I *am* bound—to—to—to quit the

premises myself!" I rather absurdly concluded, knowing
not with what possible threat to try to frighten his im-
mobility into compliance. Despairing of all further efforts,
I was precipitately leaving him, when a final thought occurred to me—one which had not been wholly unindulged
before.

"Bartleby," said I, in the kindest tone I could assume
under such exciting circumstances, "will you go home with
me now—not to my office, but my dwelling—and remain
there till we can conclude upon some convenient arrangement for you at our leisure? Come, let us start now, right
away."

"No; at present I would prefer not to make any change
at all."

I answered nothing, but, effectually dodging everyone
by the suddenness and rapidity of my flight, rushed from
the building, ran up Wall Street towards Broadway, and,
jumping into the first omnibus, was soon removed from
pursuit. As soon as tranquillity returned, I distinctly perceived that I had now done all that I possibly could, both
in respect to the demands of the landlord and his tenants,
and with regard to my own desire and sense of duty, to
benefit Bartleby, and shield him from rude persecution.
I now strove to be entirely carefree and quiescent, and
my conscience justified me in the attempt, though, indeed,
it was not so successful as I could have wished. So fearful
was I of being again hunted out by the incensed landlord
and his exasperated tenants that, surrendering my business
to Nippers for a few days, I drove about the upper part
of the town and through the suburbs in my rockaway;
crossed over to Jersey City and Hoboken, and paid fugitive
visits to Manhattanville and Astoria. In fact, I almost
lived in my rockaway for the time.

When again I entered my office, lo, a note from the
landlord lay upon the desk. I opened it with trembling
hands. It informed me that the writer had sent to the
police, and had Bartleby removed to the Tombs as a
vagrant. Moreover, since I knew more about him than
anyone else, he wished me to appear at that place and
make a suitable statement of the facts. These tidings had
a conflicting effect upon me. At first I was indignant, but
at last almost approved. The landlord's energetic, sum-

mary disposition had led him to adopt a procedure which
I do not think I would have decided upon myself; and yet,
as a last resort, under such peculiar circumstances, it
seemed the only plan.

As I afterwards learned, the poor scrivener, when told
that he must be conducted to the Tombs, offered not the
slightest obstacle, but, in his pale, unmoving way, silently
acquiesced.

Some of the compassionate and curious bystanders
joined the party, and, headed by one of the constables
arm in arm with Bartleby, the silent procession filed its
way through all the noise, and heat, and joy of the roaring
thoroughfares at noon.

The same day I received the note, I went to the Tombs,
or, to speak more properly, the Halls of Justice. Seeking
the right officer, I stated the purpose of my call, and was
informed that the individual I described was indeed within.
I then assured the functionary that Bartleby was a perfectly honest man, and greatly to be compassionated,
however unaccountably eccentric. I narrated all I knew,
and closed by suggesting the idea of letting him remain in
as indulgent confinement as possible till something less
harsh might be done—though, indeed, I hardly knew what.
At all events, if nothing else could be decided upon, the
almshouse must receive him. I then begged to have an
interview.

Being under no disgraceful charge, and quite serene
and harmless in all his ways, they had permitted him freely
to wander about the prison, and, especially, in the inclosed
grass-platted yards thereof. And so I found him there,
standing all alone in the quietest of the yards, his face
towards a high wall, while all around, from the narrow
slits of the jail windows, I thought I saw peering out upon
him the eyes of murderers and thieves.

"Bartleby!"

"I know you," he said, without looking round—"and I
want nothing to say to you."

"It was not I that brought you here, Bartleby," said I,
keenly pained at his implied suspicion. "And, to you, this
should not be so vile a place. Nothing reproachful attaches
to you by being here. And see, it is not so sad a place as

one might think. Look, there is the sky, and here is the grass."

"I know where I am," he replied, but would say nothing more, and so I left him.

As I entered the corridor again, a broad meatlike man in an apron accosted me, and, jerking his thumb over his shoulder, said—"Is that your friend?"

"Yes."

"Does he want to starve? If he does, let him live on the prison fare, that's all."

"Who are you?" asked I, not knowing what to make of such an unofficially speaking person in such a place.

"I am the grubman. Such gentlemen as have friends here hire me to provide them with something good to eat."

"Is this so?" said I, turning to the turnkey.

He said it was.

"Well, then," said I, slipping some silver into the grubman's hands (for so they called him), "I want you to give particular attention to my friend there; let him have the best dinner you can get. And you must be as polite to him as possible."

"Introduce me, will you?" said the grubman, looking at me with an expression which seemed to say he was all impatience for an opportunity to give a specimen of his breeding.

Thinking it would prove of benefit to the scrivener, I acquiesced, and, asking the grubman his name, went up with him to Bartleby.

"Bartleby, this is a friend; you will find him very useful to you."

"Your sarvant, sir, your sarvant," said the grubman, making a low salutation behind his apron. "Hope you find it pleasant here, sir; nice grounds—cool apartments—hope you'll stay with us some time—try to make it agreeable. What will you have for dinner today?"

"I prefer not to dine today," said Bartleby, turning away. "It would disagree with me; I am unused to dinners." So saying, he slowly moved to the other side of the inclosure and took up a position fronting the dead-wall.

"How's this?" said the grubman, addressing me with a stare of astonishment. "He's odd, ain't he?"

"I think he is a little deranged," said I, sadly.

"Deranged? deranged is it? Well, now, upon my word, I thought that friend of yourn was a gentleman forger; they are always pale and genteel-like, them forgers. I can't help pity 'em—can't help it, sir. Did you know Monroe Edwards?" he added, touchingly, and paused. Then, laying his hand piteously on my shoulder, sighed, "he died of consumption at Sing-Sing. So you weren't acquainted with Monroe?"

"No, I was never socially acquainted with any forgers. But I cannot stop longer. Look to my friend yonder. You will not lose by it. I will see you again."

Some few days after this, I again obtained admission to the Tombs, and went through the corridors in quest of Bartleby; but without finding him.

"I saw him coming from his cell not long ago," said a turnkey, "maybe he's gone to loiter in the yards."

So I went in that direction.

"Are you looking for the silent man?" said another turnkey, passing me. "Yonder he lies—sleeping in the yard there. 'Tis not twenty minutes since I saw him lie down."

The yard was entirely quiet. It was not accessible to the common prisoners. The surrounding walls, of amazing thickness, kept off all sounds behind them. The Egyptian character of the masonry weighed upon me with its gloom. But a soft imprisoned turf grew underfoot. The heart of the eternal pyramids, it seemed, wherein, by some strange magic, through the clefts, grass-seed, dropped by birds, had sprung.

Strangely huddled at the base of the wall, his knees drawn up and lying on his side, his head touching the cold stones, I saw the wasted Bartleby. But nothing stirred. I paused, then went close up to him, stooped over, and saw that his dim eyes were open; otherwise he seemed profoundly sleeping. Something prompted me to touch him. I felt his hand, when a tingling shiver ran up my arm and down my spine to my feet.

The round face of the grubman peered upon me now. "His dinner is ready. Won't he dine today, either? Or does he live without dining?"

"Lives without dining," said I, and closed the eyes.

"Eh!—He's asleep, ain't he?"

"With kings and counselors," murmured I.

*   *   *

There would seem little need for proceeding further in this history. Imagination will readily supply the meager recital of poor Bartleby's interment. But, ere parting with the reader, let me say that if this little narrative has sufficiently interested him to awaken curiosity as to who Bartleby was, and what manner of life he led prior to the present narrator's making his acquaintance, I can only reply that in such curiosity I fully share, but am wholly unable to gratify it. Yet here I hardly know whether I should divulge one little item of rumor which came to my ear a few months after the scrivener's decease. Upon what basis it rested, I could never ascertain, and hence how true it is I cannot now tell. But, inasmuch as this vague report has not been without a certain suggestive interest to me, however sad, it may prove the same with some others, and so I will briefly mention it. The report was this: that Bartleby had been a subordinate clerk in the Dead Letter Office at Washington, from which he had been suddenly removed by a change in the administration. When I think over this rumor, hardly can I express the emotions which seize me. Dead letters! does it not sound like dead men? Conceive a man by nature and misfortune prone to a pallid hopelessness, can any business seem more fitted to heighten it than that of continually handling these dead letters, and assorting them for the flames? For by the cartload they are annually burned. Sometimes from out the folded paper the pale clerk takes a ring—the finger it was meant for, perhaps, molders in the grave; a bank note sent in swiftest charity—he whom it would relieve nor eats nor hungers any more; pardon for those who died despairing; hope for those who died unhoping; good tidings for those who died stifled by unrelieved calamities. On errands of life, these letters speed to death.

Ah, Bartleby! Ah, humanity!

BENITO CERENO

IN the year 1799, Captain Amasa Delano, of Duxbury in Massachusetts, commanding a large sealer and general trader, lay at anchor with a valuable cargo in the harbor of St. Maria—a small, desert, uninhabited island toward the southern extremity of the long coast of Chile. There he had touched for water.

On the second day, not long after dawn, while lying in his berth, his mate came below, informing him that a strange sail was coming into the bay. Ships were then not so plenty in those waters as now. He rose, dressed, and went on deck.

The morning was one peculiar to that coast. Everything was mute and calm; everything gray. The sea, though undulated into long roods of swells, seemed fixed, and was sleeked at the surface like waved lead that has cooled and set in the smelter's mold. The sky seemed a gray surtout. Flights of troubled gray fowl, kith and kin with flights of troubled gray vapors among which they were mixed, skimmed low and fitfully over the waters, as swallows over meadows before storms. Shadows present, foreshadowing deeper shadows to come.

To Captain Delano's surprise, the stranger, viewed through the glass, showed no colors, though to do so upon entering a haven, however uninhabited in its shores, where but a single other ship might be lying, was the custom among peaceful seamen of all nations. Considering the lawlessness and loneliness of the spot, and the sort of stories at that day associated with those seas, Captain Delano's surprise might have deepened into some uneasiness had he not been a person of a singularly undistrustful good nature, not liable except on extraordinary and repeated incentives, and hardly then, to indulge in personal alarms any way involving the imputation of malign evil in man. Whether, in view of what humanity is capable, such a trait implies, along with a benevolent heart, more than ordinary quickness and accuracy of intellectual perception, may be left to the wise to determine.

But whatever misgivings might have obtruded on first seeing the stranger would almost, in any seaman's mind, have been dissipated by observing that the ship, in navigating into the harbor, was drawing too near the land, a sunken reef making out off her bow. This seemed to prove her a stranger, indeed, not only to the sealer, but the island; consequently she could be no wonted freebooter on that ocean. With no small interest Captain Delano continued to watch her—a proceeding not much facilitated by the vapors partly mantling the hull, through which the far matin light from her cabin streamed equivocally enough; much like the sun—by this time hemisphered on the rim of the horizon, and, apparently, in company with the strange ship entering the harbor—which, wimpled by the same low, creeping clouds, showed not unlike a Lima intrigante's one sinister eye peering across the Plaza from the Indian loophole of her dusk *saya-y-manta*.

It might have been but a deception of the vapors, but the longer the stranger was watched the more singular appeared her maneuvers. Erelong it seemed hard to decide whether she meant to come in or no—what she wanted, or what she was about. The wind, which had breezed up a little during the night, was now extremely light and baffling, which the more increased the apparent uncertainty of her movements.

Surmising at last that it might be a ship in distress, Captain Delano ordered his whaleboat to be dropped, and, much to the wary opposition of his mate, prepared to board her, and, at the least, pilot her in. On the night previous, a fishing party of the seamen had gone a long distance to some detached rocks out of sight from the sealer, and, an hour or two before daybreak, had returned, having set with no small success. Presuming that the stranger might have been long off soundings, the good captain put several baskets of the fish, for presents, into his boat, and so pulled away. From her continuing too near the sunken reef deeming her in danger, calling to his men he made all haste to apprise those on board of their situation. But, some time ere the boat came up, the wind, light though it was, having shifted, had headed the vessel off, as well as partly broken the vapors from about her.

Upon gaining a less remote view, the ship, when made signally visible on the verge of the leaden-hued swells, with the shreds of fog here and there raggedly furring her, appeared like a whitewashed monastery after a thunderstorm, seen perched upon some dun cliff among the Pyrenees. But it was no purely fanciful resemblance which now, for a moment, almost led Captain Delano to think that nothing less than a shipload of monks was before him. Peering over the bulwarks were what really seemed, in the hazy distance, throngs of dark cowls; while, fitfully revealed through the open portholes, other dark moving figures were dimly descried, as of Black Friars pacing the cloisters.

Upon a still nigher approach, this appearance was modified, and the true character of the vessel was plain—a Spanish merchantman of the first class, carrying Negro slaves, amongst other valuable freight, from one colonial port to another. A very large, and, in its time, a very fine vessel, such as in those days were at intervals encountered along that main; sometimes superseded Acapulco treasure ships, or retired frigates of the Spanish king's navy, which, like superannuated Italian palaces, still, under a decline of masters, preserved signs of former state.

As the whaleboat drew more and more nigh, the cause of the peculiar pipe-clayed aspect of the stranger was seen in the slovenly neglect pervading her. The spars, ropes, and great part of the bulwarks looked woolly from long unacquaintance with the scraper, tar, and the brush. Her keel seemed laid, her ribs put together, and she launched, from Ezekiel's Valley of Dry Bones.

In the present business in which she was engaged, the ship's general model and rig appeared to have undergone no material change from their original warlike and Frois-sart pattern. However, no guns were seen.

The tops were large, and were railed about with what had once been octagonal network, all now in sad disrepair. These tops hung overhead like three ruinous aviaries, in one of which was seen perched, on a ratline, a white noddy, a strange fowl so called from its lethargic, somnambulistic character, being frequently caught by hand at sea. Battered and moldy, the castellated forecastle seemed some ancient turret long ago taken by assault, and then left to decay. Toward the stern, two high-raised quarter galleries —the balustrades here and there covered with dry tindery sea moss—opening out from the unoccupied state cabin, whose deadlights, for all the mild weather, were hermetically closed and calked—these tenantless balconies hung over the sea as if it were the grand Venetian canal. But the principal relic of faded grandeur was the ample oval of the shieldlike sternpiece, intricately carved with the arms of Castile and Leon, medallioned about by groups of mythological or symbolical devices, uppermost and central of which was a dark satyr in a mask holding his foot on the prostrate neck of a writhing figure, likewise masked.

Whether the ship had a figurehead, or only a plain beak, was not quite certain, owing to canvas wrapped about that part, either to protect it while undergoing a refurbishing, or else decently to hide its decay. Rudely painted or chalked, as in a sailor freak, along the forward side of a sort of pedestal below the canvas, was the sentence, SEGUID VUESTRO JEFE ("follow your leader"); while upon the tarnished headboards near by appeared, in stately capitals, once gilt, the ship's name SAN DOMINICK, each letter streakingly corroded with tricklings of copper-spike rust; while, like mourning weeds, dark festoons of sea grass slimily swept to and fro over the name with every hearselike roll of the hull.

As, at last, the boat was hooked from the bow along toward the gangway amidship, its keel, while yet some inches separated from the hull, harshly grated as on a sunken coral reef. It proved a huge bunch of conglobated barnacles adhering below the water to the side like a wen—a token of baffling airs and long calms passed somewhere in those seas.

Climbing the side, the visitor was at once surrounded by a clamorous throng of whites and blacks, but the latter outnumbering the former more than could have been expected, Negro transportation ship as the stranger in port was. But, in one language, and as with one voice, all poured out a common tale of suffering; in which the Negresses, of whom there were not a few, exceeded the others in their dolorous vehemence. The scurvy, together with the fever, had swept off a great part of their number, more especially the Spaniards. Off Cape Horn they had narrowly escaped shipwreck; then, for days together, they had lain tranced without wind; their provisions were low; their water next to none; their lips that moment were baked.

While Captain Delano was thus made the mark of all eager tongues, his one eager glance took in all faces, with every other object about him.

Always upon first boarding a large and populous ship at sea, especially a foreign one, with a nondescript crew such as Lascars or Manila men, the impression varies in a peculiar way from that produced by first entering a strange house with strange inmates in a strange land. Both house and ship—the one by its walls and blinds, the other by its high bulwarks like ramparts—hoard from view their interiors till the last moment, but in the case of the ship there is this addition: that the living spectacle it contains, upon its sudden and complete disclosure, has, in contrast with the blank ocean which zones it, something of the effect of enchantment. The ship seems unreal; these strange costumes, gestures, and faces but a shadowy tableau just emerged from the deep, which directly must receive back what it gave.

Perhaps it was some such influence, as above is attempted to be described, which, in Captain Delano's mind, heightened whatever, upon a staid scrutiny, might have seemed unusual, especially the conspicuous figures of four elderly grizzled Negroes, their heads like black, doddered willow tops, who, in venerable contrast to the tumult below them, were couched, sphinxlike, one on the starboard cathead, another on the larboard, and the remaining pair face to face on the opposite bulwarks above the main-chains. They each had bits of unstranded old junk in their hands, and, with a sort of stoical self-content, were picking the junk into oakum, a small heap of which lay by their sides. They accompanied the task with a continuous, low, monotonous chant, droning and druling away like so many gray-headed bagpipers playing a funeral march.

The quarter-deck rose into an ample elevated poop, upon the forward verge of which, lifted, like the oakum-pickers, some eight feet above the general throng, sat along in a row, separated by regular spaces, the cross-legged figures of six other blacks, each with a rusty hatchet in his hand, which, with a bit of brick and a rag, he was engaged like a scullion in scouring, while between each two was a small stack of hatchets, their rusted edges turned forward awaiting a like operation. Though occasionally the four oakum-pickers would briefly address some person or persons in the crowd below, yet the six hatchet-polishers neither spoke to others nor breathed a whisper among themselves, but sat intent upon their task, except at intervals, when, with the peculiar love in Negroes of uniting industry with pastime, two and two they sideways clashed their hatchets together, like cymbals, with a barbarous din. All six, unlike the generality, had the raw aspect of unsophisticated Africans.

But that first comprehensive glance which took in those ten figures, with scores less conspicuous, rested but an instant upon them, as, impatient of the hubbub of voices, the visitor turned in quest of whomsoever it might be that commanded the ship.

But as if not unwilling to let nature make known her own case among his suffering charge, or else in despair of restraining it for the time, the Spanish captain, a gentlemanly, reserved-looking, and rather young man to a stranger's eye, dressed with singular richness but bearing plain traces of recent sleepless cares and disquietudes, stood passively by, leaning against the mainmast, at one moment casting a dreary, spiritless look upon his excited people, at the next an unhappy glance toward his visitor. By his side stood a black of small stature, in whose rude face, as occasionally, like a shepherd's dog, he mutely turned it up into the Spaniard's, sorrow and affection were equally blended.

Struggling through the throng, the American advanced to the Spaniard, assuring him of his sympathies, and offering to render whatever assistance might be in his power. To which the Spaniard returned for the present but grave and ceremonious acknowledgments, his national formality dusked by the saturnine mood of ill-health.

But losing no time in mere compliments, Captain Delano, returning to the gangway, had his basket of fish brought up, and as the wind still continued light, so that some hours at least must elapse ere the ship could be brought to the anchorage, he bade his men return to the sealer and fetch back as much water as the whaleboat could carry, with whatever soft bread the steward might have, all the remaining pumpkins on board, with a box of sugar and a dozen of his private bottles of cider.

Not many minutes after the boat's pushing off, to the vexation of all, the wind entirely died away, and, the tide turning, began drifting back the ship helplessly seaward. But trusting this would not long last, Captain Delano sought, with good hopes, to cheer up the strangers, feeling no small satisfaction that, with persons in their condition, he could—thanks to his frequent voyages along the Spanish Main—converse with some freedom in their native tongue.

While left alone with them, he was not long in observing some things tending to heighten his first impressions; but surprise was lost in pity, both for the Spaniards and blacks, alike evidently reduced from scarcity of water and provisions, while long-continued suffering seemed to have brought out the less good-natured qualities of the Negroes, besides at the same time impairing the Spaniard's authority over them. But, under the circumstances, precisely this condition of things was to have been anticipated. In armies,

navies, cities, or families, in nature herself, nothing more
relaxes good order than misery. Still, Captain Delano was
not without the idea that had Benito Cereno been a man
of greater energy, misrule would hardly have come to the
present pass. But the debility, constitutional or induced by
hardships bodily and mental, of the Spanish captain was
too obvious to be overlooked. A prey to settled dejection,
as if long mocked with hope he would not now indulge it
even when it had ceased to be a mock, the prospect of that
day, or evening at furthest, lying at anchor, with plenty
of water for his people, and a brother captain to counsel
and befriend, seemed in no perceptible degree to encourage
him. His mind appeared unstrung, if not still more seriously affected. Shut up in these oaken walls, chained to
one dull round of command whose unconditionality cloyed
him, like some hypochondriac abbott he moved slowly
about, at times suddenly pausing, starting, or staring, biting his lip, biting his fingernail, flushing, paling, twitching
his beard, with other symptoms of an absent or moody
mind. This distempered spirit was lodged, as before hinted,
in as distempered a frame. He was rather tall, but seemed
never to have been robust, and now with nervous suffering
was almost worn to a skeleton. A tendency to some pul-
monary complaint appeared to have been lately confirmed.
His voice was like that of one with lungs half gone—
hoarsely suppressed, a husky whisper. No wonder that, as
in this state he tottered about, his private servant appre-
hensively followed him. Sometimes the Negro gave his
master his arm, or took his handkerchief out of his pocket
for him; performing these and similar offices with that
affectionate zeal which transmutes into something filial or
fraternal acts in themselves but menial, and which has
gained for the Negro the repute of making the most pleasing body servant in the world; one, too, whom a master
need be on no stiffly superior terms with, but may treat
with familiar trust—less a servant than a devoted companion.

Marking the noisy indocility of the blacks in general,
as well as what seemed the sullen inefficiency of the whites,
it was not without humane satisfaction that Captain
Delano witnessed the steady good conduct of Babo.

But the good conduct of Babo, hardly more than the

ill-behavior of others, seemed to withdraw the half-lunatic Don Benito from his cloudy languor. Not that such precisely was the impression made by the Spaniard on the mind of his visitor. The Spaniard's individual unrest was, for the present, but noted as a conspicuous feature in the ship's general affliction. Still, Captain Delano was not a little concerned at what he could not help taking for the time to be Don Benito's unfriendly indifference towards himself. The Spaniard's manner, too, conveyed a sort of sour and gloomy disdain, which he seemed at no pains to disguise. But this the American in charity ascribed to the harassing effects of sickness, since, in former instances, he had noted that there are peculiar natures on whom prolonged physical suffering seems to cancel every social instinct of kindness, as if, forced to black bread themselves, they deemed it but equity that each person coming nigh them should, indirectly, by some slight or affront, be made to partake of their fare.

But erelong Captain Delano bethought him that, indulgent as he was at the first in judging the Spaniard, he might not after all have exercised charity enough. At bottom it was Don Benito's reserve which displeased him, but the same reserve was shown towards all but his faithful personal attendant. Even the formal reports which, according to sea usage, were, at stated times, made to him by some petty underling, either a white, mulatto, or black, he hardly had patience enough to listen to without betraying contemptuous aversion. His manner upon such occasions was, in its degree, not unlike that which might be supposed to have been his imperial countryman's, Charles V, just previous to the anchoritish retirement of that monarch from the throne.

This splenetic disrelish of his place was evinced in almost every function pertaining to it. Proud as he was moody, he condescended to no personal mandate. Whatever special orders were necessary, their delivery was delegated to his body servant, who in turn transferred them to their ultimate destination, through runners, alert Spanish boys or slave boys, like pages or pilot fish within easy call continually hovering round Don Benito. So that to have beheld this undemonstrative invalid gliding about, apathetic and mute, no landsman could have dreamed that in him

was lodged a dictatorship beyond which, while at sea, there
was no earthly appeal.

Thus the Spaniard, regarded in his reserve, seemed the
involuntary victim of mental disorder. But, in fact, his
reserve might, in some degree, have proceeded from design. If so, then here was evinced the unhealthy climax
of that icy though conscientious policy more or less
adopted by all commanders of large ships, which, except
in signal emergencies, obliterates alike the manifestation
of sway with every trace of sociality, transforming the man
into a block, or rather into a loaded cannon, which, until
there is call for thunder, has nothing to say.

Viewing him in this light, it seemed but a natural token
of the perverse habit induced by a long course of such
hard self-restraint that, notwithstanding the present condition of his ship, the Spaniard should still persist in a
demeanor which, however harmless or, it may be, appropriate, in a well-appointed vessel, such as the *San Dominick*
might have been at the outset of the voyage, was anything
but judicious now. But the Spaniard, perhaps, thought that
it was with captains as with gods: reserve, under all events,
must still be their cue. But probably this appearance of
slumbering dominion might have been but an attempted
disguise to conscious imbecility—not deep policy, but
shallow device. But be all this as it might, whether
Don Benito's manner was designed or not, the more Captain Delano noted its pervading reserve, the less he felt
uneasiness at any particular manifestation of that reserve
towards himself.

Neither were his thoughts taken up by the captain alone.
Wonted to the quiet orderliness of the sealer's comfortable
family of a crew, the noisy confusion of the *San Dominick*'s
suffering host repeatedly challenged his eye. Some promi-
nent breaches, not only of discipline but of decency, were
observed. These Captain Delano could not but ascribe, in
the main, to the absence of those subordinate deck officers
to whom, along with higher duties, is intrusted what may
be styled the police department of a populous ship. True,
the old oakum-pickers appeared at times to act the part
of monitorial constables to their countrymen, the blacks,
but though occasionally succeeding in allaying trifling outbreaks now and then between man and man, they could

do little or nothing toward establishing general quiet. The *San Dominick* was in the condition of a transatlantic emigrant ship, among whose multitude of living freight are some individuals, doubtless, as little troublesome as crates and bales, but the friendly remonstrances of such with their ruder companions are of not so much avail as the unfriendly arm of the mate. What the *San Dominick* wanted was, what the emigrant ship has, stern superior officers. But on these decks not so much as a fourth mate was to be seen.

The visitor's curiosity was roused to learn the particulars of those mishaps which had brought about such absenteeism, with its consequences, because, though deriving some inkling of the voyage from the wails which at the first moment had greeted him, yet of the details no clear understanding had been had. The best account would, doubtless, be given by the captain. Yet at first the visitor was loath to ask it, unwilling to provoke some distant rebuff. But, plucking up courage, he at last accosted Don Benito, renewing the expression of his benevolent interest, adding that, did he (Captain Delano) but know the particulars of the ship's misfortunes, he would, perhaps be better able in the end to relieve them. Would Don Benito favor him with the whole story.

Don Benito faltered, then, like some somnambulist suddenly interfered with, vacantly stared at his visitor, and ended by looking down on the deck. He maintained this posture so long that Captain Delano, almost equally disconcerted, and involuntarily almost as rude, turned suddenly from him, walking forward to accost one of the Spanish seamen for the desired information. But he had hardly gone five paces, when, with a sort of eagerness, Don Benito invited him back, regretting his momentary absence of mind, and professing readiness to gratify him.

While most part of the story was being given, the two captains stood on the after part of the main deck, a privileged spot, no one being near but the servant.

"It is now a hundred and ninety days," began the Spaniard, in his husky whisper, "that this ship, well officered and well manned, with several cabin passengers—some fifty Spaniards in all—sailed from Buenos Ayres bound to Lima, with a general cargo, hardware, Para-

guay tea and the like—and," pointing forward, "that
parcel of Negroes, now not more than a hundred and
fifty, as you see, but then numbering over three hundred
souls. Off Cape Horn we had heavy gales. In one moment,
by night, three of my best officers, with fifteen sailors,
were lost, with the mainyard, the spar snapping under them
in the slings as they sought, with heavers, to beat down
the icy sail. To lighten the hull, the heavier sacks of
maté were thrown into the sea, with most of the water
pipes lashed on deck at the time. And this last necessity it
was, combined with the prolonged detentions afterwards
experienced, which eventually brought about our chief
causes of suffering. When——"

Here there was a sudden fainting attack of his cough,
brought on, no doubt, by his mental distress. His servant
sustained him, and, drawing a cordial from his pocket,
placed it to his lips. He a little revived. But, unwilling to
leave him unsupported while yet imperfectly restored, the
black with one arm still encircled his master, at the same
time keeping his eye fixed on his face, as if to watch for
the first sign of complete restoration, or relapse, as the
event might prove.

The Spaniard proceeded, but brokenly and obscurely,
as one in a dream.

—"Oh, my God! rather than pass through what I have,
with joy I would have hailed the most terrible gales;
but——"

His cough returned and with increased violence; this
subsiding, with reddened lips and closed eyes he fell
heavily against his supporter.

"His mind wanders. He was thinking of the plague
that followed the gales," plaintively sighed the servant;
"my poor, poor master!" wringing one hand, and with
the other wiping the mouth. "But be patient, señor," again
turning to Captain Delano, "these fits do not last long;
master will soon be himself."

Don Benito reviving, went on; but, as this portion of
the story was very brokenly delivered, the substance only
will here be set down.

It appeared that after the ship had been many days
tossed in storms off the Cape, the scurvy broke out, carrying off numbers of the whites and blacks. When at last

they had worked round into the Pacific, their spars and sails were so damaged, and so inadequately handled by the surviving mariners, most of whom were become invalids, that, unable to lay her northerly course by the wind, which was powerful, the unmanageable ship for successive days and nights was blown northwestward, where the breeze suddenly deserted her, in unknown waters to sultry calms. The absence of the water pipes now proved as fatal to life as before their presence had menaced it. Induced, or at least aggravated, by the more than scanty allowance of water, a malignant fever followed the scurvy, with the excessive heat of the lengthened calm making such short work of it as to sweep away, as by billows, whole families of the Africans, and a yet larger number, proportionally, of the Spaniards, including, by a luckless fatality, every remaining officer on board. Consequently, in the smart west winds eventually following the calm, the already rent sails, having to be simply dropped, not furled, at need, had been gradually reduced to the beggars' rags they were now. To procure substitutes for his lost sailors, as well as supplies of water and sails, the captain, at the earliest opportunity, had made for Baldivia, the southernmost civilized port of Chile and South America, but upon nearing the coast the thick weather had prevented him from so much as sighting that harbor. Since which period, almost without a crew, and almost without canvas and almost without water, and at intervals giving its added dead to the sea, the *San Dominick* had been battledored about by contrary winds, inveigled by currents, or grown weedy in calms. Like a man lost in woods, more than once she had doubled upon her own track.

"But throughout these calamities," huskily continued Don Benito, painfully turning in the half-embrace of his servant, "I have to thank those Negroes you see, who, though to your inexperienced eyes appearing unruly, have, indeed, conducted themselves with less of restlessness than even their owner could have thought possible under such circumstances."

Here he again fell faintly back. Again his mind wandered, but he rallied, and less obscurely proceeded.

"Yes, their owner was quite right in assuring me that no fetters would be needed with his blacks; so that, while, as is wont in his transportation, those Negroes have always remained upon deck—not thrust below, as in the Guineamen—they have, also, from the beginning, been freely permitted to range within given bounds at their pleasure."

Once more the faintness returned—his mind roved—but, recovering, he resumed:

"But it is Babo here to whom, under God, I owe not only my own preservation, but likewise to him, chiefly, the merit is due of pacifying his more ignorant brethren, when at intervals tempted to murmurings."

"Ah, master," sighed the black, bowing his face, "don't speak of me; Babo is nothing; what Babo has done was but duty."

"Faithful fellow!" cried Captain Delano. "Don Benito, I envy you such a friend; slave I cannot call him."

As master and man stood before him, the black upholding the white, Captain Delano could not but bethink him of the beauty of that relationship which could present such a spectacle of fidelity on the one hand and confidence on the other. The scene was heightened by the contrast in dress, denoting their relative positions. The Spaniard wore a loose Chile jacket of dark velvet; white smallclothes and stockings, with silver buckles at the knee and instep; a high-crowned sombrero of fine grass; a slender sword, silver mounted, hung from a knot in his sash—the last being an almost invariable adjunct, more for utility than ornament, of a South American gentleman's dress to this hour. Excepting when his occasional nervous contortions brought about disarray, there was a certain precision in his attire curiously at variance with the unsightly disorder around, especially in the belittered ghetto, forward of the mainmast, wholly occupied by the blacks.

The servant wore nothing but wide trousers, apparently, from their coarseness and patches, made out of some old topsail; they were clean, and confined at the waist by a bit of unstranded rope, which, with his composed, deprecatory air at times, made him look something like a begging friar of St. Francis.

However unsuitable for the time and place, at least in the blunt-thinking American's eyes, and however strangely surviving in the midst of all his afflictions, the toilette of

Don Benito might not, in fashion at least, have gone beyond the style of the day among South Americans of his
class. Though on the present voyage sailing from Buenos
Ayres, he had avowed himself a native and resident of
Chile, whose inhabitants had not so generally adopted the
plain coat and once plebeian pantaloons, but, with a becoming modification, adhered to their provincial costume,
picturesque as any in the world. Still, relatively to the pale
history of the voyage, and his own pale face, there seemed
something so incongruous in the Spaniard's apparel as
almost to suggest the image of an invalid courtier tottering
about London streets in the time of the plague.

The portion of the narrative which perhaps most excited
interest, as well as some surprise, considering the latitudes
in question, was the long calms spoken of, and more
particularly the ship's so long drifting about. Without communicating the opinion, of course, the American could not
but impute at least part of the detentions both to clumsy
seamanship and faulty navigation. Eying Don Benito's
small, yellow hands, he easily inferred that the young
captain had not got into command at the hawsehole, but
the cabin window; and if so, why wonder at incompetence,
in youth, sickness, and gentility united?

But, drowning criticism in compassion, after a fresh
repetition of his sympathies, Captain Delano, having heard
out his story, not only engaged, as in the first place, to
see Don Benito and his people supplied in their immediate
bodily needs, but, also now further promised to assist him
in procuring a large permanent supply of water, as well
as some sails and rigging; and, though it would involve no
small embarrassment to himself, yet he would spare three
of his best seamen for temporary deck officers, so that
without delay the ship might proceed to Conception, there
fully to refit for Lima, her destined port.

Such generosity was not without its effect, even upon
the invalid. His face lighted up; eager and hectic, he met
the honest glance of his visitor. With gratitude he seemed
overcome.

"This excitement is bad for master," whispered the
servant, taking his arm, and with soothing words gently
drawing him aside.

When Don Benito returned, the American was pained

to observe that his hopefulness, like the sudden kindling in his cheek, was but febrile and transient.

Erelong, with a joyless mien, looking up towards the poop, the host invited his guest to accompany him there, for the benefit of what little breath of wind might be stirring.

As, during the telling of the story, Captain Delano had once or twice started at the occasional cymbaling of the hatchet-polishers, wondering why such an interruption should be allowed, especially in that part of the ship, and in the ears of an invalid; and moreover, as the hatchets had anything but an attractive look, and the handlers of them still less so, it was, therefore, to tell the truth, not without some lurking reluctance, or even shrinking, it may be, that Captain Delano, with apparent complaisance, acquiesced in his host's invitation. The more so since, with an untimely caprice of punctilio, rendered distressing by his cadaverous aspect, Don Benito, with Castilian bows, solemnly insisted upon his guest's preceding him up the ladder leading to the elevation, where, one on each side of the last step, sat for armorial supporters and sentries two of the ominous file. Gingerly enough stepped good Captain Delano between them, and in the instant of leaving them behind, like one running the gantlet, he felt an apprehensive twitch in the calves of his legs.

But when, facing about, he saw the whole file, like so many organ-grinders, still stupidly intent on their work, unmindful of everything beside, he could not but smile at his late fidgety panic.

Presently, while standing with his host looking forward upon the decks below, he was struck by one of those instances of insubordination previously alluded to. Three black boys, with two Spanish boys, were sitting together on the hatches, scraping a rude wooden platter in which some scanty mess had recently been cooked. Suddenly one of the black boys, enraged at a word dropped by one of his white companions, seized a knife, and, though called to forbear by one of the oakum-pickers, struck the lad over the head, inflicting a gash from which blood flowed.

In amazement, Captain Delano inquired what this meant. To which the pale Don Benito dully muttered that it was merely the sport of the lad.

"Pretty serious sport, truly," rejoined Captain Delano. "Had such a thing happened on board the *Bachelor's Delight*, instant punishment would have followed."

At these words the Spaniard turned upon the American one of his sudden, staring, half-lunatic looks, then, relapsing into his torpor, answered, "Doubtless, doubtless, *señor*."

Is it, thought Captain Delano, that this hapless man is one of those paper captains I've known, who by policy wink at what by power they cannot put down? I know no sadder sight than a commander who has little of command but the name.

"I should think, Don Benito," he now said, glancing toward the oakum-picker who had sought to interfere with the boys, "that you would find it advantageous to keep all your blacks employed, especially the younger ones, no matter at what useless task, and no matter what happens to the ship. Why, even with my little band, I find such a course indispensable. I once kept a crew on my quarter-deck thrumming mats for my cabin, when, for three days, I had given up my ship—mats, men, and all—for a speedy loss, owing to the violence of a gale, in which we could do nothing but helplessly drive before it."

"Doubtless, doubtless," muttered Don Benito.

"But," continued Captain Delano, again glancing upon the oakum-pickers and then at the hatchet-polishers, near by, "I see you keep some, at least, of your host employed."

"Yes," was again the vacant response.

"Those old men there, shaking their pows from their pulpits," continued Captain Delano, pointing to the oakum-pickers, "seem to act the part of old dominies to the rest, little heeded as their admonitions are at times. Is this voluntary on their part, Don Benito, or have you appointed them shepherds to your flock of black sheep?"

"What posts they fill, I appointed them," rejoined the Spaniard, in an acrid tone, as if resenting some supposed satiric reflection.

"And these others, these Ashantee conjurers here," continued Captain Delano, rather uneasily eying the brandished steel of the hatchet-polishers, where in spots, it had been brought to a shine, "this seems a curious business they are at, Don Benito?"

"In the gales we met," answered the Spaniard, "what of our general cargo was not thrown overboard was much damaged by the brine. Since coming into calm weather, I have had several cases of knives and hatchets daily brought up for overhauling and cleaning."

"A prudent idea, Don Benito. You are part owner of ship and cargo, I presume; but none of the slaves, perhaps?"

"I am owner of all you see," impatiently returned Don Benito, "except the main company of blacks, who belonged to my late friend, Alexandro Aranda."

As he mentioned this name, his air was heartbroken; his knees shook; his servant supported him.

Thinking he divined the cause of such unusual emotion, to confirm his surmise Captain Delano after a pause said: "And may I ask, Don Benito, whether—since awhile ago you spoke of some cabin passengers—the friend, whose loss so afflicts you, at the outset of the voyage accompanied his blacks?"

"Yes."

"But died of the fever?"

"Died of the fever. Oh, could I but——"

Again quivering, the Spaniard paused.

"Pardon me," said Captain Delano, lowly, "but I think that, by a sympathetic experience, I conjecture, Don Benito, what it is that gives the keener edge to your grief. It was once my hard fortune to lose, at sea, a dear friend, my own brother, then supercargo. Assured of the welfare of his spirit, its departure I could have borne like a man, but that honest eye, that honest hand—both of which had so often met mine—and that warm heart—all, all—like scraps to the dogs—to throw all to the sharks! It was then I vowed never to have for fellow voyager a man I loved, unless, unbeknown to him, I had provided every requisite, in case of a fatality, for embalming his mortal part for interment on shore. Were your friend's remains now on board this ship, Don Benito, not thus strangely would the mention of his name affect you."

"On board this ship?" echoed the Spaniard. Then, with horrified gestures, as directed against some specter, he unconsciously fell into the ready arms of his attendant, who, with a silent appeal toward Captain Delano, seemed beseeching him not again to broach a theme so unspeakably distressing to his master.

This poor fellow now, thought the pained American, is the victim of that sad superstition which associates goblins with the deserted body of man, as ghosts with an abandoned house. How unlike are we made! What to me, in like case, would have been a solemn satisfaction, the bare suggestion, even, terrifies the Spaniard into this trance. Poor Alexandro Aranda! what would you say could you here see your friend—who on former voyages, when you for months were left behind, has, I dare say, often longed and longed for one peep at you—not transported with terror at the least thought of having you anyway nigh him.

At this moment, with a dreary graveyard toll betokening a flaw, the ship's forecastle bell, smote by one of the grizzled oakum-pickers, proclaimed ten o'clock through the leaden calm, when Captain Delano's attention was caught by the moving figure of a gigantic black emerging from the general crowd below and slowly advancing towards the elevated poop. An iron collar was about his neck, from which depended a chain thrice wound round his body, the terminating links padlocked together at a broad band of iron, his girdle.

"How like a mute Atufal moves," murmured the servant.

The black mounted the steps of the poop, and, like a brave prisoner brought up to receive sentence, stood in unquailing muteness before Don Benito, now recovered from his attack.

At the first glimpse of his approach, Don Benito had started; a resentful shadow swept over his face, and, as with the sudden memory of bootless rage, his white lips glued together.

This is some mulish mutineer, thought Captain Delano, surveying, not without a mixture of admiration, the colossal form of the Negro.

"See, he waits your question, master," said the servant.

Thus reminded, Don Benito, nervously averting his glance as if shunning, by anticipation, some rebellious response, in a disconcerted voice, thus spoke:

"Atufal, will you ask my pardon now?"

The black was silent.

"Again, master," murmured the servant, with bitter upbraiding eying his countryman; "Again, master; he will bend to master yet."

"Answer," said Don Benito, still averting his glance, "say but the one word, *pardon,* and your chains shall be off."

Upon this, the black, slowly raising both arms, let them lifelessly fall, his links clanking, his head bowed; as much as to say, "No, I am content."

"Go," said Don Benito, with inkept and unknown emotion.

Deliberately as he had come, the black obeyed.

"Excuse me, Don Benito," said Captain Delano, "but this scene surprises me; what means it, pray?"

"It means that that Negro alone, of all the band, has given me peculiar cause of offense. I have put him in chains; I——"

Here he paused; his hand to his head, as if there were a swimming there, or a sudden bewilderment of memory had come over him; but meeting his servant's kindly glance seemed reassured, and proceeded:

"I could not scourge such a form. But I told him he must ask my pardon. As yet he has not. At my command, every two hours he stands before me."

"And how long has this been?"

"Some sixty days."

"And obedient in all else? And respectful?"

"Yes."

"Upon my conscience, then," exclaimed Captain Delano, impulsively, "he has a royal spirit in him, this fellow."

"He may have some right to it," bitterly returned Don Benito, "he says he was king in his own land."

"Yes," said the servant, entering a word, "those slits in Atufal's ears once held wedges of gold; but poor Babo here, in his own land, was only a poor slave; a black man's slave was Babo, who now is the white's."

Somewhat annoyed by these conversational familiarities, Captain Delano turned curiously upon the attendant, then glanced inquiringly at his master; but, as if long wonted to these little informalities, neither master nor man seemed to understand him.

"What, pray, was Atufal's offense, Don Benito?" asked

Captain Delano; "if it was not something very serious, take a fool's advice, and, in view of his general docility, as well as in some natural respect for his spirit, remit him his penalty."

"No, no, master never will do that," here murmured the servant to himself, "proud Atufal must first ask master's pardon. The slave there carries the padlock, but master here carries the key."

His attention thus directed, Captain Delano now noticed for the first that, suspended by a slender silken cord from Don Benito's neck, hung a key. At once, from the servant's muttered syllables, divining the key's purpose, he smiled and said: "So, Don Benito—padlock and key —significant symbols, truly."

Biting his lip, Don Benito faltered.

Though the remark of Captain Delano, a man of such native simplicity as to be incapable of satire or irony, had been dropped in playful allusion to the Spaniard's singularly evidenced lordship over the black, yet the hypochondriac seemed some way to have taken it as a malicious reflection upon his confessed inability thus far to break down, at least on a verbal summons, the entrenched will of the slave. Deploring this supposed misconception, yet despairing of correcting it, Captain Delano shifted the subject; but finding his companion more than ever withdrawn, as if still sourly digesting the lees of the presumed affront above mentioned, by and by Captain Delano likewise became less talkative, oppressed, against his own will, by what seemed the secret vindictiveness of the morbidly sensitive Spaniard. But the good sailor, himself of a quite contrary disposition, refrained on his part alike from the appearance as from the feeling of resentment, and if silent, was only so from contagion.

Presently the Spaniard, assisted by his servant, somewhat discourteously crossed over from his guest, a procedure which, sensibly enough, might have been allowed to pass for idle caprice of ill-humor had not master and man, lingering round the corner of the elevated skylight, began whispering together in low voices. This was unpleasing. And more: the moody air of the Spaniard, which at times had not been without a sort of valetudinarian stateliness, now seemed anything but dignified, while the menial familiarity of the servant lost its original charm of simple-hearted attachment.

In his embarrassment, the visitor turned his face to the other side of the ship. By so doing, his glance accidentally fell on a young Spanish sailor, a coil of rope in his hand, just stepped from the deck to the first round of the mizzen rigging. Perhaps the man would not have been particularly noticed were it not that, during his ascent to one of the yards, he, with a sort of covert intentness, kept his eye fixed on Captain Delano, from whom, presently, it passed, as if by a natural sequence, to the two whisperers.

His own attention thus redirected to that quarter, Captain Delano gave a slight start. From something in Don Benito's manner just then, it seemed as if the visitor had, at least partly, been the subject of the withdrawn consultation going on—a conjecture as little agreeable to the guest as it was flattering to the host.

The singular alternations of courtesy and ill-breeding in the Spanish captain were unaccountable, except on one of two suppositions—innocent lunacy, or wicked imposture.

But the first idea, though it might naturally have occurred to an indifferent observer, and, in some respect, had not hitherto been wholly a stranger to Captain Delano's mind, yet, now that, in an incipient way, he began to regard the stranger's conduct something in the light of an intentional affront, of course the idea of lunacy was virtually vacated. But if not a lunatic, what then? Under the circumstances, would a gentleman, nay, any honest boor, act the part now acted by his host? The man was an impostor. Some low-born adventurer, masquerading as an oceanic grandee, yet so ignorant of the first requisites of mere gentlemanhood as to be betrayed into the present remarkable indecorum. That strange ceremoniousness, too, at other times evinced, seemed not uncharacteristic of one playing a part above his real level. Benito Cereno—Don Benito Cereno—a sounding name. One, too, at that period, not unknown, in the surname, to supercargoes and sea captains trading along the Spanish Main, as belonging to one of the most enterprising and extensive mercantile families in all those provinces, several members of it having titles; a sort of Castilian Rothschild, with a noble brother, or cousin, in every great trading town of South

America. The alleged Don Benito was in early manhood, about twenty-nine or thirty. To assume a sort of roving cadetship in the maritime affairs of such a house, what more likely scheme for a young knave of talent and spirit? But the Spaniard was a pale invalid. Never mind. For even to the degree of simulating mortal disease, the craft of some tricksters had been known to attain. To think that, under the aspect of infantile weakness, the most savage energies might be couched—those velvets of the Spaniard but the silky paw to his fangs.

From no train of thought did these fancies come; not from within, but from without; suddenly, too, and in one throng, like hoarfrost, yet as soon to vanish, as the mild sun of Captain Delano's good nature regained its meridian.

Glancing over once more towards his host—whose side face, revealed above the skylight, was now turned towards him—he was struck by the profile, whose clearness of cut was refined by the thinness incident to ill-health, as well as ennobled about the chin by the beard. Away with suspicion. He was a true offshoot of a true hidalgo Cereno.

Relieved by these and other better thoughts, the visitor, lightly humming a tune, now began indifferently pacing the poop, so as not to betray to Don Benito that he had at all mistrusted incivility, much less duplicity; for such mistrust would yet be proved illusory, and by the event, though, for the present, the circumstance which had provoked that distrust remained unexplained. But when that little mystery should have been cleared up, Captain Delano thought he might extremely regret it did he allow Don Benito to become aware that he had indulged in ungenerous surmises. In short, to the Spaniard's black-letter text, it was best, for a while, to leave open margin.

Presently, his pale face twitching and overcast, the Spaniard, still supported by his attendant, moved over towards his guest, when, with even more than his usual embarrassment, and a strange sort of intriguing intonation in his husky whisper, the following conversation began:

"*Señor*, may I ask how long you have lain at this isle?"

"Oh, but a day or two, Don Benito."

"And from what port are you last?"

"Canton."

"And there, *señor*, you exchanged your sealskins for teas and silks, I think you said?"

"Yes. Silks, mostly."

"And the balance you took in specie, perhaps?"

Captain Delano, fidgeting a little, answered, "Yes; some silver; not a very great deal, though."

"Ah—well. May I ask how many men have you, *señor?*"

Captain Delano slightly started, but answered, "About five-and-twenty, all told."

"And at present, *señor*, all on board, I suppose?"

"All on board, Don Benito," replied the Captain, now with satisfaction.

"And will be tonight, *señor?*"

At this last question, following so many pertinacious ones, for the soul of him Captain Delano could not but look very earnestly at the questioner, who, instead of meeting the glance, with every token of craven discompo-sure dropped his eyes to the deck; presenting an unworthy contrast to his servant, who, just then, was kneeling at his feet, adjusting a loose shoe buckle, his disengaged face meantime, with humble curiosity, turned openly up into his master's downcast one.

The Spaniard, still with a guilty shuffle, repeated his question:

"And—and will be tonight, *señor?*"

"Yes, for aught I know," returned Captain Delano—"but nay," rallying himself into fearless truth, "some of them talked of going off on another fishing party about midnight."

"Your ships generally go—go more or less armed, I believe, *señor?*"

"Oh, a six-pounder or two, in case of emergency," was the intrepidly indifferent reply, "with a small stock of muskets, sealing spears, and cutlasses, you know."

As he thus responded, Captain Delano again glanced at Don Benito, but the latter's eyes were averted, while, abruptly and awkwardly shifting the subject, he made some peevish allusion to the calm, and then, without apol-ogy, once more, with his attendant, withdrew to the opposite bulwarks, where the whispering was resumed.

At this moment, and ere Captain Delano could cast a cool thought upon what had just passed, the young Spanish sailor before mentioned was seen descending from the rigging. In act of stooping over to spring inboard to the deck, his voluminous, unconfined frock, or shirt, of coarse woolen, much spotted with tar, opened out far down the chest, revealing a soiled undergarment of what seemed the finest linen, edged, about the neck, with a narrow blue ribbon, sadly faded and worn. At this moment the young sailor's eye was again fixed on the whisperers, and Captain Delano thought he observed a lurking significance in it, as if silent signs, of some Freemason sort, had that instant been interchanged.

This once more impelled his own glance in the direction of Don Benito, and, as before, he could not but infer that himself formed the subject of the conference. He paused. The sound of the hatchet-polishing fell on his ears. He cast another swift side look at the two. They had the air of conspirators. In connection with the late questionings, and the incident of the young sailor, these things now begat such return of involuntary suspicion that the singular guilelessness of the American could not endure it. Plucking up a gay and humorous expression, he crossed over to the two rapidly, saying: "Ha, Don Benito, your black here seems high in your trust, a sort of privy councilor, in fact."

Upon this, the servant looked up with a good-natured grin, but the master started as from a venomous bite. It was a moment or two before the Spaniard sufficiently recovered himself to reply; which he did, at last, with cold constraint: "Yes, *señor*, I have trust in Babo."

Here Babo, changing his previous grin of mere animal humor into an intelligent smile, not ungratefully eyed his master.

Finding that the Spaniard now stood silent and reserved, as if involuntarily, or purposely giving hint that his guest's proximity was inconvenient just then, Captain Delano, unwilling to appear uncivil even to incivility itself, made some trivial remark and moved off, again and again turning over in his mind the mysterious demeanor of Don Benito Cereno.

He had descended from the poop, and, wrapped in thought, was passing near a dark hatchway leading down into the steerage, when, perceiving motion there, he looked to see what moved. The same instant there was a sparkle

in the shadowy hatchway and he saw one of the Spanish
sailors, prowling there, hurriedly placing his hand in the
bosom of his frock, as if hiding something. Before the man
could have been certain who it was that was passing, he
slunk below out of sight. But enough was seen of him to
make it sure that he was the same young sailor before
noticed in the rigging.

What was that which so sparkled? thought Captain
Delano. It was no lamp—no match—no live coal. Could
it have been a jewel? But how come sailors with jewels?—
or with silk-trimmed undershirts either? Has he been
robbing the trunks of the dead cabin passengers? But if so
he would hardly wear one of the stolen articles on board
ship here. Ah, ah—if, now, that was indeed, a secret sign
I saw passing between this suspicious fellow and his captain awhile since; if I could only be certain that, in my
uneasiness, my senses did not deceive me, then——

Here, passing from one suspicious thing to another, his
mind revolved the strange questions put to him concerning
his ship.

By a curious coincidence, as each point was recalled,
the black wizards of Ashantee would strike up with their
hatchets, as in ominous comment on the white stranger's
thoughts. Pressed by such enigmas and portents, it would
have been almost against nature had not, even into the
least distrustful heart, some ugly misgivings obtruded.

Observing the ship, now helplessly fallen into a current,
with enchanted sails drifting with increased rapidity seaward, and noting that, from a lately intercepted projection
of the land, the sealer was hidden, the stout mariner began
to quake at thoughts which he barely durst confess to
himself. Above all, he began to feel a ghostly dread of
Don Benito. And yet, when he roused himself, dilated his
chest, felt himself strong on his legs, and coolly considered
it—what did all these phantoms amount to?

Had the Spaniard any sinister scheme, it must have
reference not so much to him (Captain Delano) as to his
ship (the *Bachelor's Delight*). Hence the present drifting
away of the one ship from the other, instead of favoring
any such possible scheme, was, for the time at least,
opposed to it. Clearly any suspicion combining such contradictions must need be delusive. Beside, was it not

absurd to think of a vessel in distress—a vessel by sickness
almost dismanned of her crew—a vessel whose inmates
were parched for water—was it not a thousand times
absurd that such a craft should, at present, be of a piratical
character; or her commander, either for himself or those
under him, cherish any desire but for speedy relief and
refreshment? But, then, might not general distress, and
thirst in particular, be affected? And might not that same
undiminished Spanish crew, alleged to have perished off
to a remnant, be at that very moment lurking in the hold?
On heartbroken pretense of entreating a cup of cold water,
fiends in human form had got into lonely dwellings, nor
retired until a dark deed had been done. And among the
Malay pirates it was no unusual thing to lure ships after
them into their treacherous harbors, or entice boarders
from a declared enemy at sea, by the spectacle of thinly
manned or vacant decks, beneath which prowled a hundred
spears with yellow arms ready to upthrust them through
the mats. Not that Captain Delano had entirely credited
such things. He had heard of them—and now, as stories,
they recurred. The present destination of the ship was the
anchorage. There she would be near his own vessel. Upon
gaining that vicinity, might not the *San Dominick,* like a
slumbering volcano, suddenly let loose energies now hid?

He recalled the Spaniard's manner while telling his
story. There was a gloomy hesitancy and subterfuge about
it. It was just the manner of one making up his tale for
evil purposes, as he goes. But if that story was not true,
what was the truth? That the ship had unlawfully come
into the Spaniard's possession? But in many of its details,
especially in reference to the more calamitous parts, such
as the fatalities among the seamen, the consequent prolonged beating about, the past sufferings from obstinate
calms and still continued suffering from thirst; in all these
points, as well as others, Don Benito's story had corrobo-
rated not only the wailing ejaculations of the indiscriminate
multitude, white and black, but likewise—what seemed
impossible to be counterfeit—by the very expression and
play of every human feature which Captain Delano saw.
If Don Benito's story was throughout an invention, then
every soul on board, down to the youngest Negress, was
his carefully drilled recruit in the plot: an incredible in-

ference. And yet, if there was ground for mistrusting his veracity, that inference was a legitimate one.

But those questions of the Spaniard. There, indeed, one might pause. Did they not seem put with much the same object with which the burglar or assassin, by daytime, reconnoiters the walls of a house? But, with ill purposes to solicit such information openly of the chief person endangered, and so, in effect, setting him on his guard—how unlikely a procedure was that? Absurd, then, to suppose that those questions had been prompted by evil designs. Thus, the same conduct which in this instance had raised the alarm, served to dispel it. In short, scarce any suspicion or uneasiness, however apparently reasonable at the time, which was not now with equal apparent reason dismissed.

At last he began to laugh at his former forebodings, and laugh at the strange ship for, in its aspect, someway siding with them, as it were; and laugh, too, at the odd-looking blacks, particularly those old scissors-grinders, the Ashantees; and those bed-ridden old knitting women, the oakum-pickers; and almost at the dark Spaniard himself, the central hobgoblin of all.

For the rest, whatever in a serious way seemed enigmatical was now good-naturedly explained away by the thought that, for the most part, the poor invalid scarcely knew what he was about; either sulking in black vapors, or putting idle questions without sense or object. Evidently, for the present the man was not fit to be intrusted with the ship. On some benevolent plea withdrawing the command from him, Captain Delano would yet have to send her to Conception, in charge of his second mate, a worthy person and good navigator—a plan not more convenient for the *San Dominick* than for Don Benito; for, relieved from all anxiety, keeping wholly to his cabin, the sick man, under the good nursing of his servant, would, probably, by the end of the passage, be in a measure restored to health, and with that he should also be restored to authority.

Such were the American's thoughts. They were tranquilizing. There was a difference between the idea of Don Benito's darkly preordaining Captain Delano's fate and Captain Delano's lightly arranging Don Benito's. Nevertheless, it was not without something of relief that the good seaman presently perceived his whaleboat in the distance.

Its absence had been prolonged by unexpected detention at the sealer's side, as well as its returning trip lengthened by the continual recession of the goal.

The advancing speck was observed by the blacks. Their shouts attracted the attention of Don Benito, who, with a return of courtesy approaching Captain Delano, expressed satisfaction at the coming of some supplies, slight and temporary as they must necessarily prove.

Captain Delano responded, but while doing so, his attention was drawn to something passing on the deck below: among the crowd climbing the landward bulwarks, anxiously watching the coming boat, two blacks, to all appearances accidentally incommoded by one of the sailors, violently pushed him aside, which the sailor someway resenting, they dashed him to the deck, despite the earnest cries of the oakum-pickers.

"Don Benito," said Captain Delano quickly, "do you see what is going on there? Look!"

But, seized by his cough, the Spaniard staggered, with both hands to his face, on the point of falling. Captain Delano would have supported him, but the servant was more alert, who, with one hand sustaining his master, with the other applied the cordial. Don Benito restored, the black withdrew his support, slipping aside a little, but dutifully remaining within call of a whisper. Such discretion was here evinced as quite wiped away, in the visitor's eyes, any blemish of impropriety which might have attached to the attendant from the indecorous conferences before mentioned, showing, too, that if the servant were to blame it might be more the master's fault than his own, since, when left to himself, he could conduct thus well.

His glance called away from the spectacle of disorder to the more pleasing one before him, Captain Delano could not avoid again congratulating his host upon possessing such a servant, who, though perhaps a little too forward now and then, must upon the whole be invaluable to one in the invalid's situation.

"Tell me, Don Benito," he added, with a smile—"I should like to have your man here myself—what will you take for him? Would fifty doubloons be any object?"

"Master wouldn't part with Babo for a thousand doubloons," murmured the black, overhearing the offer, and

taking it in earnest, and, with the strange vanity of a
faithful slave appreciated by his master, scorning to hear
so paltry a valuation put upon him by a stranger. But
Don Benito, apparently hardly yet completely restored,
and again interrupted by his cough, made but some broken
reply.

Soon his physical distress became so great, affecting his
mind, too, apparently, that, as if to screen the sad spectacle, the servant gently conducted his master below.

Left to himself, the American, to while away the time
till his boat should arrive, would have pleasantly accosted
some one of the few Spanish seamen he saw, but recalling
something that Don Benito had said touching their ill
conduct, he refrained, as a shipmaster indisposed to countenance cowardice or unfaithfulness in seamen.

While, with these thoughts, standing with eye directed
forward towards that handful of sailors, suddenly he
thought that one or two of them returned the glance and
with a sort of meaning. He rubbed his eyes and looked
again, but again seemed to see the same thing. Under a
new form, but more obscure than any previous one, the
old suspicions recurred, but, in the absence of Don Benito,
with less of panic than before. Despite the bad account
given of the sailors, Captain Delano resolved forthwith to
accost one of them. Descending the poop, he made his
way through the blacks, his movement drawing a queer cry
from the oakum-pickers, prompted by whom, the Negroes,
twitching each other aside, divided before him, but, as if
curious to see what was the object of this deliberate visit
to their ghetto, closing in behind in tolerable order, followed the white stranger up. His progress thus proclaimed
as by mounted kings-at-arms, and escorted as by a Kaffir
guard of honor, Captain Delano, assuming a good-
humored, off-handed air, continued to advance; now and
then saying a blithe word to the Negroes, and his eye
curiously surveying the white faces, here and there sparsely
mixed in with the blacks, like stray white pawns ven-
turously involved in the ranks of the chessmen opposed.

While thinking which of them to select for his purpose,
he chanced to observe a sailor seated on the deck engaged in tarring the strap of a large block, a circle of
blacks squatted round him inquisitively eying the process.

The mean employment of the man was in contrast with something superior in his figure. His hand, black with continually thrusting it into the tarpot held for him by a Negro, seemed not naturally allied to his face, a face which would have been a very fine one but for its haggardness. Whether this haggardness had aught to do with criminality could not be determined, since, as intense heat and cold, though unlike, produce like sensations, so innocence and guilt, when, through casual association with mental pain stamping any visible impress, use one seal—a hacked one.

Not again that this reflection occurred to Captain Delano at the time, charitable man as he was. Rather another idea. Because observing so singular a haggardness combined with a dark eye, averted as in trouble and shame, and then again recalling Don Benito's confessed ill opinion of his crew, insensible, he was operated upon by certain general notions which, while disconnecting pain and abashment from virtue, invariably link them with vice.

If, indeed, there be any wickedness on board this ship, thought Captain Delano, be sure that man there has fouled his hand in it, even as now he fouls it in the pitch. I don't like to accost him. I will speak to this other, this old Jack here on the windlass.

He advanced to an old Barcelona tar, in ragged red breeches and dirty nightcap, cheeks trenched and bronzed, whiskers dense as thorn hedges. Seated between two sleepy-looking Africans, this mariner, like his younger shipmate, was employed upon some rigging—splicing a cable—the sleepy-looking blacks performing the inferior function of holding the outer parts of the ropes for him.

Upon Captain Delano's approach, the man at once hung his head below its previous level; the one necessary for business. It appeared as if he desired to be thought absorbed with more than common fidelity in his task. Being addressed, he glanced up, but with what seemed a furtive, diffident air, which sat strangely enough on his weather-beaten visage, much as if a grizzly bear, instead of growling and biting, should simper and cast sheep's eyes. He was asked several questions concerning the voyage—questions purposely referring to several particulars in Don Benito's narrative, not previously corrobo-

rated by those impulsive cries greeting the visitor on
first coming on board. The questions were briefly answered, confirming all that remained to be confirmed of
the story. The Negroes about the windlass joined in with
the old sailor, but, as they became talkative, he by degrees
became mute, and at length quite glum, seemed morosely
unwilling to answer more questions, and yet, all the while,
this ursine air was somehow mixed with his sheepish one.

Despairing of getting into unembarrassed talk with such
a centaur, Captain Delano, after glancing round for a
more promising countenance but seeing none, spoke pleasantly to the blacks to make way for him, and so, amid
various grins and grimaces, returned to the poop, feeling
a little strange at first, he could hardly tell why, but upon
the whole with regained confidence in Benito Cereno.

How plainly, thought he, did that old whiskerando
yonder betray a consciousness of ill desert. No doubt when
he saw me coming he dreaded lest I, apprised by his captain
of the crew's general misbehavior, came with sharp words
for him, and so down with his head. And yet—and yet,
now that I think of it, that very old fellow, if I err not,
was one of those who seemed so earnestly eying me here
awhile since. Ah, these currents spin one's head round almost as much as they do the ship. Ha, there now's a
pleasant sort of sunny sight; quite sociable, too.

His attention had been drawn to a slumbering Negress,
partly disclosed through the lacework of some rigging,
lying, with youthful limbs carelessly disposed, under the
lee of the bulwarks, like a doe in the shade of a woodland
rock. Sprawling at her lapped breasts was her wide-awake
fawn, stark naked, its black little body half lifted from
the deck, crosswise with its dam's; its hands, like two
paws, clambering upon her; its mouth and nose ineffectually rooting to get at the mark; and meantime giving
a vexatious half-grunt, blending with the composed snore
of the Negress.

The uncommon vigor of the child at length roused the
mother. She started up, at a distance facing Captain
Delano. But as if not at all concerned at the attitude in
which she had been caught, delightedly she caught the
child up, with maternal transports, covering it with kisses.

There's naked nature, now, pure tenderness and love, thought Captain Delano, well pleased.

This incident prompted him to remark the other Negresses more particularly than before. He was gratified with their manners: like most uncivilized women, they seemed at once tender of heart and tough of constitution, equally ready to die for their infants or fight for them. Unsophisticated as leopardesses, loving as doves. Ah! thought Captain Delano, these, perhaps, are some of the very women whom Ledyard saw in Africa, and gave such a noble account of.

These natural sights somehow insensibly deepened his confidence and ease. At last he looked to see how his boat was getting on, but it was still pretty remote. He turned to see if Don Benito had returned, but he had not.

To change the scene, as well as to please himself with a leisurely observation of the coming boat, stepping over into the mizzen-chains, he clambered his way into the starboard quarter-gallery—one of those abandoned Venetian-looking water balconies previously mentioned—retreats cut off from the deck. As his foot pressed the half-damp, half-dry sea mosses matting the place, and a chance phantom cat's-paw—an islet of breeze, unheralded, unfollowed—as this ghostly cat's-paw came fanning his cheek; as his glance fell upon the row of small, round, deadlights—all closed liked coppered eyes of the coffined —and the state-cabin door, once connecting with the gallery, even as the deadlights had once looked out upon it, but now calked fast like a sarcophagus lid; and to a purple-black, tarred-over, panel, threshold, and post; and he bethought him of the time when that state cabin and this state balcony had heard the voices of the Spanish king's officers, and the forms of the Lima viceroy's daughters had perhaps leaned where he stood—as these and other images flitted through his mind as the cat's-paw through the calm, gradually he felt rising a dreamy inquietude, like that of one who alone on the prairie feels unrest from the repose of the noon.

He leaned against the carved balustrade, again looking off toward his boat, but found his eye falling upon the ribbon grass, trailing along the ship's water line, straight as a border of green box, and parterres of seaweed, broad

ovals and crescents, floating nigh and far, with what
seemed long formal alleys between, crossing the terraces
of swells, and sweeping round as if leading to the grottoes
below. And overhanging all was the balustrade by his arm,
which, partly stained with pitch and partly embossed with
moss, seemed the charred ruin of some summerhouse in
a grand garden long running to waste.

Trying to break one charm, he was but becharmed
anew. Though upon the wide sea, he seemed in some far
inland country, prisoner in some deserted château, left to
stare at empty grounds and peer out at vague roads where
never wagon or wayfarer passed.

But these enchantments were a little disenchanted as
his eye fell on the corroded mainchains. Of an ancient
style, massy and rusty in link, shackle, and bolt, they
seemed even more fit for the ship's present business than
the one for which she had been built.

Presently he thought something moved nigh the chains.
He rubbed his eyes, and looked hard. Groves of rigging
were about the chains; and there, peering from behind
a great stay, like an Indian from behind a hemlock, a
Spanish sailor, a marlinespike in his hand, was seen, who
made what seemed an imperfect gesture towards the
balcony, but immediately, as if alarmed by some advancing
step along the deck within, vanished into the recesses of
the hempen forest like a poacher.

What meant this? Something the man had sought to
communicate, unbeknown to anyone, even to his captain.
Did the secret involve aught unfavorable to his captain?
Were those previous misgivings of Captain Delano's about
to be verified? Or, in his haunted mood at the moment,
had some random, unintentional motion of the man, while
busy with the stay as if repairing it, been mistaken for a
significant beckoning?

Not unbewildered, again he gazed off for his boat. But
it was temporarily hidden by a rocky spur of the isle. As
with some eagerness he bent forward, watching for the first
shooting view of its beak, the balustrade gave way before
him like charcoal. Had he not clutched an outreaching rope
he would have fallen into the sea. The crash, though
feeble, and the fall, though hollow, of the rotten fragments,
must have been overheard. He glanced up. With sober

curiosity peering down upon him was one of the old oakum-pickers, slipped from his perch to an outside boom, while below the old Negro, and, invisible to him, reconnoitering from a porthole like a fox from the mouth of its den, crouched the Spanish sailor again. From something suddenly suggested by the man's air, the mad idea now darted into Captain Delano's mind that Don Benito's plea of indisposition, in withdrawing below, was but a pretense: that he was engaged there maturing his plot, of which the sailor, by some means gaining an inkling, had a mind to warn the stranger against, incited, it may be, by gratitude for a kind word on first boarding the ship. Was it from foreseeing some possible interference like this that Don Benito had, beforehand, given such a bad character of his sailors, while praising the Negroes, though, indeed, the former seemed as docile as the latter the contrary? The whites, too, by nature, were the shrewder race. A man with some evil design, would he not be likely to speak well of that stupidity which was blind to his depravity, and malign that intelligence from which it might not be hidden? Not unlikely, perhaps. But if the whites had dark secrets concerning Don Benito, could then Don Benito be any way in complicity with the blacks? But they were too stupid. Besides, who ever heard of a white so far a renegade as to apostatize from his very species almost, by leaguing in against it with Negroes? These difficulties recalled former ones. Lost in their mazes, Captain Delano, who had now regained the deck, was uneasily advancing along it when he observed a new face; an aged sailor seated cross-legged near the main hatchway. His skin was shrunk up with wrinkles like a pelican's empty pouch, his hair frosted, his countenance grave and composed. His hands were full of ropes, which he was working into a large knot. Some blacks were about him obligingly dipping the strands for him, here and there, as the exigencies of the operation demanded.

Captain Delano crossed over to him and stood in silence surveying the knot, his mind, by a not uncongenial transition, passing from its own entanglements to those of the hemp. For intricacy, such a knot he had never seen in an American ship, nor indeed any other. The old man looked like an Egyptian priest making Gordian knots for the temple of Ammon. The knot seemed a combination of double-bowline-knot, treble-crown-knot, back-handed-well-knot, knot-in-and-out-knot, and jamming knot.

At last, puzzled to comprehend the meaning of such a knot, Captain Delano addressed the knotter: "What are you knotting there, my man?"

"The knot," was the brief reply, without looking up.

"So it seems; but what is it for?"

"For someone else to undo," muttered back the old man, plying his fingers harder than ever, the knot being now nearly completed.

While Captain Delano stood watching him, suddenly the old man threw the knot towards him, saying in broken English—the first heard in the ship—something to this effect: "Undo it, cut it, quick." It was said lowly, but with such condensation of rapidity, that the long, slow words in Spanish, which had preceded and followed, almost operated as covers to the brief English between.

For a moment, knot in hand, and knot in head, Captain Delano stood mute, while, without further heeding him, the old man was now intent upon other ropes. Presently there was a slight stir behind Captain Delano. Turning, he saw the chained Negro, Atufal, standing quietly there. The next moment the old sailor rose, muttering, and, followed by his subordinate Negroes, removed to the forward part of the ship, where in the crowd he disappeared.

An elderly Negro, in a clout like an infant's, and with a pepper-and-salt head and a kind of attorney air, now approached Captain Delano. In tolerable Spanish, and with a good-natured, knowing wink, he informed him that the old knotter was simple-witted, but harmless, often playing his odd tricks. The Negro concluded by begging the knot, for of course the stranger would not care to be troubled with it. Unconsciously, it was handed to him. With a sort of *congé*, the Negro received it, and, turning his back, ferreted into it like a detective custom-house officer after smuggled laces. Soon, with some African words equivalent to pshaw, he tossed the knot overboard.

All this is very queer, thought Captain Delano, with a qualmish sort of emotion; but, as one feeling incipient seasickness, he strove, by ignoring the symptoms, to get rid of the malady. Once more he looked off for his boat. To his delight, it was now again in view, leaving the rocky spur astern.

The sensation here experienced, after at first relieving his uneasiness, with unforeseen efficacy soon began to remove it. The less distant sight of that well-known boat—showing it, not as before, half blended with the haze but with outline defined, so that its individuality, like a man's, was manifest; that boat, *Rover* by name, which, though now in strange seas, had often pressed the beach of Captain Delano's home, and, brought to its threshold for repairs, had familiarly lain there, as a Newfoundland dog; the sight of that household boat evoked a thousand trustful associations, which, contrasted with previous suspicions, filled him not only with lightsome confidence, but somehow with half humorous self-reproaches at his former lack of it.

"What, I, Amasa Delano—Jack of the Beach, as they called me when a lad—I, Amasa, the same that, duck-satchel in hand, used to paddle along the waterside to the schoolhouse made from the old hulk—I, little Jack of the Beach, that used to go berrying with cousin Nat and the rest—I to be murdered here at the ends of the earth on board a haunted pirate ship by a horrible Spaniard? Too nonsensical to think of! Who would murder Amasa Delano? His conscience is clean. There is someone above. Fie, fie, Jack of the Beach! you are a child indeed; a child of the second childhood, old boy; you are beginning to dote and drool, I'm afraid."

Light of heart and foot, he stepped aft, and there was met by Don Benito's servant, who, with a pleasing expression responsive to his own present feelings, informed him that his master had recovered from the effects of his coughing fit, and had just ordered him to go present his compliments to his good guest, Don Amasa, and say that he (Don Benito) would soon have the happiness to rejoin him.

There now, do you mark that? again thought Captain Delano, walking the poop. What a donkey I was. This kind gentleman who here sends me his kind compliments, he, but ten minutes ago, dark-lantern in hand, was dodging round some old grindstone in the hold, sharpening a

hatchet for me, I thought. Well, well; these long calms
have a morbid effect on the mind, I've often heard, though
I never believed it before. Ha! glancing towards the boat,
there's *Rover*, a good dog, a white bone in her mouth. A
pretty big bone though, seems to me.—What? Yes, she has
fallen afoul of the bubbling tide rip there. It sets her the
other way, too, for the time. Patience.

It was now about noon, though, from the grayness of
everything, it seemed to be getting towards dusk.

The calm was confirmed. In the far distance, away from
the influence of land, the leaden ocean seemed laid out and
leaded up, its course finished, soul gone, defunct. But the
current from landward, where the ship was, increased,
silently sweeping her further and further towards the
tranced waters beyond.

Still, from his knowledge of those latitudes, cherishing
hopes of a breeze, and a fair and fresh one, at any moment, Captain Delano, despite present prospects, buoyantly
counted upon bringing the *San Dominick* safely to anchor
ere night. The distance swept over was nothing, since,
with a good wind, ten minutes' sailing would retrace more
than sixty minutes' drifting. Meantime, one moment turning to mark *Rover* fighting the tide rip and the next to see
Don Benito approaching, he continued walking the poop.

Gradually he felt a vexation arising from the delay of
his boat; this soon merged into uneasiness, and at last—
his eye falling continually, as from a stage box into the
pit, upon the strange crowd before and below him, and
by and by recognizing there the face, now composed to
indifference, of the Spanish sailor who had seemed to
beckon from the mainchains—something of his old trepi-
dations returned.

Ah, thought he, gravely enough, this is like the ague:
because it went off, it follows not that it won't come back.

Though ashamed of the relapse, he could not altogether
subdue it; and so, exerting his good nature to the utmost,
insensibly he came to a compromise.

Yes, this is a strange craft, a strange history, too, and
strange folks on board. But—nothing more.

By way of keeping his mind out of mischief till the boat
should arrive, he tried to occupy it with turning over and
over, in a purely speculative sort of way, some lesser pe-

culiarities of the captain and crew. Among others, four curious points recurred:

First, the affair of the Spanish lad assailed with a knife by the slave boy; an act winked at by Don Benito. Second, the tyranny in Don Benito's treatment of Atufal, the black, as if a child should lead a bull of the Nile by the ring in his nose. Third, the trampling of the sailor by the two Negroes, a piece of insolence passed over without so much as a reprimand. Fourth, the cringing submission to their master of all the ship's underlings, mostly blacks, as if by the least inadvertence they feared to draw down his despotic displeasure.

Coupling these points, they seemed somewhat contradictory. But what then, thought Captain Delano, glancing towards his now nearing boat—what then? Why, Don Benito is a very capricious commander. But he is not the first of the sort I have seen, though it's true he rather exceeds any other. But as a nation—continued he in his reveries—these Spaniards are all an odd set; the very word Spaniard has a curious, conspirator, Guy-Fawkish twang to it. And yet I dare say Spaniards in the main are as good folks as any in Duxbury, Massachusetts. Ah good! At last *Rover* has come.

As, with its welcome freight, the boat touched the side, the oakum-pickers, with venerable gestures, sought to restrain the blacks, who, at the sight of three gurried water casks in its bottom and a pile of wilted pumpkins in its bow, hung over the bulwarks in disorderly raptures.

Don Benito, with his servant, now appeared, his coming, perhaps, hastened by hearing the noise. Of him Captain Delano sought permission to serve out the water, so that all might share alike, and none injure themselves by unfair excess. But sensible, and, on Don Benito's account, kind as this offer was, it was received with what seemed impatience; as if aware that he lacked energy as a commander, Don Benito, with the true jealousy of weakness, resented as an affront any interference. So, at least, Captain Delano inferred.

In another moment the casks were being hoisted in, when some of the eager Negroes accidentally jostled Captain Delano where he stood by the gangway, so that, unmindful of Don Benito, yielding to the impulse of the moment, with good-natured authority he bade the black stand back, to enforce his words making use of a half-mirthful, half-menacing gesture. Instantly the blacks paused, just where they were, each Negro and Negress suspended in his or her posture, exactly as the word had found them—for a few seconds continuing so—while, as between the responsive posts of a telegraph, an unknown syllable ran from man to man among the perched oakum-pickers. While the visitor's attention was fixed by this scene, suddenly the hatchet-polishers half rose, and a rapid cry came from Don Benito.

Thinking that at the signal of the Spaniard he was about to be massacred, Captain Delano would have sprung for his boat, but paused, as the oakum-pickers, dropping down into the crowd with earnest exclamations, forced every white and every Negro back, at the same moment, with gestures friendly and familiar, almost jocose, bidding him, in substance, not be a fool. Simultaneously the hatchet-polishers resumed their seats, quietly as so many tailors, and at once, as if nothing had happened, the work of hoisting in the casks was resumed, white and blacks singing at the tackle.

Captain Delano glanced towards Don Benito. As he saw his meager form in the act of recovering itself from reclining in the servant's arms, into which the agitated invalid had fallen, he could not but marvel at the panic by which himself had been surprised, on the darting supposition that such a commander, who, upon a legitimate occasion, so trivial too, as it now appeared, could lose all self-command, was, with energetic iniquity, going to bring about his murder.

The casks being on deck, Captain Delano was handed a number of jars and cups by one of the steward's aids, who, in the name of his captain, entreated him to do as he had proposed—dole out the water. He complied, with republican impartiality as to this republican element, which always seeks one level, serving the oldest white no better than the youngest black, excepting, indeed, poor Don Benito, whose condition, if not rank, demanded an extra allowance. To him, in the first place, Captain Delano presented a fair pitcher of the fluid, but, thirsting as he was for it, the Spaniard quaffed not a drop until after several grave bows and salutes, a reciprocation of courtesies which the sight-loving Africans hailed with clapping of hands.

Two of the less wilted pumpkins being reserved for the cabin table, the residue were minced up on the spot for the general regalement. But the soft bread, sugar, and bottled cider Captain Delano would have given the whites alone, and in chief Don Benito, but the latter objected; which disinterestedness not a little pleased the American; and so mouthfuls all around were given alike to whites and blacks, excepting one bottle of cider, which Babo insisted upon setting aside for his master.

Here it may be observed that as, on the first visit of the boat, the American had not permitted his men to board the ship, neither did he now, being unwilling to add to the confusion of the decks.

Not uninfluenced by the peculiar good humor at present prevailing, and for the time oblivious of any but benevolent thought, Captain Delano, who from recent indications counted upon a breeze within an hour or two at furthest, dispatched the boat back to the sealer, with orders for all the hands that could be spared immediately to set about rafting casks to the watering place and filling them. Likewise he bade word be carried to his chief officer that if, against present expectation, the ship was not brought to anchor by sunset, he need be under no concern; for as there was to be a full moon that night, he (Captain Delano) would remain on board ready to play the pilot, come the wind soon or late.

As the two Captains stood together observing the departing boat—the servant, as it happened, having just spied a spot on his master's velvet sleeve, and silently engaged rubbing it out—the American expressed his regrets that the *San Dominick* had no boats, none, at least, but the unseaworthy old hulk of the longboat, which, warped as a camel's skeleton in the desert and almost as bleached, lay pot-wise inverted amidships, one side a little tipped, furnishing a subterraneous sort of den for family groups of the blacks, mostly women and small children, who, squatting on old mats below, or perched above in the dark dome on the elevated seats, were descried, some distance within, like a social circle of bats sheltering in some friendly cave,

at intervals, ebon flights of naked boys and girls three or
four years old darting in and out of the den's mouth.

"Had you three or four boats now, Don Benito," said
Captain Delano, "I think that, by tugging at the oars, your
Negroes here might help along matters some. Did you sail
from port without boats, Don Benito?"

"They were stove in the gales, *señor*."

"That was bad. Many men, too, you lost then. Boats
and men. Those must have been hard gales, Don Benito."

"Past all speech," cringed the Spaniard.

"Tell me, Don Benito," continued his companion with
increased interest, "tell me, were these gales immediately
off the pitch of Cape Horn?"

"Cape Horn?—who spoke of Cape Horn?"

"Yourself did, when giving me an account of your voyage," answered Captain Delano, with almost equal astonishment at this eating of his own words, even as he ever
seemed eating his own heart, on the part of the Spaniard.
"You yourself, Don Benito, spoke of Cape Horn," he emphatically repeated.

The Spaniard turned, in a sort of stooping posture, pausing an instant as one about to make a plunging exchange
of elements, as from air to water.

At this moment a messenger boy, a white, hurried by,
in the regular performance of his function carrying the
last expired half-hour forward to the forecastle from the
cabin timepiece, to have it struck at the ship's large bell.

"Master," said the servant, discontinuing his work on
the coat sleeve and addressing the rapt Spaniard with a sort
of timid apprehensiveness, as one charged with a duty the
discharge of which, it was foreseen, would prove irksome
to the very person who had imposed it and for whose benefit it was intended, "master told me never mind where he
was, or how engaged, always to remind him, to a minute,
when shaving-time comes. Miguel has gone to strike the
half-hour afternoon. It is *now,* master. Will master go into
the cuddy?"

"Ah—yes," answered the Spaniard, starting, as from
dreams into realities, then, turning upon Captain Delano,
he said that erelong he would resume the conversation.

"Then if master means to talk more to Don Amasa,"
said the servant, "why not let Don Amasa sit by master

in the cuddy, and master can talk, and Don Amasa can
listen, while Babo here lathers and strops."

"Yes," said Captain Delano, not unpleased with this
sociable plan, "yes, Don Benito, unless you had rather not,
I will go with you."

"Be it so, *señor*."

As the three passed aft, the American could not but
think it another strange instance of his host's capriciousness, this being shaved with such uncommon punctuality
in the middle of the day. But he deemed it more than
likely that the servant's anxious fidelity had something to
do with the matter, inasmuch as the timely interruption
served to rally his master from the mood which had evidently been coming upon him.

The place called the cuddy was a light deck cabin
formed by the poop, a sort of attic to the large cabin
below. Part of it had formerly been the quarters of the
officers, but since their death all the partitionings had been
thrown down and the whole interior converted into one
spacious and airy marine hall; for absence of fine furniture and picturesque disarray of odd appurtenances, somewhat answering to the wide, cluttered hall of some eccentric
bachelor squire in the country, who hangs his shooting
jacket and tobacco pouch on deer antlers, and keeps his
fishing rod, tongs, and walking stick in the same corner.

The similitude was heightened, if not originally suggested, by glimpses of the surrounding sea, since, in one
aspect, the country and the ocean seem cousins-german.

The floor of the cuddy was matted. Overhead, four or
five old muskets were stuck into horizontal holes along
the beams. On one side was a claw-footed old table lashed
to the deck, a thumbed missal on it, and over it, a small,
meager crucifix attached to the bulkhead. Under the table
lay a dented cutlass or two with a hacked harpoon, among
some melancholy old rigging, like a heap of poor friars'
girdles. There were also two long, sharp-ribbed settees
of Malacca cane, black with age, and uncomfortable to
look at as inquisitors' racks, with a large, misshapen armchair, which, furnished with a rude barber's crotch at the
back, working with a screw, seemed some grotesque engine
of torment. A flag locker was in one corner, open, expos-
ing various colored buntings, some rolled up, others half

unrolled, still others tumbled. Opposite was a cumbrous washstand of black mahogany, all of one block, with a pedestal like a font, and over it a railed shelf, containing combs, brushes, and other implements of the toilet. A torn hammock of stained grass swung near, the sheets tossed, and the pillow wrinkled up like a brow, as if whoever slept here slept but illy, with alternate visitations of sad thoughts and bad dreams.

The further extremity of the cuddy, overhanging the ship's stern, was pierced with three openings, windows or portholes, according as men or cannon might peer, socially or unsocially, out of them. At present neither men nor cannon were seen, though huge ringbolts and other rusty iron fixtures of the woodwork hinted of twenty-four-pounders.

Glancing towards the hammock as he entered, Captain Delano said, "You sleep here, Don Benito?"

"Yes, señor, since we got into mild weather."

"This seems a sort of dormitory, sitting room, sail loft, chapel, armory, and private closet all together, Don Benito," added Captain Delano, looking round.

"Yes, señor; events have not been favorable to much order in my arrangements."

Here the servant, napkin on arm, made a motion as if waiting his master's good pleasure. Don Benito signified his readiness, when, seating him in the Malacca armchair, and for the guest's convenience drawing opposite one of the settees, the servant commenced operations by throwing back his master's collar and loosening his cravat.

There is something in the Negro which, in a peculiar way, fits him for avocations about one's person. Most Negroes are natural valets and hairdressers, taking to the comb and brush congenially as to the castinets, and flourishing them apparently with almost equal satisfaction. There is, too, a smooth tact about them in this employment, with a marvelous, noiseless, gliding briskness, not ungraceful in its way, singularly pleasing to behold, and still more so to be the manipulated subject of. And above all is the great gift of good humor. Not the mere grin or laugh is here meant. Those were unsuitable. But a certain easy cheerfulness, harmonious in every glance and gesture, as though God had set the whole Negro to some pleasant tune.

When to this is added the docility arising from the unaspiring contentment of a limited mind, and that susceptibility of blind attachment sometimes inhering in indisputable inferiors, one readily perceives why those hypochondriacs, Johnson and Byron—it may be, something like the hypochondriac Benito Cereno—took to their hearts, almost to the exclusion of the entire white race, their servingmen, the Negroes, Barber and Fletcher. But if there be that in the Negro which exempts him from the inflicted sourness of the morbid or cynical mind, how, in his most prepossessing aspects, must he appear to a benevolent one? When at ease with respect to exterior things, Captain Delano's nature was not only benign, but familiarly and humorously so. At home, he had often taken rare satisfaction in sitting in his door, watching some free man of color at his work or play. If on a voyage he chanced to have a black sailor, invariably he was on chatty and half-gamesome terms with him. In fact, like most men of a good, blithe heart, Captain Delano took to Negroes, not philanthropically, but genially, just as other men to Newfoundland dogs.

Hitherto, the circumstances in which he found the *San Dominick* had repressed the tendency. But in the cuddy, relieved from his former uneasiness, and, for various reasons, more sociably inclined than at any previous period of the day, and seeing the colored servant, napkin on arm, so debonair about his master, in a business so familiar as that of shaving too, all his old weakness for Negroes returned.

Among other things, he was amused with an odd instance of the African love of bright colors and fine shows, in the black's informally taking from the flag locker a great piece of bunting of all hues and lavishly tucking it under his master's chin for an apron.

The mode of shaving among the Spaniards is a little different from what it is with other nations. They have a basin, specifically called a barber's basin, which on one side is scooped out, so as accurately to receive the chin, against which it is closely held in lathering, which is done, not with a brush, but with soap dipped in the water of the basin and rubbed on the face.

In the present instance salt water was used for lack of

better, and the parts lathered were only the upper lip and low down under the throat, all the rest being cultivated beard.

The preliminaries being somewhat novel to Captain Delano, he sat curiously eying them, so that no conversation took place, nor, for the present, did Don Benito appear disposed to renew any.

Setting down his basin, the Negro searched among the razors, as for the sharpest, and, having found it, gave it an additional edge by expertly stropping it on the firm, smooth, oily skin of his open palm; he then made a gesture as if to begin, but midway stood suspended for an instant, one hand elevating the razor, the other professionally dabbling among the bubbling suds on the Spaniard's lank neck. Not unaffected by the close sight of the gleaming steel, Don Benito nervously shuddered; his usual ghastliness was heightened by the lather, which lather, again, was intensified in its hue by the contrasting sootiness of the Negro's body. Altogether the scene was somewhat peculiar, at least to Captain Delano, nor, as he saw the two thus postured, could he resist the vagary that in the black he saw a headsman, and in the white a man at the block. But this was one of those antic conceits, appearing and vanishing in a breath, from which, perhaps, the best-regulated mind is not always free.

Meantime the agitation of the Spaniard had a little loosened the bunting from around him, so that one broad fold swept curtainlike over the chair arm to the floor, revealing, amid a profusion of armorial bars and ground colors—black, blue, and yellow—a closed castle in a blood-red field diagonal with a lion rampant in a white.

"The castle and the lion," exclaimed Captain Delano—"why, Don Benito, this is the flag of Spain you use here. It's well it's only I, and not the King, that sees this," he added, with a smile, "but"—turning towards the black—"it's all one, I suppose, so the colors be gay"; which playful remark did not fail somewhat to tickle the Negro.

"Now, master," he said, readjusting the flag, and pressing the head gently further back into the crotch of the chair, "now, master," and the steel glanced nigh the throat.

Again Don Benito faintly shuddered.

"You must not shake so, master. See, Don Amasa,

master always shakes when I shave him. And yet master knows I never yet have drawn blood, though it's true if master will shake so I may some of these times. Now master," he continued. "And now, Don Amasa, please go on with your talk about the gale, and all that; master can hear, and, between times, master can answer."

"Ah yes, these gales," said Captain Delano; "but the more I think of your voyage, Don Benito, the more I wonder, not at the gales, terrible as they must have been, but at the disastrous interval following them. For here, by your account, have you been these two months and more getting from Cape Horn to St. Maria, a distance which I myself, with a good wind, have sailed in a few days. True, you had calms, and long ones, but to be becalmed for two months, that is, at least, unusual. Why, Don Benito, had almost any other gentleman told me such a story, I should have been half disposed to a little incredulity."

Here an involuntary expression came over the Spaniard, similar to that just before on the deck, and whether it was the start he gave, or a sudden gawky roll of the hull in the calm, or a momentary unsteadiness of the servant's hand, however it was, just then the razor drew blood, spots of which stained the creamy lather under the throat; immediately the black barber drew back his steel, and, remaining in his professional attitude, back to Captain Delano, and face to Don Benito, held up the trickling razor, saying, with a sort of half humorous sorrow, "See, master —you shook so—here's Babo's first blood."

No sword drawn before James the First of England, no assassination in that timid king's presence, could have produced a more terrified aspect than was now presented by Don Benito.

Poor fellow, thought Captain Delano, so nervous he can't even bear the sight of barber's blood; and this un-strung, sick man, is it credible that I should have imagined he meant to spill all my blood, who can't endure the sight of one little drop of his own? Surely, Amasa Delano, you have been beside yourself this day. Tell it not when you get home, sappy Amasa. Well, well, he looks like a murderer, doesn't he? More like as if himself were to be done for. Well, well, this day's experience shall be a good lesson.

Meantime, while these things were running through the

honest seaman's mind, the servant had taken the napkin from his arm, and to Don Benito had said—"But answer Don Amasa, please, master, while I wipe this ugly stuff off the razor, and strop it again."

As he said the words, his face was turned half round, so as to be alike visible to the Spaniard and the American, and seemed, by its expression, to hint that he was desirous, by getting his master to go on with the conversation, considerately to withdraw his attention from the recent annoying accident. As if glad to snatch the offered relief, Don Benito resumed, rehearsing to Captain Delano that, not only were the calms of unusual duration, but the ship had fallen in with obstinate currents, and other things he added, some of which were but repetitions of former statements, to explain how it came to pass that the passage from Cape Horn to St. Maria had been so exceedingly long, now and then mingling with his words incidental praises, less qualified than before, to the blacks, for their general good conduct. These particulars were not given consecutively, the servant, at convenient times, using his razor, and so, between the intervals of shaving, the story and panegyric went on with more than usual huskiness.

To Captain Delano's imagination, now again not wholly at rest, there was something so hollow in the Spaniard's manner, with apparently some reciprocal hollowness in the servant's dusky comment of silence, that the idea flashed across him that possibly master and man, for some unknown purpose, were acting out, both in word and deed, nay, to the very tremor of Don Benito's limbs, some juggling play before him. Neither did the suspicion of collusion lack apparent support, from the fact of those whispered conferences before mentioned. But then, what could be the object of enacting this play of the barber before him? At last, regarding the notion as a whimsey, insensibly suggested, perhaps, by the theatrical aspect of Don Benito in his harlequin ensign, Captain Delano speedily banished it.

The shaving over, the servant bestirred himself with a small bottle of scented waters, pouring a few drops on the head, and then diligently rubbing, the vehemence of the exercise causing the muscles of his face to twitch rather strangely.

His next operation was with comb, scissors, and brush,

going round and round, smoothing a curl here, clipping an unruly whisker hair there, giving a graceful sweep to the temple lock, with other impromptu touches evincing the hand of a master, while, like any resigned gentleman in barber's hands, Don Benito bore all much less uneasily, at least, than he had done the razoring; indeed, he sat so pale and rigid now that the Negro seemed a Nubian sculptor finishing off a white statue head.

All being over at last, the standard of Spain removed, tumbled up, and tossed back into the flag locker, the Negro's warm breath blowing away any stray hair which might have lodged down his master's neck, collar and cravat readjusted, a speck of lint whisked off the velvet lapel—all this being done, backing off a little space, and pausing with an expression of subdued self-complacency, the servant for a moment surveyed his master, as, in toilette at least, the creature of his own tasteful hands.

Captain Delano playfully complimented him upon his achievement, at the same time congratulating Don Benito.

But neither sweet waters, nor shampooing, nor fidelity, nor sociality, delighted the Spaniard. Seeing him relapsing into forbidding gloom, and still remaining seated, Captain Delano, thinking that his presence was undesired just then, withdrew, on pretense of seeing whether, as he had prophesied, any signs of a breeze were visible.

Walking forward to the mainmast, he stood awhile thinking over the scene, and not without some undefined misgivings, when he heard a noise near the cuddy, and, turning, saw the Negro, his hand to his cheek. Advancing, Captain Delano perceived that the cheek was bleeding. He was about to ask the cause, when the Negro's wailing soliloquy enlightened him.

"Ah, when will master get better from his sickness; only the sour heart that sour sickness breeds made him serve Babo so, cutting Babo with the razor because, only by accident, Babo had given master one little scratch, and for the first time in so many a day, too. Ah, ah, ah," holding his hand to his face.

Is it possible, thought Captain Delano; was it to wreak in private his Spanish spite against this poor friend of his that Don Benito, by his sullen manner, impelled me to

withdraw? Ah this slavery breeds ugly passions in man.—
Poor fellow!

He was about to speak in sympathy to the Negro, but
with a timid reluctance he now re-entered the cuddy.

Presently master and man came forth, Don Benito
leaning on his servant as if nothing had happened.

But a sort of love quarrel, after all, thought Captain
Delano.

He accosted Don Benito, and they slowly walked together. They had gone but a few paces, when the steward—
a tall, rajah-looking mulatto, Orientally set off with a
pagoda turban formed by three or four Madras handker-
chiefs wound about his head, tier on tier—approaching
with a saalam, announced lunch in the cabin.

On their way thither, the two captains were preceded by
the mulatto, who, turning round as he advanced, with
continual smiles and bows, ushered them on, a display
of elegance which quite completed the insignificance of
the small bareheaded Babo, who, as if not unconscious of
inferiority, eyed askance the graceful steward. But, in part,
Captain Delano imputed his jealous watchfulness to that
peculiar feeling which the full-blooded African entertains
for the adulterated one. As for the steward, his manner, if
not bespeaking much dignity of self-respect, yet evidenced
his extreme desire to please, which is doubly meritorious,
as at once Christian and Chesterfieldian.

Captain Delano observed with interest that while the
complexion of the mulatto was hybrid, his physiognomy
was European—classically so.

"Don Benito," whispered he, "I am glad to see this
usher-of-the-golden-rod of yours; the sight refutes an ugly
remark once made to me by a Barbados planter, that when
a mulatto has a regular European face, look out for him;
he is a devil. But see, your steward here has features more
regular than King George's of England, and yet there he
nods, and bows, and smiles, a king, indeed—the king of
kind hearts and polite fellows. What a pleasant voice he
has, too."

"He has, *señor*."

"But tell me, has he not, so far as you have known him,
always proved a good, worthy fellow?" said Captain Delano, pausing, while with a final genuflexion the steward

disappeared into the cabin; "come, for the reason just mentioned, I am curious to know."

"Francesco is a good man," a sort of sluggishly responded Don Benito, like a phlegmatic appreciator, who would neither find fault nor flatter.

"Ah, I thought so. For it were strange indeed, and not very creditable to us whiteskins, if a little of our blood mixed with the African's should, far from improving the latter's quality, have the sad effect of pouring vitriolic acid into black broth—improving the hue, perhaps, but not the wholesomeness."

"Doubtless, doubtless, *señor,* but"—glancing at Babo—"not to speak of Negroes, your planter's remark I have heard applied to the Spanish and Indian intermixtures in our provinces. But I know nothing about the matter," he listlessly added.

And here they entered the cabin.

The lunch was a frugal one. Some of Captain Delano's fresh fish and pumpkins, biscuit and salt beef, the reserved bottle of cider, and the *San Dominick*'s last bottle of Canary.

As they entered, Francesco, with two or three colored aids, was hovering over the table giving the last adjustments. Upon perceiving their master they withdrew, Francesco making a smiling *congé,* and the Spaniard, without condescending to notice it, fastidiously remarking to his companion that he relished not superfluous attendance.

Without companions, host and guest sat down, like a childless married couple, at opposite ends of the table, Don Benito waving Captain Delano to his place, and, weak as he was, insisting upon that gentleman being seated before himself.

The Negro placed a rug under Don Benito's feet, and a cushion behind his back, and then stood behind, not his master's chair, but Captain Delano's. At first, this a little surprised the latter. But it was soon evident that, in taking his position, the black was still true to his master, since by facing him he could the more readily anticipate his slightest want.

"This is an uncommonly intelligent fellow of yours, Don Benito," whispered Captain Delano across the table.

"You say true, *señor.*"

During the repast, the guest again reverted to parts of
Don Benito's story, begging further particulars here and
there. He inquired how it was that the scurvy and fever
should have committed such wholesale havoc upon the
whites, while destroying less than half of the blacks. As
if this question reproduced the whole scene of plague before the Spaniard's eyes, miserably reminding him of his
solitude in a cabin where before he had had so many
friends and officers round him, his hand shook, his face
became hueless, broken words escaped; but directly the
same memory of the past seemed replaced by insane ter-
rors of the present. With starting eyes he stared before him
at vacancy. For nothing was to be seen but the hand of
his servant pushing the Canary over towards him. At
length a few sips served partially to restore him. He made
random reference to the different constitution of races, enabling one to offer more resistance to certain maladies than
another. The thought was new to his companion.

Presently Captain Delano, intending to say something
to his host concerning the pecuniary part of the business
he had undertaken for him, especially—since he was
strictly accountable to his owners—with reference to the
new suit of sails, and other things of that sort, and naturally
preferring to conduct such affairs in private, was desirous
that the servant should withdraw, imagining that Don
Benito for a few minutes could dispense with his attendance. He, however, waited awhile, thinking that,
as the conversation proceeded, Don Benito, without being
prompted, would perceive the propriety of the step.

But it was otherwise. At last catching his host's eye,
Captain Delano, with a slight backward gesture of his
thumb, whispered, "Don Benito, pardon me, but there is
an interference with the full expression of what I have to
say to you."

Upon this the Spaniard changed countenance, which
was imputed to his resenting the hint, as in some way a
reflection upon his servant. After a moment's pause, he assured his guest that the black's remaining with them could
be of no disservice; because since losing his officers he had
made Babo (whose original office, it now appeared, had
been captain of the slaves) not only his constant attendant and companion, but in all things his confidant.

After this, nothing more could be said; though indeed Captain Delano could hardly avoid some little tinge of irritation upon being left ungratified in so inconsiderable a wish, by one, too, for whom he intended such solid services. But it is only his querulousness, thought he, and so, filling his glass, he proceeded to business.

The price of the sails and other matters was fixed upon. But while this was being done, the American observed that, though his original offer of assistance had been hailed with hectic animation, yet now when it was reduced to a business transaction, indifference and apathy were betrayed. Don Benito, in fact, appeared to submit to hearing the details more out of regard to common propriety than from any impression that weighty benefit to himself and his voyage was involved.

Soon his manner became still more reserved. The effort was vain to seek to draw him into social talk. Gnawed by his splenetic mood, he sat twitching his beard, while to little purpose the hand of his servant, mute as that on the wall, slowly pushed over the Canary.

Lunch being over, they sat down on the cushioned transom, the servant placing a pillow behind his master. The long continuance of the calm had now affected the atmosphere. Don Benito sighed heavily, as if for breath.

"Why not adjourn to the cuddy," said Captain Delano; "there is more air there." But the host sat silent and motionless.

Meantime his servant knelt before him with a large fan of feathers. And Francesco, coming in on tiptoes, handed the Negro a little cup of aromatic waters, with which at intervals he chafed his master's brow, smoothing the hair along the temples as a nurse does a child's. He spoke no word. He only rested his eye on his master's, as if, amid all Don Benito's distress, a little to refresh his spirit by the silent sight of fidelity.

Presently the ship's bell sounded two o'clock, and through the cabin windows a slight rippling of the sea was discerned, and from the desired direction.

"There," exclaimed Captain Delano, "I told you so, Don Benito, look!"

He had risen to his feet, speaking in a very animated tone, with a view the more to rouse his companion. But though the crimson curtain of the stern window near him that moment fluttered against his pale cheek, Don Benito seemed to have even less welcome for the breeze than the calm.

Poor fellow, thought Captain Delano, bitter experience has taught him that one ripple does not make a wind, any more than one swallow a summer. But he is mistaken for once. I will get his ship in for him, and prove it.

Briefly alluding to his weak condition, he urged his host to remain quietly where he was, since he (Captain Delano) would with pleasure take upon himself the responsibility of making the best use of the wind.

Upon gaining the deck, Captain Delano started at the unexpected figure of Atufal, monumentally fixed at the threshold, like one of those sculptured porters of black marble guarding the porches of Egyptian tombs.

But this time the start was, perhaps, purely physical. Atufal's presence, singularly attesting docility even in sullenness, was contrasted with that of the hatchet-polishers, who in patience evinced their industry; while both spectacles showed that, lax as Don Benito's general authority might be, still, whenever he chose to exert it, no man so savage or colossal but must, more or less, bow.

Snatching a trumpet which hung from the bulwarks, with a free step Captain Delano advanced to the forward edge of the poop, issuing his orders in his best Spanish. The few sailors and many Negroes, all equally pleased, obediently set about heading the ship towards the harbor.

While giving some directions about setting a lower stunsail, suddenly Captain Delano heard a voice faithfully repeating his orders. Turning, he saw Babo, now for the time acting, under the pilot, his original part of captain of the slaves. This assistance proved valuable. Tattered sails and warped yards were soon brought into some trim. And no brace or halyard was pulled but to the blithe songs of the inspirited Negroes.

Good fellows, thought Captain Delano, a little training would make fine sailors of them. Why see, the very women pull and sing too. These must be some of those Ashantee Negresses that make such capital soldiers, I've heard. But who's at the helm? I must have a good hand there.

He went to see.

The *San Dominick* steered with a cumbrous tiller, with large horizontal pulleys attached. At each pulley end stood a subordinate black, and between them, at the tillerhead, the responsible post, a Spanish seaman, whose countenance evinced his due share in the general hopefulness and confidence at the coming of the breeze.

He proved the same man who had behaved with so shamefaced an air on the windlass.

"Ah—it is you, my man," exclaimed Captain Delano—"well, no more sheep's-eyes now; look straight forward and keep the ship so. Good hand, I trust? And want to get into the harbor, don't you?"

The man assented with an inward chuckle, grasping the tillerhead firmly. Upon this, unperceived by the American, the two blacks eyed the sailor intently.

Finding all right at the helm, the pilot went forward to the forecastle to see how matters stood there.

The ship now had way enough to breast the current. With the approach of evening, the breeze would be sure to freshen.

Having done all that was needed for the present, Captain Delano, giving his last orders to the sailors, turned aft to report affairs to Don Benito in the cabin, perhaps additionally incited to rejoin him by the hope of snatching a moment's private chat while the servant was engaged upon deck.

From opposite sides, there were, beneath the poop, two approaches to the cabin, one further forward than the other, and consequently communicating with a longer passage. Marking the servant still above, Captain Delano, taking the nighest entrance—the one last named, and at whose porch Atufal still stood—hurried on his way, till, arrived at the cabin threshold, he paused an instant, a little to recover from his eagerness. Then, with the words of his intended business upon his lips, he entered. As he advanced toward the seated Spaniard, he heard another footstep, keeping time with his. From the opposite door, a salver in hand, the servant was likewise advancing.

"Confound the faithful fellow," thought Captain Delano; "what a vexatious coincidence."

Possibly the vexation might have been something different, were it not for the brisk confidence inspired by the breeze. But even as it was he felt a slight twinge, from a sudden indefinite association in his mind of Babo with Atufal.

"Don Benito," said he, "I give you joy; the breeze will hold, and will increase. By the way, your tall man and timepiece, Atufal, stands without. By your order, of course?"

Don Benito recoiled, as if at some bland satirical touch delivered with such adroit garnish of apparent good breeding as to present no handle for retort.

He is like one flayed alive, thought Captain Delano; where may one touch him without causing a shrink?

The servant moved before his master, adjusting a cushion; recalled to civility, the Spaniard stiffly replied: "You are right. The slave appears where you saw him, according to my command, which is that if at the given hour I am below he must take his stand and abide my coming."

"Ah now, pardon me, but that is treating the poor fellow like an ex-king indeed. Ah, Don Benito," smiling, "for all the license you permit in some things, I fear lest, at bottom, you are a bitter hard master."

Again Don Benito shrank, and this time, as the good sailor thought, from a genuine twinge of his conscience.

Again conversation became constrained. In vain Captain Delano called attention to the now perceptible motion of the keel gently cleaving the sea; with lackluster eye, Don Benito returned words few and reserved.

By and by, the wind having steadily risen, and still blowing right into the harbor, bore the *San Dominick* swiftly on. Rounding a point of land, the sealer at distance came into open view.

Meantime Captain Delano had again repaired to the deck, remaining there some time. Having at last altered the ship's course so as to give the reef a wide berth, he returned for a few moments below.

I will cheer up my poor friend this time, thought he.

"Better and better, Don Benito," he cried as he blithely re-entered: "there will soon be an end to your cares, at least for a while. For when, after a long, sad voyage, you know, the anchor drops into the haven, all its vast weight seems lifted from the captain's heart. We are getting on famously, Don Benito. My ship is in sight. Look through this side light here; there she is, all a-taunt-o! The *Bachelor's Delight,* my good friend. Ah, how this wind braces one up. Come, you must take a cup of coffee with me this evening. My old steward will give you as fine a cup as ever any sultan tasted. What say you, Don Benito, will you?"

At first, the Spaniard glanced feverishly up, casting a longing look towards the sealer, while, with mute concern his servant gazed into his face. Suddenly the old ague of coldness returned, and dropping back to his cushions he was silent.

"You do not answer. Come, all day you have been my host; would you have hospitality all on one side?"

"I cannot go," was the response.

"What? it will not fatigue you. The ships will lie together as near as they can without swinging foul. It will be little more than stepping from deck to deck, which is but as from room to room. Come, come, you must not refuse me."

"I cannot go," decisively and repulsively repeated Don Benito.

Renouncing all but the last appearance of courtesy, with a sort of cadaverous sullenness, and biting his thin nails to the quick, he glanced, almost glared, at his guest, as if impatient that a stranger's presence should interfere with the full indulgence of his morbid hour. Meantime the sound of the parted waters came more and more gurglingly and merrily in at the windows; as reproaching him for his dark spleen, as telling him that, sulk as he might, and go mad with it, nature cared not a jot, since whose fault was it, pray?

But the foul mood was now at its depth, as the fair wind at its height.

There was something in the man so far beyond any mere unsociality or sourness previously evinced that even the forbearing good nature of his guest could no longer endure it. Wholly at a loss to account for such demeanor, and deeming sickness with eccentricity, however extreme, no adequate excuse, well satisfied, too, that nothing in his own conduct could justify it, Captain Delano's pride began to be roused. Himself became reserved. But all seemed

one to the Spaniard. Quitting him, therefore, Captain Delano once more went to the deck.

The ship was now within less than two miles of the
sealer. The whaleboat was seen darting over the interval.

To be brief, the two vessels, thanks to the pilot's skill,
erelong in neighborly style lay anchored together.

Before returning to his own vessel, Captain Delano had
intended communicating to Don Benito the smaller details of the proposed services to be rendered. But as it
was, unwilling anew to subject himself to rebuffs, he resolved, now that he had seen the *San Dominick* safely
moored, immediately to quit her, without further allusion
to hospitality or business. Indefinitely postponing his ulterior plans, he would regulate his future actions according
to future circumstances. His boat was ready to receive
him; but his host still tarried below. Well, thought Captain
Delano, if he has little breeding, the more need to show
mine. He descended to the cabin to bid a ceremonious,
and, it may be, tacitly rebukeful adieu. But to his great
satisfaction, Don Benito, as if he began to feel the weight
of that treatment with which his slighted guest had, not
indecorously, retaliated upon him, now, supported by his
servant, rose to his feet, and grasping Captain Delano's
hand, stood tremulous, too much agitated to speak. But
the good augury hence drawn was suddenly dashed by his
resuming all his previous reserve with augmented gloom,
as, with half-averted eyes, he silently reseated himself on
his cushions. With a corresponding return of his own
chilled feelings, Captain Delano bowed and withdrew.

He was hardly midway in the narrow corridor, dim as
a tunnel, leading from the cabin to the stairs, when a
sound, as of the tolling for execution in some jailyard,
fell on his ears. It was the echo of the ship's flawed bell
striking the hour, drearily reverberated in this subterranean
vault. Instantly, by a fatality not to be withstood, his mind,
responsive to the portent, swarmed with superstitious suspicions. He paused. In images far swifter than these sentences, the minutest details of all his former distrusts swept
through him.

Hitherto, credulous good nature had been too ready to
furnish excuses for reasonable fears. Why was the Spaniard, so superfluously punctilious at times, now heedless of

common propriety in not accompanying to the side his departing guest? Did indisposition forbid? Indisposition had not forbidden more irksome exertion that day. His last equivocal demeanor recurred. He had risen to his feet, grasped his guest's hand, motioned toward his hat; then, in an instant, all was eclipsed in sinister muteness and gloom. Did this imply one brief repentant relenting at the final moment from some iniquitous plot, followed by remorseless return to it? His last glance seemed to express a calamitous yet acquiescent farewell to Captain Delano forever. Why decline the invitation to visit the sealer that evening? Or was the Spaniard less hardened than the Jew, who refrained not from supping at the board of him whom the same night he meant to betray? What imported all those daylong enigmas and contradictions, except they were intended to mystify, preliminary to some stealthy blow? Atufal, the pretended rebel but punctual shadow, that moment lurked by the threshold without. He seemed a sentry, and more. Who, by his own confession, had stationed him there? Was the Negro now lying in wait?

The Spaniard behind—his creature before: to rush from darkness to light was the involuntary choice.

The next moment, with clenched jaw and hand, he passed Atufal, and stood unharmed in the light. As he saw his trim ship lying peacefully at anchor and almost within ordinary call; as he saw his household boat, with familiar faces in it, patiently rising and falling on the short waves by the *San Dominick*'s side; and then, glancing about the decks where he stood, saw the oakum-pickers still gravely plying their fingers, and heard the low, buzzing whistle and industrious hum of the hatchet-polishers still bestirring themselves over their endless occupation; and more than all, as he saw the benign aspect of nature taking her innocent repose in the evening, the screened sun in the quiet camp of the west shining out like the mild light from Abraham's tent—as charmed eye and ear took in all these, with the chained figure of the black, clenched jaw and hand relaxed. Once again he smiled at the phantoms which had mocked him, and felt something like a tinge of remorse that, by harboring them even for a moment, he should by implication have betrayed an atheist doubt of the ever-watchful Providence above.

There was a few minutes' delay, while, in obedience to his orders, the boat was being hooked along to the gangway. During this interval, a sort of saddened satisfaction stole over Captain Delano at thinking of the kindly offices he had that day discharged for a stranger. Ah, thought he, after good actions one's conscience is never ungrateful, however much so the benefited party may be.

Presently his foot, in the first act of descent into the boat, pressed the first round of the side ladder, his face presented inward upon the deck. In the same moment he heard his name courteously sounded, and, to his pleased surprise, saw Don Benito advancing—an unwonted energy in his air, as if, at the last moment, intent upon making amends for his recent discourtesy. With instinctive good feeling, Captain Delano, withdrawing his foot, turned and reciprocally advanced. As he did so, the Spaniard's nervous eagerness increased, but his vital energy failed, so that, the better to support him, the servant, placing his master's hand on his naked shoulder, and gently holding it there, formed himself into a sort of crutch.

When the two captains met, the Spaniard again fervently took the hand of the American, at the same time casting an earnest glance into his eyes, but, as before, too much overcome to speak.

I have done him wrong, self-reproachfully thought Captain Delano; his apparent coldness has deceived me; in no instance has he meant to offend.

Meantime, as if fearful that the continuance of the scene might too much unstring his master, the servant seemed anxious to terminate it. And so, still presenting himself as a crutch, and walking between the two captains, he advanced with them towards the gangway; while still, as if full of kindly contrition, Don Benito would not let go the hand of Captain Delano but retained it in his, across the black's body.

Soon they were standing by the side, looking over into the boat, whose crew turned up their curious eyes. Waiting a moment for the Spaniard to relinquish his hold, the now embarrassed Captain Delano lifted his foot to overstep the threshold of the open gangway, but still Don Benito would not let go his hand. And yet, with an agitated tone, he said, "I can go no further; here I must bid you adieu.

Adieu, my dear, dear Don Amasa. Go—go!" suddenly tearing his hand loose, "go, and God guard you better than me, my best friend."

Not unaffected, Captain Delano would now have lingered, but, catching the meekly admonitory eye of the servant, with a hasty farewell he descended into his boat, followed by the continual adieus of Don Benito, standing rooted in the gangway.

Seating himself in the stern, Captain Delano, making a last salute, ordered the boat shoved off. The crew had their oars on end. The bowsmen pushed the boat a sufficient distance for the oars to be lengthwise dropped. The instant that was done, Don Benito sprang over the bulwarks, falling at the feet of Captain Delano; at the same time calling towards his ship, but in tones so frenzied that none in the boat could understand him. But, as if not equally obtuse, three sailors, from three different and distant parts of the ship, splashed into the sea, swimming after their captain, as if intent upon his rescue.

The dismayed officer of the boat eagerly asked what this meant. To which Captain Delano, turning a disdainful smile upon the unaccountable Spaniard, answered that, for his part, he neither knew nor cared; but it seemed as if Don Benito had taken it into his head to produce the impression among his people that the boat wanted to kidnap him. "Or else—give way for your lives," he wildly added, starting at a clattering hubbub in the ship, above which rang the tocsin of the hatchet-polishers, and seizing Don Benito by the throat he added, "this plotting pirate means murder!" Here, in apparent verification of the words, the servant, a dagger in his hand, was seen on the rail overhead, poised, in the act of leaping, as if with desperate fidelity to befriend his master to the last; while, seemingly to aid the black, the three white sailors were trying to clamber into the hampered bow. Meantime, the whole host of Negroes, as if inflamed at the sight of their jeopardized captain, impended in one sooty avalanche over the bulwarks.

All this, with what preceded and what followed, occurred with such involutions of rapidity that past, present, and future seemed one.

Seeing the Negro coming, Captain Delano had flung the

Spaniard aside, almost in the very act of clutching him, and, by the unconscious recoil shifting his place, with arms thrown up so promptly grappled the servant in his descent, that with dagger presented at Captain Delano's heart, the black seemed of purpose to have leaped there as to his mark. But the weapon was wrenched away, and the assailant dashed down into the bottom of the boat, which now, with disentangled oars, began to speed through the sea.

At this juncture, the left hand of Captain Delano, on one side, again clutched the half-reclined Don Benito, heedless that he was in a speechless faint, while his right foot, on the other side, ground the prostrate Negro, and his right arm pressed for added speed on the after oar, his eye bent forward, encouraging his men to their utmost.

But here the officer of the boat, who had at last succeeded in beating off the towing sailors, and was now, with face turned aft, assisting the bowsman at his oar, suddenly called to Captain Delano to see what the black was about, while a Portuguese oarsman shouted to him to give heed to what the Spaniard was saying.

Glancing down at his feet, Captain Delano saw the free hand of the servant aiming with a second dagger—a small one, before concealed in his wool—with this he was snakishly writhing up from the boat's bottom at the heart of his master, his countenance lividly vindictive, expressing the centered purpose of his soul; while the Spaniard, half-choked, was vainly shrinking away, with husky words, incoherent to all but the Portuguese.

That moment, across the long-benighted mind of Captain Delano, a flash of revelation swept, illuminating, in unanticipated clearness, his host's whole mysterious demeanor, with every enigmatic event of the day, as well as the entire past voyage of the *San Dominick*. He smote Babo's hand down, but his own heart smote him harder. With infinite pity he withdrew his hold from Don Benito. Not Captain Delano, but Don Benito, the black, in leaping into the boat, had intended to stab.

Both the black's hands were held, as, glancing up towards the *San Dominick*, Captain Delano, now with scales dropped from his eyes, saw the Negroes, not in misrule, not in tumult, not as if frantically concerned for Don

Benito, but, with mask torn away, flourishing hatchets and knives in ferocious piratical revolt. Like delirious black dervishes, the six Ashantees danced on the poop. Prevented by their foes from springing into the water, the Spanish boys were hurrying up to the topmost spars, while such of the few Spanish sailors not already in the sea, less alert, were descried, helplessly mixed in, on deck with the blacks.

Meantime Captain Delano hailed his own vessel, ordering the ports up, and the guns run out. But by this time the cable of the *San Dominick* had been cut, and the fag end, in lashing out, whipped away the canvas shroud about the beak, suddenly revealing, as the bleached hull swung round towards the open ocean, death for the figurehead, in a human skeleton, chalky comment on the chalked words below, FOLLOW YOUR LEADER.

At the sight, Don Benito, covering his face, wailed out: " 'Tis he, Aranda! my murdered, unburied friend!"

Upon reaching the sealer, calling for ropes, Captain Delano bound the Negro, who made no resistance, and had him hoisted to the deck. He would then have assisted the now almost helpless Don Benito up the side; but Don Benito, wan as he was, refused to move, or be moved, until the Negro should have been first put below out of view. When, presently assured that it was done, he no more shrank from the ascent.

The boat was immediately dispatched back to pick up the three swimming sailors. Meantime, the guns were in readiness, though, owing to the *San Dominick* having glided somewhat astern of the sealer, only the aftermost one could be brought to bear. With this, they fired six times, thinking to cripple the fugitive ship by bringing down her spars, but only a few inconsiderable ropes were shot away. Soon the ship was beyond the gun's range, steering broad out of the bay, the blacks thickly clustering round the bowsprit, one moment with taunting cries towards the whites, the next with upthrown gestures hailing the now dusky moors of ocean—cawing crows escaped from the hand of the fowler.

The first impulse was to slip the cables and give chase. But, upon second thoughts, to pursue with whaleboat and yawl seemed more promising.

Upon inquiring of Don Benito what firearms they had on board the *San Dominick,* Captain Delano was answered that they had none that could be used, because, in the earlier stages of the mutiny, a cabin passenger, since dead, had secretly put out of order the locks of what few muskets there were. But with all his remaining strength Don Benito entreated the Americans not to give chase, either with ship or boat, for the Negroes had already proved themselves such desperadoes that, in case of a present assault, nothing but a total massacre of the whites could be looked for. But, regarding this warning as coming from one whose spirit had been crushed by misery, the American did not give up his design.

The boats were got ready and armed. Captain Delano ordered his men into them. He was going himself when Don Benito grasped his arm.

"What! have you saved my life, *señor,* and are you now going to throw away your own?"

The officers also, for reasons connected with their interests and those of the voyage, and a duty owing to the owners, strongly objected against their commander's going. Weighing their remonstrances a moment, Captain Delano felt bound to remain; appointing his chief mate— an athletic and resolute man, who had been a privateer's-man—to head the party. The more to encourage the sailors, they were told that the Spanish captain considered his ship good as lost; that she and her cargo, including some gold and silver, were worth more than a thousand doubloons. Take her, and no small part should be theirs. The sailors replied with a shout.

The fugitives had now almost gained an offing. It was nearly night, but the moon was rising. After hard, prolonged pulling, the boats came up on the ship's quarters, at a suitable distance laying upon their oars to discharge their muskets. Having no bullets to return, the Negroes sent their yells. But upon the second volley, Indianlike, they hurtled their hatchets. One took off a sailor's fingers. Another struck the whaleboat's bow, cutting off the rope there, and remaining stuck in the gunwale like a woodman's ax. Snatching it, quivering, from its lodgment, the mate hurled it back. The returned gauntlet now stuck in the ship's broken quarter-gallery, and so remained.

The Negroes giving too hot a reception, the whites kept a more respectful distance. Hovering now just out of reach of the hurtling hatchets, they, with a view to the close encounter which must soon come, sought to decoy the blacks into entirely disarming themselves of their most murderous weapons in a hand-to-hand fight, by foolishly flinging them, as missiles, short of the mark, into the sea. But, erelong perceiving the stratagem, the Negroes desisted, though not before many of them had to replace their lost hatchets with handspikes, an exchange which, as counted upon, proved, in the end, favorable to the assailants.

Meantime, with a strong wind the ship still clove the water, the boats alternately falling behind and pulling up to discharge fresh volleys.

The fire was mostly directed towards the stern, since there, chiefly, the Negroes at present were clustering. But to kill or maim the Negroes was not the object. To take them, with the ship, was the object. To do it, the ship must be boarded, which could not be done by boats while she was sailing so fast.

A thought now struck the mate. Observing the Spanish boys still aloft, high as they could get, he called to them to descend to the yards, and cut adrift the sails. It was done. About this time, owing to causes hereafter to be shown, two Spaniards, in the dress of sailors and conspicuously showing themselves, were killed, not by volleys, but by deliberate marksman's shots; while, as it afterwards appeared, by one of the general discharges Atufal, the black, and the Spaniard at the helm likewise were killed. What, now, with the loss of the sails and loss of leaders, the ship became unmanageable to the Negroes.

With creaking masts, she came heavily round to the wind, the prow slowly swinging into view of the boats, its skeleton gleaming in the horizontal moonlight and casting a gigantic ribbed shadow upon the water. One extended arm of the ghost seemed beckoning the whites to avenge it.

"Follow your leader!" cried the mate; and, one on each bow, the boats boarded. Sealing-spears and cutlasses crossed hatchets and handspikes. Huddled upon the longboat amidships, the Negresses raised a wailing chant, whose chorus was the clash of the steel.

For a time, the attack wavered, the Negroes wedging

themselves to beat it back, the half-repelled sailors, as yet
unable to gain a footing, fighting as troopers in the saddle,
one leg sideways flung over the bulwark and one without,
plying their cutlasses like carters' whips. But in vain. They
were almost overborne, when, rallying themselves into a
squad as one man, with a huzzah they sprang inboard,
where, entangled, they involuntarily separated again. For
a few breaths' space there was a vague, muffled, inner
sound, as of submerged swordfish rushing hither and
thither through shoals of blackfish. Soon, in a reunited
band, and joined by the Spanish seamen, the whites came
to the surface, irresistibly driving the Negroes toward the
stern. But a barricade of casks and sacks, from side to
side, had been thrown up by the mainmast. Here the
Negroes faced about, and though scorning peace or truce,
yet fain would have had respite. But, without pause over-
leaping the barrier, the unflagging sailors again closed.
Exhausted, the blacks now fought in despair. Their red
tongues lolled, wolflike, from their black mouths. But the
pale sailors' teeth were set; not a word was spoken, and,
in five minutes more, the ship was won.

Nearly a score of the Negroes were killed. Exclusive of
those by the balls, many were mangled; their wounds—
mostly inflicted by the long-edged sealing-spears, resem-
bling those shaven ones of the English at Preston Pans,
made by the poled scythes of the Highlanders. On the
other side, none were killed, though several were wounded,
some severely, including the mate. The surviving Negroes
were temporarily secured, and the ship, towed back into
the harbor at midnight, once more lay anchored.

Omitting the incidents and arrangements ensuing, suffice it that, after two days spent in refitting, the ships sailed
in company for Conception, in Chile, and thence for Lima,
in Peru; where, before the viceregal courts, the whole affair, from the beginning, underwent investigation.

Though, midway on the passage, the ill-fated Spaniard,
relaxed from constraint, showed some signs of regaining
health with free-will, yet, agreeably to his own foreboding,
shortly before arriving at Lima, he relapsed, finally becoming so reduced as to be carried ashore in arms. Hearing of his story and plight, one of the many religious institutions of the City of Kings opened an hospitable refuge to

him, where both physician and priest were his nurses, and
a member of the order volunteered to be his one special
guardian and consoler, by night and by day.

The following extracts, translated from one of the official Spanish documents, will, it is hoped, shed light on the
preceding narrative, as well as, in the first place, reveal
the true port of departure and true history of the *San
Dominick*'s voyage, down to the time of her touching at
the island of St. Maria.

But ere the extracts come it may be well to preface
them with a remark.

The document selected, from among many others, for
partial translation, contains the deposition of Benito
Cereno, the first taken in the case. Some disclosures therein
were at the time held dubious, for both learned and
natural reasons. The tribunal inclined to the opinion that
the deponent, not undisturbed in his mind by recent events,
raved of some things which could never have happened.
But subsequent depositions of the surviving sailors, bearing out the revelations of their captain in several of the
strangest particulars, gave credence to the rest. So that the
tribunal, in its final decision, rested its capital sentences
upon statements which, had they lacked confirmation, it
would have deemed it but duty to reject.

———

I, DON JOSÉ DE ABOS AND PADILLA, His Majesty's
Notary for the Royal Revenue, and Register of this
Province, and Notary Public of the Holy Crusade of this
Bishopric, etc.

Do certify and declare, as much as is requisite in law,
that, in the criminal cause commenced the twenty-fourth
of the month of September, in the year seventeen hundred
and ninety-nine, against the Negroes of the ship *San
Dominick*, the following declaration before me was made:

Declaration of the first witness, DON BENITO CERENO.

The same day, and month, and year, His Honor, Doc-
tor Juan Martínez de Rozas, Councilor of the Royal
Audience of this Kingdom, and learned in the law of this
Intendency, ordered the captain of the ship *San Dominick*,

Don Benito Cereno, to appear, which he did in his litter,
attended by the monk Infelez, of whom he received the
oath, which he took by God, our Lord, and a sign of the
Cross, under which he promised to tell the truth of whatever he should know and should be asked; and being interrogated agreeably to the tenor of the act commencing
the process, he said that, on the twentieth of May last,
he set sail with his ship from the port of Valparaiso,
bound to that of Callao, loaded with the produce of the
country beside thirty cases of hardware and one hundred and sixty blacks of both sexes, mostly belonging to
Don Alexandro Aranda, gentleman, of the city of Mendoza; that the crew of the ship consisted of thirty-six
men beside the persons who went as passengers; that the
Negroes were in part as follows:

[Here, in the original, follows a list of some fifty names,
descriptions, and ages, compiled from certain recovered
documents of Aranda's, and also from recollections of
the deponent, from which portions only are extracted.]

—One, from about eighteen to nineteen years, named
José, and this was the man that waited upon his master,
Don Alexandro, and who speaks well the Spanish, having served him four or five years;*** a mulatto, named
Francesco, the cabin steward, of a good person and voice,
having sung in the Valparaiso churches, native of the
province of Buenos Ayres, aged about thirty-five years.
*** A smart Negro, named Dago, who had been for
many years a gravedigger among the Spaniards, aged
forty-six years.*** Four old Negroes, born in Africa,
from sixty to seventy, but sound, calkers by trade, whose
names are as follows: the first was named Muri, and he
was killed (as was also his son named Diamelo); the
second, Nacta; the third, Yola, likewise killed; the fourth,
Ghofan; and six full-grown Negroes, aged from thirty to
forty-five, all raw, and born among the Ashantees—
Matiluqui, Yan, Lecbe, Mapenda, Yambaio, Akim; four
of whom were killed;*** a powerful Negro named Atufal,
who being supposed to have been a chief in Africa, his
owner set great store by him. *** And a small Negro of
Senegal, but some years among the Spaniards, aged about
thirty, which Negro's name was Babo; *** that he does
not remember the names of the others, but that still
expecting the residue of Don Alexandro's papers will be
found, will then take due account of them all, and remit

to the court; *** and thirty-nine women and children of all ages.

[*The catalogue over, the deposition goes on*]

* * * That all the Negroes slept upon deck, as is customary in this navigation, and none wore fetters, because the owner, his friend Aranda, told him that they were all tractable; * * * that on the seventh day after leaving port, at three o'clock in the morning, all the Spaniards being asleep except the two officers on the watch, who were the boatswain, Juan Robles, and the carpenter, Juan Bautista Gayete, and the helmsman and his boy, the Negroes revolted suddenly, wounded dangerously the boatswain and the carpenter, and successively killed eighteen men of those who were sleeping upon deck, some with handspikes and hatchets, and others by throwing them alive overboard, after tying them; that of the Spaniards upon deck they left about seven, as he thinks, alive and tied, to maneuver the ship, and three or four more, who hid themselves, remained also alive. Although in the act of revolt the Negroes made themselves masters of the hatchway, six or seven wounded went through it to the cockpit, without any hindrance on their part; that during the act of revolt the mate and another person, whose name he does not recollect, attempted to come up through the hatchway, but, being quickly wounded, were obliged to return to the cabin; that the deponent resolved at break of day to come up the companionway, where the Negro Babo was, being the ringleader, and Atufal, who assisted him, and having spoken to them, exhorted them to cease committing such atrocities, asking them, at the same time what they wanted and intended to do, offering, himself, to obey their commands; that notwithstanding this, they threw, in his presence, three men, alive and tied, overboard; that they told the deponent to come up and that they would not kill him; which having done, the Negro Babo asked him whether there were in those seas any Negro countries where they might be carried, and he answered them, No; that the Negro Babo afterwards told him to carry them to Senegal, or to the neighboring islands of St. Nicholas, and he answered that this was impossible on account of the great distance, the necessity involved of rounding Cape Horn, the bad condition of the vessel, the want of provisions, sails, and water; but that the Negro Babo replied to him he must carry them

in anyway, that they would do and conform themselves
to everything the deponent should require as to eating
and drinking; that after a long conference, being absolutely compelled to please them, for they threatened to
kill all the whites if they were not, at all events, carried to
Senegal, he told them that what was most wanting for the
voyage was water, that they would go near the coast to
take it, and thence they would proceed on their course;
that the Negro Babo agreed to it, and the deponent steered
towards the intermediate ports, hoping to meet some
Spanish or foreign vessel that would save them; that
within ten or eleven days they saw the land, and continued their course by it in the vicinity of Nasca; that the
deponent observed that the Negroes were now restless and
mutinous because he did not effect the taking in of water,
the Negro Babo having required, with threats, that it
should be done, without fail, the following day; he told
him he saw plainly that the coast was steep, and the
rivers designated in the maps were not to be found, with
other reasons suitable to the circumstances, that the best
way would be to go to the island of Santa Maria, where
they might water easily, it being a solitary island, as the
foreigners did; that the deponent did not go to Pisco, that
was near, nor make any other port of the coast, because
the Negro Babo had intimated to him several times that
he would kill all the whites the very moment he should
perceive any city, town, or settlement of any kind on
the shores to which they should be carried; that having
determined to go to the island of Santa Maria, as the
deponent had planned, for the purpose of trying whether,
on the passage or near the island itself, they could find
any vessel that should favor them, or whether he could
escape from it in a boat to the neighboring coast of Ar-
ruco, to adopt the necessary means he immediately
changed his course, steering for the island; that the
Negroes Babo and Atufal held daily conferences, in
which they discussed what was necessary for their design of returning to Senegal, whether they were to kill
all the Spaniards, and particularly the deponent; that eight
days after parting from the coast of Nasca, the deponent being on the watch a little after daybreak, and soon
after the Negroes had their meeting, the Negro Babo
came to the place where the deponent was and told him
that he had determined to kill his master, Don Alexandro
Aranda, both because he and his companions could not
otherwise be sure of their liberty, and that, to keep the

seamen in subjection, he wanted to prepare a warning
of what road they should be made to take did they or any
of them oppose him, and that, by means of the death of
Don Alexandro, that warning would best be given, but
that what this last meant the deponent did not at the time
comprehend, nor could not, further than that the death
of Don Alexandro was intended; and moreover the Negro
Babo proposed to the deponent to call the mate Raneds,
who was sleeping in the cabin, before the thing was
done, for fear, as the deponent understood it, that the
mate, who was a good navigator, should be killed with
Don Alexandro and the rest; that the deponent, who was
the friend from youth of Don Alexandro, prayed and
conjured, but all was useless, for the Negro Babo answered him that the thing could not be prevented, and
that all the Spaniards risked their death if they should
attempt to frustrate his will in this matter or any other;
that, in this conflict, the deponent called the mate, Raneds,
who was forced to go apart, and immediately the Negro
Babo commanded the Ashantee Martinqui and the
Ashantee Lecbe to go and commit the murder; that those
two went down with hatchets to the berth of Don Alexandro, that, yet half alive and mangled, they dragged
him on deck; that they were going to throw him overboard in that state, but the Negro Babo stopped them,
bidding the murder be completed on the deck before him,
which was done, when, by his orders, the body was
carried below, forward; that nothing more was seen of
it by the deponent for three days; * * * that Don Alonzo
Sidonia, an old man, long resident at Valparaiso, and
lately appointed to a civil office in Peru, whither he had
taken passage, was at the time sleeping in the berth opposite Don Alexandro's; that awakening at his cries, surprised by them, and at the sight of the Negroes with their
bloody hatchets in their hands, he threw himself into the
sea through a window which was near him, and was
drowned, without it being in the power of the deponent
to assist or take him up; * * * that a short time after
killing Aranda, they brought upon deck his german-
cousin, of middle-age, Don Francisco Masa, of Mendoza,
and the young Don Joaquín, Marqués de Aramboalaza,
then lately from Spain, with his Spanish servant Ponce,
and the three young clerks of Aranda, José Mozairi,
Lorenzo Bargas, and Hermenegildo Gandix, all of Cádiz;
that Don Joaquín and Hermenegildo Gandix, the Negro
Babo, for purposes hereafter to appear, preserved alive,

but Don Francisco Masa, José Mozairi, and Lorenzo
Bargas, with Ponce the servant, beside the boatswain,
Juan Robles, the boatswain's mates, Manuel Viscaya and
Roderigo Hurta, and four of the sailors the Negro Babo
ordered to be thrown alive into the sea, although they
made no resistance nor begged for anything else but
mercy; that the boatswain, Juan Robles, who knew how
to swim, kept the longest above water, making acts of
contrition, and, in the last words he uttered, charged this
deponent to cause mass to be said for his soul to our
Lady of Succor; * * * that, during the three days which
followed, the deponent, uncertain what fate had befallen
the remains of Don Alexandro, frequently asked the
Negro Babo where they were, and, if still on board, whether they were to be preserved for interment ashore, entreating him so to order it; that the Negro Babo answered
nothing till the fourth day, when, at sunrise, the deponent
coming on deck, the Negro Babo showed him a skeleton,
which had been substituted for the ship's proper figurehead—the image of Christopher Colón, the discoverer of
the New World; that the Negro Babo asked him whose
skeleton that was, and whether, from its whiteness, he
should not think it a white's, that, upon discovering his
face, the Negro Babo, coming close, said words to this
effect: "Keep faith with the blacks from here to Senegal,
or you shall in spirit, as now in body, follow your leader,"
pointing to the prow; * * * that the same morning the
Negro Babo took by succession each Spaniard forward,
and asked him whose skeleton that was, and whether,
from its whiteness, he should not think it a white's; that
each Spaniard covered his face; that then to each the
Negro Babo repeated the words in the first place said to
the deponent; * * * that they (the Spaniards), being then
assembled aft, the Negro Babo harangued them, saying
that he had now done all; that the deponent (as navigator
for the Negroes) might pursue his course, warning him
and all of them that they should, soul and body, go the
way of Don Alexandro if he saw them (the Spaniards)
speak or plot anything against them (the Negroes)—a
threat which was repeated every day; that, before the
events last mentioned, they had tied the cook to throw
him overboard, for it is not known what thing they heard
him speak, but finally the Negro Babo spared his life,
at the request of the deponent; that a few days after, the deponent, endeavoring not to omit any means to preserve
the lives of the remaining whites, spoke to the Negroes

of peace and tranquillity, and agreed to draw up a paper, signed by the deponent and the sailors who could write, as also by the Negro Babo, for himself and all the blacks, in which the deponent obliged himself to carry them to Senegal, and they not to kill any more, and he formally to make over to them the ship, with the cargo, with which they were for that time satisfied and quieted. * * * But the next day, the more surely to guard against the sailors' escape, the Negro Babo commanded all the boats to be destroyed but the longboat, which was unseaworthy, and another, a cutter in good condition, which, knowing it would yet be wanted for towing the water casks, he had it lowered down into the hold.

* * * * * * * * *

[*Various particulars of the prolonged and perplexed navigation ensuing here follow, with incidents of a calamitous calm, from which portion one passage is extracted, to wit:*]

—That on the fifth day of the calm, all on board suffering much from the heat and want of water, and five having died in fits, and mad, the Negroes became irritable, and for a chance gesture, which they deemed suspicious—though it was harmless—made by the mate, Raneds, to the deponent in the act of handing a quadrant, they killed him; but that for this they afterwards were sorry, the mate being the only remaining navigator on board, except the deponent.

* * * * * * * * *

—That omitting other events which daily happened, and which can only serve uselessly to recall past misfortunes and conflicts, after seventy-three day's navigation, reckoned from the time they sailed from Nasca, during which they navigated under a scanty allowance of water, and were afflicted with the calms before mentioned, they at last arrived at the island of Santa Maria, on the seventeenth of the month of August, at about six o'clock in the afternoon, at which hour they cast anchor very near the American ship *Bachelor's Delight,* which lay in the same bay, commanded by the generous Captain Amasa Delano; but at six o'clock in the morning they had already descried the port, and the Negroes became uneasy, as soon as at distance they saw the ship, not having expected to see one there; that the Negro Babo pacified them, assuring them that no fear need be had; that straightway he ordered the figure on the bow to be covered with

canvas, as for repairs, and had the decks a little set in
order; that for a time the Negro Babo and the Negro
Atufal conferred; that the Negro Atufal was for sailing
away but the Negro Babo would not, and, by himself, cast
about what to do; that at last he came to the deponent,
proposing to him to say and do all that the deponent
declares to have said and done to the American captain;
*   *   *   *   *   *   *   that the Negro Babo
warned him that if he varied in the least, or uttered any
word, or gave any look that should give the least intimation of the past events or present state, he would
instantly kill him, with all his companions, showing a
dagger which he carried hid, saying something which,
as he understood it, meant that that dagger would be
alert as his eye; that the Negro Babo then announced the
plan to all his companions, which pleased them; that he
then, the better to disguise the truth, devised many ex-
pedients, in some of them uniting deceit and defense;
that of this sort was the device of the six Ashantees before named, who were his bravoes; that them he stationed
on the break of the poop, as if to clean certain hatchets
(in cases, which were part of the cargo), but in reality
to use them, and distribute them at need, and at a given
word he told them; that, among other devices, was the
device of presenting Atufal, his right-hand man, as
chained, though in a moment the chains could be
dropped; that in every particular he informed the deponent what part he was expected to enact in every
device, and what story he was to tell on every occasion,
always threatening him with instant death if he varied
in the least: that, conscious that many of the Negroes
would be turbulent, the Negro Babo appointed the four
aged Negroes, who were calkers, to keep what domestic
order they could on the decks; that again and again he
harangued the Spaniards and his companions, informing
them of his intent and of his devices, and of the invented
story that this deponent was to tell, charging them lest
any of them varied from that story; that these arrangements were made and matured during the interval of
two or three hours between their first sighting the ship
and the arrival on board of Captain Amasa Delano; that
this happened about half-past seven o'clock in the morning, Captain Amasa Delano coming in his boat, and all
gladly receiving him; that the deponent, as well as he
could force himself, acting then the part of principal
owner and a free captain of the ship, told Captain Amasa

Delano, when called upon, that he came from Buenos
Ayres, bound to Lima, with three hundred Negroes; that
off Cape Horn, and in a subsequent fever, many Negroes
had died; that also, by similar casualties, all the sea
officers and the greatest part of the crew had died.

*   *   *   *   *   *   *   *   *

[*And so the deposition goes on, circumstantially recounting the fictitious story dictated to the deponent by
Babo, and through the deponent imposed upon Captain
Delano, and also recounting the friendly offers of Captain
Delano, with other things, but all of which is here
omitted. After the fictitious story, etc., the deposition
proceeds:*]

*   *   *   *   *   *   *   *   *

—that the generous Captain Amasa Delano remained
on board all the day, till he left the ship anchored at six
o'clock in the evening, deponent speaking to him always
of his pretended misfortunes, under the fore-mentioned
principles, without having had it in his power to tell a
single word or give him the least hint, that he might know
the truth and state of things, because the Negro Babo,
performing the office of an officious servant with all the
appearance of submission of the humble slave, did not
leave the deponent one moment; that this was in order
to observe the deponent's actions and words, for the
Negro Babo understands well the Spanish, and besides,
there were thereabout some others who were constantly
on the watch, and likewise understood the Spanish; * * *
that upon one occasion, while deponent was standing on
the deck conversing with Amasa Delano, by a secret sign
the Negro Babo drew him (the deponent) aside, the act
appearing as if originating with the deponent; that then,
he being drawn aside, the Negro Babo proposed to him
to gain from Amasa Delano full particulars about his
ship, and crew, and arms; that the deponent asked "For
what?" that, the Negro Babo answered he might conceive; that, grieved at the prospect of what might overtake the generous Captain Amasa Delano, the deponent
at first refused to ask the desired questions, and used
every argument to induce the Negro Babo to give up this
new design; that the Negro Babo showed the point of
his dagger; that after the information had been obtained
the Negro Babo again drew him aside, telling him that
that very night he (the deponent) would be captain of
two ships, instead of one, for that, great part of the American's ship's crew being to be absent fishing, the six

Ashantees, without anyone else, would easily take it;
that at this time he said other things to the same purpose; that no entreaties availed; that, before Amasa
Delano's coming on board, no hint had been given touching the capture of the American ship; that to prevent this
project the deponent was powerless; * * * —that in some
things his memory is confused, he cannot distinctly recall every event; * * * —that as soon as they had cast
anchor at six of the clock in the evening, as has before
been stated, the American captain took leave, to return
to his vessel; that upon a sudden impulse, which the
deponent believes to have come from God and his angels,
he, after the farewell had been said, followed the generous Captain Amasa Delano as far as the gunwale, where
he stayed, under pretense of taking leave, until Amasa
Delano should have been seated in his boat; that, on
shoving off, the deponent sprang from the gunwale into
the boat, and fell into it, he knows not how, God guarding him; that—

*   *   *   *   *   *   *   *   *

[Here, in the original, follows the account of what further happened at the escape, and how the San Dominick
was retaken, and of the passage to the coast; including
in the recital many expressions of "eternal gratitude"
to the "generous Captain Amasa Delano." The deposition
then proceeds with recapitulatory remarks, and a partial
renumeration of the Negroes, making record of their individual part in the past events, with a view to furnishing,
according to command of the court, the data whereon to
found the criminal sentences to be pronounced. From this
portion is the following;]

—That he believes that all the Negroes, though not in
the first place knowing to the design of revolt, when it was
accomplished, approved it. * * * That the Negro José,
eighteen years old, and in the personal service of Don
Alexandro, was the one who communicated the information to the Negro Babo about the state of things in the
cabin, before the revolt; that this is known, because, in the
preceding midnight, he used to come from his berth, which
was under his master's, in the cabin, to the deck where the
ringleader and his associates were, and had secret conversations with the Negro Babo, in which he was several
times seen by the mate; that, one night, the mate drove
him away twice; * * that this same Negro José was the
one who, without being commanded to do so by the
Negro Babo, as Lecbe and Martinqui were, stabbed his

master, Don Alexandro, after he had been dragged half-lifeless to the deck; * * that the mulatto steward, Francesco, was of the first band of revolters, that he was, in all things, the creature and tool of the Negro Babo; that, to make his court, he, just before a repast in the cabin, proposed to the Negro Babo poisoning a dish for the generous Captain Amasa Delano; this is known and believed, because the Negroes have said it; but that the Negro Babo, having another design, forbade Francesco; * * that the Ashantee Lecbe was one of the worst of them, for that, on the day the ship was retaken, he assisted in the defense of her with a hatchet in each hand, with one of which he wounded in the breast the chief mate of Amasa Delano, in the first act of boarding; this all knew; that, in sight of the deponent, Lecbe struck with a hatchet, Don Francisco Masa, when, by the Negro Babo's orders, he was carrying him to throw him overboard alive, beside participating in the murder, before mentioned, of Don Alexandro Aranda and others of the cabin passengers; that, owing to the fury with which the Ashantees fought in the engagement with the boats, but this Lecbe and Yan survived; that Yan was bad as Lecbe; that Yan was the man who, by Babo's command, willingly prepared the skeleton of Don Alexandro, in a way the Negroes afterwards told the deponent, but which he, so long as reason is left him, can never divulge; that Yan and Lecbe were the two who, in a calm by night, riveted the skeleton to the bow; this also the Negroes told him; that the Negro Babo was he who traced the inscription below it; that the Negro Babo was the plotter from first to last; he ordered every murder, and was the helm and keel of the revolt; that Atufal was his lieutenant in all, but Atufal with his own hand committed no murder, nor did the Negro Babo; * * that Atufal was shot, being killed in the fight with the boats, ere boarding; * * that the Negresses, of age, were knowing to the revolt, and testified themselves satisfied at the death of their master, Don Alexandro; that, had the Negroes not restrained them, they would have tortured to death, instead of simply killing, the Spaniards slain by command of the Negro Babo; that the Negresses used their utmost influence to have the deponent made away with; that, in the various acts of murder, they sang songs and danced—not gaily, but solemnly, and before the engagement with the boats, as well as during the action, they sang melancholy songs to the Negroes, and that this

melancholy tone was more inflaming than a different one
would have been, and was so intended; that all this is
believed, because the Negroes have said it. * * * —that of
the thirty-six men of the crew, exclusive of the passengers
(all of whom are now dead), which the deponent had
knowledge of, six only remained alive, with four cabin
boys and ship boys, not included with the crew; * * *
—that the Negroes broke an arm of one of the cabin
boys and gave him strokes with hatchets.

[*Then follow various random disclosures referring to
various periods of time. The following are extracted;*]

—That during the presence of Captain Amasa Delano
on board, some attempts were made by the sailors, and
one by Hermenegildo Gandix, to convey hints to him of
the true state of affairs, but that these attempts were ineffectual, owing to fear of incurring death, and, furthermore, owing to the devices which offered contradictions
to the true state of affairs, as well as owing to the
generosity and piety of Amasa Delano incapable of sounding such wickedness; * * * that Luys Galgo, a sailor
about sixty years of age, and formerly of the king's navy,
was one of those who sought to convey tokens to Captain
Amasa Delano; but his intent, though undiscovered,
being suspected, he was, on a pretense, made to retire
out of sight, and at last into the hold, and there was
made away with. This the Negroes have since said; * * *
that one of the ship boys feeling, from Captain Amasa
Delano's presence, some hopes of release, and not having
enough prudence, dropped some chance word respecting
his expectations, which being overheard and understood
by a slave boy with whom he was eating at the time, the
latter struck him on the head with a knife, inflicting a bad
wound, but of which the boy is now healing; that likewise,
not long before the ship was brought to anchor, one of
the seamen steering at the time endangered himself by
letting the blacks remark some expression in his countenance, arising from a cause similar to the above, but
this sailor, by his heedful after conduct, escaped; * * *
that these statements are made to show the court that
from the beginning to the end of the revolt it was impossible for the deponent and his men to act otherwise
than they did; * * *—that the third clerk, Hermenegildo
Gandix, who before had been forced to live among the
seamen, wearing a seaman's habit, and in all respects
appearing to be one for the time, he, Gandix, was killed

by a musket ball fired through mistake from the boats before boarding; having in his fright run up the mizzen rigging, calling to the boats—"don't board," lest upon their boarding the Negroes should kill him; that this inducing the Americans to believe he some way favored the cause of the Negroes, they fired two balls at him, so that he fell wounded from the rigging, and was drowned in the sea; * * *—that the young Don Joaquín, Marqués de Aramboalaza, like Hermenegildo Gandix, the third clerk, was degraded to the office and appearance of a common seaman; that upon one occasion when Don Joaquín shrank, the Negro Babo commanded the Ashantee Lecbe to take tar and heat it, and pour it upon Don Joaquín's hands; * * *—that Don Joaquín was killed owing to another mistake of the Americans, but one impossible to be avoided, as, upon the approach of the boats, Don Joaquín, with a hatchet tied edge out and upright to his hand, was made by the Negroes to appear on the bulwarks; whereupon, seen with arms in his hands and in a questionable attitude, he was shot for a renegade seaman; * * *—that on the person of Don Joaquín was found secreted a jewel, which, by papers that were discovered, proved to have been meant for the shrine of our Lady of Mercy in Lima, a votive offering, beforehand prepared and guarded, to attest his gratitude when he should have landed in Peru, his last destination, for the safe conclusion of his entire voyage from Spain; * * * —that the jewel, with the other effects of the late Don Joaquín, is in the custody of the brethren of the Hospital de Sacerdotes, awaiting the disposition of the honorable court; * * *—that, owing to the condition of the deponent, as well as the haste in which the boats departed for the attack, the Americans were not forewarned that there were, among the apparent crew, a passenger and one of the clerks disguised by the Negro Babo; * * *—that, beside the Negroes killed in the action, some were killed after the capture and reanchoring at night, when shackled to the ringbolts on deck; that these deaths were committed by the sailors, ere they could be prevented. That so soon as informed of it, Captain Amasa Delano used all his authority, and in particular with his own hand struck down Martínez Gola, who having found a razor in the pocket of an old jacket of his which one of the shackled Negroes had on, was aiming it at the Negro's throat; that the noble Captain Amasa Delano also wrenched from the hand of Bartholomew Barlo a dagger,

secreted at the time of the massacre of the whites, with
which he was in the act of stabbing a shackled Negro,
who, the same day, with another Negro, had thrown him
down and jumped upon him; * * *—that, for all the
events, befalling through so long a time, during which
the ship was in the hands of the Negro Babo, he cannot
here give account, but that what he has said is the most
substantial of what occurs to him at present, and is the
truth under the oath which he has taken; which declaration he affirmed and ratified, after hearing it read to him.

He said that he is twenty-nine years of age, and broken
in body and mind; that when finally dismissed by the
court, he shall not return home to Chile but betake himself to the monastery on Mount Agonia without; and
signed with his honor, and crossed himself, and, for the
time, departed as he came, in his litter, with the monk
Infelez, to the Hospital de Sacerdotes.

BENITO CERENO.

DOCTOR ROZAS.

If the deposition have served as the key to fit into the
lock of the complications which precede it, then, as a
vault whose door has been flung back, the *San Dominick*'s
hull lies open today.

Hitherto the nature of this narrative, besides rendering
the intricacies in the beginning unavoidable, has more or
less required that many things, instead of being set down
in the order of occurrence, should be retrospectively or
irregularly given; this last is the case with the following
passages, which will conclude the account:

During the long, mild voyage to Lima, there was, as
before hinted, a period during which the sufferer a little
recovered his health, or, at least in some degree, his tranquillity. Ere the decided relapse which came, the two captains had many cordial conversations—their fraternal
unreserve in singular contrast with former withdrawments.

Again and again it was repeated how hard it had been
to enact the part forced on the Spaniard by Babo.

"Ah, my dear friend," Don Benito once said, "at those
very times when you thought me so morose and ungrateful, nay, when, as you now admit, you half thought me
plotting your murder, at those very times my heart was
frozen; I could not look at you, thinking of what, both on
board this ship and your own, hung, from other hands,

over my kind benefactor. And as God lives, Don Amasa, I know not whether desire for my own safety alone could have nerved me to that leap into your boat, had it not been for the thought that, did you, unenlightened, return to your ship, you, my best friend, with all who might be with you, stolen upon that night in your hammocks, would never in this world have wakened again. Do but think how you walked this deck, how you sat in this cabin, every inch of ground mined into honeycombs under you. Had I dropped the least hint, made the least advance towards an understanding between us, death, explosive death—yours as mine—would have ended the scene."

"True, true," cried Captain Delano, starting, "you have saved my life, Don Benito, more than I yours; saved it, too, against my knowledge and will."

"Nay, my friend," rejoined the Spaniard, courteous even to the point of religion, "God charmed your life, but you saved mine. To think of some things you did—those smilings and chattings, rash pointings and gesturings. For less than these, they slew my mate, Raneds; but you had the Prince of Heaven's safe conduct through all ambuscades."

"Yes, all is owing to Providence, I know: but the temper of my mind that morning was more than commonly pleasant, while the sight of so much suffering, more apparent than real, added to my good-nature, compassion, and charity, happily interweaving the three. Had it been otherwise, doubtless, as you hint, some of my interferences might have ended, unhappily enough. Besides, those feelings I spoke of enabled me to get the better of momentary distrust, at times when acuteness might have cost me my life, without saving another's. Only at the end did my suspicions get the better of me, and you know how wide of the mark they then proved."

"Wide, indeed," said Don Benito, sadly; "you were with me all day; stood with me, sat with me, talked with me, looked at me, ate with me, drank with me; and yet, your last act was to clutch for a monster, not only an innocent man, but the most pitiable of all men. To such degree may malign machinations and deceptions impose. So far may even the best man err in judging the conduct of one with the recesses of whose condition he is not acquainted. But you were forced to it, and you were in time undeceived.

Would that, in both respects, it was so ever, and with all men."

"You generalize, Don Benito; and mournfully enough. But the past is passed; why moralize upon it? Forget it. See, yon bright sun has forgotten it all, and the blue sea, and the blue sky; these have turned over new leaves."

"Because they have no memory," he dejectedly replied; "because they are not human."

"But these mild trades that now fan your cheek, do they not come with a human-like healing to you? Warm friends, steadfast friends are the trades."

"With their steadfastness they but waft me to my tomb, señor," was the foreboding response.

"You are saved," cried Captain Delano, more and more astonished and pained; "you are saved: what has cast such a shadow upon you?"

"The Negro."

There was silence, while the moody man sat, slowly and unconsciously gathering his mantle about him, as if it were a pall.

There was no more conversation that day.

But if the Spaniard's melancholy sometimes ended in muteness upon topics like the above, there were others upon which he never spoke at all; on which, indeed, all his old reserves were piled. Pass over the worst, and, only to elucidate, let an item or two of these be cited. The dress, so precise and costly, worn by him on the day whose events have been narrated, had not willingly been put on. And that silver-mounted sword, apparent symbol of despotic command, was not, indeed, a sword, but the ghost of one. The scabbard, artificially stiffened, was empty.

As for the black—whose brain, not body, had schemed and led the revolt, with the plot—his slight frame, inadequate to that which it held, had at once yielded to the superior muscular strength of his captor, in the boat. Seeing all was over, he uttered no sound, and could not be forced to. His aspect seemed to say: since I cannot do deeds, I will not speak words. Put in irons in the hold with the rest, he was carried to Lima. During the passage, Don Benito did not visit him. Nor then, nor at any time after, would he look at him. Before the tribunal he refused. When pressed by the judges he fainted. On the testimony of the sailors alone rested the legal identity of Babo.

Some months after, dragged to the gibbet at the tail of a mule, the black met his voiceless end. The body was burned to ashes; but for many days, the head, that hive of subtlety, fixed on a pole in the plaza, met, unabashed, the gazes of the whites, and across the Plaza looked towards St. Bartholomew's church, in whose vaults slept then, as now, the recovered bones of Aranda, and across the Rimac bridge looked towards the monastery, on Mount Agonia without; where, three months after being dismissed by the court, Benito Cereno, borne on the bier, did, indeed, follow his leader.

THE LIGHTNING-ROD MAN

WHAT grand irregular thunder, thought I, standing on my hearthstone among the Acroceraunian hills, as the scattered bolts boomed overhead, and crashed down among the valleys, every bolt followed by zigzag irradiations and swift slants of sharp rain, which audibly rang, like a charge of spear points, on my low shingled roof. I suppose, though, that the mountains hereabouts break and churn up the thunder, so that it is far more glorious here than on the plain. Hark!—someone at the door. Who is this that chooses a time of thunder for making calls? And why don't he, man-fashion, use the knocker, instead of making that doleful undertaker's clatter with his fist against the hollow panel? But let him in. Ah, here he comes. "Good day, sir"—an entire stranger. "Pray be seated." What is that strange-looking walking stick he carries: "A fine thunderstorm, sir."

"Fine?—Awful!"

"You are wet. Stand here on the hearth before the fire."

"Not for worlds!"

The stranger still stood in the exact middle of the cottage, where he had first planted himself. His singularity impelled a closer scrutiny. A lean, gloomy figure. Hair dark and lank, mattedly streaked over his brow. His sunken pitfalls of eyes were ringed by indigo halos, and played with an innocuous sort of lightning: the gleam without the bolt. The whole man was dripping. He stood in a puddle on the bare oak floor; his strange walking stick vertically resting at his side.

It was a polished copper rod, four feet long, lengthwise attached to a neat wooden staff, by insertion into two balls of greenish glass, ringed with copper bands. The metal rod terminated at the top, tripodwise, in three keen tines, brightly gilt. He held the thing by the wooden part alone.

"Sir," said I, bowing politely, "have I the honor of a visit from that illustrious god, Jupiter Tonans? So stood he in the Greek statue of old, grasping the lightning bolt. If you be he, or his viceroy, I have to thank you for this noble storm you have brewed among our mountains. Listen: That was a glorious peal. Ah, to a lover of the majestic, it is a good thing to have the Thunderer himself in one's cottage. The thunder grows finer for that. But pray be seated. This old rush-bottomed armchair, I grant, is a poor substitute for your evergreen throne on Olympus, but condescend to be seated."

While I thus pleasantly spoke, the stranger eyed me, half in wonder, and half in a strange sort of horror, but did not move a foot.

"Do, sir, be seated; you need to be dried ere going forth again."

I planted the chair invitingly on the broad hearth, where a little fire had been kindled that afternoon to dissipate the dampness, not the cold, for it was early in the month of September.

But without heeding my solicitation, and still standing in the middle of the floor, the stranger gazed at me portentously and spoke.

"Sir," said he, "excuse me; but instead of my accepting your invitation to be seated on the hearth there, I solemnly warn *you* that you had best accept *mine,* and stand with me in the middle of the room. Good heavens!" he cried, starting—"there is another of those awful crashes. I warn you, sir, quit the hearth."

"Mr. Jupiter Tonans," said I, quietly rolling my body on the stone, "I stand very well here."

"Are you so horridly ignorant, then," he cried, "as not to know that by far the most dangerous part of a house during such a terrific tempest as this is the fireplace?"

"Nay, I did not know that," involuntarily stepping upon the first board next to the stone.

The stranger now assumed such an unpleasant air of successful admonition, that—quite involuntarily again— I stepped back upon the hearth, and threw myself into the erectest, proudest posture I could command. But I said nothing.

"For Heaven's sake," he cried, with a stange mixture of alarm and intimidation—"for Heaven's sake, get off the hearth! Know you not that the heated air and soot are conductors—to say nothing of those immense iron fire-dogs? Quit the spot—I conjure—I command you."

"Mr. Jupiter Tonans, I am not accustomed to be commanded in my own house."

"Call me not by that pagan name. You are profane in this time of terror."

"Sir, will you be so good as to tell me your business? If you seek shelter from the storm, you are welcome, so long as you be civil, but if you come on business, open it forthwith. Who are you?"

"I am a dealer in lightning rods," said the stranger, softening his tone; "my special business is—— Merciful heaven! what a crash!—Have you ever been struck—your premises, I mean? No? It's best to be provided"—significantly rattling his metallic staff on the floor;—"by nature, there are no castles in thunderstorms; yet, say but the word, and of this cottage I can make a Gibraltar by a few waves of this wand. Hark, what Himalayas of concussions!"

"You interrupted yourself; your special business you were about to speak of."

"My special business is to travel the country for orders for lightning rods. This is my specimen rod"—tapping his staff; "I have the best of references"—fumbling in his pockets. "In Criggan last month I put up three-and-twenty rods on only five buildings."

"Let me see. Was it not at Criggan last week, about midnight on Saturday, that the steeple, the big elm, and the assembly-room cupola were struck? Any of your rods there?"

"Not on the tree and cupola, but the steeple."

"Of what use is your rod, then?"

"Of life-and-death use. But my workman was heedless. In fitting the rod at top to the steeple, he allowed a part of the metal to graze the tin sheeting. Hence the accident. Not my fault, but his. Hark!"

"Never mind. That clap burst quite loud enough to be heard without finger-pointing. Did you hear of the event at Montreal last year? A servant girl struck at her bedside with a rosary in her hand, the beads being metal. Does your beat extend into the Canadas?"

"No. And I hear that there iron rods only are in use. They should have *mine,* which are copper. Iron is easily fused. Then they draw out the rod so slender that it has not body enough to conduct the full electric current. The metal melts; the building is destroyed. My copper rods never act so. Those Canadians are fools. Some of them knob the rod at the top, which risks a deadly explosion, instead of imperceptibly carrying down the current into the earth, as this sort of rod does. *Mine* is the only true rod. Look at it. Only one dollar a foot."

"This abuse of your own calling in another might make one distrustful with respect to yourself."

"Hark! The thunder becomes less muttering. It is nearing us, and nearing the earth, too. Hark! One crammed crash! All the vibrations made one by nearness. Another flash. Hold!"

"What do you?" I said, seeing him now, instantaneously relinquishing his staff, lean intently forward towards the window, with his right fore and middle fingers on his left wrist.

But ere the words had well escaped me, another exclamation escaped him.

"Crash! only three pulses—less than a third of a mile off—yonder, somewhere in that wood. I passed three stricken oaks there, ripped out new and glittering. The oak draws lightning more than other timber, having iron in solution in its sap. Your floor here seems oak."

"Heart-of-oak. From the peculiar time of your call upon me, I suppose you purposely select stormy weather for your journeys. When the thunder is roaring you deem it an hour peculiarly favorable for producing impressions favorable to your trade."

"Hark—Awful!"

"For one who would arm others with fearlessness, you seem unbeseemingly timorous yourself. Common men choose fair weather for their travels: you choose thunderstorms; and yet——"

"That I travel in thunderstorms, I grant; but not without particular precautions, such as only a lightning-rod man may know. Hark! Quick—look at my specimen rod. Only one dollar a foot."

"A very fine rod, I dare say. But what are these particular precautions of yours? Yet first let me close yonder shutters; the slanting rain is beating through the sash. I will bar up."

"Are you mad? Know you not that yon iron bar is a swift conductor? Desist."

"I will simply close the shutters, then, and call my boy to bring me a wooden bar. Pray, touch the bellpull there."

"Are you frantic? That bell wire might blast you. Never touch bell wire in a thunderstorm, nor ring a bell of any sort."

"Nor those in belfries? Pray, will you tell me where and how one may be safe in a time like this? Is there any part of my house I may touch with hopes of my life?"

"There is; but not where you now stand. Come away from the wall. The current will sometimes run down a wall, and—a man being a better conductor than a wall—it would leave the wall and run into him. Swoop! *That* must have fallen very nigh. That must have been globular lightning."

"Very probably. Tell me at once, which is, in your opinion, the safest part of this house?"

"This room, and this one spot in it where I stand. Come hither."

"The reasons first."

"Hark!—after the flash the gust—the sashes shiver— the house, the house!—Come hither to me!"

"The reasons, if you please."

"Come hither to me!"

"Thank you again, I think I will try my old stand—the hearth. And now. Mr. Lightning-rod Man, in the pauses of the thunder, be so good as to tell me your reasons for esteeming this one room of the house the safest, and your own one standpoint there the safest spot in it."

There was now a little cessation of the storm for a while. The lightning-rod man seemed relieved, and replied:

"Your house is a one-storied house, with an attic and a cellar; this room is between. Hence its comparative safety. Because lightning sometimes passes from the clouds to the earth, and sometimes from the earth to the clouds. Do you comprehend?—and I choose the middle of the room, because, if the lightning should strike the house at all, it would come down the chimney or walls; so, obviously, the further you are from them, the better. Come hither to me, now."

"Presently. Something you just said, instead of alarming me, has strangely inspired confidence."

"What have I said?"

"You said that sometimes lightning flashes from the earth to the clouds."

"Aye, the returning stroke, as it is called; when the earth, being overcharged with the fluid, flashes its surplus upward."

"The returning stroke; that is, from earth to sky. Better and better. But come here on the hearth and dry yourself."

"I am better here, and better wet."

"How?"

"It is the safest thing you can do—hark, again!—to get yourself thoroughly drenched in a thunderstorm. Wet clothes are better conductors than the body, and so, if the lightning strike, it might pass down the wet clothes without touching the body. The storm deepens again. Have you a rug in the house? Rugs are nonconductors. Get one, that I may stand on it here, and you, too. The skies blacken— it is dusk at noon. Hark!—the rug, the rug!"

I gave him one, while the hooded mountains seemed closing and tumbling into the cottage.

"And now, since our being dumb will not help us," said I, resuming my place, "let me hear your precautions in traveling during thunderstorms."

"Wait till this one is passed."

"Nay, proceed with the precautions. You stand in the safest possible place according to your own account. Go on."

"Briefly, then. I avoid pine trees, high houses, lonely barns, upland pastures, running water, flocks of cattle and sheep, a crowd of men. If I travel on foot—as today—I do not walk fast; if in my buggy, I touch not its back or sides; if on horseback, I dismount and lead the horse. But of all things, I avoid tall men."

"Do I dream? Man avoid man? and in danger-time, too."

"Tall men in a thunderstorm I avoid. Are you so grossly ignorant as not to know that the height of a six-footer is sufficient to discharge an electric cloud upon him? Are not lonely Kentuckians, plowing, smit in the unfinished furrow? Nay, if the six-footer stand by running water, the cloud will sometimes *select* him as its conductor to that running water. Hark! Sure, yon black pinnacle is split. Yes, a man is a good conductor. The lightning goes through and through a man, but only peels a tree. But sir, you have kept me so long answering your questions that I have not yet come to business. Will you order one of my rods? Look at this specimen one. See: it is of the best of copper. Copper's the best conductor. Your house is low, but, being upon the mountains, that lowness does not one whit depress it. You mountaineers are most exposed. In mountainous countries the lightning-rod man should have most business. Look at the specimen, sir. One rod will answer for a house so small as this. Look over these recommendations. Only one rod, sir; cost, only twenty dollars. Hark! There go all the granite Taconics and Hoosics dashed together like pebbles. By the sound, that must have struck something. An elevation of five feet above the house will protect twenty feet radius all about the rod. Only twenty dollars, sir—a dollar a foot. Hark!—Dreadful!— Will you order? Will you buy? Shall I put down your

name? Think of being a heap of charred offal, like a
haltered horse burnt in his stall—and all in one flash!"

"You pretended envoy extraordinary and minister pleni-
potentiary to and from Jupiter Tonans," laughed I; "you
mere man who come here to put you and your pipestem
between clay and sky, do you think that because you can
strike a bit of green light from the Leyden jar that you
can thoroughly avert the supernal bolt? Your rod rusts, or
breaks, and where are you? Who has empowered you, you
Tetzel, to peddle round your indulgences from divine
ordinations? The hairs of our heads are numbered, and the
days of our lives. In thunder as in sunshine, I stand at ease
in the hands of my God. False negotiator, away! See, the
scroll of the storm is rolled back; the house is unharmed;
and in the blue heavens I read in the rainbow that the
Deity will not, of purpose, make war on man's earth."

"Impious wretch!" foamed the stranger, blackening in
the face as the rainbow beamed, "I will publish your infidel notions."

The scowl grew blacker on his face; the indigo circles
enlarged round his eyes as the storm rings round the midnight moon. He sprang upon me, his tri-forked thing at
my heart.

I seized it; I snapped it; I dashed it; I trod it; and,
dragging the dark lightning-king out of my door, flung his
elbowed, copper scepter after him.

But spite of my treatment, and spite of my dissuasive
talk of him to my neighbors, the lightning-rod man still
dwells in the land; still travels in storm-time, and drives
a brave trade with the fears of man.

THE ENCANTADAS;
or
ENCHANTED ISLANDS

Sketch First

THE ISLES AT LARGE

—"That may not be, said then the ferryman,
  Least we unweeting hap to be fordonne;
For those same islands seeming now and than,
  Are not firme land, nor any certein wonne,
  But stragling plots which to and fro do ronne
In the wide waters; therefore are they hight
The Wandering Islands; therefore do them shonne;
For they have oft drawne many a wandring wight
Into most deadly daunger and distressed plight;
For whosoever once hath fastened
His foot thereon may never it secure
But wandreth evermore uncertain and unsure."

    *   *   *   *   *   *   *

"Darke, dolefull, dreary, like a greedy grave,
  That still for carrion carcasses doth crave;
On top whereof ay dwelt the ghastly owl,
  Shrieking his baleful note, which ever drave
Far from that haunt all other cheerful fowl,
And all about it wandring ghosts did wayle and
    howl."

TAKE five-and-twenty heaps of cinders dumped here and there in an outside city lot, imagine some of them magnified into mountains, and the vacant lot the sea, and you will have a fit idea of the general aspect of the Encantadas, or Enchanted Isles. A group rather of extinct volcanoes than of isles, looking much as the world at large might after a penal conflagration.

It is to be doubted whether any spot of earth can, in desolateness, furnish a parallel to this group. Abandoned cemeteries of long ago, old cities by piecemeal tumbling to their ruin, these are melancholy enough; but, like all else which has but once been associated with humanity, they still awaken in us some thoughts of sympathy, however sad. Hence, even the Dead Sea, along with whatever other emotions it may at times inspire, does not fail to touch in the pilgrim some of his less unpleasurable feelings.

And as for solitariness, the great forests of the north, the expanses of unnavigated waters, the Greenland ice fields, are the profoundest of solitudes to a human observer; still the magic of their changeable tides and seasons mitigates their terror, because, though unvisited by men, those forests are visited by the May; the remotest seas reflect familiar stars even as Lake Erie does; and in the clear air of a fine Polar day, the irradiated, azure ice shows beautifully as malachite.

But the special curse, as one may call it, of the Encantadas, that which exalts them in desolation above Idumea and the Pole, is that to them change never comes; neither the change of seasons nor of sorrows. Cut by the Equator, they know not autumn, and they know not spring; while, already reduced to the lees of fire, ruin itself can work little more upon them. The showers refresh the deserts, but in these isles rain never falls. Like split Syrian gourds left withering in the sun, they are cracked by an everlasting drought beneath a torrid sky. "Have mercy upon me," the wailing spirit of the Encantadas seems to cry, "and send Lazarus that he may dip the tip of his finger in water and cool my tongue, for I am tormented in this flame."

Another feature in these isles is their emphatic uninhabitableness. It is deemed a fit type of all-forsaken overthrow that the jackal should den in the wastes of weedy

Babylon, but the Encantadas refuse to harbor even the outcasts of the beasts. Man and wolf alike disown them. Little but reptile life is here found: tortoises, lizards, immense spiders, snakes, and that strangest anomaly of outlandish nature, the *iguana*. No voice, no low, no howl is heard; the chief sound of life here is a hiss.

On most of the isles where vegetation is found at all, it is more ungrateful than the blankness of Aracama. Tangled thickets of wiry bushes, without fruit and without a name, springing up among deep fissures of calcined rock and treacherously masking them, or a parched growth of distorted cactus trees.

In many places the coast is rock-bound, or, more properly, clinker-bound; tumbled masses of blackish or greenish stuff like the dross of an iron furnace, forming dark clefts and caves here and there, into which a ceaseless sea pours a fury of foam, overhanging them with a swirl of gray, haggard mist, amidst which sail screaming flights of unearthly birds heightening the dismal din. However calm the sea without, there is no rest for these swells and those rocks; they lash and are lashed, even when the outer ocean is most at peace with itself. On the oppressive, clouded days, such as are peculiar to this part of the watery Equator, the dark, vitrified masses, many of which raise themselves among white whirlpools and breakers in detached and perilous places off the shore, present a most Plutonian sight. In no world but a fallen one could such lands exist.

Those parts of the strand free from the marks of fire stretch away in wide level beaches of multitudinous dead shells, with here and there decayed bits of sugar cane, bamboos, and coconuts, washed upon this other and darker world from the charming palm isles to the westward and southward, all the way from Paradise to Tartarus, while mixed with the relics of distant beauty you will sometimes see fragments of charred wood and moldering ribs of wrecks. Neither will anyone be surprised at meeting these last, after observing the conflicting currents which eddy throughout nearly all the wide channels of the entire group. The capriciousness of the tides of air sympathizes with those of the sea. Nowhere is the wind so light, baffling, and every way unreliable, and so given to perplexing calms,

as at the Encantadas. Nigh a month has been spent by a
ship going from one isle to another, though but ninety
miles between; for owing to the force of the current, the
boats employed to tow barely suffice to keep the craft
from sweeping upon the cliffs, but do nothing towards
accelerating her voyage. Sometimes it is impossible for
a vessel from afar to fetch up with the group itself, unless
large allowances for prospective leeway have been made
ere its coming in sight. And yet, at other times, there
is a mysterious indraft, which irresistibly draws a passing
vessel among the isles, though not bound to them.

True, at one period, as to some extent at the present
day, large fleets of whalemen cruised for spermaceti upon
what some seamen call the Enchanted Ground. But this,
as in due place will be described, was off the great outer
isle of Albemarle, away from the intricacies of the smaller
isles, where there is plenty of sea room, and hence to that
vicinity the above remarks do not altogether apply, though
even there the current runs at times with singular force,
shifting, too, with as singular a caprice.

Indeed, there are seasons when currents quite unaccountable prevail for a great distance round about the
total group, and are so strong and irregular as to change a
vessel's course against the helm, though sailing at the rate
of four or five miles the hour. The difference in the
reckonings of navigators produced by these causes, along
with the light and variable winds, long nourished a persuasion that there existed two distinct clusters of isles in the
parallel of the Encantadas, about a hundred leagues apart.
Such was the idea of their earlier visitors, the Buccaneers;
and as late as 1750 the charts of that part of the Pacific
accorded with the strange delusion. And this apparent
fleetingness and unreality of the locality of the isles was
most probably one reason for the Spaniards calling them
the Encantada, or Enchanted Group.

But not uninfluenced by their character, as they now
confessedly exist, the modern voyager will be inclined to
fancy that the bestowal of this name might have in part
originated in that air of spellbound desertness which so
significantly invests the isles. Nothing can better suggest
the aspect of once living things malignly crumbled from

ruddiness into ashes. Apples of Sodom, after touching, seem these isles.

However wavering their place may seem by reason of the currents, they themselves, at least to one upon the shore, appear invariably the same: fixed, cast, glued into the very body of cadaverous death.

Nor would the appellation "enchanted" seem misapplied in still another sense. For concerning the peculiar reptile inhabitant of these wilds—whose presence gives the group its second Spanish name, Gallipagos—concerning the tortoises found here, most mariners have long cherished a superstition not more frightful than grotesque. They earnestly believe that all wicked sea officers, more especially commodores and captains, are at death (and in some cases before death) transformed into tortoises, thenceforth dwelling upon these hot aridities, sole solitary lords of Asphaltum.

Doubtless, so quaintly dolorous a thought was originally inspired by the woebegone landscape itself; but more particularly, perhaps, by the tortoises. For, apart from their strictly physical features, there is something strangely self-condemned in the appearance of these creatures. Lasting sorrow and penal hopelessness are in no animal form so suppliantly expressed as in theirs; while the thought of their wonderful longevity does not fail to enhance the impression.

Nor even at the risk of meriting the charge of absurdly believing in enchantments can I restrain the admission that sometimes, even now, when leaving the crowded city to wander out July and August among the Adirondack Mountains, far from the influences of towns and proportionally nigh to the mysterious ones of nature; when at such times I sit me down in the mossy head of some deep-wooded gorge, surrounded by prostrate trunks of blasted pines, and recall, as in a dream, my other and far-distant rovings in the baked heart of the charmed isles, and remember the sudden glimpses of dusky shells, and long languid necks protruded from the leafless thickets; and again have beheld the vitreous inland rocks worn down and grooved into deep ruts by ages and ages of the slow draggings of tortoises in quest of pools of scanty water;

I can hardly resist the feeling that in my time I have indeed slept upon evilly enchanted ground.

Nay, such is the vividness of my memory, or the magic of my fancy, that I know not whether I am not the occasional victim of optical delusion concerning the Gallipagos. For, often in scenes of social merriment, and especially at revels held by candlelight in old-fashioned mansions, so that shadows are thrown into the further recesses of an angular and spacious room, making them put on a look of haunted undergrowth of lonely woods, I have drawn the attention of my comrades by my fixed gaze and sudden change of air, as I have seemed to see, slowly emerging from those imagined solitudes, and heavily crawling along the floor, the ghost of a gigantic tortoise, with "Memento * * * * *" burning in live letters upon his back.

Sketch Second

TWO SIDES TO A TORTOISE

"Most ugly shapes and horrible aspects,
Such as Dame Nature selfe mote feare to see,
Or shame, that ever should so fowle defects
From her most cunning hand escaped bee;
All dreadfull pourtraicts of deformitee.
Ne wonder if these do a man appall;
For all that here at home we dreadfull hold
Be but as bugs to fearen babes withall
Compared to the creatures in these isles' entrall.

　　　*　　*　　*　　*　　*　　*

Fear naught, then said the palmer, well avized,
For these same monsters are not there indeed,
But are into these fearful shapes disguized.

　　　*　　*　　*　　*　　*　　*

And lifting up his vertuous staffe on high,
Then all that dreadful armie fast gan flye
Into great Zethy's bosom, where they hidden lye."

In view of the description given, may one be gay upon the Encantadas? Yes: that is, find one the gaiety, and he will be gay. And, indeed, sackcloth and ashes as they are, the isles are not perhaps unmitigated gloom. For while no spectator can deny their claims to a most solemn and superstitious consideration, no more than my firmest

resolutions can decline to behold the specter-tortoise when
emerging from its shadowy recess; yet even the tortoise,
dark and melancholy as it is upon the back, still possesses
a bright side; its calipee or breastplate being sometimes of
a faint yellowish or golden tinge. Moreover, everyone
knows that tortoises as well as turtle are of such a make
that if you but put them on their backs you thereby expose
their bright sides without the possibility of their recovering
themselves, and turning into view the other. But after you
have done this, and because you have done this, you
should not swear that the tortoise has no dark side. Enjoy
the bright, keep it turned up perpetually if you can, but
be honest, and don't deny the black. Neither should he
who cannot turn the tortoise from its natural position so
as to hide the darker and expose his livelier aspect, like
a great October pumpkin in the sun, for that cause declare
the creature to be one total inky blot. The tortoise is both
black and bright. But let us to particulars.

Some months before my first stepping ashore upon the
group, my ship was cruising in its close vicinity. One noon
we found ourselves off the South Head of Albemarle, and
not very far from the land. Partly by way of freak, and
partly by way of spying out so strange a country, a boat's
crew was sent ashore, with orders to see all they could,
and, besides, bring back whatever tortoises they could
conveniently transport.

It was after sunset when the adventurers returned. I
looked down over the ship's high side as if looking down
over the curb of a well, and dimly saw the damp boat deep
in the sea with some unwonted weight. Ropes were dropped
over, and presently three huge antediluvian-looking tortoises, after much straining, were landed on deck. They
seemed hardly of the seed of earth. We had been broad
upon the waters for five long months, a period amply
sufficient to make all things of the land wear a fabulous
hue to the dreamy mind. Had three Spanish custom-house
officers boarded us then it is not unlikely that I should have
curiously stared at them, felt of them, and stroked them,
much as savages serve civilized guests. But instead of three
custom-house officers, behold these really wondrous tortoises—none of your schoolboy mud turtles, but black as
widower's weeds, heavy as chests of plate, with vast shells

medallioned and orbed like shields, and dented and blistered like shields that have breasted a battle, shaggy, too, here and there, with dark green moss, and slimy with the spray of the sea. These mystic creatures, suddenly translated by night from unutterable solitudes to our peopled deck, affected me in a manner not easy to unfold. They seemed newly crawled forth from beneath the foundations of the world. Yea, they seemed the identical tortoises whereon the Hindu plants this total sphere. With a lantern I inspected them more closely. Such worshipful venerableness of aspect! Such furry greenness mantling the rude peelings and healing the fissures of their shattered shells. I no more saw three tortoises. They expanded—became transfigured. I seemed to see three Roman Coliseums in magnificent decay.

Ye oldest inhabitants of this or any other isle, said I, pray, give me the freedom of your three-walled towns.

The great feeling inspired by these creatures was that of age: dateless, indefinite endurance. And in fact that any other creature can live and breathe as long as the tortoise of the Encantadas, I will not readily believe. Not to hint of their known capacity of sustaining life while going without food for an entire year, consider that impregnable armor of their living mail. What other bodily being possesses such a citadel wherein to resist the assaults of Time?

As, lantern in hand, I scraped among the moss and beheld the ancient scars of bruises received in many a sullen fall among the marly mountains of the isle—scars strangely widened, swollen, half obliterate, and yet distorted like those sometimes found in the bark of very hoary trees, I seemed an antiquary of a geologist, studying the bird tracks and ciphers upon the exhumed slates trod by incredible creatures whose very ghosts are now defunct.

As I lay in my hammock that night, overhead I heard the slow weary draggings of the three ponderous strangers along the encumbered deck. Their stupidity or their resolution was so great that they never went aside for any impediment. One ceased his movements altogether just before the mid-watch. At sunrise I found him butted like a battering ram against the immovable foot of the foremast, and still striving, tooth and nail, to force the impos-

sible passage. That that these tortoises are the victims of a
penal, or malignant, or perhaps a downright diabolical,
enchanter, seems in nothing more likely than in that strange
infatuation of hopeless toil which so often possesses them.
I have known them in their journeyings ram themselves
heroically against rocks, and long abide there, nudging,
wriggling, wedging, in order to displace them, and so hold
on their inflexible path. Their crowning curse is their
drudging impulse to straightforwardness in a belittered
world.

Meeting with no such hindrance as their companion did,
the other tortoises merely fell foul of small stumbling blocks
—buckets, blocks, and coils of rigging—and at times in
the act of crawling over them would slip with an astound-
ing rattle to the deck. Listening to these draggings and
concussions, I thought me of the haunt from which they
came: an isle full of metallic ravines and gulches, sunk
bottomlessly into the hearts of splintered mountains, and
covered for many miles with inextricable thickets. I then
pictured these three straightforward monsters, century after
century, writhing through the shades, grim as blacksmiths;
crawling so slowly and ponderously that not only did toad-
stools and all fungus things grow beneath their feet, but
a sooty moss sprouted upon their backs. With them I lost
myself in volcanic mazes, brushed away endless boughs
of rotting thickets, till finally in a dream I found myself
sitting cross-legged upon the foremost, a Brahmin similarly
mounted upon either side, forming a tripod of foreheads
which upheld the universal cope.

Such was the wild nightmare begot by my first impression of the Encantadas tortoise. But next evening, strange
to say, I sat down with my shipmates and made a merry
repast from tortoise steaks and tortoise stews; and, supper
over, out knife, and helped convert the three mighty con-
cave shells into three fanciful soup tureens, and polished
the three flat yellowish calipees into three gorgeous salvers.

Sketch Third

ROCK RODONDO

"For they this hight the Rock of vile Reproach,
  A dangerous and dreadful place,
  To which nor fish nor fowl did once approach,

But yelling meaws with sea-gulls hoars and bace
And cormoyrants with birds of ravenous race,
Which still sit waiting on that dreadful clift."

* * * * * *

"With that the rolling sea resounding soft
In his big base them fitly answered,
And on the Rock, the waves breaking aloft,
A solemn meane unto them measured."

* * * * * *

"Then he the boteman bad row easily,
And let him heare some part of that rare melody."

* * * * * *

"Suddeinly an innumerable flight
Of harmefull fowles about them fluttering cride,
And with their wicked wings them oft did smight
And sore annoyed, groping in that griesly night."

* * * * * *

"Even all the nation of unfortunate
And fatal birds about them flocked were."

To go up into a high stone tower is not only a very
fine thing in itself, but the very best mode of gaining a
comprehensive view of the region round about. It is all
the better if this tower stand solitary and alone, like that
mysterious Newport one, or else be sole survivor of some
perished castle.

Now, with reference to the Enchanted Isles, we are for-
tunately supplied with just such a noble point of observation in a remarkable rock, from its peculiar figure called of
old by the Spaniards, Rock Rodondo, or Round Rock.
Some two hundred and fifty feet high, rising straight from
the sea ten miles from land, with the whole mountainous
group to the south and east, Rock Rodondo occupies, on a
large scale, very much the position which the famous Campanile or detached Bell Tower of St. Mark does with respect
to the tangled group of hoary edifices around it.

Ere ascending, however, to gaze abroad upon the Encantadas, this sea tower itself claims attention. It is visible
at the distance of thirty miles, and, fully participating in
that enchantment which pervades the group, when first
seen afar invariably is mistaken for a sail. Four leagues
away, of a golden, hazy noon, it seems some Spanish admiral's ship, stacked up with glittering canvas. Sail ho!

Sail ho! Sail ho! from all three masts. But coming nigh, the enchanted frigate is transformed apace into a craggy keep.

My first visit to the spot was made in the gray of the morning. With a view of fishing, we had lowered three boats, and, pulling some two miles from our vessel, found ourselves just before dawn of day close under the moon-shadow of Rodondo. Its aspect was heightened, and yet softened, by the strange double twilight of the hour. The great full moon burnt in the low west like a half-spent beacon, casting a soft mellow tinge upon the sea like that cast by a waning fire of embers upon a midnight hearth; while along the entire east the invisible sun sent pallid intimations of his coming. The wind was light, the waves languid; the stars twinkled with a faint effulgence; all nature seemed supine with the long night-watch, and half-suspended in jaded expectation of the sun. This was the critical hour to catch Rodondo in his perfect mood. The twilight was just enough to reveal every striking point, without tearing away the dim investiture of wonder.

From a broken, stairlike base, washed as the steps of a water palace by the waves, the tower rose in entablatures of strata to a shaven summit. These uniform layers, which compose the mass, form its most peculiar feature. For at their lines of junction they project flatly into encircling shelves, from top to bottom, rising one above another in graduated series. And as the eaves of any old barn or abbey are alive with swallows, so were all these rocky ledges with unnumbered seafowl. Eaves upon eaves, and nests upon nests. Here and there were long birdlime streaks of a ghostly white staining the tower from sea to air, readily accounting for its saillike look afar. All would have been bewitchingly quiescent were it not for the demoniac din created by the birds. Not only were the eaves rustling with them, but they flew densely overhead, spreading themselves into a winged and continually shifting canopy. The tower is the resort of aquatic birds for hundreds of leagues around. To the north, to the east, to the west, stretches nothing but eternal ocean; so that the man-of-war hawk coming from the coasts of North America, Polynesia, or Peru, makes his first land at Rodondo. And yet, though Rodondo be terra firma, no land bird ever lighted on it.

Fancy a red robin or a canary there! What a falling into the hands of the Philistines when the poor warbler should be surrounded by such locust-flights of strong bandit birds, with long bills cruel as daggers.

I know not where one can better study the natural history of strange seafowl than at Rodondo. It is the aviary of Ocean. Birds light here which never touched mast or tree; hermit-birds, which ever fly alone; cloud-birds, familiar with unpierced zones of air.

Let us first glance low down to the lowermost shelf of all, which is the widest, too, and but a little space from high-water mark. What outlandish beings are these? Erect as men, but hardly as symmetrical, they stand all round the rock like sculptured caryatides, supporting the next range of eaves above. Their bodies are grotesquely misshapen, their bills short, their feet seemingly legless; while the members at their sides are neither fin, wing, nor arm. And truly neither fish, flesh, nor fowl is the penguin; as an edible, pertaining neither to Carnival nor Lent; without exception the most ambiguous and least lovely creature yet discovered by man. Though dabbling in all three elements, and indeed possessing some rudimental claims to all, the penguin is at home in none. On land it stumps; afloat it sculls; in the air it flops. As if ashamed of her failure, Nature keeps this ungainly child hidden away at the ends of the earth, in the Straits of Magellan, and on the abased sea-story of Rodondo.

But look, what are yon woebegone regiments drawn up on the next shelf above? what rank and file of large strange fowl? what sea Friars of Orders Gray? Pelicans. Their elongated bills, and heavy leathern pouches suspended thereto, give them the most lugubrious expression. A pensive race, they stand for hours together without motion. Their dull, ashy plumage imparts an aspect as if they had been powdered over with cinders. A penitential bird, indeed, fitly haunting the shores of the clinkered Encantadas, whereon tormented Job himself might have well sat down and scraped himself with potsherds.

Higher up now we mark the gony, or gray albatross, anomalously so called, an unsightly, unpoetic bird, unlike its storied kinsman, which is the snow-white ghost of the haunted Capes of Hope and Horn.

As we still ascend from shelf to shelf, we find the tenants
of the tower serially disposed in order of their magnitude:
gannets, black and speckled haglets, jays, sea hens, sperm-
whale birds, gulls of all varieties—thrones, princedoms,
powers, dominating one above another in senatorial array;
while, sprinkled over all, like an ever-repeated fly in a
great piece of broidery, the stormy petrel or Mother Cary's
chicken sounds his continual challenge and alarm. That
this mysterious hummingbird of ocean—which, had it but
brilliancy of hue, might, from its evanescent liveliness, be
almost called its butterfly, yet whose chirrup under the
stern is ominous to mariners as to the peasant the death-
tick sounding from behind the chimney jamb—should have
its special haunt at the Encantadas, contributes, in the
seaman's mind, not a little to their dreary spell.

As day advances the dissonant din augments. With ear-
splitting cries the wild birds celebrate their matins. Each
moment, flights push from the tower and join the aerial
choir hovering overhead, while their places below are
supplied by darting myriads. But down through all this
discord of commotion I hear clear, silver, buglelike notes
unbrokenly falling, like oblique lines of swift-slanting rain
in a cascading shower. I gaze far up, and behold a snow-
white angelic thing with one long, lancelike feather thrust
out behind. It is the bright, inspiriting chanticleer of ocean,
the beauteous bird, from its bestirring whistle of musical
invocation fitly styled the "boatswain's mate."

The winged, life-clouding Rodondo had its full counter-
part in the finny hosts which people the waters at its
base. Below the water line, the rock seemed one honey-
comb of grottoes, affording labyrinthine lurking places
for swarms of fairy fish. All were strange, many exceedingly beautiful, and would have well graced the costliest
glass globes in which goldfish are kept for a show. Nothing
was more striking than the complete novelty of many
individuals of this multitude. Here hues were seen as yet
unpainted, and figures which are unengraved.

To show the multitude, avidity, and nameless fearlessness and tameness of these fish, let me say that often,
marking through clear spaces of water—temporarily made
so by the concentric dartings of the fish above the surface
—certain larger and less unwary wights which swam slow

and deep, our anglers would cautiously essay to drop their lines down to these last. But in vain; there was no passing the uppermost zone. No sooner did the hook touch the sea, than a hundred infatuates contended for the honor of capture. Poor fish of Rodondo! in your victimized confidence, you are of the number of those who inconsiderately trust, while they do not understand, human nature.

But the dawn is now fairly day. Band after band, the seafowl sail away to forage the deep for their food. The tower is left solitary, save the fish-caves at its base. Its birdlime gleams in the golden rays like the whitewash of a tall lighthouse, or the lofty sails of a cruiser. This moment, doubtless, while we know it to be a dead desert rock, other voyagers are taking oaths it is a glad populous ship.

But ropes now, and let us ascend. Yet soft, this is not so easy.

Sketch Fourth

A PISGAH VIEW FROM THE ROCK

"That done, he leads him to the highest mount,
From whence, far off he unto him did show:"—

If you seek to ascend Rock Rodondo, take the following prescription. Go three voyages round the world as a main-royal-man of the tallest frigate that floats; then serve a year or two apprenticeship to the guides who conduct strangers up the Peak of Teneriffe; and as many more respectively to a rope-dancer, an Indian juggler, and a chamois. This done, come and be rewarded by the view from our tower. How we get there, we alone know. If we sought to tell others, what the wiser were they? Suffice it that here at the summit you and I stand. Does any balloon-ist, does the outlook man in the moon, take a broader view of space? Much thus, one fancies, looks the universe from Milton's celestial battlements. A boundless watery Kentucky. Here Daniel Boone would have dwelt content.

Never heed for the present yonder Burnt District of the Enchanted Isles. Look edgeways, as it were, past them, to the south. You see nothing; but permit me to point out the direction, if not the place, of certain interesting objects in the vast sea, which, kissing this tower's base, we behold unscrolling itself towards the Antarctic Pole.

We stand now ten miles from the Equator. Yonder, to the east some six hundred miles, lies the continent, this Rock being just about on the parallel of Quito.

Observe another thing here. We are at one of three uninhabited clusters, which, at pretty nearly uniform distances from the main, sentinel, at long intervals from each other, the entire coast of South America. In a peculiar manner, also, they terminate the South American character of country. Of the unnumbered Polynesian chains to the westward, not one partakes of the qualities of the Encantadas or Gallipagos, the isles of St. Felix and St. Ambrose, the isles Juan Fernandez and Massafuero. Of the first, it needs not here to speak. The second lie a little above the Southern Tropic, lofty, inhospitable, and uninhabitable rocks, one of which, presenting two round hummocks connected by a low reef, exactly resembles a huge double-headed shot. The last lie in the latitude of 33°, high, wild and cloven. Juan Fernandez is sufficiently famous without further description. Massafuero is a Spanish name, expressive of the fact that the isle so called lies *more without,* that is, further off the main than its neighbor Juan. This isle Massafuero has a very imposing aspect at a distance of eight or ten miles. Approached in one direction, in cloudy weather, its great overhanging height and rugged contour, and more especially a peculiar slope of its broad summits, give it much the air of a vast iceberg drifting in tremendous poise. Its sides are split with dark cavernous recesses, as an old cathedral with its gloomy lateral chapels. Drawing nigh one of these gorges from sea, after a long voyage, and beholding some tatterdemalion outlaw, staff in hand, descending its steep rocks toward you, conveys a very queer emotion to a lover of the picturesque.

On fishing parties from ships, at various times, I have chanced to visit each of these groups. The impression they give to the stranger pulling close up in his boat under their grim cliffs is that surely he must be their first discoverer, such, for the most part, is the unimpaired . . . silence and solitude. And here, by the way, the mode in, which these isles were really first lighted upon by Europeans is not unworthy of mention, especially as what is about to be said likewise applies to the original discovery of our Encantadas.

Prior to the year 1563, the voyages made by Spanish ships from Peru to Chile were full of difficulty. Along this coast, the winds from the south most generally prevail, and it had been an invariable custom to keep close in with the land, from a superstitious conceit on the part of the Spaniards that were they to lose sight of it the eternal trade wind would waft them into unending waters, from whence would be no return. Here, involved among tortuous capes and headlands, shoals and reefs, beating, too, against a continual head wind, often light and sometimes for days and weeks sunk into utter calm, the provincial vessels in many cases suffered the extremest hardships in passages which at the present day seem to have been incredibly protracted. There is on record in some collections of nautical disasters an account of one of these ships, which, starting on a voyage whose duration was estimated at ten days, spent four months at sea, and indeed never again entered harbor, for in the end she was cast away. Singular to tell, this craft never encountered a gale, but was the vexed sport of malicious calms and currents. Thrice, out of provisions, she put back to an intermediate port and started afresh, but only yet again to return. Frequent fogs enveloped her, so that no observation could be had of her place, and once, when all hands were joyously anticipating sight of their destination, lo! the vapors lifted and disclosed the mountains from which they had taken their first departure. In the like deceptive vapors she at last struck upon a reef, whence ensued a long series of calamities too sad to detail.

It was the famous pilot Juan Fernandez, immortalized by the island named after him, who put an end to these coasting tribulations, by boldly venturing the experiment—as De Gama did before him with respect to Europe—of standing broad out from land. Here he found the winds favorable for getting to the south, and by running westward till beyond the influences of the trades, he regained the coast without difficulty; making the passage which, though in a high degree circuitous, proved far more expeditious than the nominally direct one. Now it was upon these new tracks, and about the year 1670, or thereabouts, that the

Enchanted Isles, and the rest of the sentinel groups, as they may be called, were discovered. Though I know of no account as to whether any of them were found inhabited or no, it may be reasonably concluded that they have been immemorial solitudes. But let us return to Rodondo.

Southwest from our tower lies all Polynesia, hundreds of leagues away; but straight west, on the precise line of his parallel, no land rises till your keel is beached upon the Kingsmills, a nice little sail of, say, 5,000 miles.

Having thus by such distant references—with Rodondo the only possible ones—settled our relative place on the sea, let us consider objects not quite so remote. Behold the grim and charred Enchanted Isles. This nearest crater-shaped headland is part of Albemarle, the largest of the group, being some sixty miles or more long, and fifteen broad. Did you ever lay eye on the real genuine Equator? Have you ever, in the largest sense, toed the Line? Well, that identical crater-shaped headland there, all yellow lava, is cut by the Equator exactly as a knife cuts straight through the center of a pumpkin pie. If you could only see so far, just to one side of that same headland, across yon low dikey ground, you would catch sight of the isle of Narborough, the loftiest land of the cluster; no soil whatever, one seamed clinker from top to bottom, abounding in black caves like smithies, its metallic shore ringing under foot like plates of iron, its central volcanoes standing grouped like a gigantic chimney stack.

Narborough and Albemarle are neighbors after a quite curious fashion. A familiar diagram will illustrate this strange neighborhood:

$$\sqcap$$

Cut a channel at the above letter joint, and the middle transverse limb is Narborough, and all the rest is Albemarle. Volcanic Narborough lies in the black jaws of Albemarle like a wolf's red tongue in his open mouth.

If now you desire the population of Albemarle, I will give you, in round numbers, the statistics, according to the most reliable estimates made upon the spot:

Men	.	.	.	.	.	.	.	.	.	.	.	.	none
Anteaters	.	.	.	.	.	.	.	.	.	.	.	.	unknown
Man-haters	.	.	.	.	.	.	.	.	.	.	.	.	unknown
Lizards	.	.	.	.	.	.	.	.	.	.	.	.	500,000
Snakes	.	.	.	.	.	.	.	.	.	.	.	.	500,000
Spiders	.	.	.	.	.	.	.	.	.	.	.	.	10,000,000
Salamanders	.	.	.	.	.	.	.	.	.	.	.	.	unknown
Devils	.	.	.	.	.	.	.	.	.	.	.	.	unknown

Making a clean total of 11,000,000

exclusive of an incomputable host of fiends, anteaters, man-haters, and salamanders.

Albemarle opens his mouth towards the setting sun. His distended jaws form a great bay, which Narborough, his tongue, divides into halves, one whereof is called Weather Bay, the other Lee Bay; while the volcanic promontories, terminating his coasts are styled South Head and North Head. I note this because these bays are famous in the annals of the sperm whale fishery. The whales come here at certain seasons to calve. When ships first cruised hereabouts, I am told, they used to blockade the entrance of Lee Bay, when, their boats going round by Weather Bay, passed through Narborough channel, and so had the leviathans very neatly in a pen.

The day after we took fish at the base of this Round Tower, we had a fine wind, and, shooting round the north headland, suddenly descried a fleet of full thirty sail, all beating to windward like a squadron in line. A brave sight as ever man saw. A most harmonious concord of rushing keels. Their thirty kelsons hummed like thirty harp strings, and looked as straight whilst they left their parallel traces on the sea. But there proved too many hunters for the game. The fleet broke up, and went their separate ways out of sight, leaving my own ship and two trim gentlemen of London. These last, finding no luck either, likewise vanished, and Lee Bay, with all its appurtenances, and without a rival, devolved to us.

The way of cruising here is this. You keep hovering about the entrance of the bay, in one beat and out the next. But at times—not always, as in other parts of the group— a race horse of a current sweeps right across its mouth. So, with all sails set, you carefully ply your tacks. How often, standing at the foremast head at sunrise, with our

patient prow pointed in between these isles, did I gaze
upon that land, not of cakes, but of clinkers, not of streams
of sparkling water, but arrested torrents of tormented lava.

As the ship runs in from the open sea, Narborough
presents its side in one dark craggy mass, soaring up some
five or six thousand feet, at which point it hoods itself
in heavy clouds, whose lowest level fold is as clearly defined
against the rocks as the snow line against the Andes. There
is dire mischief going on in that upper dark. There toil
the demons of fire, who, at intervals, irradiate the nights
with a strange spectral illumination for miles and miles
around, but unaccompanied by any further demonstration,
or else suddenly announce themselves by terrific concussions and the full drama of a volcanic eruption. The
blacker that cloud by day, the more may you look for
light by night. Often whalemen have found themselves
cruising nigh that burning mountain when all aglow with
a ballroom blaze. Or, rather, glassworks, you may call this
same vitreous isle of Narborough, with its tall chimney
stacks.

Where we still stand, here on Rodondo, we cannot see
all the other isles, but it is a good place from which to
point out where they lie. Yonder, though, to the E.N.E.,
I mark a distant dusky ridge. It is Abington Isle, one of
the most northerly of the group, so solitary, remote, and
blank, it looks like No-Man's Land seen off our northern
shore. I doubt whether two human beings ever touched
upon that spot. So far as yon Abington Isle is concerned,
Adam and his billions of posterity remain uncreated.

Ranging south of Abington, and quite out of sight behind
the long spine of Albemarle, lies James's Isle, so called
by the early Buccaneers after the luckless Stuart, Duke of
York. Observe here, by the way, that, excepting the isles
particularized in comparatively recent times, and which
mostly received the names of famous admirals, the Encantadas were first christened by the Spaniards; but these
Spanish names were generally effaced on English charts
by the subsequent christenings of the Buccaneers, who,
in the middle of the seventeenth century, called them after
English noblemen and kings. Of these loyal freebooters
and the things which associate their name with the Encantadas, we shall hear anon. Nay, for one little item, im-

mediately; for between James's Isle and Albemarle lies a fantastic islet, strangely known as "Cowley's Enchanted Isle." But, as all the group is deemed enchanted, the reason must be given for the spell within a spell involved by this particular designation. The name was bestowed by that excellent Buccaneer himself, on his first visit here. Speaking in his published voyages of this spot, he says: "My fancy led me to call it Cowley's Enchanted Isle, for, we having had a sight of it upon several points of the compass, it appeared always in so many different forms; sometimes like a ruined fortification; upon another point like a great city," etc. No wonder though, that among the Encantadas all sorts of ocular deceptions and mirages should be met.

That Cowley linked his name with this self-transforming and bemocking isle suggests the possibility that it conveyed to him some meditative image of himself. At least, as is not impossible, if he were any relative of the mildly thoughtful and self-upbraiding poet Cowley, who lived about his time, the conceit might seem not unwarranted; for that sort of thing evinced in the naming of this isle runs in the blood, and may be seen in pirates as in poets.

Still south of James's Isle lie Jervis Isle, Duncan Isle, Crossman's Isle, Brattle Isle, Wood's Isle, Chatham Isle, and various lesser isles, for the most part an archipelago of aridities, without inhabitant, history, or hope of either in all time to come. But not far from these are rather notable isles—Barrington, Charles's, Norfolk, and Hood's. Succeeding chapters will reveal some ground for their notability.

Sketch Fifth

THE FRIGATE, AND SHIP FLYAWAY

"Looking far forth into the ocean wide,
 A goodly ship with banners bravely dight,
 And flag in her top-gallant I espide,
 Through the main sea making her merry flight."

Ere quitting Rodondo, it must not be omitted that here, in 1813, the U. S. frigate *Essex*, Captain David Porter, came near leaving her bones. Lying becalmed one morn-

ing with a strong current setting her rapidly towards the
rock, a strange sail was descried, which—not out of
keeping with alleged enchantments of the neighborhood—
seemed to be staggering under a violent wind, while the
frigate lay lifeless as if spellbound. But a light air springing
up, all sail was made by the frigate in chase of the enemy,
as supposed—he being deemed an English whaleship—but
the rapidity of the current was so great that soon all sight
was lost of him, and, at meridian, the *Essex,* spite of her
drags, was driven so close under the foam-lashed cliffs
of Rodondo that, for a time, all hands gave her up. A
smart breeze, however, at last helped her off, though the
escape was so critical as to seem almost miraculous.

Thus saved from destruction herself, she now made use
of that salvation to destroy the other vessel, if possible.
Renewing the chase in the direction in which the stranger
had disappeared, sight was caught of him the following
morning. Upon being descried he hoisted American colors
and stood away from the *Essex.* A calm ensued, when,
still confident that the stranger was an Englishman, Porter
dispatched a cutter, not to board the enemy, but drive
back his boats engaged in towing him. The cutter succeeded. Cutters were subsequently sent to capture him,
the stranger now showing English colors in place of American. But, when the frigate's boats were within a short
distance of their hoped-for prize, another sudden breeze
sprang up; the stranger, under all sail, bore off to the westward, and, ere night, was hull down ahead of the *Essex,*
which, all this time, lay perfectly becalmed.

This enigmatic craft—American in the morning, and
English in the evening, her sails full of wind in a calm—
was never again beheld. An enchanted ship, no doubt. So,
at least, the sailors swore.

This cruise of the *Essex* in the Pacific during the war
of 1812, is, perhaps, the strangest and most stirring to be
found in the history of the American navy. She captured
the furthest wandering vessels, visited the remotest seas
and isles; long hovered in the charmed vicinity of the
enchanted group, and, finally, valiantly gave up the ghost
fighting two English frigates in the harbor of Valparaiso.
Mention is made of her here for the same reason that the
Buccaneers will likewise receive record: because, like them,

by long cruising among the isles, tortoise-hunting upon their shores, and generally exploring them, for these and other reasons, the *Essex* is peculiarly associated with the Encantadas.

Here be it said that you have but three eyewitness authorities worth mentioning touching the Enchanted Isles: Cowley, the Buccaneer (1684); Colnet, the whaling-ground explorer (1798); Porter, the post captain (1813). Other than these you have but barren, bootless allusions from some few passing voyagers or compilers.

Sketch Sixth

BARRINGTON ISLE AND THE BUCCANEERS

"Let us all servile base subjection scorn,
    And as we be sons of the earth so wide,
Let us our father's heritage divide,
    And challenge to ourselves our portions dew
    Of all the patrimony, which a few
Now hold on hugger-mugger in their hand."

* * * * * *

"Lords of the world, and so will wander free,
    Whereso us listeth, uncontroll'd of any."

* * * * * *

"How bravely now we live, how jocund, how near the first inheritance, without fear, how free from little troubles!"

Near two centuries ago Barrington Isle was the resort of that famous wing of the West Indian Buccaneers, which, upon their repulse from the Cuban waters, crossing the Isthmus of Darien, ravaged the Pacific side of the Spanish colonies, and, with the regularity and timing of a modern mail, waylaid the royal treasure ships plying between Manila and Acapulco. After the toils of piratic war, here they came to say their prayers, enjoy their free-and-easies, count their crackers from the cask, their doubloons from the keg, and measure their silks of Asia with long Toledos for their yardsticks.

As a secure retreat, an undiscoverable hiding place, no spot in those days could have been better fitted. In the center of a vast and silent sea but very little traversed, surrounded by islands whose inhospitable aspect might well drive away the chance navigator and yet within a few days' sail of the opulent countries which they made

their prey, the unmolested Buccaneers found here that
tranquillity which they fiercely denied to every civilized
harbor in that part of the world. Here, after stress of
weather, or a temporary drubbing at the hands of their
vindictive foes, or in swift flight with golden booty, those
old marauders came, and lay snugly out of all harm's
reach. But not only was the place a harbor of safety, and a
bower of ease, but for utility in other things it was most
admirable.

Barrington Isle is, in many respects, singularly adapted
to careening, refitting, refreshing, and other seamen's purposes. Not only has it good water, and good anchorage,
well sheltered from all winds by the high land of Albemarle,
but it is the least unproductive isle of the group. Tortoises
good for food, trees good for fuel, and long grass good
for bedding, abound here, and there are pretty natural
walks, and several landscapes to be seen. Indeed, though
in its locality belonging to the Enchanted group, Barrington Isle is so unlike most of its neighbors that it would
hardly seem of kin to them.

"I once landed on its western side," says a sentimental
voyager long ago, "where it faces the black buttress of
Albemarle. I walked beneath groves of trees—not very
lofty, and not palm trees, or orange trees, or peach trees, to
be sure—but, for all that, after long seafaring, very beautiful to walk under, even though they supplied no fruit.
And here, in calm spaces at the heads of glades, and on
the shaded tops of slopes commanding the most quiet
scenery—what do you think I saw? Seats which might have
served Brahmins and presidents of peace societies. Fine
old ruins of what had once been symmetric lounges of stone
and turf, they bore every mark both of artificialness and
age, and were, undoubtedly, made by the Buccaneers.
One had been a long sofa with back and arms, just such
a sofa as the poet Gray might have loved to throw himself
upon, his Crebillon in hand.

"Though they sometimes tarried here for months at a
time, and used the spot for a storing place for spare spars,
sails, and casks, yet it is highly improbable that the Buccaneers ever erected dwelling houses upon the isle. They
never were here except their ships remained, and they

would most likely have slept on board. I mention this because I cannot avoid the thought that it is hard to impute the construction of these romantic seats to any other motive than one of pure peacefulness and kindly fellowship with nature. That the Buccaneers perpetrated the greatest outrages is very true, that some of them were mere cut-throats is not to be denied; but we know that here and there among their host was a Dampier, a Wafer, and a Cowley, and likewise other men, whose worst reproach was their desperate fortunes—whom persecution, or adversity, or secret and unavengeable wrongs, had driven from Christian society to seek the melancholy solitude or the guilty adventures of the sea. At any rate, long as those ruins of seats on Barrington remain, the most singular monuments are furnished to the fact that all of the Buccaneers were not unmitigated monsters.

"But during my ramble on the isle I was not long in discovering other tokens of things quite in accordance with those wild traits, popularly, and no doubt truly enough, imputed to the freebooters at large. Had I picked up old sails and rusty hoops I would only have thought of the ship's carpenter and cooper. But I found old cutlasses and daggers reduced to mere threads of rust, which, doubtless, had stuck between Spanish ribs ere now. These were signs of the murderer and robber; the reveler likewise had left his trace. Mixed with shells, fragments of broken jars were lying here and there, high up upon the beach. They were precisely like the jars now used upon the Spanish coast for the wine and pisco spirits of that country.

"With a rusty dagger fragment in one hand, and a bit of a wine jar in another, I sat me down on the ruinous green sofa I have spoken of and bethought me long and deeply of these same Buccaneers. Could it be possible that they robbed and murdered one day, reveled the next, and rested themselves by turning meditative philosophers, rural poets, and seat-builders on the third? Not very improbable, after all. For consider the vacillations of a man. Still, strange as it may seem, I must also abide by the more charitable thought, namely, that among these adventurers were some gentlemanly, companionable souls, capable of genuine tranquillity and virtue."

Sketch Seventh

CHARLES'S ISLE AND THE DOG-KING

So with outragious cry,
A thousand villeins round about him swarmed
Out of the rocks and caves adjoining nye;
Vile caitive wretches, ragged, rude, deformed;
All threatning death, all in straunge manner armed;
Some with unweldy clubs, some with long speares,
Some rusty knives, some staves in fier warmd.

*   *   *   *   *   *

We will not be of any occupation,
Let such vile vassals, born to base vocation,
  Drudge in the world, and for their living droyle,
Which have no wit to live withouten toyle.

Southwest of Barrington lies Charles's Isle. And hereby
hangs a history which I gathered long ago from a shipmate
learned in all the lore of outlandish life.

During the successful revolt of the Spanish provinces
from Old Spain, there fought on behalf of Peru a certain
Creole adventurer from Cuba, who, by his bravery and
good fortune, at length advanced himself to high rank
in the patriot army. The war being ended, Peru found itself
like many valorous gentlemen, free and independent
enough, but with few shot in the locker. In other words,
Peru had not wherewithal to pay off its troops. But the
Creole—I forget his name—volunteered to take his pay
in lands. So they told him he might have his pick of the
Enchanted Isles, which were then, as they still remain,
the nominal appanage of Peru. The soldier straightway
embarks thither, explores the group, returns to Callao, and
says he will take a deed of Charles's Isle. Moreover, this
deed must stipulate that thenceforth Charles's Isle is not
only the sole property of the Creole, but is forever free of
Peru, even as Peru of Spain. To be short, this adventurer
procures himself to be made in effect Supreme Lord of
the Island, one of the princes of the powers of the earth.*

* The American Spaniards have long been in the habit of
making presents of islands to deserving individuals. The pilot
Juan Fernandez procured a deed of the isle named after him,
and for some years resided there before Selkirk came. It is

He now sends forth a proclamation inviting subjects to his as yet unpopulated kingdom. Some eighty souls, men and women, respond, and being provided by their leader with necessaries, and tools of various sorts, together with a few cattle and goats, take ship for the promised land, the last arrival on board, prior to sailing, being the Creole himself, accompanied, strange to say, by a disciplined cavalry company of large grim dogs. These, it was observed on the passage, refusing to consort with the emigrants, remained aristocratically grouped around their master on the elevated quarter-deck, casting disdainful glances forward upon the inferior rabble there, much as, from the ramparts, the soldiers of a garrison, thrown into a conquered town, eye the inglorious citizen-mob over which they are set to watch.

Now Charles's Isle not only resembles Barrington Isle in being much more inhabitable than other parts of the group, but it is double the size of Barrington, say forty or fifty miles in circuit.

Safely debarked at last, the company, under direction of their lord and patron, forthwith proceeded to build their capital city. They make considerable advance in the way of walls of clinkers, and lava floors, nicely sanded with cinders. On the least barren hills they pasture their cattle, while the goats, adventurers by nature, explore the far inland solitudes for a scanty livelihood of lofty herbage. Meantime, abundance of fish and tortoises supply their other wants.

The disorders incident to settling all primitive regions in the present case were heightened by the peculiarly untoward character of many of the pilgrims. His Majesty was forced at last to proclaim martial law and actually hunted and shot with his own hand several of his rebellious subjects, who, with most questionable intentions, had clandestinely encamped in the interior, whence they stole by night, to prowl barefooted on tiptoe round the precincts of the lava palace. It is to be remarked, however, that prior to such stern proceedings, the more reliable men had been

---

supposed, however, that he eventually contracted the blues upon his princely property, for after a time he returned to the main, and as report goes, became a very garrulous barber in the city of Lima.

judiciously picked out for an infantry bodyguard, subordinate to the cavalry bodyguard of dogs. But the state of politics in this unhappy nation may be somewhat imagined from the circumstance that all who were not of the bodyguard were downright plotters and malignant traitors. At length the death penalty was tacitly abolished, owing to the timely thought that, were strict sportsman's justice to be dispensed among such subjects, ere long the Nimrod King would have little or no remaining game to shoot. The human part of the lifeguard was now disbanded and set to work cultivating the soil and raising potatoes, the regular army now solely consisting of the dog-regiment. These, as I have heard, were of a singularly ferocious character, though by severe training rendered docile to their master. Armed to the teeth, the Creole now goes in state, surrounded by his canine janizaries, whose terrific bayings prove quite as serviceable as bayonets in keeping down the surgings of revolt.

But the census of the isle, sadly lessened by the dispensation of justice, and not materially recruited by matrimony, began to fill his mind with sad mistrust. Some way the population must be increased. Now, from its possessing a little water, and its comparative pleasantness of aspect, Charles's Isle at this period was occasionally visited by foreign whalers. These His Majesty had always levied upon for port charges, thereby contributing to his revenue. But now he had additional designs. By insidious arts he, from time to time, cajoles certain sailors to desert their ships and enlist beneath his banner. Soon as missed, their captains crave permission to go and hunt them up. Whereupon His Majesty first hides them very carefully away, and then freely permits the search. In consequence, the delinquents are never found, and the ships retire without them.

Thus, by a two-edged policy of this crafty monarch, foreign nations were crippled in the number of their subjects, and his own were greatly multiplied. He particularly petted these renegade strangers. But alas for the deep-laid schemes of ambitious princes, and alas for the vanity of glory. As the foreign-born Pretorians, unwisely introduced into the Roman state, and still more unwisely made favorites of the emperors, at last insulted and overturned the throne, even so these lawless mariners, with all the rest of the bodyguard and all the populace, broke out into a terrible mutiny, and defied their master. He marched against them with all his dogs. A deadly battle ensued upon the beach. It raged for three hours, the dogs fighting with determined valor, and the sailors reckless of everything but victory. Three men and thirteen dogs were left dead upon the field, many on both sides were wounded, and the king was forced to fly with the remainder of his canine regiment. The enemy pursued, stoning the dogs with their master into the wilderness of the interior. Discontinuing the pursuit, the victors returned to the village on the shore, stove the spirit casks, and proclaimed a republic. The dead men were interred with the honor of war, and the dead dogs ignominiously thrown into the sea. At last, forced by stress of suffering, the fugitive Creole came down from the hills and offered to treat for peace. But the rebels refused it on any other terms than his unconditional banishment. Accordingly, the next ship that arrived carried away the ex-king to Peru.

The history of the king of Charles's Island furnishes another illustration of the difficulty of colonizing barren islands with unprincipled pilgrims.

Doubtless for a long time the exiled monarch, pensively ruralizing in Peru, which afforded him a safe asylum in his calamity, watched every arrival from the Encantadas, to hear news of the failure of the republic, the consequent penitence of the rebels, and his own recall to royalty. Doubtless he deemed the republic but a miserable experiment which would soon explode. But no, the insurgents had confederated themselves into a democracy neither Grecian, Roman, nor American. Nay, it was no democracy at all, but a permanent *riotocracy,* which gloried in having no law but lawlessness. Great inducements being offered to deserters, their ranks were swelled by accessions of scamps from every ship which touched their shores. Charles's Island was proclaimed the asylum of the oppressed of all navies. Each runaway tar was hailed as a martyr in the cause of freedom, and became immediately installed a ragged citizen of this universal nation. In vain the captains of absconding seamen strove to regain them. Their new compatriots were ready to give any number of ornamental eyes in their behalf. They had few cannon,

but their fists were not to be trifled with. So at last it came
to pass that no vessels acquainted with the character of
that country durst touch there, however sorely in want of
refreshment. It became anathema—a sea Alsatia—the un-
assailed lurking place of all sorts of desperadoes, who
in the name of liberty did just what they pleased. They
continually fluctuated in their numbers. Sailors, deserting
ships at other islands, or in boats at sea anywhere in that
vicinity, steered for Charles's Isle as to their sure home
of refuge; while, sated with the life of the isle, numbers
from time to time crossed the water to the neighboring
ones and there presenting themselves to strange captains as
shipwrecked seamen often succeeded in getting on board
vessels bound to the Spanish coast, and having a compassionate purse made up for them on landing there.

One warm night during my first visit to the group, our
ship was floating along in languid stillness when someone
on the forecastle shouted "Light ho!" We looked and saw
a beacon burning on some obscure land off the beam.
Our third mate was not intimate with this part of the
world. Going to the captain he said, "Sir, shall I put off
in a boat? These must be shipwrecked men."

The captain laughed rather grimly, as, shaking his fist
towards the beacon, he rapped out an oath, and said,
"No, no, you precious rascals, you don't juggle one of
my boats ashore this blessed night. You do well, you
thieves—you do benevolently to hoist a light yonder as
on a dangerous shoal. It tempts no wise man to pull off
and see what's the matter, but bids him steer small and
keep off shore—that is Charles's Island; brace up, Mr.
Mate, and keep the light astern."

Sketch Eighth

NORFOLK ISLE AND THE CHOLA WIDOW

"At last they in an island did espy
A seemly woman sitting by the shore,
That with great sorrow and sad agony
Seemed some great misfortune to deplore,
And loud to them for succor called evermore."

"Black his eye as the midnight sky,
White his neck as the driven snow,
Red his cheek as the morning light;—
Cold he lies in the ground below.
    My love is dead,
        Gone to his death-bedys,
All under the cactus tree."

"Each lonely scene shall thee restore,
For thee the tear be duly shed;
Belov'd till life can charm no more,
And mourned till Pity's self be dead."

Far to the northeast of Charles's Isle, sequestered from the rest, lies Norfolk Isle, and, however insignificant to most voyagers, to me, through sympathy, that lone island has become a spot made sacred by the strangest trials of humanity.

It was my first visit to the Encantadas. Two days had been spent ashore in hunting tortoises. There was not time to capture many, so on the third afternoon we loosed our sails. We were just in the act of getting under way, the uprooted anchor yet suspended and invisibly swaying beneath the wave, as the good ship gradually turned her heel to leave the isle behind, when the seaman who heaved with me at the windlass paused suddenly and directed my attention to something moving on the land, not along the beach, but somewhat back, fluttering from a height.

In view of the sequel of this little story, be it here narrated how it came to pass that an object which partly from its being so small was quite lost to every other man on board, still caught the eye of my handspike companion.

The rest of the crew, myself included, merely stood up to our spikes in heaving, whereas, unwontedly exhilarated, at every turn of the ponderous windlass, my belted comrade leaped atop of it, with might and main giving a downward, thewy, perpendicular heave, his raised eye bent in cheery animation upon the slowly receding shore. Being high lifted above all others was the reason he perceived the object, otherwise unperceivable; and this elevation of his eye was owing to the elevation of his spirits; and this again—for truth must out—to a dram of Peruvian pisco, in guerdon for some kindness done, secretly administered to him that morning by our mulatto steward. Now, certainly, pisco does a deal of mischief in the world; yet seeing that, in the present case, it was the means, though indirect, of rescuing a human being from the most dreadful fate, must we not also needs admit that sometimes pisco does a deal of good?

Glancing across the water in the direction pointed out, I saw some white thing hanging from an inland rock, perhaps half a mile from the sea.

"It is a bird, a white-winged bird, perhaps a——no; it is——it is a handkerchief!"

"Aye, a handkerchief!" echoed my comrade, and with a louder shout apprised the captain.

Quickly now—like the running out and training of a great gun—the long cabin spyglass was thrust through the mizzen-rigging from the high platform of the poop, whereupon a human figure was plainly seen upon the inland rock, eagerly waving towards us what seemed to be the handkerchief.

Our captain was a prompt, good fellow. Dropping the glass, he lustily ran forward, ordering the anchor to be dropped again, hands to stand by a boat, and lower away.

In a half-hour's time the swift boat returned. It went with six and came with seven; and the seventh was a woman.

It is not artistic heartlessness, but I wish I could but draw in crayons, for this woman was a most touching sight, and crayons, tracing softly melancholy lines, would best depict the mournful image of the dark-damasked Chola widow.

Her story was soon told, and though given in her own

strange language was as quickly understood, for our captain, from long trading on the Chilean coast, was well versed in the Spanish. A Chola, or half-breed Indian woman, of Payta in Peru, three years gone by, with her young new-wedded husband Felipe, of pure Castilian blood, and her one only Indian brother, Truxill, Hunilla had taken passage on the main in a French whaler, commanded by a joyous man, which vessel, bound to the cruising grounds beyond the Enchanted Isles, proposed passing close by their vicinity. The object of the little party was to procure tortoise oil, a fluid which for its great purity and delicacy is held in high estimation where-ever known, and it is well known all along this part of the Pacific coast. With a chest of clothes, tools, cooking utensils, a rude apparatus for trying out the oil, some casks of biscuit, and other things, not omitting two favorite dogs, of which faithful animal all the Cholos are very fond, Hunilla and her companions were safely landed at their chosen place; the Frenchman, according to the contract made ere sailing, engaged to take them off upon returning from a four months' cruise in the westward seas, which interval the three adventurers deemed quite sufficient for their purposes.

On the isle's lone beach they paid him in silver for their passage out, the stranger having declined to carry them at all except upon that condition; though willing to take every means to insure the due fulfillment of his promise. Felipe had striven hard to have this payment put off to the period of the ship's return. But in vain. Still they thought they had, in another way, ample pledge of the good faith of the Frenchman. It was arranged that the expenses of the passage home should not be payable in silver, but in tortoises—one hundred tortoises ready captured to the returning captain's hand. These the Cholos meant to secure after their own work was done, against the probable time of the Frenchman's coming back, and no doubt in prospect already felt, that in those hundred tortoises—now somewhere ranging the isle's interior—they possessed one hundred hostages. Enough: the vessel sailed; the gazing three on shore answered the loud glee of the singing crew; and, ere evening, the French craft was hull down in the distant sea, its masts three faintest lines which quickly faded from Hunilla's eye.

The stranger had given a blithesome promise, and anchored it with oaths, but oaths and anchors equally will drag; naught else abides on fickle earth but unkept promises of joy. Contrary winds from out unstable skies, or contrary moods of his more varying mind, or shipwreck and sudden death in solitary waves—whatever was the cause, the blithe stranger never was seen again.

Yet, however dire a calamity was here in store, misgivings of it ere due time never disturbed the Cholos' busy mind, now all intent upon the toilsome matter which had brought them hither. Nay, by swift doom coming like the thief at night, ere seven weeks went by, two of the little party were removed from all anxieties of land or sea. No more they sought to gaze with feverish fear, or still more feverish hope, beyond the present's horizon line, but into the furthest future their own silent spirits sailed. By persevering labor beneath that burning sun, Felipe and Truxill had brought down to their hut many scores of tortoises, and tried out the oil, when, elated with their good success, and to reward themselves for such hard work, they, too hastily, made a catamaran, or Indian raft, much used on the Spanish main, and merrily started on a fishing trip, just without a long reef with many jagged gaps, running parallel with the shore, about half a mile from it. By some bad tide or hap, or natural negligence of joyfulness (for though they could not be heard, yet by their gestures they seemed singing at the time) forced in deep water against that iron bar, the illmade catamaran was overset, and came all to pieces, when, dashed by broad-chested swells between their broken logs and the sharp teeth of the reef, both adventurers perished before Hunilla's eyes.

Before Hunilla's eyes they sank. The real woe of this event passed before her sight as some sham tragedy on the stage. She was seated on a rude bower among the withered thickets crowning a lofty cliff, a little back from the beach. The thickets were so disposed that in looking upon the sea at large she peered out from among the branches as from the lattice of a high balcony. But upon the day we speak of here, the better to watch the adventure of those two hearts she loved, Hunilla had withdrawn the branches to one side, and held them so. They formed an oval frame, through which the bluely boundless sea rolled like a painted one. And there the invisible painter painted to her view the wave-tossed and disjointed raft, its once level logs slantingly upheaved, as raking masts, and the four struggling arms undistinguishable among them, and then all subsided into smooth-flowing creamy waters, slowly drifting the splintered wreck, while, first and last, no sound of any sort was heard. Death in a silent picture, a dream of the eye, such vanishing shapes as the mirage shows.

So instant was the scene, so trancelike its mild pictorial effect, so distant from her blasted bower and her common sense of things, that Hunilla gazed and gazed, nor raised a finger or a wail. But as good to sit thus dumb, in stupor staring on that dumb show, for all that otherwise might be done. With half a mile of sea between, how could her two enchanted arms aid those four fated ones? The distance long, the time one sand. After the lightning is beheld, what fool shall stay the thunderbolt? Felipe's body was washed ashore, but Truxill's never came, only his gay, braided hat of golden straw—that same sunflower thing he waved to her, pushing from the strand—and now, to the last gallant, it still saluted her. But Felipe's body floated to the marge, with one arm encirclingly outstretched. Lockjawed in grim death, the lover-husband softly clasped his bride, true to her even in death's dream. Ah, heaven, when man thus keeps his faith, wilt thou be faithless who created the faithful one? But they cannot break faith who never plighted it.

It needs not to be said what nameless misery now wrapped the lonely widow. In telling her own story she passed this almost entirely over, simply recounting the event. Construe the comment of her features as you might, from her mere words little would you have weened that Hunilla was herself the heroine of her tale. But not thus did she defraud us of our tears. All hearts bled that grief could be so brave.

She but showed us her soul's lid, and the strange ciphers thereon engraved; all within, with pride's timidity, was withheld. Yet was there one exception. Holding out her small olive hand before her captain, she said in mild and

slowest Spanish, "*Señor,* I buried him," then paused, struggled as against the writhed coilings of a snake, and, cringing suddenly, leaped up, repeating in impassioned pain,
"I buried him, my life, my soul!"

Doubtless it was by half-unconscious, automatic mo-
tions of her hands, that this heavy-hearted one performed
the final office for Felipe, and planted a rude cross of
withered sticks—no green ones might be had—at the
head of that lonely grave, where rested now in lasting un-
complaint and quiet haven he whom untranquil seas had
overthrown.

But some dull sense of another body that should be interred, of another cross that should hallow another grave
—unmade as yet—some dull anxiety and pain touching
her undiscovered brother, now haunted the oppressed
Hunilla. Her hands fresh from the burial earth, she slowly
went back to the beach, with unshaped purposes wandering there, her spellbound eye bent upon the incessant
waves. But they bore nothing to her but a dirge, which
maddened her to think that murderers should mourn. As
time went by, and these things came less dreamingly to
her mind, the strong persuasions of her Romish faith,
which sets peculiar store by consecrated urns, prompted
her to resume in waking earnest that pious search which
had but been begun as in somnambulism. Day after day,
week after week, she trod the cindery beach, till at length
a double motive edged every eager glance. With equal
longing she now looked for the living and the dead, the
brother and the captain, alike vanished, never to return.
Little accurate note of time had Hunilla taken under such
emotions as were hers, and little, outside herself, served
for calendar or dial. As to poor Crusoe in the selfsame sea,
no saint's bell pealed forth the lapse of week or month;
each day went by unchallenged; no chanticleer announced
those sultry dawns, no lowing herds those poisonous nights.
All wonted and steadily recurring sounds, human, or
humanized by sweet fellowship with man, but one stirred
that torrid trance—the cry of dogs; save which naught
but the rolling sea invaded it, an all-pervading monotone,
and to the widow that was the least loved voice she could
have heard.

No wonder that, as her thoughts now wandered to the

unreturning ship and were beaten back again, the hope against hope so struggled in her soul that at length she desperately said, "Not yet, not yet; my foolish heart runs on too fast." So she forced patience for some further weeks. But to those whom earth's sure indraft draws, patience or impatience is still the same.

Hunilla now sought to settle precisely in her mind, to an hour, how long it was since the ship had sailed, and then, with the same precision, how long a space remained to pass. But this proved impossible. What present day or month it was she could not say. Time was her labyrinth, in which Hunilla was entirely lost.

And now follows——

Against my own purposes a pause descends upon me here. One knows not whether nature doth not impose some secrecy upon him who has been privy to certain things. At least, it is to be doubted whether it be good to blazon such. If some books are deemed most baneful and their sale forbid, how, then, with deadlier facts, not dreams of doting men? Those whom books will hurt will not be proof against events. Events, not books, should be forbid. But in all things man sows upon the wind, which bloweth just there whither it listeth; for ill or good, man cannot know. Often ill comes from the good, as good from ill.

When Hunilla——

Dire sight it is to see some silken beast long dally with a golden lizard ere she devour. More terrible to see how feline Fate will sometimes dally with a human soul, and by a nameless magic make it repulse a sane despair with a hope which is but mad. Unwittingly I imp this catlike thing, sporting with the heart of him who reads, for if he feel not he reads in vain.

—"The ship sails this day, today," at last said Hunilla to herself; "this gives me certain time to stand on; without certainty I go mad. In loose ignorance I have hoped and hoped; now in firm knowledge I will but wait. Now I live and no longer perish in bewilderings. Holy Virgin, aid me! Thou wilt waft back the ship. Oh, past length of weary weeks—all to be dragged over—to buy the certainty of today, I freely give ye, though I tear ye from me!"

As mariners, tossed in tempest on some desolate ledge, patch them a boat out of the remnants of their vessel's

wreck, and launch it in the selfsame waves, see here
Hunilla, this lone shipwrecked soul, out of treachery invoking trust. Humanity, thou strong thing, I worship thee,
not in the laureled victor, but in this vanquished one.

Truly Hunilla leaned upon a reed, a real one—no
metaphor; a real Eastern reed. A piece of hollow cane,
drifted from unknown isles, and found upon the beach,
its once jagged ends rubbed smoothly even as by sand-
paper, its golden glazing gone. Long ground between the
sea and land, upper and nether stone, the unvarnished
substance was filed bare, and wore another polish now,
one with itself, the polish of its agony. Circular lines at
intervals cut all round this surface, divided it into six
panels of unequal length. In the first were scored the days,
each tenth one marked by a longer and deeper notch; the
second was scored for the number of seafowl eggs for
sustenance, picked out from the rocky nests; the third, how
many fish had been caught from the shore; the fourth,
how many small tortoises found inland; the fifth, how
many days of sun; the sixth, of clouds; which last, of the
two, was the greater one. Long night of busy numbering,
misery's mathematics, to weary her too-wakeful soul to
sleep; yet sleep for that was none.

The panel of the days was deeply worn—the long tenth
notches half effaced, as alphabets of the blind. Ten thousand times the longing widow had traced her finger over
the bamboo—dull flute, which, played on, gave no sound—
as if counting birds flown by in air would hasten tortoises
creeping through the woods.

After the one hundred and eightieth day no further
mark was seen; that last one was the faintest, as the first
the deepest.

"There were more days," said our captain; "Many, many
more; why did you not go on and notch them, too,
Hunilla?"

"*Señor,* ask me not."

"And meantime, did no other vessel pass the isle?"

"Nay, *señor;* —but——"

"You do not speak; but *what,* Hunilla?"

"Ask me not, *señor.*"

"You saw ships pass, far away; you waved to them;
they passed on—was that it, Hunilla?"

"*Señor,* be it as you say."

Braced against her woe, Hunilla would not, durst not, trust the weakness of her tongue. Then when our captain asked whether any whaleboats had—

But no, I will not file this thing complete for scoffing souls to quote, and call it firm proof upon their side. The half shall here remain untold. Those two unnamed events which befell Hunilla on this isle, let them abide between her and her God. In nature, as in law, it may be libelous to speak some truths.

Still, how it was that, although our vessel had lain three days anchored nigh the isle, its one human tenant should not have discovered us till just upon the point of sailing, never to revisit so lone and far a spot, this needs explaining ere the sequel come.

The place where the French captain had landed the little party was on the further and opposite end of the isle. There too it was that they had afterwards built their hut. Nor did the widow in her solitude desert the spot where her loved ones had dwelt with her, and where the dearest of the twain now slept his last long sleep, and all her plaints awaked him not, and he of husbands the most faithful during life.

Now, high broken land rises between the opposite extremities of the isle. A ship anchored at one side is invisible from the other. Neither is the isle so small but a considerable company might wander for days through the wilderness of one side and never be seen, or their halloos heard, by any stranger holding aloof on the other. Hence Hunilla, who naturally associated the possible coming of ships with her own part of the isle, might to the end have remained quite ignorant of the presence of our vessel, were it not for a mysterious presentiment, borne to her, so our mariners averred, by this isle's enchanted air. Nor did the widow's answer undo the thought.

"How did you come to cross the isle this morning, then, Hunilla?" said our captain.

"*Señor,* something came flitting by me. It touched my cheek, my heart, *señor.*"

"What do you say, Hunilla?"

"I have said, *señor,* something came through the air."

It was a narrow chance. For when in crossing the isle

Hunilla gained the high land in the center, she must then
for the first have perceived our masts, and also marked
that their sails were being loosed, perhaps even heard
the echoing chorus of the windlass song. The strange ship
was about to sail, and she behind. With all haste she now
descends the height on the hither side, but soon loses sight
of the ship among the sunken jungles at the mountain's
base. She struggles on through the withered branches,
which seek at every step to bar her path, till she comes to
the isolated rock, still some way from the water. This she
climbs, to reassure herself. The ship is still in plainest
sight. But now, worn out with overtension, Hunilla all
but faints; she fears to step down from her giddy perch;
she is fain to pause, there where she is, and as a last resort
catches the turban from her head, unfurls and waves it
over the jungles towards us.

During the telling of her story the mariners formed a
voiceless circle round Hunilla and the captain, and when
at length the word was given to man the fastest boat, and
pull round to the isle's thither side, to bring away Hunilla's
chest and the tortoise oil, such alacrity of both cheery and
sad obedience seldom before was seen. Little ado was
made. Already the anchor had been recommitted to the
bottom, and the ship swung calmly to it.

But Hunilla insisted upon accompanying the boat as
indispensable pilot to her hidden hut. So being refreshed
with the best the steward could supply, she started with
us. Nor did ever any wife of the most famous admiral, in
her husband's barge, receive more silent reverence of
respect than poor Hunilla from this boat's crew.

Rounding many a vitreous cape and bluff, in two hours'
time we shot inside the fatal reef, wound into a secret
cove, looked up along a green many-gabled lava wall,
and saw the island's solitary dwelling.

It hung upon an impending cliff, sheltered on two sides
by tangled thickets, and half-screened from view in front
by juttings of the rude stairway, which climbed the prec-
ipice from the sea. Built of canes, it was thatched with
long, mildewed grass. It seemed an abandoned hayrick,
whose haymakers were now no more. The roof inclined
but one way, the eaves coming to within two feet of the
ground. And here was a simple apparatus to collect the

dews, or rather doubly-distilled and finest winnowed rains, which, in mercy or in mockery, the night skies sometimes drop upon these blighted Encantadas. All along beneath the eaves a spotted sheet, quite weather-stained, was spread, pinned to short, upright stakes, set in the shallow sand. A small clinker, thrown into the cloth, weighed its middle down, thereby straining all moisture into a calabash placed below. This vessel supplied each drop of water ever drunk upon the isle by the Cholos. Hunilla told us the calabash would sometimes, but not often, be half filled overnight. It held six quarts, perhaps. "But," said she, "we were used to thirst. At sandy Payta, where I live, no shower from heaven ever fell; all the water there is brought on mules from the inland vales."

Tied among the thickets were some twenty moaning tortoises, supplying Hunilla's lonely larder, while hundreds of vast tableted black bucklers, like displaced, shattered tombstones of dark slate, were also scattered round. These were the skeleton backs of those great tortoises from which Felipe and Truxill had made their precious oil. Several large calabashes and two goodly kegs were filled with it. In a pot near by were the caked crusts of a quantity which had been permitted to evaporate. "They meant to have strained it off next day," said Hunilla, as she turned aside.

I forgot to mention the most singular sight of all, though the first that greeted us after landing.

Some ten small, soft-haired, ringleted dogs, of a beautiful breed peculiar to Peru, set up a concert of glad welcomings when we gained the beach, which was responded to by Hunilla. Some of these dogs had, since her widowhood, been born upon the isle, the progeny of the two brought from Payta. Owing to the jagged steeps and pitfalls, tortuous thickets, sunken clefts, and perilous intricacies of all sorts in the interior, Hunilla, admonished by the loss of one favorite among them, never allowed these delicate creatures to follow her in her occasional birds'-nests climbs and other wanderings; so that, through long habitation, they offered not to follow when that morning she crossed the land, and her own soul was then too full of other things to heed their lingering behind. Yet, all along she had so clung to them that, besides what moisture they lapped up at early daybreak from the small

scoop holes among the adjacent rocks, she had shared
the dew of her calabash among them; never laying by
any considerable store against those prolonged and utter
droughts which, in some disastrous seasons, warp these
isles.

Having pointed out, at our desire, what few things she
would like transported to the ship—her chest, the oil,
not omitting the live tortoises which she intended for a
grateful present to our captain—we immediately set to
work, carrying them to the boat down the long, sloping
stair of deeply shadowed rock. While my comrades were
thus employed, I looked and Hunilla had disappeared.

It was not curiosity alone, but, it seems to me, something
different mingled with it which prompted me to drop my
tortoise and once more gaze slowly around. I remembered
the husband buried by Hunilla's hands. A narrow pathway
led into a dense part of the thickets. Following it through
many mazes, I came out upon a small, round, open space,
deeply chambered there.

The mound rose in the middle; a bare heap of finest
sand, like that unverdured heap found at the bottom of
an hourglass run out. At its head stood the cross of withered sticks, the dry, peeled bark still fraying from it, its
transverse limb tied up with rope and forlornly adroop
in the silent air.

Hunilla was partly prostrate upon the grave, her dark
head bowed, and lost in her long, loosened Indian hair,
her hands extended to the cross-foot with a little brass
crucifix clasped between—a crucifix worn featureless, like
an ancient graven knocker long plied in vain. She did not
see me, and I made no noise, but slid aside and left the spot.

A few moments ere all was ready for our going, she
reappeared among us. I looked into her eyes, but saw no
tear. There was something which seemed strangely haughty
in her air, and yet it was the air of woe. A Spanish and an
Indian grief, which would not visibly lament. Pride's
height in vain abased to proneness on the rack; nature's
pride subduing nature's torture.

Like pages the small and silken dogs surrounded her,
as she slowly descended towards the beach. She caught
the two most eager creatures in her arms: "Mia Teeta!

Mia Tomoteeta!" and, fondling them, inquired how many
could we take on board.

The mate commanded the boat's crew—not a hard-
hearted man, but his way of life had been such that in
most things, even in the smallest, simple utility was his
leading motive.

"We cannot take them all, Hunilla; our supplies are
short; the winds are unreliable; we may be a good many
days going to Tombez. So take those you have, Hunilla,
but no more."

She was in the boat; the oarsmen, too, were seated; all
save one, who stood ready to push off and then spring
himself. With the sagacity of their race, the dogs now
seemed aware that they were in the very instant of being
deserted upon a barren strand. The gunwales of the boat
were high; its prow—presented inland—was lifted; so,
owing to the water, which they seemed instinctively to
shun, the dogs could not well leap into the little craft.
But their busy paws hard scraped the prow, as it had
been some farmer's door shutting them out from shelter
in a winter storm. A clamorous agony of alarm. They did
not howl, or whine; they all but spoke.

"Push off! Give way!" cried the mate. The boat gave
one heavy drag and lurch, and next moment shot swiftly
from the beach, turned on her heel, and sped. The dogs
ran howling along the water's marge, now pausing to gaze
at the flying boat, then motioning as if to leap in chase,
but mysteriously withheld themselves, and again ran
howling along the beach. Had they been human beings,
hardly would they have more vividly inspired the sense
of desolation. The oars were plied as confederate feathers
of two wings. No one spoke. I looked back upon the beach,
and then upon Hunilla, but her face was set in a stern
dusky calm. The dogs crouching in her lap vainly licked
her rigid hands. She never looked behind her, but sat
motionless till we turned a promontory of the coast and
lost all sights and sounds astern. She seemed as one who,
having experienced the sharpest of mortal pangs, was
henceforth content to have all lesser heartstrings riven, one
by one. To Hunilla, pain seemed so necessary that pain
in other beings, though by love and sympathy made her
own, was unrepiningly to be borne. A heart of yearning

in a frame of steel. A heart of earthy yearning, frozen by the frost which falleth from the sky.

The sequel is soon told. After a long passage, vexed by calms and baffling winds, we made the little port of Tombez in Peru, there to recruit the ship. Payta was not very distant. Our captain sold the tortoise oil to a Tombez merchant, and adding to the silver a contribution from all hands, gave it to our silent passenger, who knew not what the mariners had done.

The last seen of lone Hunilla she was passing into Payta town, riding upon a small gray ass; and before her on the ass's shoulders, she eyed the jointed workings of the beast's armorial cross.

Sketch Ninth

HOOD'S ISLE AND THE HERMIT OBERLUS

> "That darkesome glen they enter, where they find
> That cursed man low sitting on the ground,
> Musing full sadly in his sullein mind;
> His griesly lockes long grouen and unbound,
> Disordered hong about his shoulders round,
> And hid his face, through which his hollow eyne
> Lookt deadly dull, and stared as astound;
> His raw-bone cheekes, through penurie and pine,
> Were shronke into the jawes, as he did never dine.
> His garments nought but many ragged clouts,
> With thornes together pind and patched reads,
> The which his naked sides he wrapt abouts."

Southeast of Crossman's Isle lies Hood's Isle, or McCain's Beclouded Isle, and upon its south side is a vitreous cove with a wide strand of dark pounded black lava, called Black Beach, or Oberlus's Landing. It might fitly have been styled Charon's.

It received its name from a wild white creature who spent many years here, in the person of a European bringing into this savage region qualities more diabolical than are to be found among any of the surrounding cannibals.

About half a century ago, Oberlus deserted at the above-named island, then, as now, a solitude. He built himself a den of lava and clinkers, about a mile from the Landing, subsequently called after him, in a vale, or expanded gulch, containing here and there among the rocks about two acres of soil capable of rude cultivation, the only place on the isle not too blasted for that purpose. Here he succeeded in raising a sort of degenerate potatoes and pumpkins, which from time to time he exchanged with needy whalemen passing, for spirits or dollars.

His appearance, from all accounts, was that of the victim of some malignant sorceress; he seemed to have drunk of Circe's cup; beastlike; rags insufficient to hide his nakedness; his befreckled skin blistered by continual exposure to the sun; nose flat; countenance contorted, heavy, earthy; hair and beard unshorn, profuse, and of fiery red. He struck strangers much as if he were a volcanic creature thrown up by the same convulsion which exploded into sight the isle. All bepatched and coiled asleep in his lonely lava den among the mountains, he looked, they say, as a heaped drift of withered leaves, torn from autumn trees, and so left in some hidden nook by the whirling halt for an instant of a fierce night wind, which then ruthlessly sweeps on, somewhere else to repeat the capricious act. It is also reported to have been the strangest sight, this same Oberlus, of a sultry, cloudy morning, hidden under his shocking old black tarpaulin hat, hoeing potatoes among the lava. So warped and crooked was his strange nature that the very handle of his hoe seemed gradually to have shrunk and twisted in his grasp, being a wretched bent stick, elbowed more like a savage's war sickle than a civilized hoe handle. It was his mysterious custom upon a first encounter with a stranger ever to present his back, possibly because that was his better side, since it revealed the least. If the encounter chanced in his garden, as it sometimes did—the new-landed strangers going from the seaside straight through the gorge, to hunt up the queer greengrocer reported doing business here—Oberlus for a time hoed on, unmindful of all greeting, jovial or bland; as the curious stranger would turn to face him, the recluse, hoe in hand, as diligently would avert himself, bowed over, and sullenly revolving round his murphy hill. Thus far for hoeing. When planting, his whole aspect and all his gestures were so malevolently and uselessly sinister and secret that he seemed rather in act of dropping poison into wells than potatoes into soil. But among his lesser and more harmless marvels was an idea he ever had that his visitors came

equally as well led by longings to behold the mighty hermit
Oberlus in his royal state of solitude as simply to obtain
potatoes, or find whatever company might be upon a
barren isle. It seems incredible that such a being should
possess such vanity, a misanthrope be conceited; but
he really had his notion, and, upon the strength of it, often
gave himself amusing airs to captains. But after all this
is somewhat of a piece with the well-known eccentricity
of some convicts, proud of that very hatefulness which
makes them notorious. At other times, another unaccountable whim would seize him, and he would long dodge advancing strangers round the clinkered corners of his hut;
sometimes, like a stealthy bear, he would slink through
the withered thickets up the mountains and refuse to see
the human face.

Except his occasional visitors from the sea, for a long
period the only companions of Oberlus were the crawling
tortoises, and he seemed more than degraded to their
level, having no desires for a time beyond theirs, unless
it were for the stupor brought on by drunkenness. But,
sufficiently debased as he appeared, there yet lurked in
him, only awaiting occasion for discovery, a still further
proneness. Indeed, the sole superiority of Oberlus over
the tortoises was his possession of a larger capacity of
degradation, and, along with that, something like an intelligent will to it. Moreover, what is about to be revealed
perhaps will show that selfish ambition, or the love of rule
for its own sake, far from being the peculiar infirmity of
noble minds, is shared by beings which have no mind at
all. No creatures are so selfishly tyrannical as some brutes,
as anyone who has observed the tenants of the pasture
must occasionally have observed.

"This island's mine by Sycorax my mother," said Oberlus to himself, glaring round upon his haggard solitude.
By some means, barter or theft—for in those days ships
at intervals still kept touching at his Landing—he obtained
an old musket, with a few charges of powder and ball.
Possessed of arms, he was stimulated to enterprise, as a
tiger that first feels the coming of its claws. The long habit
of sole dominion over every object round him, his almost
unbroken solitude, his never encountering humanity except
on terms of misanthropic independence or mercantile

craftiness, and even such encounters being comparatively but rare—all this must have gradually nourished in him a vast idea of his own importance, together with a pure animal sort of scorn for all the rest of the universe.

The unfortunate Creole who enjoyed his brief term of royalty at Charles's Isle was perhaps in some degree influenced by not unworthy motives, such as prompt other adventurous spirits to lead colonists into distant regions and assume political pre-eminence over them. His summary execution of many of his Peruvians is quite pardonable, considering the desperate characters he had to deal with, while his offering canine battle to the banded rebels seems under the circumstances altogether just. But for this King Oberlus and what shortly follows, no shade of palliation can be given. He acted out of mere delight in tyranny and cruelty, by virtue of a quality in him inherited from Sycorax his mother. Armed now with that shocking blunderbuss, strong in the thought of being master of that horrid isle, he panted for a chance to prove his potency upon the first specimen of humanity which should fall unbefriended into his hands.

Nor was he long without it. One day he spied a boat upon the beach, with one man, a Negro, standing by it. Some distance off was a ship, and Oberlus immediately knew how matters stood. The vessel had put in for wood, and the boat's crew had gone into the thickets for it. From a convenient spot he kept watch of the boat, till presently a straggling company appeared loaded with billets. Throwing these on the beach, they again went into the thickets, while the Negro proceeded to load the boat.

Oberlus now makes all haste and accosts the Negro, who, aghast at seeing any living being inhabiting such a solitude, and especially so horrific a one, immediately falls into a panic, not at all lessened by the ursine suavity of Oberlus, who begs the favor of assisting him in his labors. The Negro stands with several billets on his shoulder, in act of shouldering others, and Oberlus, with a short cord concealed in his bosom, kindly proceeds to lift those other billets to their place. In so doing, he persists in keeping behind the Negro, who, rightly suspicious of this, in vain dodges about to gain the front of Oberlus; but Oberlus dodges also, till at last, weary of this bootless

attempt at treachery, or fearful of being surprised by the
remainder of the party, Oberlus runs off a little space to
a bush, and, fetching his blunderbuss, savagely commands
the Negro to desist work and follow him. He refuses.
Whereupon, presenting his piece, Oberlus snaps at him.
Luckily the blunderbuss misses fire, but by this time,
frightened out of his wits, the Negro, upon a second intrepid summons, drops his billets, surrenders at discretion,
and follows on. By a narrow defile familiar to him, Oberlus speedily removes out of sight of the water.

On their way up the mountains, he exultingly informs
the Negro that henceforth he is to work for him and be his
slave, and that his treatment would entirely depend on
his future conduct. But Oberlus, deceived by the first impulsive cowardice of the black, in an evil moment slackens
his vigilance. Passing through a narrow way, and perceiving his leader quite off his guard, the Negro, powerful
fellow, suddenly grasps him in his arms, throws him
down, wrests his musketoon from him, ties his hands with
the monster's own cord, shoulders him, and returns with
him down to the boat. When the rest of the party arrive,
Oberlus is carried on board the ship. This proved an
Englishman, and a smuggler, a sort of craft not apt to
be overcharitable. Oberlus is severely whipped, then hand-
cuffed, taken ashore, and compelled to make known his
habitation and produce his property. His potatoes, pumpkins, and tortoises, with a pile of dollars he had hoarded
from his mercantile operations, were secured on the spot.
But while the too vindictive smugglers were busy destroying his hut and garden, Oberlus makes his escape into the
mountains, and conceals himself there in impenetrable
recesses, only known to himself, till the ship sails, when
he ventures back, and by means of an old file which he
sticks into a tree, contrives to free himself from his hand-
cuffs.

Brooding among the ruins of his hut, and the desolate
clinkers and extinct volcanoes of this outcast isle, the insulted misanthrope now meditates a signal revenge upon
humanity, but conceals his purposes. Vessels still touch
the Landing at times, and by-and-by Oberlus is enabled
to supply them with some vegetables.

Warned by his former failure in kidnaping strangers,

he now pursues a quite different plan. When seamen come ashore, he makes up to them like a free-and-easy comrade, invites them to his hut, and with whatever affability his redhaired grimness may assume, entreats them to drink his liquor and be merry. But his guests need little pressing, and so, soon as rendered insensible, are tied hand and foot, and, pitched among the clinkers, are there concealed till the ship departs, when, finding themselves entirely dependent upon Oberlus, alarmed at his changed demeanor, his savage threats, and above all, that shocking blunderbuss, they willingly enlist under him, becoming his humble slaves, and Oberlus the most incredible of tyrants. So much so that two or three perish beneath his initiating process. He sets the remainder—four of them—to breaking the caked soil, transporting upon their backs loads of loamy earth, scooped up in moist clefts among the mountains; keeps them on the roughest fare; presents his piece at the slightest hint of insurrection; and in all respects converts them into reptiles at his feet—plebeian garter snakes to this Lord Anaconda.

At last Oberlus contrives to stock his arsenal with four rusty cutlasses and an added supply of powder and ball intended for his blunderbuss. Remitting in good part the labor of his slaves, he now approves himself a man, or rather devil, of great abilities in the way of cajoling or coercing others into acquiescence with his own ulterior designs, however at first abhorrent to them. But indeed, prepared for almost any eventual evil by their previous lawless life, as a sort of ranging cowboys of the sea, which had dissolved within them the whole moral man so that they were ready to concrete in the first offered mold of baseness now; rotted down from manhood by their hopeless misery on the isle, wonted to cringe in all things to their lord, himself the worst of slaves, these wretches were now become wholly corrupted to his hands. He used them as creatures of an inferior race; in short, he gaffles his four animals and makes murderers of them, out of cowards fitly manufacturing bravos.

Now, sword or dagger, human arms are but artificial claws and fangs, tied on like false spurs to the fighting cock. So, we repeat, Oberlus, tsar of the isle, gaffles his four subjects; that is, with intent of glory, puts four rusty cutlasses into their hands. Like any other autocrat, he had a noble army now.

It might be thought a servile war would hereupon ensue. Arms in the hands of trodden slaves? how indiscreet of Emperor Oberlus! Nay, they had but cutlasses—sad old scythes enough—he a blunderbuss, which by its blind scatterings of all sorts of boulders, clinkers, and other scoria would annihilate all four mutineers, like four pigeons at one shot. Besides, at first he did not sleep in his accustomed hut; every lurid sunset, for a time, he might have been seen wending his way among the riven mountains, there to secrete himself till dawn in some sulphurous pitfall, undiscoverable to his gang; but finding this at last too troublesome, he now each evening tied his slaves hand and foot, hid the cutlasses, and thrusting them into his barracks, shut to the door, and, lying down before it, beneath a rude shed lately added, slept out the night, blunderbuss in hand.

It is supposed that not content with daily parading over a cindery solitude at the head of his fine army, Oberlus now meditated the most active mischief, his probable object being to surprise some passing ship touching at his dominions, massacre the crew, and run away with her to parts unknown. While these plans were simmering in his head, two ships touch in company at the isle, on the opposite side to his, when his designs undergo a sudden change.

The ships are in want of vegetables, which Oberlus promises in great abundance, provided they send their boats round to his Landing, so that the crews may bring the vegetables from his garden, informing the two captains, at the same time, that his rascals—slaves and soldiers —had become so abominably lazy and good-for-nothing of late, that he could not make them work by ordinary inducements, and did not have the heart to be severe with them.

The arrangement was agreed to, and the boats were sent and hauled upon the beach. The crews went to the lava hut, but to their surprise nobody was there. After waiting till their patience was exhausted, they returned to the shore, when lo, some stranger—not the Good Samaritan either—seems to have very recently passed that way. Three of the boats were broken in a thousand pieces, and the fourth was missing. By hard toil over the mountains and through the clinkers, some of the strangers succeeded in returning to that side of the isle where the ships lay, when fresh boats are sent to the relief of the rest of the hapless party.

However amazed at the treachery of Oberlus, the two captains, afraid of new and still more mysterious atrocities —and indeed, half imputing such strange events to the enchantments associated with these isles—perceive no security but in instant flight, leaving Oberlus and his army in quiet possession of the stolen boat.

On the eve of sailing they put a letter in a keg, giving the Pacific Ocean intelligence of the affair, and moored the keg in the bay. Some time subsequent, the keg was opened by another captain chancing to anchor there, but not until after he had dispatched a boat round to Oberlus's Landing. As may be readily surmised, he felt no little inquietude till the boat's return, when another letter was handed him, giving Oberlus's version of the affair. This precious document had been found pinned half-mildewed to the clinker wall of the sulphurous and deserted hut. It ran as follows: showing that Oberlus was at least an accomplished writer, and no mere boor, and what is more, was capable of the most tristful eloquence.

"Sir: I am the most unfortunate ill-treated gentleman that lives. I am a patriot, exiled from my country by the cruel hand of tyranny.

"Banished to these Enchanted Isles, I have again and again besought captains of ships to sell me a boat, but always have been refused, though I offered the handsomest prices in Mexican dollars. At length an opportunity presented of possessing myself of one, and I did not let it slip.

"I have been long endeavoring, by hard labor and much solitary suffering, to accumulate something to make myself comfortable in a virtuous though unhappy old age; but at various times have been robbed and beaten by men professing to be Christians.

"Today I sail from the Enchanted group in the good boat Charity bound to the Feejee Isles.

"FATHERLESS OBERLUS.

"*P.S.*—Behind the clinkers, nigh the oven, you will find the old fowl. Do not kill it; be patient; I leave it setting; if it shall have any chicks, I hereby bequeath them to you, whoever you may be. But don't count your chicks before they are hatched."

The fowl proved a starveling rooster, reduced to a sitting posture by sheer debility.

Oberlus declares that he was bound to the Feejee Isles; but this was only to throw pursuers on a false scent. For, after a long time, he arrived, alone in his open boat, at Guayaquil. As his miscreants were never again beheld on Hood's Isle, it is supposed, either that they perished for want of water on the passage to Guayaquil, or, what is quite as probable, were thrown overboard by Oberlus, when he found the water growing scarce.

From Guayaquil Oberlus proceeded to Payta, and there, with that nameless witchery peculiar to some of the ugliest animals, wound himself into the affections of a tawny damsel, prevailing upon her to accompany him back to his Enchanted Isle; which doubtless he painted as a Paradise of flowers, not a Tartarus of clinkers.

But unfortunately for the colonization of Hood's Isle with a choice variety of animated nature, the extraordinary and devilish aspect of Oberlus made him to be regarded in Payta as a highly suspicious character. So that being found concealed one night, with matches in his pocket, under the hull of a small vessel just ready to be launched, he was seized and thrown into jail.

The jails in most South American towns are generally of the least wholesome sort. Built of huge cakes of sunburnt brick, and containing but one room, without windows or yard, and but one door heavily grated with wooden bars, they present both within and without the grimmest aspect. As public edifices they conspicuously stand upon the hot and dusty Plaza, offering to view, through the gratings, their villainous and hopeless inmates, burrowing in all sorts of tragic squalor. And here, for a long time, Oberlus was seen, the central figure of a mongrel and assassin band, a creature whom it is religion to detest, since it is philanthropy to hate a misanthrope.

Note.—They who may be disposed to question the possibility of the character above depicted, are referred to the 2d vol. of Porter's Voyage into the Pacific, where they will recognize many sentences, for expedition's sake derived verbatim from thence and incorporated here; the main difference—save a few passing reflections—between the two accounts being that the present writer has added to Porter's facts accessory ones picked up in the Pacific from reliable sources, and, where facts conflict, has naturally preferred his own authorities to Porter's. As, for instance, *his* authorities place Oberlus on Hood's Isle: Porter's, on Charles's Isle. The letter found in the hut is also somewhat different, for while at the Encantadas he was informed that, not only did it evince a certain clerkliness, but was full of the strangest satiric effrontery which does not adequately appear in Porter's version. I accordingly altered it to suit the general character of its author.

Sketch Tenth

RUNAWAYS, CASTAWAYS, SOLITARIES, GRAVESTONES, ETC.

> "And all about old stocks and stubs of trees,
> Whereon nor fruit nor leaf was ever seen,
> Did hang upon ragged knotty knees,
> On which had many wretches hanged been."

Some relics of the hut of Oberlus partially remain to this day at the head of the clinkered valley. Nor does the stranger, wandering among other of the Enchanted Isles, fail to stumble upon still other solitary abodes, long abandoned to the tortoise and the lizard. Probably few parts of earth have, in modern times, sheltered so many solitaries. The reason is that these isles are situated in a distant sea, and the vessels which occasionally visit them are mostly all whalers, or ships bound on dreary and protracted voyages, exempting them in a good degree from both the oversight and the memory of human law. Such is the character of some commanders and some seamen that under these untoward circumstances it is quite impossible but that scenes of unpleasantness and discord should occur between them. A sullen hatred of the tyran-

nic ship will seize the sailor, and he gladly exchanges it
for isles, which, though blighted as by a continual sirocco
and burning breeze, still offer him, in their labyrinthine
interior, a retreat beyond the possibility of capture. To
flee the ship in any Peruvian or Chilean port, even the
smallest and most rustical, is not unattended with great
risk of apprehension, not to speak of jaguars. A reward
of five pesos sends fifty dastardly Spaniards into the wood,
who, with long knives, scour them day and night in eager
hopes of securing their prey. Neither is it, in general, much
easier to escape pursuit at the isles of Polynesia. Those of
them which have felt a civilizing influence present the
same difficulty to the runaway with the Peruvian ports,
the advanced natives being quite as mercenary and keen
of knife and scent as the retrograde Spaniards; while, owing to the bad odor in which all Europeans lie, in the minds
of aboriginal savages who have chanced to hear aught
of them, to desert the ship among primitive Polynesians,
is, in most cases, a hope not unforlorn. Hence the Enchanted Isles become the voluntary tarrying place of all
sorts of refugees; some of whom too sadly experience the
fact that flight from tyranny does not of itself insure a
safe asylum, far less a happy home.

Moreover, it has not seldom happened that hermits
have been made upon the isles by the accidents incident
to tortoise hunting. The interior of most of them is
tangled and difficult of passage beyond description; the
air is sultry and stifling; an intolerable thirst is provoked,
for which no running stream offers its kind relief. In a
few hours, under an equatorial sun, reduced by these
causes to entire exhaustion, woe betide the straggler at
the Enchanted Isles! Their extent is such as to forbid an
adequate search, unless weeks are devoted to it. The impatient ship waits a day or two, when, the missing man
remaining undiscovered, up goes a stake on the beach,
with a letter of regret, and a keg of crackers and another
of water tied to it, and away sails the craft.

Nor have there been wanting instances where the in-
humanity of some captains has led them to wreak a secure revenge upon seamen who have given their caprice

or pride some singular offense. Thrust ashore upon the scorching marl, such mariners are abandoned to perish outright, unless by solitary labors they succeed in discovering some precious dribblets of moisture oozing from a rock or stagnant in a mountain pool.

I was well acquainted with a man who, lost upon the Isle of Narborough, was brought to such extremes by thirst that at last he only saved his life by taking that of another being. A large hair seal came upon the beach. He rushed upon it, stabbed it in the neck, and then throwing himself upon the panting body quaffed at the living wound; the palpitations of the creature's dying heart injected life into the drinker.

Another seaman, thrust ashore in a boat upon an isle at which no ship ever touched, owing to its peculiar sterility and the shoals about it, and from which all other parts of the group were hidden—this man, feeling that it was sure death to remain there, and that nothing worse than death menaced him in quitting it, killed two seals, and, inflating their skins, made a float, upon which he transported himself to Charles's Island, and joined the republic there.

But men not endowed with courage equal to such desperate attempts find their only resource in forthwith seeking some watering place, however precarious or scanty, building a hut, catching tortoises and birds, and in all respects preparing for a hermit life, till tide or time, or a passing ship, arrives to float them off.

At the foot of precipices on many of the isles, small rude basins in the rocks are found, partly filled with rotted rubbish or vegetable decay, or overgrown with thickets, and sometimes a little moist, which, upon examination, reveal plain tokens of artificial instruments employed in hollowing them out, by some poor castaway or still more miserable runaway. These basins are made in places where it was supposed some scanty drops of dew might exude into them from the upper crevices.

The relics of hermitages and stone basins are not the only signs of vanishing humanity to be found upon the isles. And, curious to say, that spot which of all others in settled communities is most animated, at the Enchanted

Isles presents the most dreary of aspects. And though it may seem very strange to talk of post offices in this barren region, yet post offices are occasionally to be found there. They consist of a stake and a bottle. The letters being not only sealed, but corked. They are generally deposited by captains of Nantucketers for the benefit of passing fishermen, and contain statements as to what luck they had in whaling or tortoise hunting. Frequently, however, long months and months, whole years, glide by and no applicant appears. The stake rots and falls, presenting no very exhilarating object.

If now it be added that gravestones, or rather graveboards, are also discovered upon some of the isles, the picture will be complete.

Upon the beach of James's Isle, for many years was to be seen a rude fingerpost, pointing inland. And, perhaps, taking it for some signal of possible hospitality in this otherwise desolate spot—some good hermit living there with his maple dish—the stranger would follow on in the path thus indicated, till at last he would come out in a noiseless nook and find his only welcome, a dead man—his sole greeting the inscription over a grave. Here, in 1813, fell, in a daybreak duel, a lieutenant of the U.S. frigate *Essex,* aged twenty-one—attaining his majority in death.

It is but fit that, like those old monastic institutions of Europe whose inmates go not out of their own walls to be inurned but are entombed there where they die, the Encantadas, too, should bury their own dead, even as the great general monastery of earth does hers.

It is known that burial in the ocean is a pure necessity of seafaring life, and that it is only done when land is far astern, and not clearly visible from the bow. Hence, to vessels cruising in the vicinity of the Enchanted Isles, they afford a convenient Potter's Field. The interment over, some good-natured forecastle poet and artist seizes his paint brush and inscribes a doggerel epitaph. When, after a long lapse of time, other good-natured seamen chance to come upon the spot, they usually make a table of the mound, and quaff a friendly can to the poor soul's repose.

As a specimen of these epitaphs, take the following, found in a bleak gorge of Chatham Isle:

"Oh, Brother Jack, as you pass by,
As you are now, so once was I.
Just so game, and just so gay,
But now, alack, they've stopped my pay.
No more I peep out of my blinkers,
Here I be—tucked in with clinkers!"

THE BELL-TOWER

In the south of Europe, nigh a once frescoed capital, now with dank mold cankering its bloom, central in a plain, stands what, at distance, seems the black mossed stump of some immeasurable pine, fallen, in forgotten days, with Anak and the Titan.

As all along where the pine tree falls, its dissolution leaves a mossy mound—last-flung shadow of the perished trunk; never lengthening, never lessening; unsubject to the fleet falsities of the sun; shade immutable, and true gauge which cometh by prostration—so westward from what seems the stump, one steadfast spear of lichened ruin veins the plain.

From that treetop, what birded chimes of silver throats had rung. A stone pine, a metallic aviary in its crown: the Bell-Tower, built by the great mechanician, the unblest foundling, Bannadonna.

Like Babel's, its base was laid in a high hour of reno-

vated earth, following the second deluge, when the waters
of the Dark Ages had dried up and once more the green
appeared. No wonder that, after so long and deep sub-
mersion, the jubilant expectation of the race should, as
with Noah's sons, soar into Shinar aspiration.

In firm resolve, no man in Europe at that period went
beyond Bannadonna. Enriched through commerce with
the Levant, the state in which he lived voted to have the
noblest Bell-Tower in Italy. His repute assigned him to
be architect.

Stone by stone, month by month, the tower rose. Higher,
higher, snaillike in pace, but torch or rocket in its pride.

After the masons would depart, the builder, standing
alone upon its ever-ascending summit at close of every
day, saw that he overtopped still higher walls and trees.
He would tarry till a late hour there, wrapped in schemes
of other and still loftier piles. Those who of saints' days
thronged the spot—hanging to the rude poles of scaffold-
ing like sailors on yards or bees on boughs, unmindful of
lime and dust, and falling chips of stone—their homage
not the less inspirited him to self-esteem.

At length the holiday of the Tower came. To the sound
of viols, the climax-stone slowly rose in air, and, amid the
firing of ordnance, was laid by Bannadonna's hands upon
the final course. Then mounting it, he stood erect, alone,
with folded arms, gazing upon the white summits of blue
inland Alps, and whiter crests of bluer Alps offshore—
sights invisible from the plain. Invisible, too, from thence
was that eye he turned below, when, like the cannon
booms, came up to him the people's combustions of applause.

That which stirred them so was seeing with what serenity the builder stood three hundred feet in air, upon an un-
railed perch. This none but he durst do. But his periodic
standing upon the pile, in each stage of its growth—such
discipline had its last result.

Little remained now but the bells. These, in all respects, must correspond with their receptacle.

The minor ones were prosperously cast. A highly enriched one followed, of a singular make, intended for suspension in a manner before unknown. The purpose of this
bell, its rotary motion and connection with the clockwork,

also executed at the time, will, in the sequel, receive mention.

In the one erection, bell-tower and clock-tower were united, though, before that period, such structures had commonly been built distinct; as the Campanile and Torre del Orologio of St. Mark to this day attest.

But it was upon the great state bell that the founder lavished his more daring skill. In vain did some of the less elated magistrates here caution him, saying that though truly the tower was titanic, yet limit should be set to the dependent weight of its swaying masses. But, undeterred, he prepared his mammoth mold, dented with mythological devices; kindled his fires of balsamic firs; melted his tin and copper, and, throwing in much plate contributed by the public spirit of the nobles, let loose the tide.

The unleashed metals bayed like hounds. The workmen shrunk. Through their fright, fatal harm to the bell was dreaded. Fearless as Shadrach, Bannadonna, rushing through the glow, smote the chief culprit with his ponderous ladle. From the smitten part, a splinter was dashed into the seething mass, and at once was melted in.

Next day a portion of the work was heedfully uncovered. All seemed right. Upon the third morning, with equal satisfaction, it was bared still lower. At length, like some old Theban king, the whole cooled casting was disinterred. All was fair except in one strange spot. But as he suffered no one to attend him in these inspections, he concealed the blemish by some preparation which none knew better to devise.

The casting of such a mass was deemed no small triumph for the caster; one, too, in which the state might not scorn to share. The homicide was overlooked. By the charitable that deed was but imputed to sudden transports of esthetic passion, not to any flagitious quality. A kick from an Arabian charger; not sign of vice, but blood.

His felony remitted by the judge, absolution given him by the priest, what more could even a sickly conscience have desired.

Honoring the tower and its builder with another holiday, the republic witnessed the hoisting of the bells and clockwork amid shows and pomps superior to the former.

Some months of more than usual solitude on Bannadonna's part ensued. It was not unknown that he was engaged upon something for the belfry, intended to complete it and surpass all that had gone before. Most people imagined that the design would involve a casting like the bells. But those who thought they had some further insight would shake their heads, with hints that not for nothing did the mechanician keep so secret. Meantime, his seclusion failed not to invest his work with more or less of that sort of mystery pertaining to the forbidden.

Erelong he had a heavy object hoisted to the belfry, wrapped in a dark sack or cloak—a procedure sometimes had in the case of an elaborate piece of sculpture, or statue, which, being intended to grace the front of a new edifice, the architect does not desire exposed to critical eyes till set up, finished, in its appointed place. Such was the impression now. But, as the object rose, a statuary present observed, or thought he did, that it was not entirely rigid, but was, in a manner, pliant. At last, when the hidden thing had attained its final height, and, obscurely seen from below, seemed almost of itself to step into the belfry, as if with little assistance from the crane, a shrewd old blacksmith present ventured the suspicion that it was but a living man. This surmise was thought a foolish one, while the general interest failed not to augment.

Not without demur from Bannadonna, the chief magistrate of the town, with an associate—both elderly men—followed what seemed the image up the tower. But, arrived at the belfry, they had little recompense. Plausibly entrenching himself behind the conceded mysteries of his art, the mechanician withheld present explanation. The magistrates glanced toward the cloaked object, which, to their surprise, seemed now to have changed its attitude, or else had before been more perplexingly concealed by the violent muffling action of the wind without. It seemed now seated upon some sort of frame, or chair, contained within the domino. They observed that nigh the top, in a sort of square, the web of the cloth, either from accident or design, had its warp partly withdrawn, and the cross threads plucked out here and there, so as to form a sort of woven grating. Whether it were the low wind or no, stealing through the stone latticework, or only their own perturbed imaginations, is uncertain, but they thought they discerned a slight sort of fitful, springlike motion in the domino. Nothing, however incidental or insignificant, escaped their uneasy eyes. Among other things, they pried out, in a corner, an earthen cup, partly corroded and partly encrusted, and one whispered to the other that this cup was just such a one as might, in mockery, be offered to the lips of some brazen statue, or, perhaps, still worse.

But, being questioned, the mechanician said that the cup was simply used in his founder's business, and described the purpose—in short, a cup to test the condition of metals in fusion. He added that it had got into the belfry by the merest chance.

Again and again they gazed at the domino, as at some suspicious incognito at a Venetian mask. All sorts of vague apprehensions stirred them. They even dreaded lest, when they should descend, the mechanician, though without a flesh-and-blood companion, for all that, would not be left alone.

Affecting some merriment at their disquietude, he begged to relieve them, by extending a coarse sheet of workman's canvas between them and the object.

Meantime he sought to interest them in his other work, nor, now that the domino was out of sight, did they long remain insensible to the artistic wonders lying round them —wonders hitherto beheld but in their unfinished state, because, since hoisting the bells, none but the caster had entered within the belfry. It was one trait of his, that, even in details, he would not let another do what he could, without too great loss of time, accomplish for himself. So, for several preceding weeks, whatever hours were unemployed in his secret design had been devoted to elaborating the figures on the bells.

The clock bell, in particular, now drew attention. Under a patient chisel, the latent beauty of its enrichments, before obscured by the cloudings incident to casting, that beauty in its shyest grace, was now revealed. Round and round the bell, twelve figures of gay girls, garlanded, hand-in-hand, danced in a choral ring—the embodied hours.

"Bannadonna," said the chief, "this bell excels all else. No added touch could here improve. Hark!" hearing a sound, "was that the wind?"

"The wind, Excellenza," was the light response. "But

the figures, they are not yet without their faults. They need some touches yet. When those are given, and the——— block yonder," pointing towards the canvas screen, "when Haman there, as I merrily call him—him? *it,* I mean——— when Haman is fixed on this, his lofty tree, then, gentlemen, will I be most happy to receive you here again."

The equivocal reference to the object caused some return of restlessness. However, on their part, the visitors forbore further allusion to it, unwilling, perhaps, to let the foundling see how easily it lay within his plebeian art to stir the placid dignity of nobles.

"Well, Bannadonna," said the chief, "how long ere you are ready to set the clock going, so that the hour shall be sounded? Our interest in you, not less than in the work itself, makes us anxious to be assured of your success. The people, too—why, they are shouting now. Say the exact hour when you will be ready."

"Tomorrow, Excellenza, if you listen for it—or should you not, all the same—strange music will be heard. The stroke of one shall be the first from yonder bell," pointing to the bell adorned with girls and garlands, "that stroke shall fall there, where the hand of Una clasps Dua's. The stroke of one shall sever that loved clasp. Tomorrow, then, at one o'clock, as struck here, precisely here," advancing and placing his finger upon the clasp, "the poor mechanic will be most happy once more to give you liege audience, in this his littered shop. Farewell till then, illustrious magnificoes, and hark ye for your vassal's stroke."

His still, Vulcanic face hiding its burning brightness like a forge, he moved with ostentatious deference towards the scuttle, as if so far to escort their exit. But the junior magistrate, a kind-hearted man, troubled at what seemed to him a certain sardonical disdain lurking beneath the foundling's humble mien, and in Christian sympathy more distressed at it on his account than on his own, dimly surmising what might be the final fate of such a cynic solitaire, nor perhaps uninfluenced by the general strangeness of surrounding things, this good magistrate had glanced sadly, sideways from the speaker, and thereupon his foreboding eye had started at the expression of the unchanging face of the Hour Una.

"How is this, Bannadonna," he lowly asked, "Una looks unlike her sisters."

"In Christ's name, Bannadonna," impulsively broke in the chief, his attention for the first attracted to the figure by his associate's remark. "Una's face looks just like that of Deborah, the prophetess, as painted by the Florentine, Del Fonca."

"Surely, Bannadonna," lowly resumed the milder magistrate, "you meant the twelve should wear the same jocundly abandoned air. But see, the smile of Una seems but a fatal one. 'Tis different."

While his mild associate was speaking, the chief glanced inquiringly from him to the caster, as if anxious to mark how the discrepancy would be accounted for. As the chief stood, his advanced foot was on the scuttle's curb.

Bannadonna spoke:

"Excellenza, now that, following your keener eye, I glance upon the face of Una, I do, indeed perceive some little variance. But look all round the bell, and you will find no two faces entirely correspond. Because there is a law in art——but the cold wind is rising more; these lattices are but a poor defense. Suffer me, magnificoes, to conduct you at least partly on your way. Those in whose well-being there is a public stake, should be heedfully attended."

"Touching the look of Una, you were saying, Bannadonna, that there was a certain law in art," observed the chief, as the three now descended the stone shaft, "pray, tell me, then——"

"Pardon; another time, Excellenza—the tower is damp."

"Nay, I must rest, and hear it now. Here,—here is a wide landing, and through this leeward slit, no wind, but ample light. Tell us of your law, and at large."

"Since, Excellenza, you insist, know that there is a law in art which bars the possibility of duplicates. Some years ago, you may remember, I graved a small seal for your republic, bearing, for its chief device, the head of your own ancestor, its illustrious founder. It becoming necessary, for the customs' use, to have innumerable impressions for bales and boxes, I graved an entire plate, containing one hundred of the seals. Now, though, indeed, my object was to have those hundred heads identical, and though, I dare say, people think them so, yet, upon closely scanning an uncut impression from the plate, no two of those five-score faces, side by side, will be found alike. Gravity is the air of all, but diversified in all. In some, benevolent; in some, ambiguous; in two or three, to a close scrutiny, all but incipiently malign, the variation of less than a hair's breadth in the linear shadings round the mouth sufficing to all this. Now, Excellenza, transmute that general gravity into joyousness, and subject it to twelve of those variations I have described, and tell me, will you not have my hours here, and Una one of them? But I like——"

"Hark! is that——a footfall above?"

"Mortar, Excellenza; sometimes it drops to the belfry floor from the arch where the stonework was left undressed. I must have it seen to. As I was about to say: for one, I like this law forbidding duplicates. It evokes fine personalities. Yes, Excellenza, that strange, and—to you —uncertain smile, and those forelooking eyes of Una, suit Bannadonna very well."

"Hark!—sure we left no soul above?"

"No soul, Excellenza; rest assured, no *soul*.—Again the mortar."

"It fell not while we were there."

"Ah, in your presence, it better knew its place, Excellenza," blandly bowed Bannadonna.

"But Una," said the milder magistrate, "she seemed intently gazing on you; one would have almost sworn that she picked you out from among us three."

"If she did, possibly it might have been her finer apprehension, Excellenza."

"How, Bannadonna? I do not understand you."

"No consequence, no consequence, Excellenza—but the shifted wind is blowing through the slit. Suffer me to escort you on, and then, pardon, but the toiler must to his tools."

"It may be foolish, signor," and the milder magistrate, as, from the third landing, the two now went down unescorted, "but, somehow, our great mechanician moves me strangely. Why, just now, when he so superciliously replied, his walk seemed Sisera's, God's vain foe, in Del Fonca's painting. And that young, sculptured Deborah, too. Aye, and that——"

"Tush, tush, signor!" returned the chief. "A passing whim. Deborah?—Where's Jael, pray?"

"Ah," said the other, as they now stepped upon the sod, "ah, signor, I see you leave your fears behind you with the chill and gloom; but mine, even in this sunny air, remain. Hark!"

It was a sound from just within the tower door, whence they had emerged. Turning, they saw it closed.

"He has slipped down and barred us out," smiled the chief; "but it is his custom."

Proclamation was now made that the next day, at one hour after meridian, the clock would strike, and—thanks to the mechanician's powerful art—with unusual accompaniments. But what those should be, none as yet could say. The announcement was received with cheers.

By the looser sort, who encamped about the tower all night, lights were seen gleaming through the topmost blind-work, only disappearing with the morning sun. Strange sounds, too, were heard, or were thought to be, by those whom anxious watching might not have left mentally undisturbed—sounds, not only of some ringing implement, but also, so they said, half-suppressed screams and plainings, such as might have issued from some ghostly engine overplied.

Slowly the day drew on, part of the concourse chasing the weary time with songs and games, till, at last, the great blurred sun rolled, like a football, against the plain.

At noon, the nobility and principal citizens came from the town in cavalcade, a guard of soldiers, also, with music, the more to honor the occasion.

Only one hour more. Impatience grew. Watches were held in hands of feverish men, who stood, now scrutinizing their small dial-plates, and then, with neck thrown back, gazing toward the belfry, as if the eye might foretell that which could only be made sensible to the ear, for, as yet, there was no dial to the tower clock.

The hour hands of a thousand watches now verged within a hair's breadth of the figure 1. A silence, as of the expectations of some Shiloh, pervaded the swarming plain. Suddenly a dull, mangled sound, naught ringing in it, scarcely audible, indeed, to the outer circles of the people—that dull sound dropped heavily from the belfry.

At the same moment, each man stared at his neighbor blankly. All watches were upheld. All hour hands were at —had passed—the figure 1. No bell stroke from the tower. The multitude became tumultuous.

Waiting a few moments, the chief magistrate, commanding silence, hailed the belfry to know what thing unforeseen had happened there.

No response.

He hailed again and yet again.

All continued hushed.

By his order, the soldiers burst in the tower door, when, stationing guards to defend it from the now surging mob, the chief, accompanied by his former associate, climbed the winding stairs. Halfway up, they stopped to listen. No sound. Mounting faster, they reached the belfry, but, at the threshold, started at the spectacle disclosed. A spaniel, which, unbeknown to them, had followed them thus far, stood shivering as before some unknown monster in a brake, or, rather, as if it snuffed footsteps leading to some other world.

Bannadonna lay, prostrate and bleeding, at the base of the bell which was adorned with girls and garlands. He lay at the feet of the hour Una; his head coinciding, in a vertical line, with her left hand, clasped by the hour Dua. With downcast face impending over him, like Jael over nailed Sisera in the tent, was the domino; now no more becloaked.

It had limbs, and seemed clad in a scaly mail, lustrous as a dragon-beetle's. It was manacled, and its clubbed arms were uplifted, as if, with its manacles, once more to smite its already smitten victim. One advanced foot of it was inserted beneath the dead body, as if in the act of spurning it.

Uncertainty falls on what now followed.

It were but natural to suppose that the magistrates would, at first, shrink from immediate personal contact with what they saw. At the least, for a time, they would stand in involuntary doubt, it may be, in more or less of horrified alarm. Certain it is that an arquebuss was called for from below. And some add that its report, followed by a fierce whiz, as of the sudden snapping of a mainspring, with a steely din, as if a stack of sword blades should be dashed upon a pavement; these blended sounds came ringing to the plain, attracting every eye far upward to the belfry, whence, through the latticework, thin wreaths of smoke were curling.

Some averred that it was the spaniel, gone mad by fear, which was shot. This, others denied. True it was, the spaniel never more was seen; and, probably for some unknown reason, it shared the burial now to be related of the domino. For, whatever the preceding circumstances may have been, the first instinctive panic over, or else all ground of reasonable fear removed, the two magistrates, by themselves, quickly rehooded the figure in the dropped cloak wherein it had been hoisted. The same night, it was secretly lowered to the ground, smuggled to the beach, pulled far out to sea, and sunk. Nor to any after urgency, even in free convivial hours, would the twain ever disclose the full secrets of the belfry.

From the mystery unavoidably investing it, the popular solution of the foundling's fate involved more or less of supernatural agency. But some few less unscientific minds pretended to find little difficulty in otherwise accounting for it. In the chain of circumstantial inferences drawn, there may or may not have been some absent or defective links. But, as the explanation in question is the only one which tradition has explicitly preserved, in dearth of better, it will here be given. But, in the first place, it is requisite to present the supposition entertained as to the entire motive and mode, with their origin, of the secret design of Bannadonna, the minds above-mentioned assuming to penetrate as well into his soul as into the event. The disclosure will indirectly involve reference to peculiar matters, none of the clearest, beyond the immediate subject.

At that period, no large bell was made to sound otherwise than as at present, by agitation of a tongue within by means of ropes, or percussion from without, either from cumbrous machinery, or stalwart watchmen, armed with heavy hammers, stationed in the belfry or in sentry boxes on the open roof, according as the bell was sheltered or exposed.

It was from observing these exposed bells, with their watchmen, that the foundling, as was opined, derived the first suggestion of his scheme. Perched on a great mast or spire, the human figure, viewed from below, undergoes such a reduction in its apparent size as to obliterate its intelligent features. It evinces no personality. Instead of bespeaking volition, its gestures rather resemble the automatic ones of the arms of a telegraph.

Musing, therefore, upon the purely Punchinello aspect of the human figure thus beheld, it had indirectly occurred to Bannadonna to devise some metallic agent which should strike the hour with its mechanic hand, with even greater precision than the vital one. And, moreover, as the vital watchman on the roof, sallying from his retreat at the given periods, walked to the bell with uplifted mace to smite it, Bannadonna had resolved that his invention should likewise possess the power of locomotion, and, along with that, the appearance, at least, of intelligence and will.

If the conjectures of those who claimed acquaintance with the intent of Bannadonna be thus far correct, no unenterprising spirit could have been his. But they stopped not here; intimating that though, indeed, his design had, in the first place, been prompted by the sight of the watchman, and confined to the devising of a subtle substitute for him, yet, as is not seldom the case with projectors, by insensible gradations proceeding from comparatively pigmy aims to titanic ones, the original scheme had, in its anticipated eventualities, at last attained to an unheard-of degree of daring. He still bent his efforts upon the locomotive figure for the belfry, but only as a partial type of an ulterior creature, a sort of elephantine helot, adapted to further, in a degree scarcely to be imagined, the universal conveniences and glories of humanity; supplying nothing less than a supplement to the Six Days' Work; stocking the earth with a new serf, more useful than the ox, swifter than the dolphin, stronger than the lion, more cunning than the ape, for industry an ant, more fiery than serpents, and yet, in patience, another ass. All excellences of all God-made creatures which served man were here to receive advancement, and then to be combined in one. Talus was to have been the all-accomplished helot's name. Talus, iron slave to Bannadonna, and, through him, to man.

Here, it might well be thought that, were these last conjectures as to the foundling's secrets not erroneous, then

must he have been hopelessly infected with the craziest
chimeras of his age; far outgoing Albert Magus and Cor-
nelius Agrippa. But the contrary was averred. However
marvelous his design, however apparently transcending not
alone the bounds of human invention, but those of divine
creation, yet the proposed means to be employed were alleged to have been confined within the sober forms of
sober reason. It was affirmed that, to a degree of more
than skeptic scorn, Bannadonna had been without sympathy for any of the vainglorious irrationalities of his
time. For example, he had not concluded, with the vision-
aries among the metaphysicians, that between the finer
mechanic forces and the ruder animal vitality some germ
of correspondence might prove discoverable. As little did
his scheme partake of the enthusiasm of some natural
philosophers, who hoped, by physiological and chemical
inductions, to arrive at a knowledge of the source of life,
and so qualify themselves to manufacture and improve
upon it. Much less had he aught in common with the tribe
of alchemists, who sought by a species of incantations to
evoke some surprising vitality from the laboratory. Neither
had he imagined, with certain sanguine theosophists, that,
by faithful adoration of the Highest, unheard-of powers
would be vouchsafed to man. A practical materialist, what
Bannadonna had aimed at was to have been reached, not
by logic, not by crucible, not by conjuration, not by altars,
but by plain vise-bench and hammer. In short, to solve
nature, to steal into her, to intrigue beyond her, to procure someone else to bind her to his hand—these, one and
all, had not been his objects, but, asking no favors from
any element or any being, of himself to rival her, outstrip
her, and rule her. He stooped to conquer. With him, common sense was theurgy; machinery, miracle; Prometheus,
the heroic name for machinist; man, the true God.

Nevertheless, in his initial step, so far as the experimen-
tal automaton for the belfry was concerned, he allowed
fancy some little play, or, perhaps, what seemed his fanci-
fulness was but his utilitarian ambition collaterally extended. In figure, the creature for the belfry should not
be likened after the human pattern, nor any animal one,
nor after the ideals, however wild, of ancient fable, but

equally in aspect as in organism be an original production —the more terrible to behold, the better.

Such, then, were the suppositions as to the present scheme, and the reserved intent. How, at the very threshold, so unlooked-for a catastrophe overturned all, or rather, what was the conjecture here, is now to be set forth.

It was thought that on the day preceding the fatality, his visitors having left him, Bannadonna had unpacked the belfry image, adjusted it, and placed it in the retreat provided—a sort of sentry box in one corner of the belfry; in short, throughout the night, and for some part of the ensuing morning, he had been engaged in arranging everything connected with the domino: the issuing from the sentry box each sixty minutes; sliding along a grooved way, like a railway; advancing to the clock bell with uplifted manacles; striking it at one of the twelve junctions of the four-and-twenty hands; then wheeling, circling the bell, and retiring to its post, there to bide for another sixty minutes, when the same process was to be repeated; the bell, by a cunning mechanism, meantime turning on its vertical axis, so as to present, to the descending mace, the clasped hands of the next two figures, when it would strike two, three, and so on, to the end. The musical metal in this time bell being so managed in the fusion, by some art perishing with its originator, that each of the clasps of the four-and-twenty hands should give forth its own peculiar resonance when parted.

But on the magic metal, the magic and metallic stranger never struck but that one stroke, drove but that one nail, served but that one clasp, by which Bannadonna clung to his ambitious life. For, after winding up the creature in the sentry box, so that, for the present, skipping the intervening hours, it should not emerge till the hour of one, but should then infallibly emerge, and, after deftly oiling the grooves whereon it was to slide, it was surmised that the mechanician must then have hurried to the bell, to give his final touches to its sculpture. True artist, he here became absorbed, and absorption still further intensified, it may be, by his striving to abate that strange look of Una, which, though, before others, he had treated with

such unconcern, might not, in secret, have been without
its thorn.

And so, for the interval, he was oblivious of his creature, which, not oblivious of him, and true to its creation,
and true to its heedful winding up, left its post precisely
at the given moment, along its well-oiled route, slid noiselessly towards its mark, and, aiming at the hand of Una
to ring one clangorous note, dully smote the intervening
brain of Bannadonna, turned backwards to it, the manacled
arms then instantly upspringing to their hovering poise.
The falling body clogged the thing's return, so there it
stood, still impending over Bannadonna, as if whispering
some post-mortem terror. The chisel lay dropped from the
hand, but beside the hand; the oil-flask spilled across the
iron track.

In his unhappy end, not unmindful of the rare genius
of the mechanician, the republic decreed him a stately
funeral. It was resolved that the great bell—the one whose
casting had been jeopardized through the timidity of the
ill-starred workman—should be rung upon the entrance
of the bier into the cathedral. The most robust man of
the country round was assigned the office of bell ringer.

But as the pallbearers entered the cathedral porch,
naught but a broken and disastrous sound, like that of
some lone Alpine landslide, fell from the tower upon their
ears. And then all was hushed.

Glancing backwards, they saw the groined belfry crashed
sideways in. It afterwards appeared that the powerful
peasant who had the bell rope in charge, wishing to test
at once the full glory of the bell, had swayed down upon
the rope with one concentrate jerk. The mass of quaking
metal, too ponderous for its frame, and strangely feeble
somewhere at its top, loosed from its fastening, tore sideways down, and, tumbling in one sheer fall three hundred
feet to the soft sward below, buried itself inverted and half
out of sight.

Upon its disinterment, the main fracture was found to
have started from a small spot in the ear, which, being
scraped, revealed a defect, deceptively minute, in the
casting, which defect must subsequently have been pasted
over with some unknown compound.

The remolten metal soon reassumed its place in the

tower's repaired superstructure. For one year the metallic choir of birds sang musically in its belfry boughwork of sculptured blinds and traceries. But on the first anniversary of the tower's completion—at early dawn, before the concourse had surrounded it—an earthquake came; one loud crash was heard. The stone pine, with all its bower of songsters, lay overthrown upon the plain.

So the blind slave obeyed its blinder lord, but, in obedience, slew him. So the creator was killed by the creature. So the bell was too heavy for the tower. So the bell's main weakness was where man's blood had flawed it. And so pride went before the fall.

The *Town-Ho's* Story

(CHAPTER 54 of *Moby-Dick*)

[*As told at the Golden Inn*]

THE Cape of Good Hope, and all the watery region round about there, is much like some noted four corners of a great highway, where you meet more travellers than in any other part.

It was not very long after speaking the Goney that another homeward-bound whaleman, the *Town-Ho*,* was encountered. She was manned almost wholly by Polynesians. In the short Gam that ensued she gave us strong news of Moby-Dick. To some the general interest in the White Whale was now wildly heightened by a circumstance of the *Town-Ho's* story, which seemed obscurely to involve with the whale a certain wondrous, inverted visitation of one of those so-called judgments of God which at

---

* The ancient whale-cry upon first sighting a whale from the masthead, still used by whalemen in hunting the famous Gallipagos terrapin. [Melville's note.]

times are said to overtake some men. This latter circumstance, with its own particular accompaniments, forming what may be called the secret part of the tragedy about to be narrated, never reached the ears of Captain Ahab or his mates. For that secret part of the story was unknown to the captain of the *Town-Ho* himself. It was the private property of three confederate white seamen of that ship, one of whom, it seems, communicated it to Tashtego with Romish injunctions of secrecy, but the following night Tashtego rambled in his sleep, and revealed so much of it in that way, that when he was wakened he could not well withhold the rest. Nevertheless, so potent an influence did this thing have on those seamen in the Pequod who came to the full knowledge of it, and by such a strange delicacy, to call it so, were they governed in this matter, that they kept the secret among themselves so that it never transpired abaft the Pequod's mainmast. Interviewing in its proper place this darker thread with the story as publicly narrated on the ship, the whole of this strange affair I now proceed to put on lasting record.

For my humor's sake, I shall preserve the style in which I once narrated it at Lima, to a lounging circle of my Spanish friends, one saint's eve, smoking upon the thick-gilt tiled piazza of the Golden Inn. Of those fine cavaliers, the young Dons, Pedro and Sebastian, were on the closer terms with me; and hence the interluding questions they occasionally put, and which are duly answered at the time.

"Some two years prior to my first learning the events which I am about rehearsing to you, gentlemen, the *Town-Ho,* Sperm Whaler of Nantucket, was cruising in your Pacific here, not very many days' sail eastward from the eaves of this good Golden Inn. She was somewhere to the northward of the Line. One morning upon handling the pumps, according to daily usage, it was observed that she made more water in her hold than common. They supposed a swordfish had stabbed her, gentlemen. But the captain, having some unusual reason for believing that rare good luck awaited him in those latitudes; and therefore being very averse to quit them, and the leak not being then considered at all dangerous, though, indeed, they could not find it after searching the hold as low down as was possible in rather heavy weather, the ship still continued her

cruisings, the mariners working at the pumps at wide and
easy intervals; but no good luck came; more days went by,
and not only was the leak yet undiscovered, but it sensibly
increased. So much so, that now taking some alarm, the
captain, making all sail, stood away for the nearest harbor
among the islands, there to have his hull hove out and
repaired.

"Though no small passage was before her, yet, if the
commonest chance favored, he did not at all fear that his
ship would founder by the way, because his pumps were
of the best, and being periodically relieved at them, those
six-and-thirty men of his could easily keep the ship free;
never mind if the leak should double on her. In truth, well
nigh the whole of this passage being attended by very
prosperous breezes, the *Town-Ho* had all but certainly
arrived in perfect safety at her port without the occurrence
of the least fatality, had it not been for the brutal over-
bearing of Radney, the mate, a Vineyarder, and the bitterly
provoked vengeance of Steelkilt, a Lakeman and desperado
from Buffalo.

" 'Lakeman!—Buffalo! Pray, what is a Lakeman, and
where is Buffalo?' said Don Sebastian, rising in his swinging mat of grass.

"On the eastern shore of our Lake Erie, Don; but—I
crave your courtesy—may be, you shall soon hear further
of all that. Now, gentlemen, in square-sail brigs and three-
masted ships, well nigh as large and stout as any that ever
sailed out of your old Callao to far Manila; this Lakeman,
in the land-locked heart of our America, had yet been
nurtured by all those agrarian free-booting impressions
popularly connected with the open ocean. For in their
interflowing aggregate, those grand fresh-water seas of
ours,—Erie, and Ontario, and Huron, and Superior, and
Michigan,—possess an oceanlike expansiveness, with
many of the ocean's noblest traits; with many of its rimmed
varieties of races and of climes. They contain round archi-
pelagoes of romantic isles, even as the Polynesian waters
do; in large part, are shored by two great contrasting nations, as the Atlantic is; they furnish long maritime approaches to our numerous territorial colonies from the
East, dotted all round their banks; here and there are
frowned upon by batteries, and by the goatlike craggy

guns of lofty Mackinaw; they have heard the fleet thunder-
ings of naval victories; at intervals, they yield their beaches
to wild barbarians, whose red painted faces flash from out
their peltry wigwams; for leagues and leagues are flanked
by ancient and unentered forests, where the gaunt pines
stand like serried lines of kings in Gothic genealogies; those
same woods harboring wild Afric beasts of prey, and
silken creatures whose exported furs give robes to Tartar
Emperors; they mirror the paved capitals of Buffalo and
Cleveland, as well as Winnebago villages; they float alike
the full-rigged merchant ship, the armed cruiser of the
State, the steamer, and the beech canoe; they are swept
by Borean and dismasting blasts as direful as any that lash
the salted wave; they know what shipwrecks are, for out
of sight of land, however inland, they have drowned full
many a midnight ship with all its shrieking crew. Thus,
gentlemen, though an inlander, Steelkilt was wild-ocean
born, and wild-ocean nurtured; as much of an audacious
mariner as any. And for Radney, though in his infancy
he may have laid him down on the lone Nantucket beach,
to nurse at his maternal sea; though in after life he had
long followed our austere Atlantic and your contemplative
Pacific; yet was he quite as vengeful and full of social
quarrel as the backwoods seaman, fresh from the latitudes
of buck-horn handled bowie knives. Yet was this Nan-
tucketer a man with some good-hearted traits; and this
Lakeman, a mariner, who though a sort of devil indeed,
might yet by inflexible firmness, only tempered by that
common decency of human recognition which is the
meanest slave's right; thus treated, this Steelkilt had long
been retained harmless and docile. At all events, he had
proved so thus far; but Radney was doomed and made
mad, and Steelkilt—but, gentlemen, you shall hear.

"It was not more than a day or two at the furthest after
pointing her prow for her island haven, that the *Town-
Ho*'s leak seemed again increasing, but only so as to
require an hour or more at the pumps every day. You
must know that in a settled and civilized ocean like our
Atlantic, for example, some skippers think little of pumping
their whole way across it; though of a still, sleepy night,
should the officer of the deck happen to forget his duty
in that respect, the probability would be that he and his

shipmates would never again remember it, on account of all hands gently subsiding to the bottom. Nor in the solitary and savage seas far from you to the westward, gentlemen, is it altogether unusual for ships to keep clanging at their pump handles in full chorus even for a voyage of considerable length; that is, if it lie along a tolerably accessible coast, or if any other reasonable retreat is afforded them. It is only when a leaky vessel is in some very out of the way part of those waters, some really landless latitude, that her captain begins to feel a little anxious.

"Much this way had it been with the *Town-Ho;* so when her leak was found gaining once more, there was in truth some small concern manifested by several of her company; especially by Radney the mate. He commanded the upper sails to be well hoisted, sheeted home anew, and every way expanded to the breeze. Now this Radney, I suppose, was as little of a coward, and as little inclined to any sort of nervous apprehensiveness touching his own person as any fearless, unthinking creature on land or on sea that you can conveniently imagine, gentlemen. Therefore when he betrayed this solicitude about the safety of the ship, some of the seamen declared that it was only on account of his being a part owner in her. So when they were working that evening at the pumps, there was on this head no small gamesomeness slily going on among them, as they stood with their feet continually overflowed by the rippling clear water; clear as any mountain spring, gentlemen—that bubbling from the pumps ran across the deck, and poured itself out in steady spouts at the lee scupper holes.

"Now, as you well know, it is not seldom the case in this conventional world of ours—watery or otherwise; that when a person placed in command over his fellow men finds one of them to be very significantly his superior in general pride of manhood, straightway against that man he conceives an unconquerable dislike and bitterness; and if he have a chance he will pull down and pulverize that subaltern's tower, and make a little heap of dust of it. Be this conceit of mine as it may, gentlemen, at all events Steelkilt was a tall and noble animal with a head like a Roman, and a flowing golden beard like the tasseled housings of your last viceroy's snorting charger; and a brain, and a heart, and a soul in him, gentlemen, which had made Steelkilt Charlemagne, had he been born son to Charlemagne's father. But Radney, the mate, was ugly as a mule; yet as hardy, as stubborn, as malicious. He did not love Steelkilt, and Steelkilt knew it.

"Espying the mate drawing near as he was toiling at the pump with the rest, the Lakeman affected not to notice him, but unawed, went on with his gay banterings.

" 'Aye, aye, my merry lads, it's a lively leak this; hold a cannikin, one of ye, and let's have a taste. By the Lord, it's worth bottling! I tell ye what, men, old Rad's investment must go for it! he had best cut away his part of the hull and tow it home. The fact is, boys, that swordfish only began the job; he's come back again with a gang of ship carpenters, sawfish, and filefish, and what not; and the whole posse of 'em are now hard at work cutting and slashing at the bottom; making improvements, I suppose. If old Rad were here now, I'd tell him to jump overboard and scatter 'em. They're playing the devil with his estate, I can tell him. But he's a simple old soul,—Rad, and a beauty too. Boys, they say the rest of his property is invested in looking glasses. I wonder if he'd give a poor devil like me the model of his nose.'

" 'Damn your eyes! what's that pump stopping for?' roared Radney, pretending not to have heard the sailors' talk. 'Thunder away at it!'

" 'Aye, aye, sir,' said Steelkilt, merry as a cricket. 'Lively, boys, lively, now!' And with that the pump clanged like fifty fire engines; the men tossed their hats off to it, and erelong that peculiar gasping of the lungs was heard which denotes the fullest tension of life's utmost energies.

"Quitting the pump at last, with the rest of his band, the Lakeman went forward all panting, and sat himself down on the windlass; his face fiery red, his eyes bloodshot, and wiping the profuse sweat from his brow. Now what cozening fiend it was, gentlemen, that possessed Radney to meddle with such a man in that corporeally exasperated state, I know not; but so it happened. Intolerably striding along the deck, the mate commanded him to get a broom and sweep down the planks, and also a shovel, and remove some offensive matters consequent upon allowing a pig to run at large.

"Now, gentlemen, sweeping a ship's deck at sea is a

piece of household work which in all times but raging gales is regularly attended to every evening; it has been known to be done in the case of ships actually foundering at the time. Such, gentlemen, is the inflexibility of sea usages and the instinctive love of neatness in seamen; some of whom would not willingly drown without first washing their faces. But in all vessels this broom business is the prescriptive province of the boys, if boys there be aboard. Besides, it was the stronger men in the *Town-Ho* that had been divided into gangs, taking turns at the pumps; and being the most athletic seaman of them all, Steelkilt had been regularly assigned captain of one of the gangs; consequently he should have been freed from any trivial business not connected with truly nautical duties, such being the case with his comrades. I mention all these particulars so that you may understand exactly how this affair stood between the two men.

"But there was more than this: the order about the shovel was almost as plainly meant to sting and insult Steelkilt, as though Radney had spat in his face. Any man who has gone sailor in a whaleship will understand this; and all this and doubtless much more, the Lakeman fully comprehended when the mate uttered his command. But as he sat still for a moment, and as he steadfastly looked into the mate's malignant eye and perceived the stacks of powder casks heaped up in him and the slow match silently burning along towards them; as he instinctively saw all this, that strange forbearance and unwillingness to stir up the deeper passionateness in any already ireful being—a repugnance most felt, when felt at all, by really valiant men even when aggrieved—this nameless phantom feeling, gentlemen, stole over Steelkilt.

"Therefore, in his ordinary tone, only a little broken by the bodily exhaustion he was temporarily in, he answered him saying that sweeping the deck was not his business, and he would not do it. And then, without at all alluding to the shovel, he pointed to three lads as the customary sweepers; who, not being billeted at the pumps, had done little or nothing all day. To this, Radney replied with an oath, in a most domineering and outrageous manner unconditionally reiterating his command; meanwhile advancing upon the still seated Lakeman, with an uplifted cooper's club hammer which he had snatched from a cask near by.

"Heated and irritated as he was by his spasmodic toil at the pumps, for all his first nameless feeling of forbearance the sweating Steelkilt could but ill brook this bearing in the mate; but somehow still smothering the conflagration within him, without speaking he remained doggedly rooted to his seat, till at last the incensed Radney shook the hammer within a few inches of his face, furiously commanding him to do his bidding.

"Steelkilt rose, and slowly retreating round the windlass, steadily followed by the mate with his menacing hammer, deliberately repeated his intention not to obey. Seeing, however, that his forbearance had not the slightest effect, by an awful and unspeakable intimation with his twisted hand he warned off the foolish and infatuated man; but it was to no purpose. And in this way the two went once slowly round the windlass; when, resolved at last no longer to retreat, bethinking him that he had now forborne as much as comported with his humor, the Lakeman paused on the hatches and thus spoke to the officer:

" 'Mr. Radney, I will not obey you. Take that hammer away, or look to yourself.' But the predestinated mate coming still closer to him, where the Lakeman stood fixed, now shook the heavy hammer within an inch of his teeth; meanwhile repeating a string of insufferable maledictions. Retreating not the thousandth part of an inch; stabbing him in the eye with the unflinching poniard of his glance, Steelkilt, clenching his right hand behind him and creepingly drawing it back, told his persecutor that if the hammer but grazed his check he (Steelkilt) would murder him. But, gentlemen, the fool had been branded for the slaughter by the gods. Immediately the hammer touched the cheek; the next instant the lower jaw of the mate was stove in his head; he fell on the hatch spouting blood like a whale.

"Ere the cry could go aft Steelkilt was shaking one of the backstays leading far aloft to where two of his comrades were standing their mastheads. They were both Canallers.

" 'Canallers!' cried Don Pedro. 'We have seen many whaleships in our harbors, but never heard of your Canallers. Pardon: who and what are they?'

" 'Canallers, Don, are the boatmen belonging to our grand Erie Canal. You must have heard of it.'

" 'Nay, senor; hereabouts in this dull, warm, most lazy, and hereditary land, we know but little of your vigorous North.'

" 'Aye? Well then, Don, refill my cup. Your chicha's very fine; and ere proceeding further I will tell ye what our Canallers are; for such information may throw sidelight upon my story.'

"For three hundred and sixty miles, gentlemen, through the entire breadth of the state of New York; through numerous populous cities and most thriving villages; through long, dismal uninhabited swamps, and affluent, cultivated fields, unrivalled for fertility; by billiard room and barroom; through the holy-of-holies of great forests; on Roman arches over Indian rivers; through sun and shade; by happy hearts or broken; through all the wide contrasting scenery of those noble Mohawk counties; and especially, by rows of snow-white chapels, whose spires stand almost like milestones, flows one continual stream of Venetianly corrupt and often lawless life. There's your true Ashantee, gentlemen; there howl your pagans; where you ever find them, next door to you; under the long-flung shadow, and the snug patronizing lee of churches. For by some curious fatality, as it is often noted of your metropolitan freebooters that they ever encamp around the halls of justice, so sinners, gentlemen, most abound in holiest vicinities.

" 'Is that a friar passing?' said Don Pedro, looking downwards into the crowded plazza, with humorous concern.

" 'Well for our northern friend, Dame Isabella's Inquisition wanes in Lima,' laughed Don Sebastian. 'Proceed, senor.'

" 'A moment! Pardon!' cried another of the company. 'In the name of all us Limeese, I but desire to express to you, sir sailor, that we have by no means overlooked your delicacy in not substituting present Lima for distant Venice in your corrupt comparison. Oh! do not bow and look surprised; you know the proverb all along this coast— "Corrupt as Lima." It but bears out your saying, too; churches more plentiful than billiard tables, and forever open—and "Corrupt as Lima." So, too, Venice; I have been there; the holy city of the blessed evangelist, St. Mark!

—St. Dominic, purge it! Your cup! Thanks: here I refill; now, you pour out again.'

"Freely depicted in his own vocation, gentlemen, the Canaller would make a fine dramatic hero, so abundantly and picturesquely wicked is he. Like Mark Antony, for days and days along his green-turfed, flowery Nile, he indolently floats, openly toying with his red-cheeked Cleopatra, ripening his apricot thigh upon the sunny deck. But ashore, all this effeminacy is dashed. The brigandish guise which the Canaller so proudly sports; his slouched and gaily-ribboned hat betoken his grand features. A terror to the smiling innocence of the villages through which he floats; his swart visage and bold swagger are not unshunned in cities. Once a vagabond on his own canal, I have received good turns from one of these Canallers; I thank him heartily; would fain be not ungrateful; but it is often one of the prime redeeming qualities of your man of violence, that at times he has as stiff an arm to back a poor stranger in a strait, as to plunder a wealthy one. In sum, gentlemen, what the wildness of this canal life is, is emphatically evinced by this; that our wild whalefishery contains so many of its most finished graduates, and that scarce any race of mankind, except Sydney men, are so much distrusted by our whaling captains. Nor does it at all diminish the curiousness of this matter, that to many thousands of our rural boys and young men born along its line, the probationary life of the Grand Canal furnishes the sole transition between quietly reaping in a Christian cornfield, and recklessly ploughing the waters of the most barbaric seas.

"'I see! I see!' impetuously exclaimed Don Pedro, spilling his chicha upon his silvery ruffles. 'No need to travel! The world's one Lima. I had thought, now, that at your temperate North the generations were cold and holy as the hills.—But the story.'

"I left off, gentlemen, where the Lakeman shook the backstay. Hardly had he done so, when he was surrounded by the three junior mates and the four harpooneers, who all crowded him to the deck. But sliding down the ropes like baleful comets, the two Canallers rushed into the uproar, and sought to drag their man out of it towards the forecastle. Others of the sailors joined with them in this attempt, and a twisted turmoil ensued; while standing out of harm's way, the valiant captain danced up and down with a whalepike, calling upon his officers to manhandle that atrocious scoundrel, and smoke him along to the quarter-deck. At intervals, he ran close up to the revolving border of the confusion, and prying into the heart of it with his pike, sought to prick out the object of his resentment. But Steelkilt and his desperadoes were too much for them all; they succeeded in gaining the forecastle deck, where, hastily slewing about three or four large casks in a line with the windlass, these sea-Parisians entrenched themselves behind the barricade.

" 'Come out of that, ye pirates!' roared the captain, now menacing them with a pistol in each hand, just brought to him by the steward. 'Come out of that, ye cut-throats!'

"Steelkilt leaped on the barricade, and striding up and down there, defied the worst the pistols could do; but gave the captain to understand distinctly, that his (Steelkilt's) death would be the signal for a murderous mutiny on the part of all hands. Fearing in his heart lest this might prove but too true, the captain a little desisted, but still commanded the insurgents instantly to return to their duty.

" 'Will you promise not to touch us, if we do?' demanded their ringleader.

" 'Turn to! turn to!—I make no promise;—to your duty! Do you want to sink the ship, by knocking off at a time like this? Turn to!' and he once more raised a pistol.

" 'Sink the ship?' cried Steelkilt. 'Aye, let her sink. Not a man of us turns to, unless you swear not to raise a rope-yarn against us. What say ye, men?' turning to his comrades. A fierce cheer was their response.

"The Lakeman now patrolled the barricade, all the while keeping his eye on the captain, and jerking out such sentences as these:—'It's not our fault; we didn't want it; I told him to take his hammer away; it was boy's business; he might have known me before this; I told him not to prick the buffalo; I believe I have broken a finger here against his cursed jaw; ain't those mincing knives down in the forecastle there, men? look to those handspikes, my hearties. Captain, by God, look to yourself; say the word; don't be a fool; forget it all; we are ready to turn to; treat us decently, and we're your men; but we won't be flogged.'

" 'Turn to! I make no promises, turn to, I say!'

" 'Look ye, now,' cried the Lakeman, flinging out his arm towards him, 'there are a few of us here (and I am one of them) who have shipped for the cruise, d'ye see; now as you well know, sir, we can claim our discharge as soon as the anchor is down; so we don't want a row; it's not our interest; we want to be peaceable; we are ready to work, but we won't be flogged.'

" 'Turn to!' roared the captain.

"Steelkilt glanced round him a moment, and then said:— 'I tell you what it is now, Captain, rather than kill ye, and be hung for such a shabby rascal, we won't lift a hand against ye unless ye attack us; but till you say the word about not flogging us, we don't do a hand's turn.'

" 'Down into the forecastle then, down with ye, I'll keep ye there till ye're sick of it. Down ye go.'

" 'Shall we?' cried the ringleader to his men. Most of them were against it; but at length, in obedience to Steelkilt, they preceded him down into their dark den, growlingly disappearing, like bears into a cave.

"As the Lakeman's bare head was just level with the planks, the captain and his posse leaped the barricade, and rapidly drawing over the slide of the scuttle, planted their group of hands upon it, and loudly called for the steward to bring the heavy brass padlock belonging to the companionway. Then opening the slide a little, the captain whispered something down the crack, closed it, and turned the key upon them—ten in number—leaving on deck some twenty or more, who thus far had remained neutral.

"All night a wide-awake watch was kept by all the officers, forward and aft, especially about the forecastle scuttle and fore hatchway; at which last place it was feared the insurgents might emerge, after breaking through the bulkhead below. But the hours of darkness passed in peace; the men who still remained at their duty toiling hard at the pumps, whose clinking and clanking at intervals through the dreary night dismally resounded through the ship.

"At sunrise the captain went forward, and knocking on the deck, summoned the prisoners to work; but with a yell they refused. Water was then lowered down to them, and a couple of handfuls of biscuit were tossed after it; when again turning the key upon them and pocketing it, the

captain returned to the quarter-deck. Twice every day for
three days this was repeated; but on the fourth morning a
confused wrangling, and then a scuffling was heard, as the
customary summons was delivered; and suddenly four men
burst up from the forecastle, saying they were ready to
turn to. The fetid closeness of the air, and a famishing diet,
united perhaps to some fears of ultimate retribution, had
constrained them to surrender at discretion. Emboldened
by this, the captain reiterated his demand to the rest, but
Steelkilt shouted up to him a terrific hint to stop his bab-
bling and betake himself where he belonged. On the fifth
morning three others of the mutineers bolted up into the
air from the desperate arms below that sought to restrain
them. Only three were left.

" 'Better turn to, now?' said the captain with a heartless
jeer.

" 'Shut us up again, will ye!' cried Steelkilt.

" 'Oh! certainly,' said the captain, and the key clicked.

"It was at this point, gentlemen, that enraged by the
defection of seven of his former associates, and stung by
the mocking voice that had last hailed him, and maddened
by his long entombment in a place as black as the bowels
of despair; it was then that Steelkilt proposed to the two
Canallers, thus far apparently of one mind with him, to
burst out of their hole at the next summoning of the garrison; and armed with their keen mincing knives (long,
crescentic, heavy implements with a handle at each end)
run amuck from the bowsprit to the taffrail; and if by any
devilishness of desperation possible, seize the ship. For
himself, he would do this, he said, whether they joined him
or not. That was the last night he should spend in that den.
But the scheme met with no opposition on the part of the
other two; they swore they were ready for that, or for any
other mad thing, for anything in short but a surrender.
And what was more, they each insisted upon being the first
man on deck, when the time to make the rush should come.
But to this their leader as fiercely objected, reserving that
priority for himself; particularly as his two comrades would
not yield, the one to the other, in the matter; and both of
them could not be first, for the ladder would but admit
one man at a time. And here, gentlemen, the foul play
of these miscreants must come out.

"Upon hearing the frantic project of their leader, each in his own separate soul had suddenly lighted, it would seem, upon the same piece of treachery, namely: to be foremost in breaking out, in order to be the first of the three, though the last of the ten, to surrender; and thereby secure whatever small chance of pardon such conduct might merit. But when Steelkilt made known his determination still to lead them to the last, they in some way, by some subtle chemistry of villainy, mixed their before secret treacheries together; and when their leader fell into a doze, verbally opened their souls to each other in three sentences; and bound the sleeper with cords, and gagged him with cords; and shrieked out for the captain at midnight.

"Thinking murder at hand, and smelling in the dark for the blood, he and all his armed mates and harpooneers rushed for the forecastle. In a few minutes the scuttle was opened, and, bound hand and foot, the still struggling ringleader was shoved up into the air by his perfidious allies, who at once claimed the honor of securing a man who had been fully ripe for murder. But all these were collared, and dragged along the deck like dead cattle; and, side by side, were seized up into the mizen rigging, like three quarters of meat, and there they hung till morning. 'Damn ye,' cried the captain, pacing to and fro before them, 'the vultures would not touch ye, ye villains!'

"At sunrise he summoned all hands; and separating those who had rebelled from those who had taken no part in the mutiny, he told the former that he had a good mind to flog them all round—thought, upon the whole, he would do so—he ought to—justice demanded it; but for the present, considering their timely surrender, he would let them go with a reprimand, which he accordingly administered in the vernacular.

" 'But as for you, ye carrion rogues,' turning to the three men in the rigging—'for you, I mean to mince ye up for the try pots'; and, seizing a rope, he applied it with all his might to the backs of the two traitors, till they yelled no more, but lifelessly hung their heads sideways, as the two crucified thieves are drawn.

" 'My wrist is sprained with ye!' he cried, at last; 'but there is still rope enough left for you, my fine bantam, that wouldn't give up. Take that gag from his mouth, and let us hear what he can say for himself.'

"For a moment the exhausted mutineer made a tremulous motion of his cramped jaws, and then painfully twisting round his head, said in a sort of hiss, 'What I say is this—and mind it well—if you flog me, I murder you!'

" 'Say ye so? then see how ye frighten me'—and the captain drew off with the rope to strike.

" 'Best not,' hissed the Lakeman.

" 'But I must,'—and the rope was once more drawn back for the stroke.

"Steelkilt here hissed out something, inaudible to all but the captain; who, to the amazement of all hands, started back, paced the deck rapidly two or three times, and then suddenly throwing down his rope, said, 'I won't do it—let him go—cut him down: d'ye hear?'

"But as the junior mates were hurrying to execute the order, a pale man, with a bandaged head, arrested them—Radney the chief mate. Ever since the blow, he had lain in his berth; but that morning, hearing the tumult on the deck, he had crept out, and thus far had watched the whole scene. Such was the state of his mouth, that he could hardly speak; but mumbling something about *his* being willing and able to do what the captain dared not attempt, he snatched the rope and advanced to his pinioned foe.

" 'You are a coward!' hissed the Lakeman.

" 'So I am, but take that.' The mate was in the very act of striking, when another hiss stayed his uplifted arm. He paused: and then pausing no more, made good his word, spite of Steelkilt's threat, whatever that might have been. The three men were then cut down, all hands were turned to, and, sullenly worked by the moody seamen, the iron pumps clanged as before.

"Just after dark that day, when one watch had retired below, a clamor was heard in the forecastle; and the two trembling traitors running up, besieged the cabin door, saying they durst not consort with the crew. Entreaties, cuffs, and kicks could not drive them back, so at their own instance they were put down in the ship's run for salvation. Still, no sign of mutiny reappeared among the rest. On the contrary, it seemed, that mainly at Steelkilt's instigation, they had resolved to maintain the strictest peacefulness, obey all order to the last, and, when the ship reached port, desert her in a body. But in order to insure the speediest end to the voyage, they all agreed to another thing— namely, not to sing out for whales, in case any should be discovered. For, spite of her leak, and spite of all her other perils, the *Town-Ho* still maintained her mastheads, and her captain was just as willing to lower for a fish that moment, as on the day his craft first struck the cruising ground; and Radney the mate was quite as ready to change his berth for a boat, and with his bandaged mouth seek to gag in death the vital jaw of the whale.

"But though the Lakeman had induced the seamen to adopt this sort of passiveness in their conduct, he kept his own counsel (at least till all was over) concerning his own proper and private revenge upon the man who had stung him in the ventricles of his heart. He was in Radney the chief mate's watch; and as if the infatuated man sought to run more than half way to meet his doom, after the scene at the rigging, he insisted, against the express counsel of the captain, upon resuming the head of his watch at night. Upon this, and one or two other circumstances, Steelkilt systematically built the plan of his revenge.

"During the night, Radney had an unseamanlike way of sitting on the bulwarks of the quarter-deck, and leaning his arm upon the gunwale of the boat which was hoisted up there, a little above the ship's side. In this attitude, it was well known, he sometimes dozed. There was a considerable vacancy between the boat and the ship, and down between this was the sea. Steelkilt calculated his time, and found that his next trick at the helm would come round at two o'clock, in the morning of the third day from that in which he had been betrayed. At his leisure, he employed the interval in braiding something very carefully in his watches below.

"'What are you making there?' said a shipmate.

"'What do you think? what does it look like?'

"'Like a lanyard for your bag; but it's an odd one, seems to me.'

"'Yes, rather oddish,' said the Lakeman, holding it at arm's length before him; 'but I think it will answer. Ship- mate, I haven't enough twine,—have you any?'

"But there was none in the forecastle.

" 'Then, I must get some from old Rad;' and he rose to go aft.

" 'You don't mean to go a begging to *him!*' said a sailor.

" 'Why not? Do you think he won't do me a turn, when it's to help himself in the end, shipmate?' and going to the mate, he looked at him quietly, and asked him for some twine to mend his hammock. It was given him—neither twine nor lanyard were seen again; but the next night an iron ball, closely netted, partly rolled from the pocket of the Lakeman's monkey jacket, as he was tucking the coat into his hammock for a pillow. Twenty-four hours after, his trick at the silent helm—nigh to the man who was apt to doze over the grave always ready dug to the seaman's hand—that fatal hour was then to come; and in the fore-ordaining soul of Steelkilt, the mate was already stark and stretched as a corpse, with his forehead crushed in.

"But, gentlemen, a fool saved the would-be murderer from the bloody deed he had planned. Yet complete revenge he had, and without being the avenger. For by a mysterious fatality, Heaven itself seemed to step in to take out of his hands into its own the damning thing he would have done.

"It was just between daybreak and sunrise of the morning of the second day, when they were washing down the decks, that a stupid Teneriffe man, drawing water in the mainchains, all at once shouted out, 'There she rolls! there she rolls!' Jesu, what a whale! It was Moby-Dick.

" 'Moby-Dick!' cried Don Sebastian; 'St. Dominic! Sir sailor, but do whales have christenings? Whom call you Moby-Dick?'

" 'A very white, and famous, and most deadly immortal monster, Don;—but that would be too long a story.'

" 'How? how?' cried all the young Spaniards, crowding.

" 'Nay, Dons, Dons—nay, nay! I cannot rehearse that now. Let me get more into the air, sirs.'

" 'The chicha! the chicha!' cried Don Pedro; 'our vigorous friend looks faint;—fill up his empty glass!'

"No need, gentlemen; one moment, and I proceed.— Now, gentlemen, so suddenly perceiving the snowy whale within fifty yards of the ship—forgetful of the compact among the crew—in the excitement of the moment, the Teneriffe man had instinctively and involuntarily lifted his

voice for the monster, though for some little time past it
had been plainly beheld from the three sullen mastheads.
All was now a frenzy. 'The White Whale—the White
Whale!' was the cry from captain, mates, and harpooneers,
who, undeterred by fearful rumors, were all anxious to
capture so famous and precious a fish; while the dogged
crew eyed askance, and with curses, the appalling beauty of
the vast milky mass, that lit up by a horizontal spangling
sun, shifted and glistened like a living opal in the blue
morning sea. Gentlemen, a strange fatality pervades the
whole career of these events, as if verily mapped out before
the world itself was charted. The mutineer was the bowsman of the mate, and when fast to a fish, it was his duty to
sit next him, while Radney stood up with his lance in the
prow, and haul in or slacken the line, at the word of command. Moreover, when the four boats were lowered, the
mate's got the start; and none howled more fiercely with
delight than did Steelkilt, as he strained at his oar. After a
stiff pull, their harpooneer got fast, and, spear in hand,
Radney sprang to the bow. He was always a furious man, it
seems, in a boat. And now his bandaged cry was, to beach
him on the whale's topmost back. Nothing loath, his bowsman hauled him up and up, through a blinding foam that
blent two whitenesses together; till of a sudden the boat
struck as against a sunken ledge, and keeling over, spilled
out the standing mate. That instant, as he fell on the
whale's slippery back, the boat righted, and was dashed
aside by the swell, while Radney was tossed over into the
sea, on the other flank of the whale. He struck out through
the spray, and, for an instant, was dimly seen through that
veil, wildly seeking to remove himself from the eye of
Moby-Dick. But the whale rushed round in a sudden mael-
strom; seized the swimmer between his jaws; and rearing
high up with him, plunged headlong again, and went down.
    "Meantime, at the first tap of the boat's bottom, the
Lakeman had slackened the line, so as to drop astern from
the whirlpool; calmly looking on, he thought his own
thoughts. But a sudden, terrific, downward jerking of the
boat, quickly brought his knife to the line. He cut it; and
the whale was free. But, at some distance, Moby-Dick rose
again, with some tatters of Radney's red woolen shirt,
caught in the teeth that had destroyed him. All four boats

gave chase again; but the whale eluded them, and finally wholly disappeared.

"In good time, the *Town-Ho* reached her port—a savage, solitary place—where no civilized creature resided. There, headed by the Lakeman, all but five or six of the foremastmen deliberately deserted among the palms; eventually, as it turned out, seizing a large double war canoe of the savages, and setting sail for some other harbor.

"The ship's company being reduced to but a handful, the captain called upon the Islanders to assist him in the laborious business of heaving down the ship to stop the leak. But to such unresting vigilance over their dangerous allies was this small band of whites necessitated, both by night and by day, and so extreme was the hard work they underwent, that upon the vessel being ready again for sea, they were in such a weakened condition that the captain durst not put off with them in so heavy a vessel. After taking counsel with his officers, he anchored the ship as far offshore as possible; loaded and ran out his two cannon from the bows; stacked his muskets on the poop; and warning the Islanders not to approach the ship at their peril, took one man with him, and setting the sail of his best whaleboat, steered straight before the wind for Tahiti, five hundred miles distant, to procure a reinforcement to his crew.

"On the fourth day of the sail, a large canoe was descried, which seemed to have touched at a low isle of corals. He steered away from it; but the savage craft bore down on him; and soon the voice of Steelkilt hailed him to heave to, or he would run him under water. The captain presented a pistol. With one foot on each prow of the yoked war canoes, the Lakeman laughed him to scorn; assuring him that if the pistol so much as clicked in the lock, he would bury him in bubbles and foam.

"'What do you want of me?' cried the captain.

"'Where are you bound? and for what are you bound?' demanded Steelkilt; 'no lies.'

"'I am bound to Tahiti for more men.'

"'Very good. Let me board you a moment—I come in peace.' With that he leaped from the canoe, swam to the boat; and climbing the gunwale, stood face to face with the captain.

" 'Cross your arms, sir; throw back your head. Now, repeat after me. As soon as Steelkilt leaves me, I swear to beach this boat on yonder island, and remain there six days. If I do not, may lightnings strike me!'

" 'A pretty scholar,' laughed the Lakeman. 'Adios, *señor!*' and leaping into the sea, he swam back to his comrades.

"Watching the boat till it was fairly beached, and drawn up to the roots of the coconut trees, Steelkilt made sail again, and in due time arrived at Tahiti, his own place of destination. There, luck befriended him; two ships were about to sail for France, and were providentially in want of precisely that number of men which the sailor headed. They embarked; and so forever got the start of their former captain, had he been at all minded to work them legal retribution.

"Some ten days after the French ships sailed, the whale-boat arrived, and the captain was forced to enlist some of the more civilized Tahitians, who had been somewhat used to the sea. Chartering a small native schooner, he returned with them to his vessel; and finding all right there, again resumed his cruisings.

"Where Steelkilt now is, gentlemen, none know; but upon the island of Nantucket, the widow of Radney still turns to the sea which refuses to give up its dead; still in dreams sees the awful White Whale that destroyed him. * * *

" 'Are you through?' said Don Sebastian, quietly.

" 'I am, Don.'

" 'Then I entreat you, tell me if to the best of your own convictions, this your story is in substance really true? It is so passing wonderful! Did you get it from an unquestionable source? Bear with me if I seem to press.'

" 'Also bear with all of us, sir sailor; for we all join in Don Sebastian's suit,' cried the company, with exceeding interest.

" 'Is there a copy of the Holy Evangelists in the Golden Inn, gentlemen?'

" 'Nay,' said Don Sebastian; 'but I know a worthy priest near by, who will quickly procure one for me. I go for it; but are you well advised? this may grow too serious.'

" 'Will you be so good as to bring the priest also, Don?'

" 'Though there are no Auto-da-Fés in Lima now,' said one of the company to another; 'I fear our sailor friend runs risk of the archiepiscopacy. Let us withdraw more out of the moonlight. I see no need of this.'

" 'Excuse me for running after you, Don Sebastian; but may I also beg that you will be particular in procuring the largest sized Evangelists you can.'

* * *

" 'This is the priest, he brings you the Evangelists,' said Don Sebastian, gravely, returning with a tall and solemn figure.

" 'Let me remove my hat. Now, venerable priest, further into the light, and hold the Holy Book before me that I may touch it.'

" 'So help me, Heaven, and on my honor the story I have told ye, gentlemen, is in substance and its great items, true. I know it to be true; it happened on this ball; I trod the ship; I knew the crew; I have seen and talked with Steelkilt since the death of Radney.' "

AFTERWORD

In 1850 Herman Melville was one of the most successful of American novelists. Of his five novels, four were much liked, and his readers wanted more stories of the same kind. Instead he gave them *Moby-Dick* (1851) which was thought by most reviewers to be incomprehensible. Melville refused to retreat. His next novel, *Pierre,* was even more unacceptable. The kind of novel Melville wanted to write could not succeed.

What was he to do? Since his marriage, in 1847, he had tried to support his family by writing, and writing was his trade. His family and friends busied themselves trying to find a consular post for him. How much Melville heard about their behind-the-scenes maneuvers is not known. In any event they came to nothing. But Melville had plans of his own. He had not yet tried the magazines, then as now in America a source of income for a fiction writer. For years his friend Nathaniel Hawthorne, before the publication of *The Scarlet Letter* in 1850, had been a magazinist, though he had not made much money in the business. Melville lost no time. Between the last months of 1853, when "Bartleby" appeared in *Putnam's Monthly Magazine* (November, December), and May, 1856, when "The Apple-Tree Table" appeared in the same magazine, he published thirteen stories, some of them of novella length.

In May, 1856, five of the seven stories which had appeared in *Putnam's* were issued by Dix and Edwards as *The Piazza Tales.* (A prefatory sketch, "The Piazza," was written by Melville for the collection.) The stories there collected are: "The Piazza," "Bartleby," "Benito Cereno," "The Lightning-Rod Man," "The Encantadas; or Enchanted Islands," and "The Bell Tower." On the whole *The Piazza Tales* was well received, but the firm of Dix and Edwards (publishers of *Putnam's*) was dissolved in the panic of 1857 and there were no profits from the book.

The payments Melville had received for the magazine publication of his stories averaged about $240 a year!

325

Though Melville did not make money by story writing, he did prove that his talent was by no means exhausted. His imagination was as inventive as ever and more wide-ranging. In this new venture, too, he learned how to tell a tale concisely and how to keep the required tone throughout. Into these stories Melville released many of the tensions of those difficult years. Some of his themes are the fear of isolation, the dislike of taking charity, the inviolate sanctity of the human heart.

"The Piazza"

Like most of the stories written in the 1850's "The Piazza" is a "teaser." There are autobiographical certainties in it. Melville did buy a farm-house near Pittsfield, Massachusetts (in 1850), and he did add a piazza facing his favorite mountain, Greylock. But what of the deeper meaning; of the distant gleam up the mountain which comes from the house of a woodsman and his lonely sister Marianna? Are the words at the end of the story Melville's comment on his career as a writer, particularly his recent career?—"Enough. Launching my yawl no more for fairyland, I stick to the piazza. It is my box-royal, and this amphitheater, my theater of San Carlo." There will not be another *Moby-Dick,* Melville seems to be saying, but life as seen from the piazza suffices for his art. As he walks its deck, he is haunted by Marianna's face "and many as real a story." When the curtain falls in his new theater, "truth comes in with darkness."

"Bartleby"

In "Bartleby" Melville is doing several things at the same time, but so adroitly is the story constructed that the reader will not notice any joints. In the first place, it is a kind of mystery story. Where does this strange man Bartleby come from? Why does he increasingly act in so antisocial a fashion? Why does he finally "prefer" to go to prison (the notorious Tombs, built in "Egyptian" style, which stood just north of New York's City Hall) rather than accept the charity of his former employer? Melville does not solve the mystery for us but he provides all the materials for a solution, *if* we can guess the meaning of the lawyer's spoken epitaph for Bartleby: "Ah, Bartleby! Ah, humanity!"

Just beneath the surface is considerable covert satire of American business success. The lawyer for whom Bartleby and the other scriveners work is, we note, a *Wall Street* lawyer with a thriving practice. He had once been employed by John Jacob Astor and he is proud to add "that I was not insensible to the late John Jacob Astor's good opinion." Benevolent though the lawyer is, his office is a prison. His scriveners look out on no green space but on walls thrust close up to them. The one that Bartleby gazes at is only three feet away.

Melville is also saying something about writers and the task of writing—the tedious "copying" which the scriveners perform with varying degrees of adaptability. The clue to this version of the meaning comes at the end, when the lawyer learns that Bartleby had once been a clerk in the Dead Letter Office at Washington. There he had sorted for the flames letters full of human woe or charity or love which had never reached the receiver (reader?). Are these dead letters Melville's own novels which had been "missent"?

Bartleby's "I would prefer not to" can be related to a strain in Melville's own make-up. He was a stubborn man and often said No to his family and close friends. Some light on this aspect of the story is cast by a passage in the letter Melville wrote to Hawthorne to thank him for a copy of *The House of the Seven Gables.* "There is the grand truth about Nathaniel Hawthorne. He says No! in thunder; but the Devil himself cannot make him say *yes.* For all men who say *yes,* lie; and all men who say *no*—why, they are in the happy condition of judicious, unincumbered travelers in Europe; they cross the frontiers into Eternity with nothing but a carpetbag—that is to say, the Ego."

"Benito Cereno"

In the present critical interest in Melville's stories, none of them except "Billy Budd" has been so much argued about as "Benito Cereno." In the shouted arguments—

about Absolute Evil, Melville's views on slavery, the effeteness of old Spain *vs.* New-World virtue—the excellence of the story, as story, has been neglected.

"Benito Cereno" is one of the most exciting mystery stories in the English language. Captain Delano thinks, at the end, that all the relevant facts have come out, but the reader guesses, through Melville's ironic treatment of Delano's investigations aboard the *San Dominick,* that there is a deeper mystery here which no Yankee sea captain and no vice-regal court can penetrate. Time after time, while Delano is on board the Spanish ship, he thinks he has got to the heart of the matter. Then some new piece of unsettling evidence comes to his attention and he has to change course. Nothing works the way it should. As Delano's bafflement increases, so do his twinges of fear. At the climax of the story when Captain Don Benito leaps into the whaleboat in a desperate effort to escape his black captors, and Babo leaps after him intending murder, a flash of revelation sweeps across the "long benighted mind of Captain Delano." He had—thus far—got everything wrong. Don Benito, his friend Aranda, and the crew, have been victims of a terrible slave revolt. The innocent-seeming blacks are organized and disciplined murderers.

So Delano finally believes. But is this all? In the trial Babo refuses to speak. We never know his story. What is left of him after his execution, his head, "that hive of subtlety," is fixed on a pole in the Plaza. It stares in death across the Rimac bridge to the monastery where Don Benito—in what degree guilty?—has taken refuge and where he dies.

Melville found the germ of his story in Chapter XVIII of Amasa Delano's *A Narrative of Voyages and Travels in the Northern and Southern Hemispheres* (1817), but he made Delano's story his own, adding such significant details as the following: the sinister description of the *San Dominick;* the dark row of the Ashantee hatchet-polishers; the creation of the character and acts of Babo (Muri in the original), including the superb shaving scene; Babo's leap into the boat; the chance revelation of the skeleton figurehead; and all the symbols which give the story its sinister tone.

Melville's most important change is his transformation

of the character of Delano. In the *Narrative* Delano pictures himself as a capable, shrewd, benevolent Yankee sea captain who goes about his business of restoring order on the Spanish ship in accordance with accepted naval procedures. Once the job is done, he is most concerned to get the money due him for services rendered. Melville keeps Delano as his "central intelligence" through whose eyes we witness all the events. But with what a difference! His ironic treatment of Delano invites us, indeed compels us, to go beyond the captain's "evidence" at every stage, in order that we may imagine the total truth. We cannot be content with what one critic has rightly termed "the enduring innocence of Captain Amasa Delano."

"The Lightning-Rod Man"

At first glance this short tale seems to be an amusing but uncomplicated account of the attempt by a salesman of lightning rods to sell his wares to the sales-resistant narrator while a terrific thunder storm rages around the house. In 1853 householders in the Pittsfield region had gone daft over lightning rods, as the result of a strenuous advertising campaign. According to family legend, Melville was visited by one of the salesmen and based his story on this encounter.

But this story has a subsurface meaning. Melville is satirizing ministers of the Calvinist persuasion who preach hell-fire and damnation while at the same time they exhort their congregations to buy a lightning rod (conversion to Christianity) in order to escape God's wrath. The narrator's (and Melville's) position is stated at the end of the story. "The hairs of our heads are numbered, and the days of our lives. In thunder as in sunshine, I stand at ease in the hands of my God. False negotiator, away! See, the scroll of the storm is rolled back; the house is unharmed; and in the blue heavens I read in the rainbow that the Deity will not, of purpose, make war on man's earth."

"The Encantadas, or Enchanted Islands"

In the ten sketches that make up "The Encantadas" Melville employs again the method which had served him well in writing *Typee, Omoo, White Jacket,* and *Moby-Dick.* Basing his stories on his own experiences in the South Seas, he filled out and enriched them with material drawn from many sources. Few writers have so skillfully "plagiarized" from their reading.

The Enchanted Islands (or Galápagos), lying six hundred miles off the coast of Ecuador and cut in two by the equator, were first described in 1535 by Fray Tomás de Berlanga, Bishop of Panama, in a letter to His Majesty, the King of Spain. In this document begins the legend of the infernolike barrenness of the islands. Until the end of the eighteenth century, when the whalers arrived, they were avoided by mariners because of the contrary winds and unpredictable currents encountered there. In the seventeenth century English buccaneers had made the islands their hideout, from which they sallied forth to seize Spanish ships venturing near. The navigator of one of these freebooting vessels gave the islands their English names and charted them for the first time.

With the arrival of the whalers, the Encantadas became a way station in the Pacific, where news and letters could be exchanged and the giant tortoises taken on board for food. In the early years whales abounded in the region. The *Acushnet,* the whaler on which Melville sailed from New Bedford early in 1841, arrived at the Islands in October of that year, cruised in the vicinity for several weeks, and returned in the following January. Thus Melville knew the islands at first hand. In these sketches he used the scenes he remembered and legends he picked up from other sailors. He also relied heavily on authorities, particularly Captain David Porter's *Journal of a Cruise Made to the Pacific Ocean* (1822). (See Sketches V, IX, X.)

The epigraphs which preface the sketches, most of them extracted from Spenser's *Faerie Queene,* set the various tones Melville wished to create: of mystery, fear, enchantment, of humanity reduced to the lowest level of existence.

"The Bell-Tower"

Melville appropriately chose Renaissance Italy for the

time and setting of this story. As a Renaissance man, Bannadonna, ambitious, inventive, confident of his powers, seeks to perform three incredible creative acts: to build a bell tower which shall be the noblest ever attempted; to place in its belfry a huge and beautifully wrought state bell; and—his secret project—to mold a mechanical figure in the shape of a manacled man, which shall advance on rails each hour and strike the bell. Man, as bell ringer, is to be supplanted by machine-man.

Bannadonna fails. He is killed by his slave-machine at the moment of his triumph. All three of his creations are destroyed. Melville neatly sums up the total action for us at the conclusion of the story in a *haec fabula docet* (this is what the fable teaches). Yet, as in most of these stories, he conceals his deeper meaning.

Bannadonna's failure and death cannot be explained by the simple "pride went before the fall" of the conclusion. Melville wishes us to ask what is *particular* about Bannadonna's pride. This is the secret meaning which the reader must puzzle out. The surest clue is given in the paragraph describing the ways in which Bannadonna differs from his fellow artists and inventors: "With him, common sense was theurgy; machinery, miracle; Prometheus, the heroic name for machinist; man, the true God."

There is more than a hint here that Melville is commenting on the confidence of his own age in rationally conceived scientific and mechanical marvels. The atomic bomb and the digital computer were yet to come, but Melville would have understood the implications for humanity in these inventions.

"The Town-Ho's *Story"*

Chapter 54 of *Moby-Dick,* "The *Town-Ho's* Story," can stand by itself. Whether Melville wrote it as a short story and then fitted it into the action of the novel is not known. Probably he did not. Yet he realized that it could stand alone and published it in two places before *Moby-Dick* was issued: *Harper's New Monthly Magazine,* October, 1851, and the *Baltimore Weekly Sun,* November 8, 1851.

"The *Town-Ho's* Story" is picked up by Tashtego, one

of the harpooners of the *Pequod,* in the second of the nine gams (social meetings of two or more whale ships) which occur in the course of the novel. From four of the whalers which the *Pequod* meets something is learned about the ferocity of the terrible white whale, Moby-Dick, but the account from the *Town-Ho* is the longest. Captain Ahab, so eager for news of Moby-Dick, never hears it.

Melville probably chose Lima as the place where his narrator, Ishmael, retells the story because the setting adds an exotic touch. For some reason this Peruvian city fascinated Melville. He had visited it on a forty-eight-hours leave early in 1844, when he was a seaman on the frigate *United States.*

"Billy Budd"

Five months before he died Melville completed a short novel to which he gave the tentative title "Billy Budd, Foretopman." The manuscript was not ready to be published, for there are many cancellations and variant readings in it. But the draft must have been near to his final intention because he concluded it with "End of Book. April 19th, 1891." Possibly he had undertaken the story because there had recently been in the journals a revival of interest in a famous case of alleged mutiny on an American naval vessel, the so-called *Somers* affair of 1842, in which Melville's cousin Lieutenant Guert Gansevoort played an accusatory role somewhat like Claggart's in "Billy Budd."

Whatever use Melville was making of the *Somers* affair, it is abundantly clear why he created a new setting for his story. He needed the background of England's naval war against the French after the Revolution and the anxieties of the British officers following the mutinies at Spithead and the Nore. In time of war there can be no delay in imposing sentence, no mercy for a seaman who kills his superior, even though the murder is committed without malice or premeditation. So Captain Vere argues, and with these arguments he persuades his reluctant drumhead court to sentence Billy to be hanged. Without these arguments Captain Vere would be a monster.

The implications of "Billy Budd," allegorical, symbolic, ethical, are many and subtle, but the lines of the story are clear. Melville is pursuing themes here which he had tackled before: the conflict between innocence and depravity, the "mystery of iniquity," the dilemma of the just man who has heavenly insights but must act in accord with earthly standards (the Articles of War).

Billy, who is Adam before the Fall, primitive man impressed into the world of war from the *Rights of Man*, Isaac made ready for sacrifice, stands at the end of a long line of Melville's innocents. In his early novels, *Typee*, *Redburn*, *White-Jacket*, he presents his hero as a young man, inexperienced but eager for experience, and sends him through adventures which open his eyes to the depravity as well as the heroism of which man is capable. Only in *Pierre* does he turn on his innocent hero and mock him as the Fool of Virtue.

There had been other Claggarts—Jackson in *Redburn* and Bland in *White-Jacket*—but Claggart's depravity is of a different sort from theirs, not sordid or sensual, mercenary or avaricious. Claggart's pride is Satanic. He looks on Billy's goodness with "pale ire, envy and despair." Through "natural depravity" he brings on Billy's death.

There is no clear analogue to Captain Vere in the other works, but Melville had approached Vere's problem many times. There is something of Starbuck (of *Moby-Dick*) in Vere; something, strangely enough, of that bewildered innocent, Pierre. And the total argument of the long poem *Clarel* (1876), in the variety of the ethical problems it raises (and does not solve), leads on to "Starry Vere."

In watching the course of the story, we must be sure to note with what deliberateness Melville defines the characters of Billy, Claggart, and Vere. It is as if he knew he was having his last say about these archetypal men and that he must tell the truth about them as he had learned it. Yet, could the truth be told, by however conscientious a novelist? In Chapter XIV of *The Confidence Man* (1857) Melville satirizes novelists who neatly sum up their characters, reconciling all inconsistencies of nature. This is not Melville's way. The ultimate human ambiguities cannot be resolved. The answers lie elsewhere; perhaps in heaven.

One human certainty, nevertheless, Melville offers us at the end of "Billy Budd." The naval chronicles brand Billy as a traitor. His shipmates will not have it so. They keep track of the spar from which he was hanged until it becomes a "mere dock-yard boom." Soon a chip from it is "as a piece of the Cross." The legend of Billy's innocence will not die. Is not Melville saying that true goodness, aspersed by a Satanic Claggart and doomed to

SELECTED BIBLIOGRAPHY

Works by Herman Melville

Typee, 1846   Novel   (Signet Classic 0451-525183)
Omoo, 1847   Novel
Mardi, 1849   Novel
Redburn, 1849   Novel
White-Jacket, 1850   Novel   (Meridian Classic 0452-010640)
Moby Dick, 1841   Novel   (Signet Classic 0451-524551)
Pierre; or, The Ambiguities, 1852   Novel   (Meridian Classic 0452-009960)
Israel Potter, 1855   Novel
The Piazza Tales, 1856   Stories   (Signet Classic 0451-524462)
The Confidence-Man: His Masquerade, 1857   Novel   (Meridian Classic 0452-008948)
Battle-Pieces and Aspects of the War, 1866   Poems
Clarel: A Poem and Pilgrimage in the Holy Land, 1876   Poem
John Marr and Other Sailors, 1888   Poems
Timoleon and Other Poems, 1891   Poems
Billy Budd, Sailor, 1924   Novel   (Signet Classic 0451-524462)

Biography and Criticism

Allen, Gay Wilson, *Melville and His World*. New York: Viking Press, 1971.
Anderson, Charles Roberts. *Melville in the South Seas*. New York: Columbia Univ. Press, 1939.
Berthoff, Warner. *The Example of Melville*. Princeton: Princeton Univ. Press, 1963.
Chase, Richard. *Herman Melville: A Critical Study*. New York: Macmillan, 1949.
————, ed. *Melville: A Collection of Critical Essays*. Englewood Cliffs, N.J.: Prentice-Hall, 1962.
Dryden, Edgar A. *Melville's Thematics of Form: The Great Art of Telling the Truth*. Baltimore: Johns Hopkins Press, 1968.
Fidelson, Charles. *Symbolism and American Literature*. Chicago: Univ. of Chicago Press, 1953.
Franklin, H. Bruce. *The Wake of the Gods: Melville's Mythology*. Stanford: Stanford Univ. Press, 1967.
Howard, Leon. *Herman Melville: A Biography*.Berkeley: Univ. of California Press; London: Cambridge Univ. Press, 1951.
Lawrence, D. H. *Studies in Classic American Literature*. New York: Thomas Seltzer, 1923.
Levin, Harry. *The Power of Blackness: Hawthorne, Poe, Melville*. New York: Alfred A. Knopf, 1958.
Matthiessen, F. O. *American Renaissance*. New York and London: Oxford Univ. Press, 1941.

Hillway, Tyrus. *Herman Melville*. New York: Twayne, 1963.

Howard, Leon. *Herman Melville: A Biography*. Berkeley: Univ. of California Press; London: Cambridge Univ. Press, 1951.

Lawrence, D. H. *Studies in Classic American Literature*. New York: Thomas Seltzer, 1923.

Levin, Harry. *The Power of Blackness: Hawthorne, Poe, Melville*. New York: Alfred A. Knopf, 1958.

Leydan, Jay. *The Melville Log: A Documentary Life of Herman Melville, 1819-1891*. 2 vols. New York: Harcourt, Brace, 1951.

Matthiessen, F. O. *American Renaissance*. New York and London: Oxford Univ. Press, 1941.

Metcalf, Eleanor Melville. *Herman Melville: Cycle and Epicycle*. Cambridge: Harvard Univ. Press, 1953.

Miller, James E. Jr. *A Reader's Guide to Herman Melville*. New York: Farrar, Straus, and Cudahy, 1962.

Miller, Perry. *The Raven and the Whale: The War of Words and Wits in the Era of Poe and Melville*. New York: Harcourt, Brace, 1956.

Mumford, Lewis. *Herman Melville*. New York: Harcourt, Brace, 1929. Rev. ed., 1962.

Olson, Charles. *Call Me Ismael*. New York: Reynal and Hitchcock, 1947.

Parker, Hershel, ed. *The Recognition of Herman Melville: Selected Criticism Since 1846*. Ann Arbor: Univ. of Michigan Press, 1967.

Pavese, Cesare. "Herman Melville." In *American Literature: Essays and Opinions*. Trans. Edwin Fussell. Berkeley: Univ. of California Press, 1970, pp. 55-68.

Pullin, Faith, ed. *New Perspectives on Melville*. Edinburgh: Edinburgh Univ. Press, 1978.

Sedgwick, William Ellery. *Melville: The Tragedy of Mind*. Cambridge: Harvard Univ. Press, 1944.

Seelye, John D. *Melville: The Ironic Diagram*. Evanston: Northwestern Univ. Press, 1970.

Smith, Henry Nash. "The Madness of Ahab." In *Democracy and the Novel: Popular Resistance to Classic American Writers*. New York: Oxford Univ. Press, 1978, pp. 35-55.

Stern, Milton R. *The Fine Hammered Steel of Herman Melville*. Urbana: Univ. of Illinois Press, 1957.

Thompson, Lawrence. *Melville's Quarrel with God*. Princeton: Princeton Univ. Press, 1952.

A Note on the Text

Billy Budd, which was first published after Herman Melville's death, has been available in many versions. The text included in this book follows the definitive Harvard University Press edition, edited by F. Barron Freeman (1948), and revised by Elizabeth Treeman (1956). Miss Treeman's revision, indicated in her corrigenda, have been incorporated here. The six stories from *The Piazza Tales* are reprinted from the first (1856) edition, which Melville himself revised and saw through the press. Inconsistencies of spelling, punctuation and typography, in all the tales, have been brought into conformity with modern American usage.